YOUR DEEPEST FEAR

David Jackson

ZAFFRE

First published in Great Britain in 2019 by

ZAFFRE
80–81 Wimpole St, London W1G 9RE

Copyright © David Jackson, 2019

A CIP catalogue record for this book is
available from the British Library.

Paperback ISBN: 978-1-78576-556-8

Also available as an ebook

1 3 5 7 9 10 8 6 4 2

Typeset by IDSUK (Data Connection) Ltd
Printed and bound in Great Britain by Clays Ltd, Elcograf S.p.A.

MIX
Paper from
responsible sources
FSC® C018072

Zaffre is an imprint of Bonnier Books UK
www.bonnierbooks.co.uk

YOUR DEEPEST FEAR

David Jackson is the bestselling author of *Cry Baby*. His debut novel, *Pariah*, was Highly Commended in the Crime Writers' Association Debut Dagger Awards. He lives on the Wirral peninsula with his wife and two daughters. Follow David on Twitter: @Author_Dave, or via his website davidjacksonbooks.com.

This one's for Peter,
who deserves much more

1

The regrets will come later.

She will wish she had responded to the light more quickly. The tiny blinking light, insistently proclaiming the reason for its existence.

But then she will reason about this, and accept that it would have made no difference. The outcome would have been just as devastating.

If she had come home a day earlier, though – yes, that might have been a completely different matter. Or if she had not gone at all. She hadn't really wanted to go. If the situation had been happier here, she wouldn't have left. Either way, she would have been here to take the call, and maybe, just maybe, she could have intervened.

But then she will realise that real happiness would have meant not needing to take the call in the first place. He would have been here, with her.

She will wish she had tried much harder with him. She will wonder if she surrendered him to his fate too easily.

Those thoughts will haunt her for ever.

But before the regrets will come the anger.

And before the anger will come the tears.

Sara Prior smiles when the house comes into view. It always has this effect on her.

It's a small detached cottage on the outskirts of Halewood, long neglected by the previous owners when she and Matthew bought it. She visualised the potential as soon as she saw it. Its isolation worried her a little, but Matthew craved the peace and quiet.

The house can hardly be called grand or even noteworthy in appearance, but it is her home. *Their* home. She and Matthew put a lot of effort into getting this place into shape. Hour upon hour each evening. They made it perfect.

Matthew is here. He is everywhere in this house. He is in the doors he stripped, the floorboards he mended, the wiring he installed. When they met, he knew nothing of DIY. When he left, he had become an expert.

When he left . . .

She sighs. Wishes he were inside the house as he always used to be, waiting excitedly at the window for her return, then racing to the front door to greet her, all wide eyes and daft grin.

One day soon, she thinks, it'll be like that again. If only he could use his DIY skills to fix himself.

She parks the car on the patch of gravel in front of the house and gets out. She opens up the boot and takes out her case. Cabin baggage, to avoid having to wait at the airport carousels.

She locks the car and drags the case to the house. Finds her key and opens up. Picks up her post and free newspapers from behind the door.

Inside, the smell is familiar and welcoming. A Molton Brown diffuser on the sideboard in the hallway. Next to that, a light on the telephone is winking at her, notifying her that she has messages on the answering machine.

They can wait. They will be automated sales calls, or reminders to pay bills. That's all they ever are.

She leaves her case in the hall and proceeds to the kitchen. Tea is her top priority. The lukewarm brown muck they served her on the flight didn't qualify.

While the kettle boils, she takes off her coat and opens her mail. Junk, mostly, but also two tickets for *West Side Story* at the Liverpool Empire. A surprise for Matthew. She expects him to say no, but she's going to try anyway. He likes musicals. And if he does say no, she'll find someone else to go with her.

No. She won't do that. It's Matthew or nobody. If he says no, she'll give the tickets away. That's the truth of it.

Her father wouldn't understand. He has never hidden his dislike of Matthew. He regards her husband as weak and spineless. He wanted her to marry someone more stereotypically macho.

She nearly did, of course. It wasn't to be.

She thinks that sometimes these things happen for a reason. Good can come out of bad. Matthew was the good.

'Why are you even going back there?' her father asked last night. 'He left you. You could come back to live with us. Or I'll buy you a place of your own. What has Liverpool got to offer you now?'

She made it clear to him that she has no intention of moving back to Copenhagen. She has her own life now. She likes it here.

Besides, this is where Matthew lives, and she's not giving up on him just yet. Tomorrow she will call round to his place with the tickets. She will talk to him, because she thinks that's what he really needs. It has been four months now, and she still doesn't fully understand why he felt the need to move out.

She thinks he needs her. She brought him out of himself. She taught him about life, about living. She gave him purpose and happiness. She even schooled him in sex.

And then something happened to him. Something he won't talk about.

She has made it her mission to find out what it was.

She drinks her tea and tries to recall the contents of her freezer. She doesn't really want to go shopping. The four-day trip to Copenhagen has drained her. She knew it would, which is why she put it off for so long. Her parents had wanted her there for Christmas and New Year, but there was no way she was going to be so far away from Matthew then. The festive period is a trigger for so many to commit suicide.

No shopping today, she decides. I'll make do.

She heads back into the hall. As she reaches for her case, she notices the blinking white light on the phone again.

She reaches across and jabs the play button on the phone's base station. A voice tells her that she has three new messages.

She lays the bag down and starts to unzip it.

The first message plays. It's the tail end of a recording informing her of the benefits of a boiler replacement scheme.

She shakes her head, then starts pulling her dirty clothes out of the case.

Second message: the gas company, asking for the householder to call them back. Their phone number is announced twice, just in case she has forgotten how to replay messages.

She makes a mental note to pay the gas bill. Gathers up her clothes. Walks back towards the kitchen.

Halts when she hears the next voice.

What stops her is not just that it's Matthew's voice, but also that his words are being fired at her in a tone of sheer unadulterated terror.

'*Sara! Remember! Victoria and Albert. All I can say. They're here! They're— Sara, I love you. I—*'

It is interrupted by a fumbling noise, and then what sounds like the beginning of a blood-curdling scream . . .

And then the line goes dead.

2

Sara turns slowly on her heel, the clothes still clutched in arms that are now dotted with goose pimples.

What the hell was that?

And then she is flinging the washing onto the floor, racing to the phone, scanning the infernal device for the buttons that will make it replay the latest message.

She stabs out what she thinks is the correct sequence, praying that it doesn't delete anything. She holds her breath . . .

'Sara! Remember! Victoria and Albert. All I can say. They're here! They're— Sara, I love you. I—'

And then the noises again. As though someone snatched the phone out of his hand. And as though they . . .

They were hurting him. Someone was hurting my Matthew!

Her brain is filled with questions about what the message might mean, but right now is not the time to dissect it. The pleading in Matthew's voice overrides all that. Now is the time to respond, to act.

She plucks the receiver from its cradle. Flicks through her contacts until she finds Matthew. Presses the call button.

She listens to the maddening chirrup as Matthew's phone rings.

'Come on, come on!' she urges.

But she gets no answer.

She ends the call as another thought occurs to her. She replays Matthew's message again, but this time she is more interested in what the answering machine has to say about it.

Just after ten o'clock this morning. That's when the call came in. And now it's – she checks her watch – past two o'clock.

That's four fucking hours!

She races back to the kitchen. Grabs her coat and keys. Dashes out of the house and leaps into the car.

As she drives, she makes use of the hands-free to call Matthew's number. Again and again she calls him, and each time she fails to get a response.

This is bad, she thinks. This is so, so wrong.

I knew it! I knew I shouldn't have gone to fucking Copenhagen. What the hell has Matthew got himself involved in?

She breaks all the speed limits, and yet still the journey to Matthew's house seems to take far too long. Why did he have to move all the way to a shitty little terraced dump in Aintree?

She knows the answer to that one. It wasn't just because it was all he could afford. It wasn't, as he claimed, that it was closer to his place of work in Bootle. It was because it put distance between them. That was the real reason.

When she finally screeches to a halt, she leaps out of the car and dashes up to the white PVC front door. She rings the bell, pounds the knocker.

There is no response.

She drops to her knees, flips open the letter box and looks inside.

It is eerily quiet in there. No sign of life whatsoever.

She brings her mouth to the letter slot. 'Matthew! Are you in there? Come to the door!'

Again nothing.

And now she's not sure what to do. Call the police? Get them to knock the door down?

Maybe. But first . . .

The house stands next to a beauty parlour, shuttered and closed now as it's a Sunday. On the other side is an alleyway.

Trust Matthew to pick somewhere without immediate neighbours!

Sara moves down the alley to the rear of the house. She tries the yard door. It's locked.

She looks up and down the alleyway. Nobody watching. The other buildings visible here are mostly shops, their walls topped by broken glass or barbed wire. Sara walks away from Matthew's wall, turns.

And then a sudden sprint. A leap. Her hands just manage to grasp the top edge of the wall. She clings there as she walks her feet up the brick wall, wishing she were wearing jogging bottoms and trainers instead of the smart trousers and shoes she still has on.

She swings one leg over the wall, straddling it for a second, then brings the other leg over and drops down on the other side.

Matthew's backyard is tiny. Mostly concrete, but with a rectangle of lawn so small it seems pointless.

The house appears lifeless. Sara steps up to the kitchen window and peers inside.

It's a wreck.

Many of the drawers and cupboards are open. Much of their content – cutlery, tins, household cleansers – has been pulled out and is littering the tiled floor. Boxes of cereal have been tipped out onto the counter.

Sara continues up the yard, stopping at the window looking into the living room. It's just as chaotic in there. Cushions have been sliced open. Books have been taken from the shelves and tossed to the floor. Pictures have been ripped out of their frames.

She turns to the back door, and that's when she knows for certain that the madness inside wasn't caused by Matthew in a fit of rage.

One of the panes of glass in the door has been smashed.

Someone broke in to this house.

Sara feels the goosebumps returning. She reaches for the door handle. Turns it. The door opens.

She steps inside, hears the fragments of glass crunching beneath her feet. She pauses there for a second, listening, alert to any signs of danger.

She looks again at the devastation in the kitchen. The freezer door has been left open, and the appliance is emitting an irritating beep as it complains about its temperature. On the floor in front of it is a pile of boxes and packets of food, sitting in a puddle from a bag of melted ice cubes. The sink is full of a mixture of pasta and rice and flour, the empty bags tossed aside onto the draining board.

Sara sees a knife block on the counter. She moves quickly across to it and slides out the biggest knife it contains.

Her heart pounding, she exits the kitchen. In the hallway are two doors to her right and a stairway to her left. She steps quietly up to the first door, which is partly open. It leads to the living room she observed from the yard, so she knows there's nobody in there. All the same, she pushes the door open and gives it a quick once-over.

The next room is a different matter. Again, the door is slightly ajar, and she can hear nothing from inside, but she's taking no chances.

She brings her eyes to the narrow gap, checking for moving shadows on the other side. As she does this, she searches her memory in an effort to build a mental map of the room before exposing herself to possible danger.

She flattens herself against the wall so as not to present a clear target in the doorway. Knife tightly clutched in one hand, she nudges the door with the other.

It opens more swiftly than she expects, but then stops with a thud, followed by the clatter of objects tumbling to the floor.

Shit!

She risks a glance inside. Then another. Finally she steps in, knife at the ready.

There is nobody here.

Sara sees that the door has hit a small table that had been shifted away from its usual position. The collision caused a lamp and wooden ornament to topple to the floor, but that's the least of the turmoil in here. Matthew has an extensive collection of CDs, collected over many years, but Sara can see that every CD case that once sat on the shelves has been opened and flung onto the floor.

Sara stares down at the heap. Sees album covers that unreel threads of memory in her mind. Those were good times. Seeing all those shared songs tossed away like this brings a lump to her throat.

But now is not the time for sentimentality. There may be people in this house. People who have heard the noise she has just made, and who are now awaiting their opportunity to break her skull open.

She leaves the room and approaches the staircase. Slow, careful steps.

She pauses there for a few seconds, listening intently. Then she begins her ascent, her gaze glued to the landing above.

When she reaches the top of the stairs, she halts and performs another scan. The door to the small bathroom is wide open, and she can see that nobody is in there. That's one room down, two to go.

The door to the rear bedroom – the spare one that Matthew uses as an office – is fully closed; she can't get in there without making further noise.

She decides to leave that room till last.

She treads softly along the landing. When she gets to the front bedroom, she takes some deep but quiet breaths, then repeats her earlier manoeuvre of squashing herself against the wall while she pushes the door open. It opens with a slight creak, but there is no sudden rush of intruders towards her.

She slides silently into the room. Sees that it's like the others. Sheets and mattress on the floor; clothes dragged out of the wardrobes; drawers tipped upside down.

So, on to the final room.

She retraces her steps along the landing, then stares long and hard at the closed door. She presses her ear to the varnished wood, but hears nothing on the other side. She stares at it again, then grabs the handle and takes some deep breaths.

Here we go, then.

She turns the handle, pushes the door open.

Straight ahead is Matthew's computer desk. The drawers have been turned out, and there is no sign of his laptop.

Sara leaps into the room, knife arm in front of her. She is ready. If they are here, she is ready to fight, to maim, to—

No.

She is not ready for this.

Please, God, not this.

Matthew is here.

She goes to him. Puts the knife down, freeing up hands that she doesn't know what to do with in this situation. She doesn't know how to help. This is beyond anything she has ever experienced, and she has experienced much.

Matthew is on the floor. He is naked and spreadeagled.

And dead. Very dead. She has seen enough of death to know that.

For Matthew, it is probably a blessing. He has been nailed to the floor. Huge steel nails have been driven through his arms, his legs and even his genitals. Rivulets of bright blood have coursed across his pallid flesh and pooled beneath him. His mouth is open, as if in a final agonising scream, and his eyes have rolled back in their sockets.

He must have suffered greatly. There is no pretending otherwise.

'Matthew,' she says. 'I am so sorry. So sorry.'

She reaches a hand to his face and closes his eyelids. And then she cries. And when it hits her yet again that tears accomplish nothing, she digs deep and finds the anger, the drive, the essence of survival, and she picks up the knife and stabs it again and again into the floorboards.

3

Detective Sergeant Nathan Cody isn't certain how he's going to play this, but he's willing to give it a try.

He pulls up behind one of the many marked police vehicles, then gets out of his car and strides quickly along the street. When he gets to the house, he sees the figures of Webley and Ferguson, familiar even through their white protective Tyvek suits.

'What took you so long?' says Webley. 'We were beginning to think you'd decided not to bother.'

Megan Webley gets away with quite a lot when it comes to her sergeant. It has nothing to do with Cody being a soft touch, and everything to do with the fact that she was once the love of his life. That was years ago, but since she and Cody were thrown together again on the Major Incident Team they have endured much turmoil, both physical and emotional. Through choice or not, bonds have been re-formed and continue to strengthen. Most of the time, Cody chooses to bury his head in the sand about it, but sometimes his strength of feeling for Webley surprises him.

'Had a few matters to attend to,' says Cody, although he knows it's a crap answer that isn't going to convince anyone. 'The boss here?'

Webley eyes him with suspicion. 'She's inside. Are you okay?'

'Yeah, fine. Why shouldn't I be?'

Webley exchanges glances with the towering figure of Neil 'Footlong' Ferguson next to her.

'No reason,' she says.

It occurs to Cody that this isn't going as planned. 'You been in there yet?'

'No. Weird one, apparently. Bloke's been nailed to his floor.'

'Jesus.'

'No,' says Footlong. 'They used a cross for him. Similar idea, though.'

'Who is he?'

'Name's Matthew Prior. He lived here alone, separated from his wife. She's the one who found the body and called it in.'

'Possible crime of passion, you think?'

Footlong shrugs. 'Maybe. Her story is she was on a flight into Manchester when it happened. Doesn't mean she didn't get someone else to do it for her, though. I always get suspicious when people have airtight alibis, forgive the pun.'

Cody nods. 'Right. I'll get suited up, then.'

He starts to walk away. Halts when he hears the bellow behind him.

'Cody!'

He turns around again. Sees the stocky figure of DCI Stella Blunt coming out of the house towards him.

'What are you doing here?' she asks him.

Cody contorts his features into his best look of innocence. 'Ma'am?'

'Don't play games with me,' she says. She turns to Webley and Ferguson. 'You two, get inside and do something useful.'

Cody sees how his two colleagues look at him before reluctantly abandoning him to his fate. Their faces hold the promise of a barrage of questions later.

Blunt waits until they have disappeared, then pulls down the hood of her white suit. 'I thought I left you with plenty of things to get on with.'

'You did, but I thought you could do with me here.'

'You did, did you?'

'Yes.'

'Cody, we've already had this conversation. I thought I made it perfectly plain that you are not to go anywhere near crime scenes involving fatalities until I give you the all clear.'

'Ma'am, I'm not a child. If I didn't think I could cope with this, I'd say so.'

'No. That's just it. You wouldn't say so. You'd keep it to yourself, just like you always do. You have just returned from leave after a pretty traumatic ordeal that landed you in hospital.'

'It was precautionary, that's all. There was nothing wrong with me.'

'I think the doctors would disagree. By all accounts you were in pretty bad shape. And anyway, it's not the physical injuries I'm talking about.' She taps her own temple. 'It's what's happening up here that concerns me.'

'I've been through worse.'

'Yes, I know you've been through worse, and that's my point. Anyone experiencing what you've been through cannot be unaffected. I have a duty of care, Nathan. Much as I'd like my best detectives on this case, I have to think about their welfare too. I am not risking causing you permanent mental damage.'

'So what does that mean? You're keeping me tied to a desk?'

'Of course not. I want your assistance. I just don't want to put you slap bang in the middle of a scene that might turn you into a gibbering wreck.'

'For how long? I mean, how long will it take for you to believe I can do my job properly?'

'Again, we've discussed this. Have you booked yourself in yet?'

Cody looks away. Taps his foot.

'Not yet. I've been a little busy with all that paperwork you've given me.'

'I thought as much. Good job I've done it for you, then, isn't it?'

He turns to her again. 'What? Ma'am, I do not need to see a shrink.'

'Yes, Nathan, you do. That's exactly what you need if you're to remain on my team. Your first session is tomorrow morning, nine o'clock.'

'*First* session? How many—?'

'Her practice is on Rodney Street. The street where you live. That means there's no excuse not to be there. The force uses her a lot for this type of thing, and she doesn't come cheap, so if I find out you've skipped the meeting, you'll be out on your ear. Is that understood?'

Cody looks into the distance again. He's fuming now. But he's been given little choice.

'And until then? How do I occupy myself while you're all in there doing what I should be doing?'

'Don't be petulant, Nathan. It's not an attractive quality in anyone. You can help to organise the house-to-house. After that, you can head back to the station and interview the victim's wife.'

'Great,' says Cody.

Blunt takes a step closer to Cody and lowers her voice. 'Look, Nathan, I'm not doing this as a way of getting rid of you. That's the last thing I want. But you and I both know that this was always on the cards. You have to admit that your behaviour can be a little . . . *erratic* at times. Do this for me, get yourself signed off as fit for duty, and I won't bother you again. Deal?'

Cody looks at her. 'Fine,' he says. 'Whatever it takes.'

But he's still angry.

And more than a little scared.

4

'First impressions, Rory?'

Rory Stroud turns his vast bulk towards Blunt, his inquisitor. 'I can do a mean Cary Grant. *Judy, Judy, Judy.* What do you think?'

'Don't give up the day job. Besides, Cary Grant never actually said those words.'

'He didn't?'

'No. Now can we stick to impressions of the case in hand, please?'

'For you, Stella, anything.'

Webley can tell that behind Stroud's face mask he is wearing a huge grin. The forensic pathologist is famed for his way with the ladies.

Stroud waves a gloved hand towards the corpse on the floor. 'Not a pleasant way to go. Someone has made damn sure this fellow didn't die quickly.'

'How quickly?'

Stroud sucks air noisily through his mask. 'Hard to say. Could have been hours. You see the way most of the nails have been driven through the fleshy edges of the limbs, rather than the head or torso? That suggests the attackers were trying to avoid hitting major arteries and internal organs. They wanted him alive and in pain.'

'So what killed him?'

'Again, not easy to say before I do the PM. There's a lot of blood here, so could be exsanguination. It's also perfectly possible that his heart just gave out. His system would have been under an immense amount of stress. To be honest, I think he would have been praying for a way out.'

Webley keeps her eyes on the body. She has seen some shocking sights, but this one is way up in the rankings. How could anyone do something like this to another human being?

Blunt says, 'I know how you're going to answer, but for the sake of completeness I'm going to ask you anyway. Do you have anything to contribute about time of death?'

Stroud laughs. 'Let it never be said that you aren't thorough, my dear Stella. You know the pathologist's standard response to that, yes?'

'It's engraved on my heart. Find out when the victim was last seen alive, find out when the body was discovered, and voila, the time of death was somewhere between the two. Are you going to surprise me today?'

'Depends. Am I right in thinking that this man's wife received a phone call from him this morning?'

'A message was left on her answering machine at about ten o'clock.'

'And she found the body at . . . ?'

'About two forty-five.'

'Then my answer is no – I am not going to surprise you. Those timings are consistent with my preliminary assessment of the deceased.'

Blunt sighs heavily. 'What about the number of assailants?'

'Difficult to say. The house looks like a rugby team has rampaged through it, but it's possible that one person could have done it all. You see these marks on the victim's head? If they were the initial blows, they may have been enough to subdue him, perhaps even render him unconscious. Once the first few nails were pounded in, he'd have been unable to move.'

Blunt stares again at the body. 'Poor bugger.'

Stroud nods. 'Problem I've got now is unsticking him from the floor so I can get him back to the mortuary.'

'Good luck with that,' says Blunt.

Webley watches as her boss scans the room. She wonders what's going through Blunt's mind. All those years of expertise brought to bear on her surroundings. What is she seeing? What conclusions is she already drawing?

Webley has huge admiration for Blunt. More so since she learned about her greatest vulnerability. Even Cody doesn't know about that particular skeleton in Blunt's closet.

Although something's going on between the pair of them, she thinks. Why was Cody prevented from coming into the house? And where is he now?

Blunt moves carefully across the stepping plates to another white-suited figure. 'Dev? What can you tell me?'

Dev Chandra, the crime scene manager, turns to Blunt. 'On the face of it, it seems that someone was looking for something and wanted it very badly. Clear signs of a break-in through the back door, the ransacking of the house, and then the torture of the victim, as though they were desperate to get information out of him. That said, appearances can be deceptive.'

'Anything missing, as far as you can tell?'

Chandra gestures towards the office desk. 'The computer. We can't find that anywhere. Without a full inventory of the house contents, though, it's difficult to know what else might have been taken. We're searching it as best we can, but as you've seen, the place is a tip.'

'I understand. What about forensics?'

'Tons of it. Fibres, blood spatters, fingerprints, footprints, DNA – you name it. What we don't know yet is who they belong to. Could be the attackers, could be the victim, could be the wife, could be previous visitors. There is one standout item, though.'

'Which is?'

'Walk this way.'

Chandra leads Blunt out of the room. Webley follows.

'Here,' says Chandra. He pulls out a torch, switches it on and focuses its beam on the bannister post. 'See?'

Webley shuffles up behind Blunt and cranes forward for a closer look.

'A fingerprint,' says Blunt. 'In blood.'

'Certainly is,' says Chandra. 'If it's Prior's own blood from the recent attack, then there's no way he could have left the print here.'

'Is it a good print?'

'It's partial, but it looks pretty well-defined to me. Let's just hope we can match it up to a known criminal.'

Blunt straightens up. 'Thanks, Dev. Good work. Keep me informed.'

When Chandra has returned to his evidence collection duties, Blunt turns to Webley.

'Seen enough?' she asks. 'I for one could do with some fresh air.'

Webley nods, then follows Blunt downstairs and out of the house. They both pull off their hoods and face masks.

'Okay, Megan,' says Blunt. 'You've seen what I've seen. What do you think?'

'I think . . . I think Dev has got to be right about this. Someone was looking for something. They've gone through every room, trashing the place to find it. And they tortured Prior to get him to talk, to tell them where it is.'

'Okay, so my next question. What is *it*? What were they after?'

Webley shakes her head. 'I've no idea.' She looks back at the small unassuming house. 'What could this guy possibly own that's worth that much trouble?'

'And,' Blunt adds, 'why wouldn't he tell them what he knew? I can assure you now, you'd only have to *show* me one of those nails before I started blurting out answers to everything I was asked.'

5

Cody's fear has taken a tighter grip of him since he got back to the station.

He's in a no-win situation. Until he undergoes the sessions with a head doctor, he's not going to be allowed to participate fully in investigations. On the other hand, what if the doc finds something? What if Cody finds it impossible to keep in all the things he must?

The enforced leave of absence didn't help. He has been a wreck since his last case. All his problems returning with a vengeance. The insomnia, the anxiety, the hallucinations. Blunt made a good call this afternoon; he's not sure he would have coped well with a scene that sounded like something straight out of Dante or Bosch.

So yes, he thinks. I'm ill. As bad as ever.

And my biggest worry is that a shrink will spot it from a mile away.

'Could I have some water, please?'

The voice jolts him back into the here and now. He's in an interview room – one of the less imposing ones in the station, with comfy chairs and plants and pictures on the wall. Sitting across from him is Sara Prior. Slim and blonde, wolf-blue eyes and with an accent that Cody can't quite place. And there's something else about this woman. A distancing he can't quite fathom.

'Sorry,' he says. 'Yes, of course. You wouldn't prefer tea, or coffee?'

She shakes her head. 'Water's fine.'

He picks up the jug and pours water into a plastic beaker, which he passes across to her.

She nods her gratitude.

'I know this must be difficult for you,' he says, 'but the quicker we move, the more likely it is we'll catch whoever did this terrible thing.'

'It's not difficult for me,' she says. 'Ask your questions.'

Her response surprises Cody. She seems so calm, so rational.

'Okay,' he says. 'But I'll understand if you find this upsetting. If you need a break at any point, please let me—'

'I'm fine. Please, what do you want to know?'

He stares into those lupine eyes. She does not flinch, but sends back her own challenging gaze. Cody suspects many would crumble under such scrutiny.

He checks the few notes he has in front of him. 'Matthew Prior was your husband, yes?'

'That's correct.'

'But you haven't been living with him?'

'No.' She flicks a hand towards the paperwork in front of Cody. 'My address is on your form there. I live in Halewood.'

'How long have you lived apart from each other?'

'About four months.'

'And before that, you both lived at the Halewood address?'

'Yes.'

'How long were you married?'

'About three years.'

'Were you intending to get divorced?'

'No.'

'Then can I ask why you separated?'

'No, you may not. I really don't see why that's relevant to Matthew's murder. In fact, I don't see why any of these questions about my relationship with Matthew are relevant.'

Cody finds a smile for her. She's not making it easy for him, but a smile can work wonders sometimes.

'I'm sorry. Perhaps it would help if I explain how we do things. I'm not just being nosey. I'm trying to build a picture of Matthew's life. How he lived, his likes and dislikes, who he came into contact with, who might have had reason to kill him. Right now, I don't know what's relevant and what's not. It's possible that ninety-nine per cent of what you tell me in this interview won't have any bearing on the investigation whatsoever. But the other one per cent might crack the case. I'm trying to find that one per cent.'

She remains quiet for a few seconds, then nods her head. 'You're right. I can see that you're just doing your job. Please go ahead.'

Cody feels he has just been granted royal assent to enter an area not normally open to commoners. He clears his throat.

'Okay, so about the separation? If you don't mind.'

She takes a sip of her water. 'No real reason. No affairs or domestic violence, if that's what you're asking. We just needed some time apart.'

'After only three years?'

'It happens.' She considers her answer for a moment. 'Perhaps it would be more accurate to say that Matthew needed some space.'

'Space? Why? Was something bothering him?'

'Nothing specific. What you have to understand about Matthew is that he is – *was* – a very private person. He was socially awkward. He would get anxious about the smallest of things. If a taxi was a minute late he would pace up and down with worry. Or if he had a headache he would think it was a brain tumour. He was very introverted. When we met, it was me who had to invite him out on a date.'

'You found him hard work, then?'

'Not at all. I found him very easy to be with. And actually, I believe he appreciated what I brought him.'

'Which was?'

'A life. I know that sounds very dramatic, but Matthew had no real life before we got together. He was so used to his own company. Apart from work, he didn't go anywhere or do anything. He'd never had a long-term girlfriend. His only social activity was computer gaming.'

Cody chews this over and tastes the bitter familiarity. His own life now is not so different from what poor Matthew's was.

'But you changed all that? You made him happy?'

'Yes. It may sound conceited, but I think I did. We were opposites in many ways, but that's what brought us together. I wanted someone who wasn't pretentious or ambitious or arrogant. Matthew wanted someone to bring him out of his shell and show him that life can be fun if you're willing to take a few risks.'

'Sounds like a perfect match. So when did it go wrong?'

'I suppose about the start of last year. He became very . . . morose. Very withdrawn. He stopped talking to me. He stopped wanting to spend time with me.'

'But you don't know what might have caused it?'

'No. I have no idea. I tried to get him to explain, but he refused to speak about it. I offered to go to marriage guidance counselling with him, but he didn't want that either.'

'Did you argue?'

'Not really. Sometimes I lost my temper with him, but mostly I was just upset that I couldn't help him. He could see how unhappy it was making me, and that's when he told me he was moving out.'

'What did you say?'

'What could I say? He told me he needed time to sort himself out. I had to go along with it. I wasn't given a choice. I always hoped he would come back.'

'After he left, did you continue to see each other?'

'Yes. I went to his house every couple of days. I bought shopping and gifts for him. I tried talking things over with him.'

'Did it work?'

She blinks. 'I . . . I wish I could say yes, but it wouldn't be true. He seemed to get unhappier each day.'

'But he never gave you any clues as to what was wrong?'

'No. Now I wish I'd pushed harder. I think if he'd told me, I could have done something about it. But now . . .'

'Yes?'

'Now it's too late.'

6

Cody thinks there's something wrong here. Something about the way Sara Prior is acting.

He's seen it all in rooms like this, talking to bereaved family members. The full gamut of emotions. Some wail; some go into shock or denial; some faint; some rant or become violent.

Sara does none of these things. She seems so relaxed in her chair, sipping her water and answering his questions. Cody has seen people in job interviews who are more nervous than this. She claims to have been devoted to her husband, so why isn't her severance from him causing her more distress? What is she holding back?

'Tell me about what happened today. How did you find out about Matthew?'

'There was a message on my telephone answering machine. I—'

'You'd just returned from the airport, is that right?'

'Yes. Manchester.'

'Where had you been?'

'Copenhagen. I'm from there originally. I was visiting family. My maiden name is Olsen.'

'Ah, you're Danish. I was trying to place the accent. Your English is excellent.'

'Almost everyone in Copenhagen speaks some English. My father insisted we speak it as much as possible. He had grand ideas of a future for me in global financing.'

Cody notices how she doesn't even seem to register his compliment. Not so much as a nod of appreciation.

'Okay,' he continues. 'So you got home . . .'

'Yes, and I saw that I had messages. I ignored them at first. I made a cup of tea and just forgot about them. But then I went back to the hall for my suitcase. That's when I listened to the calls.'

'How many calls were there?'

'Three, but only one from Matthew.'

'What did he say?'

'It was . . . It was very strange. He was clearly anxious about something. He said something like, "They're here." He said it a couple of times. But he also said . . .'

'Go on.'

'I'm finding it hard to believe now, but he said something like, "Remember Victoria and Albert."'

Cody pauses with his pen in mid-sentence on his notepad. 'Can you repeat that, please?'

'Yes. He said, "Remember Victoria and Albert." I'm sure it was that.'

Cody frowns, but jots it down. 'What else?'

'Nothing, really. He said he had no more time to speak, and then . . . and then it was like somebody took the phone off him, and . . .'

Cody says nothing. Just lets her find the words.

'And then he screamed. I heard the start of a scream. That was all.'

Cody observes her for a few long seconds. Waits for tears that don't fall, a quivering lip that doesn't happen. All so matter-of-fact.

'It must have scared you,' he says. But the prompt goes unanswered.

He says, 'This thing about Victoria and Albert. Do you know what he meant by that?'

'No.'

'Something to do with the Victoria and Albert Museum?'

'I don't think so. I've never been there, and as far as I know, neither had Matthew.'

'People, then. Do you know anyone called Victoria and Albert?'

A slow shake of the head. 'No. That doesn't ring any bells with me.'

'Can you think of any other reason why he'd ask you to remember those names?'

'None at all.'

Cody taps his pen on his chin. 'The phone message. Any idea why he left it on your landline instead of calling you on your mobile?'

'He was terrified. I think he just panicked and picked the first number on his speed dial.'

'Is the message still on your answering machine? You didn't delete it?'

'No. It's still there.'

'Good. I'd like to send someone over to make a copy of it, if that's all right with you.'

'Yes. That's fine.'

'All right, so you listened to the call from Matthew. Then what?'

'I went straight over there.'

'That was your first impulse? You didn't call the police?'

'I didn't know what was happening. Matthew had changed so much since he moved out. I thought perhaps he was having some kind of breakdown. And anyway, do you think the police would have been interested? What would you have done if I had called you and said my husband rang to say something about Victoria and Albert before screaming down the phone at me?'

Cody smiles. 'When you put it like that . . . Okay, so you drove to his house, yes?'

'Yes. I confess I broke the speed limit a few times. You might find me on one or two of those traffic cameras of yours.'

'I think you had a pretty good excuse. How did things look when you got to Matthew's house?'

'You mean inside?'

'No. Before then. When you got out of your car.'

'It looked normal. No sign of anything strange.'

'Was the front door open?'

'No. It was closed. I rang the doorbell, and I tried shouting through the letter box, but nobody came.'

'Do you have a key to the house?'

'No. Matthew would have hated the thought of someone coming into his home without his knowledge. I once asked him what I was supposed to do if he had an accident or something, but he still refused.'

'So how did you get inside?'

'I went round to the back of the house.'

Cody consults his notes again. 'We checked the yard door. It was locked.'

She seems unfazed. 'Yes. I climbed the wall.'

'You climbed the wall?'

'Yes.'

'It's a pretty high wall.'

'Yes, it is.'

Cody almost expects her to break into a laugh, to tell him that she's pulling his leg. But she's deadly serious.

'All right, so you climbed over the wall. Then what did you do?'

'I looked through the windows. I could see all the mess in there. And then I saw that the glass in the back door was smashed. Someone had broken into the house.'

'Yes, that's how it looked to us.'

'So I went in.'

Cody tries to take her answer in his stride. Fails miserably.

'You went straight in?'

'Yes.'

'Did you have your mobile phone with you?'

'Yes.'

'But you didn't try calling the police?'

'I didn't want to wait. Matthew might have been hurt. In his call he sounded in pain.'

'The house had been broken into. There could have been intruders still in there.'

'I picked up a knife in the kitchen.' A thought suddenly occurs to her. 'There'll be a knife with my fingerprints on it. You should probably know that.'

Cody is dumbfounded. She keeps surprising him. He would have been satisfied with an answer like, 'I didn't know what I was doing. I was in a state of shock.' But she seems to have known exactly what she was doing, and had no hesitation in doing it.

'What did you do after you picked up the knife?'

'I searched the house. The back bedroom was the last one I went into. That's where I found Matthew.'

'That must have been a hell of a shock.'

Again no response. No confirmation that she experienced emotions of any kind.

Cody still senses he's missing something here.

'I'm sorry, Mrs Prior,' he says. 'Forgive me if this sounds a little insensitive, but I don't quite get the sequence of events as you've described them.'

'What is it you don't get, Sergeant Cody?'

'I don't get why it took you so long to call the police. I don't get the fact that you climbed a brick wall and went alone into a house to face possible intruders.'

And then she hits him with the question that floors him.

'Is it because I'm a woman?'

'What?'

'I'm asking you whether you would find my account as difficult to believe if it came from the mouth of a man.'

Cody considers this carefully. He thinks, Is she right? Am I just being sexist?

'To be honest,' he says, 'I don't know many people, male or female, who would do what you did today. I have to take my hat off to you for your bravery.'

'I did what was necessary. But I would like to see some bravery in return. I want you to be brave enough to believe me. I can see in your eyes that you have your doubts. I didn't do what you expect women in my position to do, and I'm not acting now in the way you expect women to behave.'

'Mrs Prior, I really hope you don't think—'

'I'm not going to cry, here in front of you. I'm not going to fall to pieces just to satisfy your preconceived notions. I won't do any of that, Sergeant Cody. I will grieve in my own way, if that's all right with you. If that's something you can't accept, then we may as well terminate the interview right now.'

Cody wants to laugh out loud. He realises he has just been told off, and that he thoroughly deserved it. He also realises that he likes this woman. Likes her a lot, even though he doesn't fully understand her.

'I can accept that,' he tells her.

'Good. Then please continue.'

'Tell me a little more about Matthew. What was his job?'

'He worked for the tax office. When I met him he was based in Newcastle, but then he was offered a promotion. It meant transferring to the Bootle office, so that's when we moved to Liverpool.'

'When was this?'

'About two years ago.'

'Did you make many friends here?'

'A few. Not many.'

'What about enemies? Did Matthew ever fall out with anybody? Anyone ever threaten him?'

She shakes her head. 'Matthew didn't get into fights. He hated confrontation. He was nice to everyone he met.'

'Any money problems?'

'No. He had a good job, and so do I.'

'What do you do?'

'I'm a personal trainer.'

'Really? I could do with one of those myself.'

She eyes him up. 'My rates are reasonable.'

Cody clears his throat again. He would have preferred an answer along the lines of, *You look in pretty good shape already.*

'You saw the house,' he says. 'Somebody searched every inch of it. Any idea what they might have been looking for?'

'No. He had nothing valuable. His money went on books and CDs and computer games.'

'What type of games?'

She shrugs. 'I didn't take much interest. They had lots of people shooting at each other. It's how he got his thrills.'

'What else did he use his computer for?'

'I don't know. The usual, I suppose. Email, the web – that kind of thing.'

'The reason I ask is because there's no sign of his computer in the house. Can you think of any reason why someone might have wanted to steal it?'

She shakes her head. 'Sergeant Cody, I don't think you have fully understood what I have been trying to tell you about my husband. Matthew was kind and gentle and shy. That wasn't a disguise. He wasn't really a spy for MI5 or an assassin or whatever. He was just a normal man who had a few problems coping with life. I loved him deeply. And you know what?'

'What?'

'He loved me too. He told me so. You said something earlier about my bravery in going into his house. It wasn't because of courage; it was because of something else he said in his phone message. He said he loved me. I hadn't heard those words from Matthew for a long time, but he said them then. He was scared for his life – perhaps he even knew he was about to be killed – but his last thought was to let me know he still loved me. If you have ever been in love, Sergeant Cody, you will understand that that's the only explanation you need for my actions.'

7

The house seems so empty.

Even though Matthew hasn't lived here for months, Sara feels his absence more keenly now. She has always clung to a thread of hope that he would return one day – that he would fill the Matthew-shaped hole in her life and her home.

But now that hope has gone. Matthew has been snatched away from her. And so cruelly, too.

The violence makes it so much worse. If he had died in an accident, or perhaps even taken his own life, she believes she might have come to terms with it more easily. But this! Why would anyone treat him so sadistically? What could he possibly have done?

She feels sorry for that policeman. Cody. He was doing his best, but she really couldn't help him. She told him the truth: Matthew was a lovely man who just needed someone by his side.

I should have been there, she thinks. I should have protected him.

She is standing in the hall. Her suitcase is still open on the floor, her dirty washing still heaped in the doorway to the kitchen. Cody brought her home, along with a technician who took a copy of Matthew's phone message. They have gone now, leaving her in the emptiness.

She expects that they will look into her background. They will treat her as a suspect. It's only natural, and she's not worried about it. Let them think what they like.

Perhaps I should have acted more like a distraught widow, she thinks. Perhaps I should have screamed and pulled out my hair in clumps. Maybe then they would have believed me.

No matter. I'm not a performing seal. Crying won't fix a thing. It didn't fix Svend and it won't fix Matthew.

She decides she won't ever love another man. It always leads to too much pain – for them and for her.

I must be cursed, she thinks. There's a spell on me. I am a – what is the English word? – a *jinx*, that's it.

They couldn't have been any more different from each other, Svend and Matthew, and yet the outcome was the same. Svend she can understand – the danger was always hovering on the horizon in his case. But not Matthew. Matthew was the stereotypical mild-mannered public servant. Matthew was a man whose definition of risk was shelling out for a lottery ticket, or opting for a pizza topping he'd never tried before. Matthew's only exposure to violence prior to his death was in the form of animated pixels on his computer screen.

So it must be me, she thinks. I'm the link. I'm the reason why those around me get killed.

And yet . . .

The message. On the phone.

She looks at the phone again now. It sits there, defying her to listen again to the closing words of her now dead husband.

She steps across to it. Commands it to replay the last message.

'Sara! Remember! Victoria and Albert. All I can say. They're here! They're— Sara, I love you. I—'

His terror is almost tangible. It infects her. She feels the familiar surge of adrenaline as it readies her to fight for her life.

She takes a few deep breaths. I'm safe, she tells herself. I'm at home. Nothing can get to me here.

She plays the message again, forcing herself to focus on the words rather than the emotion.

Remember! Victoria and Albert.

What the hell does that mean?

She wracks her brain for conversations – *snippets* of conversations – anything that might have related to those two names during her brief time with Matthew.

Nothing comes to mind.

But what if it's associated with the future rather than the past? What if Matthew wants her to bear the names in mind for some event that is yet to occur?

What could that possibly be? And how will she know when it's happening? How can she be sure to call up those names at the precise moment they are needed?

It doesn't make any sense.

She moves on to the next part of the message. The bit about *they*. *They're here!*

Who? Who were there? And why was Matthew so terrified of them? It seems clear that he knew their identities and their aim. He knew his hourglass was running out.

Shocking images jump into her mind. She sees Matthew desperately stabbing at the buttons of his phone as he hears his attackers breaking into his house. She sees him crying, hears his sobbing when the call isn't answered immediately.

And then the sudden outpouring of words when the answering machine eventually grants its permission to talk. The rushed burble as the intruders appear in his sights, see what he is doing, and snatch his lifeline away from him.

Lifeline – ha! If only. If only she had been on the other end of that line rather than a fucking machine.

And then more images. Of torture, of interrogation, of immense unendurable agony. She sees his blood, feels his humiliation, hears his prayers for an end to his torment.

And then the pictures in her head become confused, jumbled with others. Memories and imaginings conjoin in a maelstrom of death and injury, until she doesn't know what is real and what is not.

She releases a yell. A long, drawn-out scream of fury and anguish that echoes around a house that now seems just a hollow shell.

A full two minutes pass while she sits kneeling on the wooden floor of the hallway, staring but not seeing.

She plays the recorded message again. This time she concentrates on the end of it. The part where Matthew tells her unequivocally that he loves her.

She has sometimes feared that she would never hear those words again. When he moved out of this house, Matthew seemed so damaged, so not in control of himself. She hoped that he would eventually find peace, but there was always a nagging doubt that it might be beyond his enfeebled reach.

And here it is. The confirmation of his devotion to her. It took his imminent death to squeeze it out of him, but here it is.

She plays the message again and again. She no longer hears the fear, the cries. She blots those out and hears only him assuring her of his love.

And what she produces in response is what she told DS Cody she was denying him. Tears in abundance – evidence of a fragility that she will let no man see again.

8

Monday morning on Rodney Street, the Harley Street of the North. The Georgian doors open. Doctors, dentists, therapists, acupuncturists and other highly paid private sector professionals welcome in the clients who line their pockets so readily.

Cody just wants to get this over with. There's a case to be solved, and over at the station his colleagues will be taking steps towards solving it. Without him. It doesn't seem right. It feels like missing an important lesson at school – so important that he cannot hope to catch up on his return.

And besides, this is a waste of everyone's time. He's going to lie through his teeth no matter what this particular professional asks, and hope that his story is swallowed without catching in the throat. But even if it isn't, what can the psychologist prove? What Cody keeps telling himself is that this is just a matter of putting himself in the shoes of someone who doesn't have a problem. This is a test of his acting ability, and nothing more.

The waiting room is plush and modern. Even the magazines here are this month's. No television, though. Cody guesses that's so it doesn't show something that might upset a patient.

He hears the rapid click of heels as a woman strides briskly into the waiting area. She looks about the same age as Cody, which somehow makes him more agitated. He had hoped for someone much older – someone close to retirement who has nothing to prove with over-zealous probing.

'Mr Cody?'

'Yes,' he says. 'Hi.'

She proffers a hand, together with a smile that is meant to be welcoming but which he doesn't find a comfort.

'I'm Gem Falstaff. Would you like to come through?'

He'd like to say, *No, I'd rather leave now, if it's all the same to you*, but he doesn't think it will help in getting signed off. He also doesn't like the name Gem. Nobody calls themselves Gem.

She leads him into an office that has the expected exhibits of expertise: framed certificates on the wall, shelves of boring-looking academic tomes, and *objets d'art* attesting to wealth derived from success. She waves him into a low chair alongside a coffee table that holds a framed photograph of a smiling family that look nothing like her. She sits opposite him and crosses her legs before resting a folder of papers on them.

Cody wonders what is already in that folder, and what will be added to it by the end of the session.

'Okay,' she says. 'Do you mind if I call you Nathan?'

'Uhm—'

'I can call you Mr Cody if you prefer. I just think that's a little—'

'Cody. Everyone calls me Cody. Except my mum. And sometimes my boss.'

She smiles at him, and he wishes he hadn't just told her about how Blunt addresses him. She might be seeing all kinds of Oedipus stuff in his words.

'Cody it is, then. You've been told about the purpose of these sessions, I take it?'

He shrugs. 'I got the gist. You want to check I'm fit for duty. Which I am, by the way.'

'Well, great. In that case, this should be a breeze.'

She looks down at her folder, flips a page.

'I see you've filled out the pre-assessment form. Nothing out of the ordinary here. In fact, you could say it's extraordinarily ordinary.'

She smiles again, but Cody is certain she is making a criticism. He's beginning to wonder if he should have ticked a few more of the boxes at the extreme ends of the responses. Given her something to get her teeth into, however untrue.

'You say you haven't experienced any suicidal tendencies.'

'That's right.'

'Insomnia?'

'No.'

'Depression or anxiety?'

'No.'

'Panic attacks?'

'No.'

'Do you drink much?'

'Hardly ever.'

'Really? Why's that?'

Damn, thinks Cody. Have I just fallen into a trap?

'What do you mean?'

'Well, a guy your age, working in the police force . . . Your colleagues must try to drag you to the pub now and again, no?'

Shit.

'Yes. I mean, I have the occasional drink. Just not very often.'

'Ever have enough to get drunk?'

He thinks about lying, but he's already told her he hardly ever drinks.

'No. Not now.'

'But you used to?'

'Yes.'

'So what changed?'

'I . . . I decided I needed to adopt a healthier lifestyle. I saw what drink was doing to people around me.'

'You mean your colleagues?'

'Yes. And my dad.'

'Your dad's a heavy drinker?'

'He can be.'

She nods. Clicks her pen and makes a note in her paperwork. 'We'll come back to your family later.'

Thought we might, Cody thinks.

She says, 'When was it you decided to go on the wagon?'

'About a year ago.'

'A year ago. Okay.'

Another scribbled note. Cody would love to know what she's writing.

'But I'm not exactly on the wagon,' he adds. 'I just drink much less now.'

'Uh-huh,' she says. He senses they'll probably return to this topic later, too.

She leans back in her chair. Studies him for a few seconds. 'I want you to know,' she says, 'that I'm not trying to catch you out in these sessions. I'm here to help you.'

'I thought your job was to assess me.'

'That too. But at the heart of all this is your welfare. You have a very demanding job. You must see some gruesome sights.'

'I'm used to it.'

'They don't bother you?'

'Not at all. It comes with the job.'

'I know, but that doesn't mean it can't affect you. I've met some very experienced police officers who have been severely traumatised by their work. The problem is they don't always realise it at the time.' She pauses. 'Are you working on a case at the moment?'

'Yes.'

'Is it a murder?'

'Yes.'

'Did you view the body?'

Cody shifts in his seat. 'No.'

'No? Isn't that unusual?'

'Depends. On this occasion, I was asked to perform other duties.'

'You were asked not to attend the crime scene?'

'Yes.'

'Who gave you that order?'

'My commanding officer. DCI Blunt.'

Falstaff looks down at her notes and makes a ticking motion with her pen, as if confirming the story already present there.

'Why did she do that?'

'She . . . she was worried it might affect me adversely.'

'I see. I assume she wouldn't normally do that, so why was she so worried this time?'

'Because of what I'd been through on a previous case. I'm sure this is in your notes, but I've just returned from leave.'

Falstaff flips through her pages again. 'You were hospitalised.'

'Yes. But I was okay. Nothing serious.'

Falstaff continues reading for a while, then looks straight at Cody. 'Some would say you went through quite an ordeal.'

'I like to get my hands dirty,' says Cody.

'Which is fine when things go well, but sometimes they don't. Are you comfortable with talking about those times when your best-laid plans haven't worked out?'

'Sure,' he says, because he knows it's the only answer he can give.

'Good. If at any time you feel you want to take a break, just let me know, okay?'

He nods, but he has already decided he's not going to request a timeout. That would be a big mistake.

'All right,' says Falstaff. 'Let's begin at the beginning.'

'I was working on a child abduction case. A six-year-old girl called—'

'Sorry,' says Falstaff. 'You're talking about the last case you worked on. I wanted to take you back a bit further in time, to when you were on that undercover operation that went wrong.'

Cody blinks. 'That was quite a while ago.'

'Year before last. Not so long, really.'

'Okay, but I've already seen a psychologist for that one.'

'Yes,' says Falstaff. She consults her notes again. 'Who was it you saw?'

'Er . . . I forget his name. Oldish guy, glasses, beard . . .'

'Dr Rimmer.'

'Could be. Yes.'

Falstaff takes a while formulating her next response. As if what she really wants to say is something like, *Yeah, I know Rimmer, and he's a useless old fart who just nods and puts down whatever it is the patient wants his bosses to hear, but don't even think about me doing the same thing because it wouldn't be very professional.*

'I like to get the full picture,' she says. 'Every event in our lives connects to every other. Sorry if that means going over old ground, but I think it would be helpful.'

'Right,' says Cody, although he doesn't think this is going to be the least bit helpful to himself. 'What do you want to know?'

'Well, let's start with the facts. What happened exactly?'

Cody collects his thoughts as he decides how to launch into his story. It's not one he often tells.

'I was working undercover with a partner called Jeff Vance. We'd infiltrated a gang led by a man called Barry Duffy.'

'What were they doing, this gang?'

'Whatever they could. Drugs, guns, robbery. We were building evidence, but we also knew there were bigger fish to fry above Duffy. We were hoping to get to them.'

'Did Duffy believe your cover story?'

Cody shrugs. 'We thought so at the time. Maybe he didn't, though. Maybe he always knew the truth. Or else somebody told him.'

'So how did he react?'

'He didn't – at least not directly. Looking back, it's one of the weird things about it. What you have to understand is that

Duffy was a vicious bastard. He'd have happily torn me limb from limb once he knew I was a copper. But he chose not to do that. Instead, he brought in outside help.'

'Go on.'

Cody takes a deep breath. This is where it gets uncomfortable. This is the bit he prefers not to relive, even though it constantly intrudes into his dreams and his thoughts.

'Duffy and one of his deputies came to us with a proposition. Duffy told us he wanted to introduce us to his boss, to discuss a new business venture. He wanted an answer there and then. No time to think about it, no time for us to contact our superiors. Our options were to play safe and miss the big opportunity we'd been waiting for, or take a gamble.'

'And you chose to take the gamble?'

'I have a tendency to do that. So did Jeff.'

'So you went to the meeting. And no other police officers knew you were there?'

Cody shakes his head. 'They took extra precautions to ensure we weren't followed. They drove us to a warehouse on the docks.'

'You didn't suspect anything?'

Cody thinks about this, as he has done thousands of times before.

'*Suspect* would be the wrong word. I worried we'd been rumbled, but that worry is always there in undercover work. Every time you do a drug deal you worry that you'll say or do the wrong thing, or that someone will recognise you. You just have to push the thought aside and carry on.'

'But on this occasion you'd have been correct.'

'Actually, I'm still not sure. I still wonder if even Duffy knew exactly what was about to happen. I don't think he could have been that good an actor.'

Falstaff nods, and he can tell that she has already become fascinated by the details of the case, even though she needs to move on to its psychological ramifications.

'All right. You go to the warehouse. Duffy and his man are with you. What happens next?'

'We chat, we joke, we wait. Jeff and Duffy light up cigarettes. It all seems fine. And then the door bursts open.'

Cody can still hear the resounding bang of that door. He remembers his heart leaping in his chest. He can see Jeff's cigarette being dropped to the concrete floor.

'Who is it? Who comes in?'

'The clowns.'

'The clowns?'

'Four men. They're dressed in overalls and wearing clown masks. One of them is carrying a sawn-off shotgun.'

'Duffy's boss?'

'I don't think so. It was obvious from Duffy's reaction that he'd been expecting someone to arrive, but even he seemed surprised at what turned up. I think he and his mate were actually glad to get out of there.'

'They left you alone with the clowns?'

'Yes.'

'What did the clowns want? Did they say?'

'They didn't say anything the whole time they were there.'

'Not a word?'

'Not one word. That wasn't their aim. Their aim was to hurt us.'

Falstaff nods slowly, thoughtfully. 'Can you talk about it? About what they did to you?'

'They tied us to chairs. Then they watched us for a while.'

'They watched you? You mean they just stared at you?'

'Yes. At first they just stood looking at us, but then Waldo gave them a signal and they—'

'Waldo?'

'Sorry, yes. He was the one in charge. I don't know why, but I gave him a name. Waldo seemed to fit.'

'All right, so Waldo gave them a signal . . .'

'Yes. And then they started circling us. They walked around and around us for ages.'

'Did you try talking to them?'

'Yes. I asked them what this was about. I told them they'd made a mistake. They didn't listen.'

'And how did you feel at that stage?'

'Terrified. Convinced we were about to die.'

'The most frightened you'd ever been in your life?'

'Probably.'

'What happened next?'

'They suddenly stopped walking. It was weird. Like they all knew exactly when to stop. Then Waldo waved one of his men over. He pointed down at my feet.'

'Your feet?'

'Yes. He wanted the other guy to remove my shoes and socks.'

'And did he?'

'Yes.'

'Why? Why did he do that?'

A twitch tugs at Cody's lip. He senses that it wants to grow into a tremble. His eyes are beginning to sting.

'So that . . . so that . . .'

'What? What did he do?'

'He called over another of his men. The man passed him something.'

'What was that something?'

'A pair of garden loppers.'

'Loppers?'

'Yes. You know those long-handled tools for snipping through branches?'

Falstaff goes quiet. Cody wonders how much of this is already in the report, because it seems to come as a shock to her.

She says, 'And . . . what did he do with them?'

'He, uhm, he . . . he started cutting off my toes.'

Snip!

Cody hears it. He hears the crunch of his toe being removed and his scream reverberating around the warehouse. He feels the intense stab of pain that shoots up through his body.

There is disbelief on Falstaff's face as she stares wide-eyed at Cody's feet.

'He cut off your toes?'

'Yes.'

'How . . . how many?'

'Four in total. Two from each foot.'

Falstaff appears to struggle to find her next question. She looks as though she would prefer to emit something like 'Fucking hell!' Instead, she says, 'How did you get him to stop?'

'I didn't. Jeff did.'

'How?'

Cody swallows hard. 'He, uhm, he gave up. He told them we were police officers. He started telling them everything about the operation.'

'Is that what they were waiting to hear? A confession?'

'No. I don't think so. Jeff's words meant nothing to Waldo. He should have stayed silent. He should have kept it to himself. He ...'

'What?'

'He shouldn't have distracted Waldo. That's all he was achieving, only he didn't realise. He was bringing himself to Waldo's attention. I tried telling him. I yelled at him to keep quiet. But it was too late. I could see that it was too late to stop Waldo.'

'Stop him doing what?'

'From leaving me. I wanted him to stay where he was, to leave Jeff out of this. But he was already on his way. There was nothing I could do to prevent it happening.'

'What? What couldn't you stop?'

'I couldn't ... I couldn't ...'

It's as clear as day. He sees the steady, irrevocable movement of Waldo towards his new prey. He sees how Waldo slips his hand into his overalls and pulls out a massive knife, its crescent blade glinting in the fluorescent light. He sees the instant of realisation on Jeff's face – the moment he apprehends the enormity of his mistake. And then he sees what happens next. It could be happening here and now, in this room, because it is so fresh and raw in Cody's mind.

And then all of Cody's promises to himself go to shit, because he can prevent the tears no longer. Much though he didn't want it, he has been given an opportunity to open up, to let out some of his pain. He knows he should spurn the offer, but instead he finds himself taking it, grasping it with both hands, despite what it might mean for his career. His words are strangled by his cries, and he doesn't know if he is making any sense, but he knows that mere words could never do justice to the event, to the sheer visceral imagery of a living human being having his face sliced from his skull.

9

It's like when the stranger walks into a bar in one of those old western movies. Cody feels the eyes on him, the rhythmic tapping of his shoes the only sound as he approaches his desk in the incident room. If there were a piano player here, even he would fall silent.

Webley in particular carries an expression filled with questions. She will hold on to them, then come to him later to let them spill out.

At the front of the room, Blunt stands imperiously and observes like an interrupted schoolteacher, waiting for Cody to find his seat. As she resumes speaking, Cody knows he ought to listen, but he quickly finds himself zoning out. He is still shaken by his session with Falstaff. She got to him, in a way he never believed she would. He dropped his guard, allowed her inside. He did that once with Webley. Told her everything. About the clowns, about their effects on him. Back then it felt good, it felt like a release. But this, this feels like the thin end of a wedge between him and the police force. Falstaff has his career in her hands, for God's sake. What was he thinking? And how much further will she hammer in that wedge during their next encounter?

He becomes aware of movement. Blunt stepping out of the limelight and a man taking her place. Cody recognises him as Dev Chandra, the crime scene manager.

'I'd just like to give you a brief update on the CSI findings so far,' says Chandra. 'The first thing I'd like to mention is the fingerprint found at the top of the stairs, on the bannister post. Although it's only a partial print, it's very well defined. It's possible to see a thin scar running diagonally across it. Unfortunately, the print doesn't throw up a match on any of our databases.'

'That's the print that was formed from blood, right?' Blunt asks.

'Yes. We've run a comparison, and it's definitely Mathew Prior's blood. What's odd, though, is that there are no other matching prints anywhere else in the house.'

'Not even in the bedroom?'

'Nope.'

'Odd indeed. Do you have an explanation?'

Chandra smiles, as though he's been hoping for that question. 'Gloves.'

Blunt shakes her head. 'I don't understand.'

'We've searched every inch of that house. Almost all of the fingerprints belong to Prior. There are also some left by Prior's wife. There are a few others we haven't identified yet, but the likelihood is that they belong to previous occupants of the property, tradesmen and so on, rather than the intruders.'

'Why do you say that?'

'Because there are no alien prints where we'd hope to find them. Take the drawers, for example. They were all pulled open to see what was inside, and yet the only prints on those drawers belong to Prior. Same goes for things like the CDs and books. They were all picked up and inspected by the intruders, but again the only prints those items hold are Prior's. We even examined each one of the nails driven into Prior's body. Not a single fingerprint on any of them. The killers had to have been wearing gloves.'

'Okay, so explain the print on the bannister.'

'Someone got careless. When they'd finished with Prior, they left the bedroom, and one of the attackers took off their gloves. There would certainly have been blood on the outside of the killer's gloves; probably on their clothes too. All it took was for him – or her – to touch a spot of that blood before coming into contact with the bannister . . .'

Blunt frowns. 'But no match.'

'Not yet. But find me some suspects and that could quickly change.'

'All right. Well, that's something. What else?'

'Plenty. Fibres of wool, dyed maroon. Possibly from a sweater or similar. We went through Prior's clothes and found no such garment. However, there were plenty of them around and on his corpse. We need to do more analysis, but we're hoping that'll tell us where the item might have been bought.'

'Good. What else?'

'Human hairs. Dark brown and recently cut short. There's evidence of a wax grooming product on them. Again, we're analysing it to see if we can work out the precise brand. We're also doing DNA tests on the hairs, as well as the bottle.'

'Bottle?'

Chandra smiles again. 'The intruders were extremely thorough. They even checked the contents of Prior's fridge. In doing so, they pulled out a six-pack of bottled water and tossed it on the floor. However, it looks like one of the attackers got thirsty.

The plastic wrapping holding the bottles together had been ripped open, and some of the fragments left on the floor. One of the bottles was missing. We found it in the wastepaper basket in Prior's study.'

'How do you know it's the same bottle, and not one that Prior put there earlier?'

'Batch numbers on the bottles. Plus, the bottle has no fingerprints on it. What it probably will have on it, however, is traces of saliva from whoever drank its contents.'

Blunt nods appreciatively. 'Excellent work, Dev. Please let the CSIs know how much we rely on them.'

As Chandra returns to his seat, Blunt addresses the room. 'You heard what Dev said. We've got hairs, a fingerprint, clothing fibres and DNA. Lots of evidence to make a match on suspects, but first you've got to round some up and bring them in! It would be nice if we had a motive. Clearly, the attackers were looking for something. Are we any closer to working out what it was?'

Footlong is the first to respond. 'The only thing we know that's definitely missing is Prior's laptop, but that was in plain sight. They didn't have to rip the house apart to find that.'

Blunt casts her eyes to the back of the room. 'Grace, you're the computer whiz. Any way we can find out what might have been on Prior's laptop?'

Grace Meade, the intelligence analyst, raises herself tentatively from her chair. 'It's a difficult one. We can probably get some data from Prior's internet service provider, and we might be able to look at whatever Prior may have backed up to the cloud, but it's not going to be a complete picture. It's also possible that the intruders may have taken the computer as a last resort, simply because they couldn't find what they were looking for in the house. There might be nothing of value on it whatsoever.'

Blunt sighs and turns her focus on Cody. 'You've spoken to the wife. Did she give you anything we can use?'

'Not a lot. According to her, Prior was just a humble, introverted civil servant, interested only in books, music and computer games. She did hint at something happening to him that wrecked their marriage, but she claims she has no idea what it was.'

'Do you believe her?'

'I think so. She seemed genuine enough. Full of surprises, though.'

'In what way?'

'Her bravery, for one thing. I've never seen a wife cope so well with the violent loss of a spouse. But it's not just that. She went into that house alone, knowing full that there may have been a gang of violent criminals inside. She scaled the back wall, went inside, picked up a knife and searched the property room by room. I have to say I'm incredibly impressed by Sara Prior.'

Cody catches a sidelong glance from Webley, and wonders what it means.

'There is another explanation, of course,' says Blunt. 'Which is that she's handling her loss so well because it's something she wanted – maybe even planned. Perhaps she knew all along that her husband's killers had long gone before she went into his house.'

Cody shakes his head. 'I don't think so. I think it's more likely that she was running on adrenaline. It's like the old story of a mother lifting a car to rescue her trapped child. My feeling is that she really loved her husband and wanted to do everything in her power to protect him.'

'If I may . . .'

This from Chandra again. Blunt looks across to him. 'Dev?'

'I didn't mention it earlier, but it's in my written report. I realise most of you won't have had a chance to look at it yet . . .'

'Go on.'

'With regard to Sara Prior, we needed her fingerprints to work out which of those in the house were hers and which belonged to the killers.'

'Okay.'

'That's standard, of course. It's also normal operating procedure to check all prints against those stored on our computer systems.'

Silence now. Everyone realises what's coming next.

'In Sara Prior's case we got a match.'

Cody's stomach lurches. A match? She's a criminal?

'She's known to us?' says Blunt.

'Not *us*, exactly,' Chandra answers. 'She cropped up on an international search. Specifically, the Danish military.'

'She's in the forces?'

'Used to be. And not just in support. She was infantry. She has done tours of duty in Kosovo and Helmand. If anyone knows about killing, it's Sara Prior.'

10

'Well, that explains it,' says Cody.

Blunt locks her eyes on him. 'Explains what?'

'Why she didn't hesitate in going into that house. She knows how to handle herself.'

'That's one way of looking at it. Alternatively, it tells us that the person closest to our murder victim has ample experience and training in how to eliminate people.'

Cody opens his mouth to object, but Blunt hasn't finished.

'Tell me,' she says. 'Did Sara Prior supply you with any of this information about being in the Danish army?'

Cody swallows. 'No. No, she didn't.'

'No. A fairly significant omission, don't you think?'

'Maybe. But I got the impression that she likes to keep herself to herself. She—'

'I don't care what she *likes*. This is a homicide investigation, and she needs to go along with what *we* like. Talk to her again, Cody. I want to know what else she's decided isn't worth telling us.'

'Yes, ma'am.'

Cody feels like a scolded schoolboy. He catches Webley looking at him again.

'And while you're at it,' Blunt adds, 'what about this telephone message?'

'Ma'am?'

Blunt gestures towards Grace Meade. 'Grace, play it once more, will you?'

Grace fiddles with her computer. Over the room speakers comes the recorded message left by Prior for his wife.

'We were talking about this before you got here,' says Blunt, almost as though it's Cody's fault that he was unable to attend earlier. 'We can't make head nor tail of it, probably because it obviously relies on some knowledge shared only by Prior and his wife.'

'She said she has no idea what it means,' says Cody.

'Yes. And we've also established that Sara Prior is adept at being economical with the truth. Her husband was trying to tell her something, in a way that meant something to her but would not be understood by the people breaking into his room to murder him. He wasn't just tossing out random phrases. Whether she realises it or not, she holds the key to this mystery. Get it out of her, Cody.'

The discussion moves on. Plans are made, actions identified, tasks assigned. When the meeting finally breaks up, Webley sidles over to Cody's desk.

'Everything all right?' she asks.

'Yeah, why?'

'Well, for one thing, you were late coming in this morning. The last time that happened, you were in deep shit.'

He laughs, but he realises how hollow it sounds. 'Nothing like that. I had an appointment I couldn't break, that's all.'

'In the first twenty-four hours of a murder inquiry? That's not like you. Normally, it'd be impossible to tear you away from—'

'Yeah, well this one was different.'

His words slice not only through Webley's sentence, but through the atmosphere.

'Okay,' she says. Then, after a lengthy pause: 'Is something going on?'

'What do you mean?'

'Yesterday, at the house. One minute you were getting suited up to view the crime scene, and the next you just disappeared.'

'Blunt had other ideas for me.'

'It seemed very sudden. What was the problem?'

'No problem. She made a suggestion, I thought it was a good idea, and . . . and that's it.'

'I see,' says Webley, patently unconvinced. 'You didn't prefer to see for yourself what they did to Prior?'

'I've seen the reports. It's all there.'

'Hmm.'

She stands at his desk for a while longer, and he wishes she would just give up and walk away.

'What time are you going to see Sara Prior?' she asks.

'Soon as I've caught up on these reports.'

'Want me to come with you?'

'I can manage. Why do you ask?'

'I just thought . . . well . . .'

'What?'

'I dunno. I just wonder if she might be a little bit more forth-coming if there were two of us in there. You know: good cop, bad cop.'

'She doesn't need the third degree right now. She's just lost her husband.'

'Yeah, I know. But you heard what the boss said. She seems to be playing with us.'

'Us? Do you mean me?'

'Well . . . you were pretty defensive of her.'

'Defensive?'

'Yes. Surely you can't deny—'

'I wasn't being defensive. I just happen to believe what she told me. She convinced me.'

'Come on, Cody. This isn't like you. If this had been anyone else you were interviewing—'

'What do you mean, anyone else? Are you accusing me of bias?'

Webley clamps her mouth shut, but Cody can see in her eyes what she thinks. She thinks his head has been turned. She thinks he has fallen under the spell of an attractive blonde Scandinavian woman.

'I will talk to her,' says Cody. 'I will interview her again, using exactly the same approach I would use for anybody else on any other homicide investigation. I expect the outcome to be the same, but I will follow orders, and I will do so in a professional manner. Is that good enough for you?'

Webley straightens up. She wants to say more, but then she shifts her gaze and realises that others are tuning in to this strained conversation.

She nods and walks stiffly away, and Cody is left feeling that he no longer knows how to deal with people.

11

She seems surprised to see him at her door, but not alarmed. She doesn't appear to be thinking something like, *Shit, I've been rumbled*. Or whatever the Danish equivalent of that might be.

She even offers him a smile as she says, 'Sergeant Cody. Please, come in.'

So he does. He enters a home that is filled with varnished wooden floors and doors, oak furniture, massive candles, flowers, tasteful framed paintings.

Sara Prior is wearing a baggy sweater in powder blue, black leggings and big fluffy slippers. When they get to the living room, she kicks off the slippers and sits cross-legged on the cream sofa. She beckons Cody to take the armchair opposite. In the background, soft piano music is being played.

'This is a lovely house,' says Cody. 'It's very relaxing.'

'Thank you. You've probably heard the Danish word *hygge*, describing feelings of comfort and contentment. It's been all the rage. That's what Matthew and I were aiming for here.'

He watches her for a second, finding it hard to reconcile what he sees here with the image of her dressed in combat uniform and firing a rifle with the intention of blowing the enemy's brains out.

'How are you today?' he asks.

Her eyes seem suddenly to fill with sadness. '*Hygge* is also about being with the one you love,' she says. 'Unfortunately, that has been taken away from me now.'

'I'm sorry. I didn't mean to—'

She waves it away. 'It's okay. It's for me to deal with. Time is the great healer, is it not?'

'So they say. I hope so.'

'I hope so, too. But . . .'

'What?'

'You said it as though it might apply to you, too.'

'Did I? Maybe it applies to all of us, in one way or another. Life isn't always completely smooth.'

'No.' She pauses. 'I'm sorry, I'm being a terrible host. Would you like some tea or coffee?'

'Not for me, thank you. I don't want to intrude.'

He realises he hasn't been forceful enough in his answer when she slips from the sofa and back into her slippers.

'Nonsense,' she says. 'The company will probably do me some good. I won't be a minute.'

When she has disappeared from the room, Cody thinks to himself, She's different today. Not the Scandinavian Ice Queen she seemed to be yesterday. There's more warmth there now, and maybe even a hint of vulnerability.

And then he shakes himself out of it. He thinks, What the hell am I doing? Why am I being like this? I'm supposed to be giving her hard stares and threatening language, not admiring her soft furnishings and drinking her tea.

She re-enters the room. Says, 'Kettle's on!'

Cody waits for her to sit down again, then leans forward in an attempt to make himself more confrontational.

'I hope you don't mind,' he says, 'but I'd like to ask you a few more questions.'

'I don't mind. And I'm sorry if I gave you a hard time yesterday. I realise you were only doing your job.'

He nods, but wishes that she would stop being so nice to him.

'The first thing is about the message that Matthew left on your telephone answering machine.'

'Yes. It's very strange.'

'Have you given it any more thought? Any idea what it might mean?'

She turns her head towards the hallway, where the phone is. As though all that's left of her husband is out there.

'I've listened to it a lot. Mainly to hear Matthew's voice again. But I still don't know what he was talking about.'

'He was very specific about Victoria and Albert. Very clear about those names. As if you'd know what he meant. Are you sure it doesn't ring any bells?'

She shakes her head slowly.

'They aren't people you know, perhaps?' Cody asks. 'Maybe under a slightly different version of the names, like Vicky and Bert? Or do you have relatives with names like that?'

More head shaking. 'No. I've gone through all possible combinations. Sometimes I wonder if Matthew was trying to prepare me for something.'

'What do you mean?'

'I don't know. Maybe he wanted me to remember those names for something that's about to happen, not that's already happened. Does that make sense?'

'What kind of thing?'

'I have no idea. A password? "Victoria and Albert" could be a password, couldn't it? Or does he want me to go to the Victoria and Albert Museum?'

'Why would he ask you to do that?'

'I don't know. This morning I had the idea that I was going to take a train down to London to visit the museum, just in case that's what he was saying. All of these crazy ideas are running around my head because I'm trying so hard to work out what Matthew wanted from me.'

Cody is convinced she is telling him the truth. It's so easy for them back at the station, he thinks. They look at the facts through their cynical eyes and they say, *Of course she knows. She's lying through her Danish teeth. Shine a light in her eyes, Cody. Get out the rubber truncheon.*

But they're not sitting here now, in front of this woman. They're not looking into her fjord-blue eyes and hearing the undercurrents of love and sadness in her words. They can't see the things that won't appear in any police report.

'There's something else I'd like to ask you about,' he says.

'All right, but first tea, yes?'

She gets up and leaves the room again, leaving Cody scrambling for the best way to put his next line of questioning. This one is going to be harder, because it's going to suggest that she could be something other than what she is portraying.

And yet, isn't that what makes Sara Prior so intriguing? The way in which she has shifted lives so radically? The way in which she has shed combat fatigues and a bullet-proof vest in favour of comfy sweaters and slippers?

Sara returns with a tray in her hands. She sets it down on the glass-topped coffee table, then serves the tea from its pot. She hands the bone china cup and saucer to Cody, then puts a plate of confectionery in front of him.

'You must try one of these,' she says.

'What are they?'

'A selection of Danish pastries. One of the things for which we are justifiably famous.'

'What else are you famous for?'

'Oh, lots of things. Lurpak. Sandi Toksvig. The list is endless.'

Cody laughs. He takes a sip of his steaming tea, but doesn't pick up one of the pastries.

'Now then,' she says to him. 'You were about to ask me something.'

'Yes. Something came up on our computers. Something about you.'

'Okay.'

'You haven't always been a personal trainer, have you?'

'No. But I didn't say I had.'

'No. No, you didn't. But you also didn't tell me that you used to be in the army.'

She doesn't appear shocked that he knows this. If anything, she seems faintly amused.

'You didn't ask about my previous careers.'

'You're absolutely right. I didn't. But you did have opportunities to mention it. For example, when I questioned you about climbing the back wall of your husband's house, going inside alone, searching the place . . .'

'Are we back to that again, Sergeant Cody?'

'Back to what?'

'Your unwillingness to accept that a woman can be capable of such things. Your desperate need for an explanation for behaviour that doesn't fit your expected pattern.'

'No, it's not about that.'

'Then what is it about?'

He has to think about this. Yes, what is it about? So, she was in the army. She knows how to kill – possibly has killed. But she certainly didn't hammer those nails into her husband. Why would being a soldier make her more likely to get somebody else to do her dirty work?

It's starting to irritate him that, yet again, his questioning is being driven by a bunch of people who have already formulated their judgment about a woman they have never seen or spoken to. Their logic seems to be: *she's a wife who's been dumped, she's a trained killer, do the maths.*

Well, guess what, guys? Life isn't always logical.

Trying to rescue himself, he says, 'It just seems . . . a significant piece of information you might have mentioned.'

'You mean because I trained to kill people for a living?'

So there it is. She's come right out and said it. No beating around the bush here.

'Well . . . when you put it like that, I hope you can see how your reluctance to mention it might have seemed a little odd. To some people.'

'As I've already told you, Sergeant Cody, I don't like to do what people expect of me.'

'No. I've learned that about you.'

'And what else would you like to learn about me?'

'How you and Matthew met. I mean, you're in the army, Afghanistan or wherever. Matthew is working for the tax office in England. How did your paths cross?'

'Actually, we didn't meet until after I left the army.'

'Did you come on a visit to England?'

'Not at first. This might sound a little weird, but we met on the internet.'

'The internet? Really?'

'Yes. We got talking on a forum. We shared a mutual interest.'

'Which was?'

'Don't laugh. We were huge David Bowie fans. We used to spend ages online, talking about his music and his life.'

'I'm not laughing. I like his music too. Quite a shock when he died.'

'Yes. We played his music endlessly for days afterwards.'

'So Bowie brought you together?'

'He did. Matthew accepted my invitation to come to Copenhagen. I showed him the sights. He fell in love with the place. I fell in love with him.'

'As simple as that.'

'Yes. As simple as that.'

'I've never been to Copenhagen.'

'You should go. It's beautiful, especially at Christmas. That's when Matthew first came. He wanted to do all the usual tourist things, so I showed him the Tivoli Gardens and the Christmas markets. We took a boat ride at Nyhavn. We drank Gluhwein and ate German sausages. We strolled through the town and admired the shop displays. I bought Matthew a model of Tintin to bring home. You'll probably find it somewhere in all that mess at his house.'

Cody tries to picture them together, hand in hand, looking lovingly into each other's eyes, but he still finds it a struggle. He has seen photographs of Matthew when he was alive. In nearly all of them, Matthew couldn't look directly at the camera, but stared down at his shoes, or off to one side. Cody has also seen photographs of Matthew's naked dead body. He was not a slight man, but his bulk was built from flab rather than muscle.

'Forgive me,' he says, 'but from what you've told me, you seem so very different from each other.'

She laughs. 'You think I would have gone for a more macho, sporty type? Is that what you're thinking?'

'Well, yes.'

'I thought so too, at first. In fact, I did.'

'What?'

'I fell in love once before. I shouldn't have.'

'Why do you say that?'

'He was a soldier too. In my unit. That's why it was a mistake. You should never fall in love with a work colleague.'

'No. So what happened?'

'We were on patrol in Helmand Province. We were laughing, joking. Svend said something crude, so I punched him playfully. He pretended to be hurt and staggered away. Straight onto an IED.'

'A landmine.'

'Yes. A landmine.'

'Jesus.'

'The bottom half of him was completely gone. We did what we could for him, but there was too much damage. He died after a few minutes.'

'That's . . . that's awful. I'm so sorry.'

'It's okay. I can say that now, but when it happened it affected me greatly. The doctors said I was traumatised. I didn't stay long in the army after that.'

Cody cannot help but see the parallels with his own experience. The trauma he suffered, and the way it affected him. He knows he still has a long way to go on his road to recovery, and he wonders if that is true for Sara also.

Sara takes a deep breath. A cleansing breath. 'But out of bad sometimes comes good. I changed. I wanted the opposite of army life. Matthew was that opposite. He wasn't interested in aggression or fighting, except in his beloved computer games. He wanted only peace, and someone to love him and take care of him.'

'That's not a bad aim in life,' says Cody.

She smiles wistfully. 'No. It isn't.'

12

Only minutes after Cody has left her house, Sara decides she needs to get out of there too. She has had enough of this isolation. She needs people around her. Sights and sounds to take her mind off things.

She jumps in the car and drives into the city. Parks at the Liverpool One shopping centre. She spends some time there, wandering from shop to shop, looking but not seeing, listening in to random snippets of conversation.

When she comes out of Debenhams and onto Lord Street, she makes a left turn without even thinking about it and heads towards James Street. It's only as she passes the railway station there that she realises where her feet are taking her.

The Mersey.

One of her favourite things about Copenhagen is the sight and smell of water. She loves the canals, the bridges, the houseboats, the open sea. Here in Liverpool, she makes a trip down to the dock area as often as she can to keep those feelings of her birthplace fresh.

She crosses the busy Strand and passes the Port of Liverpool Building, one of the 'Three Graces' characterising the city's distinctive waterfront. When she reaches the Naval War Memorial, she ascends its few steps, then leans her arms on the steel railings and stares out across the leaden river. She remains there for some time, her nose streaming as blasts of cold air push at her. She watches a ferry forging its way steadily across to Birkenhead. Overhead, seagulls call mournfully.

She wonders how long she will stay here. Not here at this precise spot, but here in England. What reason is there to stay, now that Matthew is gone?

She thinks back to her conversation with Sergeant Cody, when she was telling him about Matthew's first trip to Copenhagen. The rekindled memories bring a smile to her face. She remembers how anxious Matthew was when she took him on a rollercoaster ride at the Tivoli Gardens. He spent most of the ride clutching her hand tightly in his own, and the photograph of them displayed at the booth showed clearly how terrified he was.

She remembers also a later Christmas visit, when they went to the Rundetaarn – the round tower – when he proposed to her after they kissed under the mistletoe in one of the windows.

Yes, they had some wonderful times together.

Sara steps back, away from the railings. She stares at the inscription on the base of the memorial's stone column:

These officers and men of the Merchant Navy died while serving with the Royal Navy and have no grave but the sea.

Matthew will have no grave either. Not until he provides some answers. Not until he reveals to the world the reason for his death.

Sara needs that explanation. She will not do anything about leaving this country until it is given to her. And if the police can't unearth it, she will do so herself. That's the promise she makes to Matthew.

She closes her eyes for a few seconds and breathes heavily. Then, slowly, she moves away from the memorial.

She's not sure where to go next but doesn't want to return home just yet. She continues along the riverfront, ending up in the coffee shop at the Tate. She orders a large cappuccino and a chocolate muffin, then takes a seat at a window table.

She stares out at the water again, calmer here in the dock. The bobbing boats dotted all around the edges. The converted warehouses supported by thick, cast iron pillars painted in salmon pink. A Japanese couple move in front of her, blocking her view while they snap some selfies. She smiles at them, but they don't seem to notice, and they move on.

She thinks again about Matthew's first trip to Copenhagen. There was a choir in one of the market squares. They held candles and sang Christmas carols. She and Matthew stood there for a long time, listening and occasionally singing along. She ventured a glance towards him, and saw how entranced he was, like a little boy.

It was only about a month later that she made her first trip to England. Newcastle at first. But when the job came up in Liverpool, he brought her along to show her what it had to offer. She instantly fell in love with the place.

A sudden feeling of déjà vu dances up her spine, and she realises that she sat here in this café with Matthew on that initial visit. His job had brought him here many times, and he knew all the touristy things to see and do. He told her about the announcement of the *Titanic*'s sinking being made from what used to be the White Star headquarters at the bottom of James Street. He told her about the docklands, and the history of this particular dock. How it was opened during the very first state visit to the city by a member of the royal family. Prince Albert was the dignitary, and the dock was forever named after him. Matthew also told her about—

The memory scampers away quickly as the questions invade her mind.

Prince Albert. The Albert Dock. Could it be?

Sara! Remember! Victoria and Albert. All I can say. They're here! They're— Sara, I love you. I—

No. It still doesn't make any sense. What possible connection . . . ?

She stares out of the window again. Not idly this time, but looking for something – anything – that might complete the circle her brain is struggling to construct. She looks at the shopfronts and reads their signage, tries to make out the names on the boats. Nothing jumps out at her, and so she turns back to her recollection of that day. What did they talk about, here in this café? What did they do?

She thinks back to the beginning of that visit to the docks. They took the train that time. Got off at James Street. Turned right towards the river . . .

No. Wait. We didn't. Not straightaway. We made a slight detour first. We crossed the road, heading towards the crown courts. He wanted to show me something. A monument. A statue.

Sara's hand jumps to her mouth.

The statue on James Street. It's of Queen Victoria.

Remember! Victoria and Albert.

Yes, that's right. We went to see the statue first. Matthew wanted to show me how, from a certain angle, it appears as though Victoria is endowed with massive male genitalia. Except that, Matthew being Matthew, he couldn't get the words out. He could only keep pointing and giggling while I struggled to work out what he was trying to tell me, and—

Victoria and Albert.

Is that it, Matthew? Is that what you were trying to get me to think about? My first trip to the city? What we did on that day?

She stares unseeing into her coffee cup, her mind feverishly working to dredge up images from all that time ago. The Victoria Monument, the Albert Dock, and then . . .

And then?

The Walker Art Gallery, wasn't it?

No. Not quite. There was one other stop along the route.

And then it all comes together. All the pieces fall into place in a gigantic mental thunderclap that leaves her visibly trembling.

Sara grabs her bag and gets up abruptly from her chair. She leaves the coffee and muffin unfinished. She has somewhere else she needs to be.

The place that Matthew was telling her to go to.

13

A pathway of titles.

She spent a while here when she first came with Matthew. A long line of familiar titles from books, movies and music, set into the pavement outside Liverpool Central Library. *The African Queen. A Tale of Two Cities. The Godfather. Citizen Kane. The Mikado. Apocalypse Now. A Bear Called Paddington.* And at the top of the list, *Pride and Prejudice* rubbing shoulders with *Robinson Crusoe.*

She doesn't even see the words now. Doesn't notice the homeless man on the steps to the right, or the tourists pointing up at the architecture. Her eyes are locked on the automatic doors as she heads straight for them, her mind busily occupied with thoughts of what she might find here.

Inside, she doesn't feel the splendour that washed over her that first time. Back then, she was stunned at how completely the aged exterior belied the bright, futuristic layout within, as though it were a Tardis. She stood on Levi Tafari's poem on the floor of the atrium and stared right up to the glass dome on the roof of the building, the vast space above criss-crossed by staircases on the intervening floors.

She takes the escalator up to the first floor, edging past other travellers in her hurry to get to her destination. When she gets to the top, she heads to the right-hand side of the floor, then passes through the entrance to the adjoining room.

The transition is startling. A demonstration of this Tardis's power to transport its occupants from an intensely high-tech present to a more sedate, lavish past. The Picton Reading Room is a vast circular chamber with a domed ceiling. It has oak shelves and globe lighting and ornate wrought iron spiral staircases. The circumference of the room is lined with three tiers of books, stretching from the floor to the bottom edge of the ceiling, with more shelves radiating inwards like wheel spokes, pointing towards an oak-built lighting column at the central axis of the space.

Sara stands next to the column and slowly turns, taking in the vast numbers of books here.

Where to start?

She knows it wasn't at floor level: she remembers ascending one of the narrow staircases. And it can't have been on the top level either, because that's reserved for staff.

But that still leaves a hell of a lot of books.

She chews on her lip. Think, Sara, think! Which way did we go?

She could ask for assistance, but she wants that to be a last resort. She doesn't want anyone else involved in this if she can avoid it. Matthew was being cryptic for a reason.

And then she remembers. The clock!

They went up the staircase to the left of the clock – she's sure of that now.

She moves quickly to the steps, but then has to wait while a large, middle-aged woman comes down them.

Sara races up the stairs.

Which way now?

Left. I'm sure of it. We went anti-clockwise.

She starts walking, scanning the shelves as she goes. So many books. But she recalls that they didn't go very far before her eye was caught by one particular title, high on a shelf of books that are not allowed out on loan.

It has to be close by, she thinks. Unless, of course, they have completely moved everything since then. What if it's in a totally different position now? What if . . . what if they got rid of it?

Her stomach lurches at the thought.

But then she sees it.

There. Probably where it's always been. It has a dull beige cover, the writing on its spine in an unobtrusive font. It doesn't call attention to itself. It's possible that the only person to have touched it since she last laid her fingers on it was Matthew.

She pulls it down from the shelf. Stares at its title.

Memories cascade in. She remembers stifled giggling, made worse by the room's funereal atmosphere. She'd had too much wine with her lunch, and she had been laughing at Matthew's gaucheness over Victoria's seemingly male appendage. In fact, he had used that very word – *appendage* – rather than anything more direct or crude.

Things got worse when she happened to see the book. The wine had already caused her to feel a little naughty, a little puerile. At any other time, the book might not have led to the unrestrained explosion of mirth that it did, prompting those at the reading desks below to glare up at her with unconcealed hostility.

Matthew rounded on her with a loud 'Shush!', but there was a smile playing on his lips.

She pulled the book down in explanation. 'Look,' she whispered, still chuckling.

Matthew squinted myopically. 'What?'

'The author's name. Cockburn.'

She sniggered again as she said the word out loud. She enjoyed the sound of it so much she had to say it again and again. 'Cockburn. Cockburn. Cockburn.'

By now, she was in hysterics, but Matthew merely rolled his eyes.

'It's pronounced Co-burn, not Cock-burn.'

'What?' she said, the tears rolling down her cheeks. 'What are you talking about? It's got a *c* and a *k* in it. That's cock. That's very definitely a cock. Like Queen Victoria's.'

She started laughing again. She remembers laughing so hard that her stomach hurt, and she remembers how Matthew couldn't help but be infected by the hilarity.

'What is that book anyway?' he had said, prising it from her grasp while she pinched her nose in an effort to contain herself. 'You know what I'm going to do? If you ever get sad or depressed, I'm going to bring you here to take another look at this. I've never seen you so tickled.'

He brought the book closer to his face. '*All I Can Say: A Personal Journey Through Language and Dialect*. By Jeremiah Cockburn.'

Another snort of laughter from Sara. 'Cock-Burn,' she whispered, almost losing control again.

'Come on,' he said, putting the book back on its shelf. 'Let's get you out of here before someone chucks us out.'

And that was it. That was the event. Of seemingly little importance back then, but now . . .

Sara! Remember! Victoria and Albert. All I can say.

It was a list. The Victoria monument, then the Albert Dock, and then the book – this book. *All I Can Say*. Matthew wanted to lead her back to this book, but without being so explicit about it that his attackers would comprehend.

She holds the book firmly in her hands. Looks around her in fear that someone might be about to pounce on her for daring to touch this special volume.

She opens the cover, starts turning the pages. She sees only page after page of dense text.

She flips to the end, then uses her thumb to riffle through the whole book. Nothing jumps out at her. She's not sure what she expects – some scribbled annotations in a margin, perhaps, or a turned-down corner of a page – but she gets nothing.

She flicks through it again, and then again. All she sees is boring typeset prose.

No, Matthew, she thinks. Please don't tell me that all you were doing was fulfilling your promise. Please don't let this be just your way of cheering me up because I'm devastated to lose you. It has to be more than that. You have to be telling me more. You didn't go to all the trouble of delivering your final message in the form of a puzzle just to let me know you wanted me to be happy.

And then something occurs to her. She thinks, What if some-body has been here before me? What if there *was* something hidden between these pages, but another visitor came across it and removed it?

No. It can't be that. Who else would pick up this book, this special book that means so much to me and Matthew?

But whatever the explanation, it seems that there is nothing to be found here, and Sara's eyes well up with the frustration of the moment. She opens the book one last time, grabbing it by the front and back covers and shaking the pages violently, not caring whether this is an expensive or rare volume, not caring whether her act is being witnessed by staff or security cameras.

Nothing drops to the floor.

She is done here. It is time to go home. It is time to accept that whatever secrets Matthew was trying to divulge will never reach her. It is time to move on with her life.

She stretches up her arm to replace the book on the shelf.

And then she sees it.

A white triangle, jutting out from between the dustjacket and the back cover. She lowers her arm again. Tugs gently on the triangle.

It's the corner of an envelope. She pulls it all the way out. Written on its front, in Matthew's characteristic longhand, are the words, 'To my darling Sara.'

14

Cody feels a little sheepish as he climbs in behind the wheel of the unmarked saloon. In the passenger seat, Webley sits patiently and quietly, as if awaiting Cody's apology before normal service is resumed.

He knows he has to issue it, of course. He cannot deny that he gave her a hard time this morning. The question is how to go about it.

He starts driving. He always prefers to do the driving.

After a painful period of silence, he says, 'About this morning . . .'

He hopes that's all he needs to say. That she'll jump in at that point and dismiss it with a cheery, 'Not a problem. I understand.' Or something of that nature.

But she doesn't. She simply turns her head in his direction and waits for him to continue.

'I was an arsehole,' he says. 'And I'm sorry. Okay?'

'All right,' she says. 'Apology accepted. Are you going to tell me what's going on?'

'What do you mean?'

'I mean about the reason for your arseholeness. What got into you?'

'I was . . . I was uptight about something.'

'What? Did it have something to do with why you were late coming in?'

'Kind of. Yes. I'd been to a meeting.'

'A meeting?'

'Well, a session. With a psychologist.'

She touches his arm. 'Cody, that's brilliant. You're seeking help? You're—'

'No, it's not brilliant. I'm doing it under duress. I'm doing it because Blunt has forced my hand. She insists on seeing a formal validation of my mental health before I'm allowed anywhere near another victim.'

'Oh.'

'Yes, oh.'

Webley turns towards him as much as her seatbelt allows. 'Well, maybe it's nothing to get worked up about. I mean, you've been a lot better lately, haven't you? I haven't seen you throttle any newspaper reporters lately.'

She laughs, but Cody doesn't see the funny side of the reminder.

'I cried,' he tells her.

'What?'

'In the session this morning. I told the psychologist about what happened to me when I was working undercover, and I broke down.'

'Well . . . that's natural, isn't it? Anyone who'd been through something like that would find it distressing to talk about it. Doesn't mean you're not fit for the job.'

He lapses into silence for a few seconds, and then he says, 'It's got worse again lately.'

'What has?'

'The nightmares. The hallucinations.'

'Since you ended up in hospital?'

'Yes. It kind of brought it all back.'

'Again, surely that's only natural? That was quite an ordeal. You wouldn't be human if it didn't affect you. Anyone would be traumatised after that.'

'I'm worried she's going to sign me off work. Send me for treatment or something. Maybe even medication.'

'You're jumping to conclusions. Let her do her job and stop worrying about it. And if she recommends a little therapy, so what? Maybe that would be for the best.'

'Or maybe she recommends that I'm not fit for duty. I've already had a couple of weeks off, and it drove me nuts. I need this job, Megan.'

She touches his arm again. 'Stop worrying. It'll be fine.'

He's not convinced. And telling Megan the reasons for his erratic behaviour hasn't helped in the slightest. It has only made him feel more uneasy about his future.

'What about Sara Prior?' Webley asks.

'What about her?'

'The way you're treating her with kid gloves. Does that have anything to do with your sessions?'

'No. I don't know. Maybe.'

'Is that multiple choice? I just pick an answer?'

'There's something about Sara. I get her – do you know what I mean? There's something different about her.'

'Cody, I hope you're not saying what I think you're saying.'

'What? No! Not that. I just feel a certain . . . *affinity* with her.'

'An affinity.'

'Yeah. When I went back to speak to her at her house, she told me that she saw an old boyfriend of hers blown to bits in Afghanistan. It changed her whole world view. I can relate to that.'

Webley looks out at the traffic for a minute. Then she says, 'Be careful, Cody. Okay? With Sara Prior, I mean. Just be careful.'

15

Lewis Fulton is a man who, it seems to Cody, is full of his own self-importance. He takes great delight in announcing to everyone in earshot that he will be in the meeting room, helping out the police with their enquiries, as if he alone may hold the key to breaking the case.

The room is starkly functional. A long table surrounded by about a dozen chairs, a computer and projection system, and a smaller table supporting some white cups and an empty coffee jug. Fulton slouches down on one of the chairs and puts his hands behind his head, trying too hard to give the impression of being at ease and in control.

'So,' he says, 'how can I help you?'

Cody begins the questioning. 'Tell us about Matthew Prior. What sort of employee was he?'

'Good man. Solid. Reliable. Not so hot in terms of social skills, but I can't fault his work.'

'Did you like him?'

'I'm not sure I'd use the word "like". I mean, I wouldn't class him as a friend. We got on well enough, though.'

'Ever argue with him? Ever have to tear a strip off him?'

'No, not at all. Matthew wasn't the argumentative type. He avoided confrontation. But, to be honest, I can't recall a single occasion where I had to get tough with him. Like I say, his work was impeccable.'

'Ever see him get into a fight with anybody else here? Any friction you noticed?'

'Can't say I did. He pretty much kept himself to himself. He wouldn't even go out for coffee with the others. Most of the time he ate his lunch alone at his desk.'

'You make him sound a little eccentric.'

'That's probably a good word for it. Painfully shy, maybe. An introvert. He would never say much in our team meetings.'

'Did his anti-social behaviour ever get anyone's back up that you know of?'

'If it did, nobody complained to me about it. I think they mostly just left him to his own devices.'

'What about customers?'

'Customers?'

'Yes. Many people don't like having to pay tax. For some of them, the taxman is like a traffic warden or a bailiff.'

Fulton laughs. 'Matthew wasn't a tax inspector. God, there's no way he could have dealt with queries about tax returns.'

'No? What did he do, then?'

'He was what we call a designer. He created e-learning pack-ages for internal training. Generic stuff on diversity, health and safety, and so on, but also more specialist aids to explain processes and systems.'

'He came here as a part of a promotion package, didn't he?'

'Yes, that's right. It was advertised internally. Matthew applied, and he was clearly the best person for the job.'

'Any others from this branch apply?'

'A couple.'

'Is it possible they might have been miffed at being passed over for promotion? That they might have wanted to take it out on Matthew?'

Fulton shakes his head vigorously. 'I really don't think so.' He lowers his voice and leans forward conspiratorially. 'To be frank, I think the other applicants were just dipping their toes in the water. I don't think they ever believed they were in with a chance.'

'Do you know much about what went on in Matthew's personal life?' Webley asks.

Fulton sits up straight again as he eyes Webley. 'Not a lot. Only that he was married.' He turns back to Cody. 'Have you met his wife?' he says, obviously intending it as a man to man thing.

'I've met her, yes,' Cody says.

'She's something, isn't she?'

Cody makes no reply.

'I mean, come on. Matthew was punching above his weight there, don't you think? Lucky bastard.'

'He's dead, Mr Fulton,' says Webley.

Fulton returns his gaze to Webley, his eyelids fluttering now. 'Yes. Sorry, I didn't mean—'

'When did you meet his wife?'

'When he first came to Liverpool, just over two years ago. I was having my thirtieth birthday party and most of the team were invited, so I asked him to come along with his wife.'

'And he came?'

'Jumped at the chance. Thinking about it, he was a different person then. Happier. I think he really wanted to try to fit in.'

'When did it all change? When did he become less happy?'

'I'm not sure. Probably less than a year later. He seemed to stop trying. Not in his work, though. In fact, I'd say he threw himself into that even more. What I mean is, he just didn't seem to want to mix with anybody else.'

'Did you ever discuss it with him?'

Fulton puts up his hands. 'Not my business. My job is to make sure he does the work. I stay out of personal lives.'

'Did you know he'd left his wife and moved out?'

'Really? No, I didn't. I'm shocked.'

Cody waits for him to add something like, *How could anyone leave a stunner like that?* To Fulton's credit, he seems to realise it wouldn't be appropriate.

'Is it possible that Matthew might have spoken to anyone else about his personal problems?'

'Well, there's Ann.'

'Ann?'

'Ann Staples. She's another team member. I think she felt a bit sorry for Matthew. She spent a lot of her free time trying to talk to him. Sometimes she'd sit at his desk and have lunch with him.'

'Can we speak to her?'

'She's not around today. She only found out about Matthew when she came in this morning. She got so upset I had to send her home.'

'We'd like her address, if that's all right.'

'Yeah, sure.'

Fulton looks down at the table for a moment. Then he says, 'The news reports are saying that Matthew was *brutally* murdered. Not just murdered, but *brutally* murdered.'

'Yes,' says Webley. 'I'd say that was an accurate term.'

Fulton nods. 'Poor guy. I'll miss having him around.'

I can tell, thinks Cody. Look at how upset you are.

16

She decides she will wait until she gets home.

She puts the letter in her pocket. On the walk back to her car, she keeps her hand on it constantly for fear it may somehow escape and be carried away on a freak gust of wind. It seems almost to be burning her fingers, singeing her with its demand for its content to be revealed. But she knows she has to wait.

She is afraid of what her reaction might be. Afraid of the stares in the library or from other drivers as she sobs uncontrollably. Afraid, too, of what secrets are in this letter – of what drove Matthew to adopt such a clandestine means of communication.

And so she waits until she is home.

She stares at the envelope now, at the writing on its front.

To my darling Sara.

Undeniably Matthew's handwriting. So precise, so florid.

She picks up the letter opener. Slices it carefully through the top edge of the envelope. Inside is a single piece of paper. She unfolds it, sees that it has been laser-printed. Taking a deep breath, she begins to read.

To my darling Sara,

If you are reading this letter, it can only be because something terrible has happened to me. I might even be dead. Which is pretty weird when you think about it. But then if there's one thing I've learned from being with you, it's that life can be unpredictable and dangerous and scary and exciting – all the things I never experienced before you came into my life.

I want you to know first and foremost that I love you. That I loved you from the moment I first set eyes on you. That I have never stopped loving you, even during those times when it must have seemed that nothing could have been further from the truth. My love for you is total.

I also want you to know that I am so, so sorry for what I have put you through. I did what I thought was for the best, but it was impossible for me to tell you why. Now, finally, I can explain.

I'm in trouble, Sara. I made a mistake. The biggest mistake I've ever made. I thought I needed to change. If there's one thing you've taught me, it's that I need to have more courage, that I need to stop hiding from myself and the world. I've tried to do that, and now I'm paying the price.

They're after me, Sara. They're coming for me. You're reading this letter because I have given you a message that only you will understand, and that's because they must be right on my tail. I'm sorry for my cryptic message, but I know they're watching and listening. They will search my house and my computer. They mustn't be allowed to know I've contacted you. You mustn't tell the police either, because that could put your own life at risk.

I'm telling you all this as a warning. They will want to cover their tracks, and that might mean making sure that I haven't passed any information about them to you. They may come looking for you, and I want you to be prepared for that. I want you to be on your guard. To be honest, I'd prefer it if you would go back to Copenhagen. You'll be safer there. But I know you won't listen to me!

If they do come, you may be left with no choice but to go to the police. Tell them they need to find a man who goes by the name 'Metro'. They should start their search in The Tar Barrel pub in Bootle.

I realise I'm not giving you much detail, but to be honest it's much better for you not to know. I just want you to understand that it's the reason I've been so miserable. It's nothing you did, or a reflection on our relationship. I desperately wanted to continue my life with you, but it would have been unfair to put you in danger like that.

You made me so happy, and I threw it all away. I hope you'll forgive me one day.

Stay safe. I'd like to think you won't forget me, but you should move on with your life now. You deserve much better than me.

Your loving husband,

Matthew

The letter ends with Matthew's extravagant signature in blue ink. He always liked to use a fountain pen to sign letters.

A tear tumbles from Sara's cheek and splashes onto the page. She wipes it away quickly, before it can soak into the paper. This is Matthew's last gift to her. It's precious.

She places the letter carefully on the coffee table, then stands up and walks to the window. She doesn't see what is outside; her vision is too blurred.

As she cries, she realises that it is partly through relief. On many occasions she assumed the fault for their separation must be hers. She worried that she must have pushed him too much, taken him too far beyond his comfort zone.

But now she knows. Matthew has confirmed that it was nothing to do with her. There were other things going on in his life. A secret world of which she was completely unaware.

She goes back to the coffee table and picks up the letter again. It throws up more questions than answers. Who are these mysterious people who were coming after Matthew? What did they want from him? What knowledge or item in his possession was of such importance that he had to die for it?

She knows she should take this to the police, to Detective Sergeant Cody. This is vital information. It might possibly lead them directly to Matthew's killers.

But then she focuses on the sentence that pleads with her not to say anything to the authorities, because that might endanger her.

She isn't worried about danger. She has walked, slept and eaten in the fiery furnace of danger. What concerns her more is that informing the police might lead to a flurry of activity that could tip off the killers. They might go into hiding. Or the police might fuck it all up and the suspects would literally get away with murder.

That's not going to happen, she tells herself. They're not getting away with this. Somebody killed my husband, and they're going to pay for it.

Even if it's the last thing I do.

17

They have to ring and knock several times before they can get Ann Staples to come to the door. When she finally does appear, she keeps the chain on the door, leaving just a crack through which to fix a single beady eye on the two detectives.

'Hello?' she says. 'What is it?'

Cody presents his warrant card. 'Police, Mrs Staples. We're here to talk to you about Matthew.'

'Miss,' she says.

'I'm sorry?'

'I'm a Miss. Not a Mrs.'

'Ah, okay. Sorry. I'm DS Cody and this is DC Webley. May we come in?'

'I suppose so.'

Ann closes the door while she removes the chain, then opens it again. Cody gets a view of a short woman in her early forties. She is wearing a green cardigan, a tartan skirt, and pale green tights. Around her neck is a multi-coloured knitted scarf that is so long its ends trail along the floor.

Ann catches him looking at the scarf. 'I have the hat too,' she says.

'Er, right,' Cody says.

He has no idea what she's talking about, but his attention is shoved elsewhere as soon as he enters the house.

In the hallway is a Tardis.

Not the real thing, obviously – Ann Staples doesn't convince as a Time Lord – but a persuasive replica, nonetheless.

Cody exchanges glances with Webley.

'What do you think?' says Ann.

Cody turns to see that she is now wearing a wide-brimmed hat.

'Er, very nice,' Cody says.

'Tom Baker,' she informs him.

'The fashion designer?'

'No, silly. He played Doctor Who. Always wore a hat and a scarf like these.'

'I see.'

'Yes. Anyway, go into the living room. Mind the Dalek.'

She ushers them through to the living room, where the first thing Cody sees is a large red Dalek in the middle of the floor, its single 'eye' aimed disconcertingly in his direction. Scattered around the room are numerous scale models and other items of *Doctor Who* memorabilia, while on the wall are a large number of framed photographs of actors from the series.

'Please,' says Ann, 'take a seat.'

While Cody lowers himself onto the sofa, Webley looks warily at the decapitated head of a Cyberman on the sideboard alongside her own chair.

'So,' says Cody, 'I take it you're a Whover.'

'A what?'

'A . . . Whover?'

'No, I think you'll find that's a type of vacuum cleaner. If you mean Whovian, then yes, I'm one of the most devoted fans. I go to all the conventions. Most of these photographs are signed by the actors. I even got to meet Bernard Cribbins. Did you know he's the only actor to have played two of the Doctor's companions?'

'No, I didn't know that.'

'Yes. He was so lucky. I'd do anything to travel with the Doctor.'

It occurs to Cody to suggest his own psychologist as a suitable doctor for Ann Staples. She seems to have only one foot in reality.

He clears his throat. 'As you may have gathered, we've come here today to talk about Matthew Prior.'

She nods. 'It's very upsetting. I had to leave work when I heard. Why do humans insist on doing such horrible things to each other?'

'I understand you knew Matthew pretty well.'

'What makes you think that?'

'We spoke to your boss. Mr Fulton.'

Ann's expression hardens. 'I see.'

'Are you annoyed that he told us that?'

'Let's just say that Lewis and I don't always see eye to eye. He's not a nice man.'

'In what way?'

'He makes snide remarks. Says things that a boss shouldn't. He can be really immature sometimes.'

'These remarks – does he only make them about you?'

'No. He does it to everyone. Except his own bosses, of course. Never has a bad word to say about them, especially when they're on site. Personally, I can cope, but when he says things about people like Jodie . . .'

Cody sees the sudden blazing in Ann's eyes.

'Jodie?'

'Jodie Whittaker.'

'I'm sorry, who?'

'The first female Doctor. I mean, why can't the Doctor be a woman? Why can't the Doctor be black or gay or whatever? It's called "regeneration" for a purpose. Lewis should bloody well keep his misogynistic views to himself.' She blinks at Cody. 'I'm sorry. I shouldn't swear, but, well, he really does push my buttons.'

Cody grants her a second to calm down and hopes that she won't keep dragging every question back to her fantasy world.

'Did Lewis make comments about Matthew?'

'Oh, yes. More than anyone else, probably.'

'What did he say?'

Ann hesitates. 'Lots of little things. If they happened just once, you might dismiss them, but they all added up over time. Like Matthew would be talking to me and another woman, and Lewis would walk in and say, "Hello, ladies." Just last week, he announced that the ladies' loos were out of action, but he looked directly at Matthew when he said it.'

'In other words, he made a habit of challenging Matthew's masculinity?'

'Yes. It was always very subtle. Nothing that would stand up if a formal complaint was made. But he knew what he was doing, and I know for a fact that Matthew noticed.'

'Why do you think Mr Fulton was doing that? He told us he had nothing bad to say about Matthew's work.'

'Oh, he definitely couldn't fault Matthew's work. It was his personality he didn't like. He was all over him when he first arrived, inviting him to parties and stuff. Truth be told, I think he was more interested in getting his chance to talk to Matthew's wife. Sara is very attractive, you know.'

'Yes,' says Cody, feeling the heat of Webley's eyes on him. 'But then it all turned sour, right?'

'Yes. I think it was partly jealousy over Sara, but also because Matthew wasn't one of the lads, you know? He didn't like football or boxing or heavy drinking, didn't talk about women in a demeaning way. He was more of a quiet, sensitive type.' She pauses. 'I don't like to talk about my boss in this way, but to be honest I think he was bullying Matthew because he knew Matthew wouldn't stand up to him.'

'Was Matthew upset about it?'

'He didn't actually say he was, but I could tell it bothered him.'

'Did he ever give you his opinion of Fulton?'

Ann shakes her head. 'Matthew wouldn't do that. He wouldn't speak ill of people, even if he didn't like them.'

'What's your view? Do you think he might have hated Fulton? Enough to make trouble for him?'

'I don't think Matthew was capable of hating. He didn't do strong emotion, and he found it difficult to act on whatever feelings he had.'

Webley says, 'How did you get to know Matthew?'

Ann turns to face her. 'We work in the same office. I liked him as soon as I met him. I could tell he was my sort of person. I once asked him to name all the people who'd played the Doctor, and he only forgot one. That's pretty good going.'

'What about others in the office? Did he get on with them?'

'I think they liked him at first, but gradually they started to ignore him. I didn't. I made sure he always had someone to talk to.'

'Did he open up to you?'

'Sometimes.'

'About his personal life?'

'Sometimes.'

'What about recently? Did he talk about anyone that might want to hurt him?'

'No. Not that.'

'What, then?'

Ann considers this. 'Matthew had been troubled for a long time. He'd been very unhappy.'

'Do you know why?'

'Not really. I got the feeling he did something. Something he regretted.'

'What kind of thing?'

'I'm not sure. Matthew was never comfortable in his own skin. I think he wanted to make a change, to turn from a caterpillar into a butterfly, if that makes any sense. I think he believed he'd never be good enough for Sara.'

'He said this?'

'Yes. Several times. He would say how strong Sara is, how fearless. He wished he could be more like her, but he knew he wasn't capable of it.'

'Did you know that he and Sara had separated?'

Ann hangs her head. She looks deeply sorrowful. 'Yes. Such a shame. Whatever it was that Matthew did, it destroyed him, and that destroyed his marriage.'

'Did he talk to you about Sara? About what she meant to him?'

'Yes. He loved her deeply. But something got in the way.'

Cody resumes the questioning. 'Do you think it's what led to his murder?'

Ann shrugs. 'I have no idea, but . . .'

'But what?'

'The last time we had a proper heart to heart, he told me he'd made a decision.'

'A decision?'

'Yes. An important decision. He said he was going to fix things, no matter what the cost.'

Cody exchanges glances with Webley. 'And that's it? He didn't tell you what the decision was, or what it was supposed to fix?'

Ann's eyes glint with tears. 'No. But you know what I think? I think he'd decided to be brave for once, to do what was right. I believe Matthew was killed because, for the first time in his life, he decided not to back down.'

18

Sara sits in her car and watches the comings and goings on the other side of the street. The Tar Barrel doesn't look the sort of place she would ever consider going for a night out, or even a single drink for that matter. It sits between a fenced-off derelict building and a graffiti-adorned house with the flag of St George hanging from one window. Tracksuits seem to be the attire of choice of its shaven-headed patrons. Congregated in front of the entrance, a small knot of young men puff on hand-rolled cigarettes and compete over how many f-words they can fit into a sentence.

Sara wonders whatever possessed Matthew to set foot beyond the peeling door of this place. Okay, it's only a ten-minute stroll from his office building, but Matthew didn't like pubs at the best of times. He couldn't relax in the midst of alcohol-fuelled displays of aggression and brashness and lack of inhibition. He preferred people to remain in full control of their faculties at all times. From what Sara can see of those who frequent The Tar Barrel, Matthew might as well have painted 'Victim' across his forehead when he decided to walk in there. They would have been on him like piranhas.

She waits for the men to finish their roll-ups and head back inside. She gives them a couple of minutes, then gets out of her car and locks it up. She hopes it will be here when she gets back.

She crosses the street. She has dressed down for the occasion – jogging bottoms and a hoody – but she suspects it's not enough to blend in. She's not turning back now, though.

Before she reaches the door, her nostrils are assailed by the pungent odour of weed, left behind by the lads who were just here. Further unsavoury smells greet her as she enters and moves past the gents' toilet: a mixture of stale beer and bleach, with undertones of urine and vomit.

Nice, she thinks.

A head turns. Then another. Someone nudges someone else, who nudges someone else, and attentions fall like dominoes. In all corners of the room, eyes follow her as she makes her way towards the bar. She has to squeeze past a gang of girls who make no attempt to get out of her way. Their orange faces, with their plumped-up lips and heavy eyebrows, carry more hostility than those of the lascivious males. Their examination of this stranger in their midst is more probing, more distrustful.

When she reaches the bar, nobody rushes across to serve her. The only staff member in sight is a huge bald man in a tight-fitting T-shirt displaying the contours beneath. Sara can't decide whether more work has gone into developing his biceps or the pot belly. A tattoo of a snake is wrapped around his forearm.

The man glances in her direction, then returns to talking to one of his customers.

Sara waits.

When he looks her way a second time, she smiles and raises her index finger. Somewhat reluctantly, the man hefts his bulk away from the counter and saunters towards her. She can see now that his T-shirt is emblazoned with a cartoon image of a Second World War German fighter plane and the message 'Cheeky Fokka'. She decides not to tell him that it doesn't seem appropriate.

The bartender squares up to her and rests hands that are like bear paws on the sticky counter. He doesn't speak; his invitation for her to do so comes in the form of a chin-tilt towards her.

Great customer interface skills, she thinks.

'Hi,' she says. 'I'd like some information, please.'

He shakes his head. 'I think you've taken a wrong turning, love. The tourist information office is miles away.'

He doesn't smile as he says this, but Sara hears the unsubtle laughs of others around the bar.

'I'm looking for someone.'

'Aren't we all, love? But we're not a dating agency, either. We're a pub. We serve drinks. Look around you. Do you think we make massive profits here? On a good day I might make enough to keep the bailiffs off my back. So unless you're intending to brighten my day with a picture of the Queen, I've got nothing to say to you.'

'A picture of the Queen?'

'Yes, love. I don't know where you're from, but over here we carry her picture on little bits of paper called money.'

'Ah, yes.' Sara digs a ten-pound note out of her pocket, unfolds it and shows it to the barman. 'I think she has a nice face, don't you?'

The man sighs heavily. 'What'll it be?'

'Er, a Coke, please. Diet.'

Sara hears sniggers behind her. Someone mutters, 'Jesus.'

'A Diet Coke? And that's it? No brandy in it? No vodka?'

She shrugs. 'I'm driving.'

The barman shakes his head. 'One Diet Coke coming up.' He quickly fills a glass with ice, opens a bottle, and then slams the two items down on the counter in front of her.

Sara smiles as she passes her money across. As she receives her change she says, 'About my information—'

Before she can get any further, another customer shouts over: 'Two pints of lager when you're ready, Billy.'

Billy the barman gives Sara an unapologetic look. 'Maybe later. I talk more when I'm not worrying about the bailiffs, if you catch my drift.'

His drift flies by very much uncaught by Sara, who stares at him uncomprehendingly. In return he widens his eyes and turns them on the change still clutched in her hand. Then he moves away to his beckoning customer.

Sara picks up the glass and bottle, then turns and moves away from the bar. She tries not to catch any of the many eyes still locked onto her, but instead zeroes in on an empty table in the corner of the room. She takes a seat facing the bar, her back to the wall, and pours her drink.

And then she waits.

19

It's not long before she has company.

A young buck plonks himself down on the chair opposite her. He could be good-looking if he tried, but he has the pallor of someone who has just been let out of jail after a long sentence, and there are shiny stains of uncertain origin on his top.

'All right, girl,' he says. 'Don't mind if I join you, do you?'

'Am I coming apart?' she replies.

He looks mystified.

'Joke,' she says.

It takes a second or two to penetrate to his brain, then another second for his brain to contort his rubbery lips into an inane grin. He looks over his shoulder at his mates, who raise their glasses, egging him on after his apparent initial success.

'That's a weird accent you've got. Where you from, girl?' he asks.

'Wales,' she says.

'Yeah? I shoulda realised. Been there loads of times. We used to go to a caravan in Llandudno. Do you know it?'

'You'd have to give me a few more details. Caravans all look the same to me.'

'No . . . I meant Llandudno.'

She shakes her head as she tries to see past him to the bar. 'I'm from the other side of Wales.'

'Oh. The other side, eh? I haven't been there. What're you doing here, then?'

'I'm studying,' she says.

'Studying? You a student, then? Are you at the uni?'

'No. It's just a hobby.'

He looks confused again. 'What is?'

'Studying. I study people.'

'Why?'

'I'm trying to understand what makes them tick. I'm interested in the nature of social intercourse.'

He laughs, then his mouth opens and closes a few times before he says, 'Er, okay. What?'

'Social intercourse. Like we're having now.'

'We are?'

'Yes. Hadn't you realised? It's artificial, though.'

He nods sagely, then frowns. 'How do you mean?'

'We have different agenda. Yours is to chat me up. Mine is to put you under the microscope.'

He leans back in his chair, smiling and splaying his legs. 'You won't need no microscope with me, girl.'

Sara looks across at the bar again. She's beginning to tire of this game. Pulling the strings of this drunken moron is too easy. Her anger and frustration are growing too. Matthew deserves more than this.

She gets up from her chair, starts to head towards the bar.

'Hang on, girl. Where you going?'

He grabs hold of her wrist. She halts, looks down at him.

'Let go now, or I'll break every one of your fingers.'

Even through his haze, he can see that she means it, and he releases her.

'Bit strong, isn't it?' he says. 'I was only being friendly.'

But his voice is already lost to her, drowned out by the jeers of his mates, deriding his performance.

Sara reaches the bar. Billy the bartender squares up to her again.

'Don't tell me,' he says. 'Another Diet Coke, right?'

'No,' she answers. 'Six pints of lager.'

He stares at her, checking to see if she is taking the piss.

'Six pints of lager.'

'Yes.'

'I thought you were driving.'

'I am.'

'But you're going to drink six pints of lager?'

'No.'

Billy sighs again. 'You're not going to drink the lager?'

'No.'

'Then why are you ordering six pints of lager that you're not going to drink?'

'I'm keeping the bailiffs off your back, and I'm keeping you in front of me for the time that it takes to serve the drinks.' She pulls some more money out of her pocket and places it on the table. 'You can give the beer to your other customers, or you can drink it yourself, or you can throw it down the drain. I really don't care. You can also keep the change. All I want in return is for you to give me some information while you're pouring the beer.'

Billy looks down at the money. 'What kind of information?'

'I'm looking for someone.'

'Who?'

'I don't know his real name. I think he gets called Metro.'

She sees the hesitation, the flicker of the eyes to Sara's right.

He shakes his head, but he finds it difficult to look her in the face. 'Sorry, I don't know anyone by that name.'

Sara turns and looks to her right. Two young men are watching her closely. One of the men blinks incessantly, as though he is wearing contacts that are irritating him. The other has short-cropped ginger hair and a million freckles.

Sara faces the bartender again. Slides the money towards him on the counter.

'Think harder. Metro. He's been here, hasn't he? Is he here now?'

'I've told you. I've never heard of him.'

She searches his face for a few seconds and realises this is going nowhere.

'I'm changing my order,' she says. She jerks her thumb towards the two men on surveillance. 'Whatever they're having. It's on me for the rest of the night.' And then she turns and walks back to her table.

The lothario who was here earlier has disappeared. Sara picks up her drink and sips at it, her eyes on the bar. She sees the two men swagger over to fill the space she vacated in front of Billy. Despite being much bigger than his questioners, Billy seems a little afraid of them. He is suddenly a lot more talkative, although Sara cannot hear what he is saying. When he gestures in her direction, the two men turn and give her a hard stare. Then the one with freckles says something else to Billy and points to his beer bottle. Billy immediately fetches two more bottles from his fridge, opens them, and sets them in front of the lads.

Sara realises she has lit a fuse. What the other end is attached to is anyone's guess.

The two men come across to her table, their faces set. Sara sips her Coke. She expects them to sit on the hard chairs opposite, but instead they plonk themselves down on the cushioned bench she is on, one on each side. They sit very close, their thighs in contact with hers.

Sara swirls the ice cubes in her drink. Takes another sip.

'All right, darling,' says Freckles to her right. 'Thought we'd better come across and say thank you.'

'For the drinks,' says Blinky. 'It's only good manners.'

'Is right,' says Freckles. 'That's how we were brought up. Never does any harm to be polite, my mam used to say.' He slides his arm along the backrest of the bench, so that it's poised just above Sara's shoulders. ''Course, the question in my mind is why would you be buying us drinks?'

'It's a natural enough question,' says Blinky. 'We don't know each other, do we? It's very weird when some foreign bird comes in here and pays for our drinks all night.'

'Very weird,' Freckles echoes. 'It's almost as if you want something from us. Is that right, darling? Have we got something you want?'

'I hope so,' Sara says. 'The barman over there seems to think so.'

'Does he now? I didn't hear him say anything like that.'

'He didn't need to. I can read him like a book.'

'Really? Mind-reader, are you?'

'Telepathic, are you?' says Blinky.

'I have my moments,' says Sara. 'Like now, for instance. I can tell what you're both thinking.'

'Is that right? Go 'ead, then. Do your stuff. What am I thinking right now?'

As he says this, Freckles makes a show of turning his eyes on Sara's chest.

Sara thinks, You're not intimidating me, little boy.

'You're afraid,' she says.

'You what?' Freckles splutters. 'Afraid?'

'Yes. You're afraid of a man called Metro, and you're afraid of me because I'm asking about Metro. And your mate here,' – she indicates Blinky on her left – 'is scared of both of those things, but he's also afraid of you, which is why he's playing second fiddle.'

As psychology goes, it's fundamental stuff. It was driven into her hard in her army days. When faced with an angry rabble, you need to assess instantly what is really bothering them, and who speaks for them. Deal with the organ grinder, not the monkey, as the curious English expression has it.

There follows much hollow laughter. The two minions trying to show how tough they are.

'She thinks we're frightened,' says Freckles. 'Look at me, quaking in my boots.'

'I'm terrified, me,' says Blinky. 'I think I might wet myself in a minute.'

And then the laughing stops, and the two become deadly serious.

'Okay, darling, what's going on? Why all the fucking questions? Are you a bizzy?'

'A what?'

'A copper. A policewoman. Jesus, you really are from another planet, aren't you?'

'No, I'm not from the police. I'm here for a friend. Someone who got hurt.'

'I see. And you think this Metro person had something to do with it?'

Sara turns her head and looks Freckles directly in the eye. 'Did he?'

Keep looking at me, she thinks. Stare right at me while you deny all knowledge, and then I might believe you.

Freckles breaks eye contact and takes a swig of his beer. 'You're in the wrong place, darling. Asking the wrong questions. You could get into trouble doing that.'

'Big trouble,' says Blinky.

She turns towards the sidekick. 'Why do you do that with your eyes? Are you nervous around women?'

She sees his mouth tighten, and wonders if she's pushed too far. But then she feels the touch of a hand in her hair. She whips her head right to face Freckles, who is leaning in towards her.

'A good-looking tart like you shouldn't be in here, all by yourself, asking about people you know nothing about. You never know what might happen. We could do what we like with you, do you realise that? Nobody here would lift a finger to help you. In fact, they'd probably cheer us on while we had our bit of fun. And afterwards they'd all go deaf, dumb and blind, unable to answer any questions about what happened here. Is that what you want?' He continues to twirl his fingers in her hair. 'Yeah, maybe it is. Maybe it's getting you all hot and bothered, the thought of us doing stuff to you while everyone watches. Am I right about that? Am I?'

She feels it, then. The cold wetness. She jumps and pushes the man's bottle away. Stares down at the beer stain in her lap.

Freckles explodes into laughter. 'Oh, crap,' he says. 'I've got her too excited. Have you seen this?'

His mate looks down, then whoops and claps his hands. 'Shit, you've got her all moist, lad. Nice one!'

Sara stands up and tries to brush the beer away. Her action serves only to make others aware of her predicament, and they join in the laughter.

'I think she needs to take them off and dry them,' says Blinky.

Freckles stands up and speaks quietly in her ear again. 'I think you'd better leave, love. While you're still wearing clothes. Know what I mean?'

Sara looks at him again. Weighs up her chances. They're not good.

She walks away. Past the leering males and the clucking females, and out into the cold darkness.

20

Cody is late getting home. It's always the same in the early days of a murder investigation. All the balls are in the air; all the cogs are in motion; nothing is yet resolved. The cops can't afford to relax, to let anything escape their attention in this crucial phase. Given time, evidence will deteriorate or be corrupted; suspects will disappear or cover their tracks; witness memories will fade or become confused. And so the detectives will work until they drop in this first couple of days.

Cody is ready to drop now. With a bit of luck, he might even get a few hours of precious sleep tonight.

Sleep is not the close companion it used to be. Now it often prefers to dance just beyond Cody's reach, teasing him with its promises. He has learnt to cope with the scant time it begrudgingly grants him.

It goes through peaks and troughs. Six months ago, he was at his lowest. Night terrors kept him awake, and the sleep deprivation helped to fuel hallucinations in a vicious cycle that threatened to dismantle his sanity beyond repair.

Then things changed.

He didn't tell the psychologist about this change, of course, and has no intention of ever doing so. It's always on his mind, but that's where it will stay.

He thinks about it now as he unlocks his front door on Rodney Street. It used to be the case that he would just wander in, pick up his mail, head upstairs, eat, drink and relax.

Not anymore.

Now, he half-expects someone to jump out at him. He tenses at every noise, however slight. Before he can do anything else, he has to check every room of the flat for unwanted surprises.

He's not being paranoid.

They've been here.

Waldo and his pals have been here.

It started with the phone calls. They occurred regularly for months. Nothing was said during the calls, and no matter what questions or insults Cody fired down the line, he got nothing in return. But Cody had an idea who was making them.

His suspicions were confirmed when his own screams were played back at him over the door intercom. Then, on later occasions, there were signs that Waldo had entered his building. Had even been into his apartment.

He is undeniably terrified that the clowns are back in his life. He never knows when they will come knocking again.

But here's the thing . . .

It's what he wants.

As scared as he is of Waldo and his followers, Cody welcomes their return. It means he has a chance of catching them, of carrying out some kind of retribution he has yet to decide upon. It means he may finally achieve closure.

That is everything to Cody. Without that prospect, he knows his mind would crumble and his career would be over. His life would be over.

So bring it on, Waldo.

Are you here? Hiding in the shadows of the ground-floor hallway? Behind one of those doors belonging to the dental practice, perhaps? Or that particularly scary door that leads down to the basement?

Or here, on the next floor up, just waiting for me to pass so that you can leap out at me?

Are you on the other side of this door I'm unlocking now – the one that leads up to my flat?

No? Then what about the flat itself? In my bedroom? The kitchen? The living room?

No. Waldo isn't here. Not this time. But he'll be back.

Of that, Cody has no doubt.

Cody reheats some leftover Bolognese he made at the weekend and eats it with some penne pasta and grated cheese. He doesn't accompany it with wine or beer – not because of the guff he gave the psychologist, but because alcohol worsens his already sporadic sleep pattern.

He relaxes in the living room with a book. Although he has a television, he rarely watches it. Too much of what it beams out at him is irritating. He'd much rather read or play his guitar. If it were earlier in the evening, he'd use the gym equipment he installed in one of the bedrooms.

But not tonight. It's too late, and he really is tired. Sleep – the old tease – is beckoning, and this time she seems genuine. It would be an insult to refuse her.

And then the phone rings.

Cody glances at the clock, sees that it's close to 11 p.m.

There are generally only two reasons his phone rings at this time of night. One is because of a work-related emergency. DCI Blunt commanding him to get his arse back out on the street because there's been another murder, or because there's been a sudden development in an existing case and it can't wait while he lounges about in his scruffy pit of a bed. Something along those lines.

The other reason is Waldo.

Cody gets up and goes over to the phone in its charging station. The caller display tells him the number is unavailable. Which in turn tells him this is likely to be Waldo.

Cody is suddenly alert. It'll be a long time before he relaxes enough for sleep again.

He picks up the phone and presses the call answer button.

'Hello?'

Nothing.

So, the silent treatment again. Ho hum.

Cody sits down on his sofa, the phone clamped to his ear.

'Hello?' he says again. 'Clown central here. You want to report a clown-related incident?'

He knows he won't get an answer. It doesn't work like that. He won't even hear breathing. Just silence until he gets bored and hangs up.

He has thought often about the reasons for these calls – what they are meant to achieve – and has decided that it's simply to keep him on his toes, to keep the memories of the clowns fresh in his mind. Waldo wants to be a constant presence.

Well, he's succeeding.

'Tell me,' says Cody. 'What size shoes do clowns wear? I mean, as a minimum? Gotta be pretty large, right? Much larger than mine. But then I've got a few toes missing, so I'm not a standard comparison. Of course, you already know that, don't you? You probably remember how—'

And then Cody thinks he hears something. A noise. A muffled scrape, and then possibly a click of a switch. And he begins to suspect that this call might be different. He begins to wonder if—

'Hello, Cody,' says the caller.

21

It's a cliché, but Cody really does feel the hairs on his neck and his arms stand to rigid attention.

The voice has been disguised. Put through a machine or computer to give it a deep, sinister sound. It would be impossible to work out what the original voice sounded like. But what has got Cody really spooked is that he is being spoken to at all. This is a live human being. This is the person to whom Cody has been desperate to speak outside of his nightmares.

'Who is this?' he asks, almost breathlessly.

'I think you know,' says the voice. 'We've already been introduced.'

It takes a few seconds for Cody to reply. He needs to be certain this isn't some kind of sadistic prank.

'When? How did we meet?'

'At the warehouse. We had a party. I brought three friends. You brought one. He didn't last the course, unfortunately. You, on the other hand, got almost legless.'

The slow, booming laugh that follows could belong to the devil himself. Cody feels his mouth go dry. There's a phantom throbbing where his severed toes should be.

'A lot of people know that story. Doesn't prove anything about you.'

'You're right. It doesn't. Perhaps this will help.'

There's a pause. A click. And then the screaming.

Not Cody's own cries this time – they were bad enough. No, these are the screams of Jeff Vance, his partner, calling out for God's intervention while his face is parted from his skull.

Cody wants to drop the phone and run to the bathroom to be sick. He forces himself to remain, to try to think rationally. To keep his mind from breaking under the pressure of this bombardment of evil.

The voice comes back on the line. 'Enough of a hint, Cody? Know who I am now?'

Cody swallows. 'Yes. You're . . . You're Waldo.'

'Waldo?'

'Yes. I needed to call you something. It's what I came up with.'

'Waldo. Waldo. Hmm, yes, I like it.'

'You can give me your real name if you prefer.'

'All in good time, Cody. All in good time. When we get to know each other a bit better.'

'Is this your way of setting up a date? I don't come cheap, you know.'

Another rumble of laughter. 'I love it. You're so transparent. A display of humour to hide your terror.'

'You don't frighten me.'

'Oh, but I think I do. I think I frighten you more than anything in this world. I'll bet there isn't a day that goes by when I don't pop up in your head.'

'How about popping up in the real world? Why don't you do that? Come on. Right now. You and me.'

'Don't get all ridiculously macho, Cody. Believe me, a fight with me is the last thing you want. You need to start being careful what you wish for.'

'Yeah, right. Who's scared now, huh? And why the fuck are you calling me anyway? Got nobody to play with right now?'

'Actually, I'm here to offer you some help.'

'I don't need any help from you.'

'On this matter, I think you do.'

'Really? Enlighten me.'

'I want to offer you something.'

'The only thing you can offer me is your stupid clown head on a plate.'

The laugh again. 'Good job that's what I had in mind, then.'

Cody frowns. 'What? What are you talking about?'

'I'm talking about me, Cody. I'm calling to give you the once in a lifetime opportunity to catch me.'

22

'Why?' Cody asks. 'Why would you want me to catch you?'

'I think you deserve a break. You've had a hard time of it lately.'

'What makes you think that?'

'I read the papers. I saw the reports of what you went through in that child abduction case. Must have been tough.'

'All part of the job,' Cody says casually.

'If you say so. But I also feel I owe you one. It's been too easy for me so far. As sporting challenges go, I have to say you've been a little bit disappointing. I thought you'd be a lot closer to finding me by now.'

'Maybe I'm closer than you think.'

'And maybe you're not. Maybe you're light years away. I'm starting to get bored. It's like when you play hide-and-seek, and you hear the person who's looking for you walking off in completely the wrong direction. You feel the need to build the excitement by calling out to them or whistling. Well, here I am, Cody, whistling to you.'

'Is that what this is to you? Just a game?'

'Of course. It's been a game all along. It was a game when we first met in the warehouse. That's what I do: I play games with people.'

'And if I don't want to play?'

'You don't get a choice. You're already in the middle of the game. Besides, something tells me you don't want to resign just yet.'

'Are you going to tell me what the rules of this game are?'

'There are no rules. Anything goes. There is, however, an objective.'

'Which is?'

'Isn't it obvious? To find me. To catch me. To take out your revenge on me, in whatever form you think is suitable. Surely that's a game worth playing?'

'And what's your own objective?'

'Oh, just to have fun. To watch you dance and jump through hoops for my amusement. I'm not just a clown, you know. I'm also the circus master and the audience. You are simply a part of the entertainment.'

'No. Don't get ideas above your station. You're Waldo the Clown, and that's all you are. And when I take you down, I'll be the one doing all the laughing.'

'That's the spirit, Cody! That's more like it. You know, it's just occurred to me how appropriate the name Waldo is. There's a set of books called *Where's Wally?* – have you heard of it? – and in the US it's called *Where's Waldo?* So that's what we're doing: we're playing *Where's Waldo?* Don't you think that's such a delicious coincidence?'

'Actually, I think you're a dick. But keep playing with yourself if that's how you like to get your kicks. Now, are you going to tell me where you are or not?'

'Patience, Cody. You don't think I'm just going to blurt out my address, do you? Where would be the fun in that? No, I'm afraid you're going to have to work for your prize.'

'Why am I not surprised?'

'Don't worry. It's nothing too taxing at this time of night. You must be tired, ready for bed. By the way, what are you reading at the moment? There are a lot of good books on those shelves of yours.'

Cody flinches at the stark reminder that Waldo has been inside the apartment. He has been in this very room. He may even have sat exactly where Cody is now.

The thought sends a shiver up his spine.

He says, 'I'm reading *It*, by Stephen King. You should try it. You might pick up some tips on how to be scary instead of a complete joke.'

'Ah, there you go with the bravado again. I'm sure you haven't forgotten, but I can play the recording of you when I was snipping away at your toes if you like. You weren't so cocksure then, were you?'

Cody doesn't feel so cocksure now either. He thinks he's putting up a brave front, but front is what it is. When he looks down at his free hand resting on his lap, he sees how it's trembling.

He says, 'Get to the point, will you?'

'All right, I will. Have you ever seen *Silence of the Lambs*, Cody?'

'That's what you call getting to the point?'

'Bear with me. Well, have you?'

'Yes, I've seen it.'

'Good. Then you'll know there's a scene where Hannibal Lecter offers to help Clarice catch a serial killer, but only after she tells him something personal about herself.'

'I remember.'

'Excellent. Then off you go.'

'What? You want to know something personal about me? Like what? How many times I've been to the toilet today?'

'I was thinking something more profound. Something about what makes you tick, or a deeply held belief.'

'What I absolutely believe right now is that I need to put you behind bars.'

'Enough of the flippancy, Cody. If you want my help, you need to do this. Tell me about something that happened to you today.'

'I was at work. I can't talk to you about police business.'

'No. And to be candid, I'm not very interested in the misadventures of the Merseyside Police Farce. What about *before* you went to work?'

'I got up, showered, had breakfast. If you're interested, I mixed two types of cereal in the same bowl. Is that Freudian enough for you?'

'And after breakfast?'

'I drove to work.'

'No, Cody, you didn't.'

The shiver again. He knows. Waldo knows.

'I didn't?'

'No. You went to see a psychologist.'

'How do you know that? Have you been following me?'

'I often watch you. You'd be surprised how many times I've been only yards away from you. Now tell me about the psychologist. Why did you go to see her?'

Cody finds it difficult to concentrate. He's too busy thinking about all the possible occasions on which he might have been able to catch a glimpse of his enemy, and about how much of his life story is now known to Waldo.

'I . . . It's standard procedure.'

'Standard procedure for what?'

'For when an officer has been through a traumatic event. You said yourself you've been reading about me in the papers.'

'And that's what you talked about?'

'Yes.'

'No.'

'What?'

'That's not what you talked about, is it?'

'Yes, it is. Like I just told you, officers who—'

'Don't lie, Cody. You talked about me, didn't you?'

'Why would I talk about you? That was ages ago. The child abduction case put me in hospital. It—'

'That case was a walk in the park compared to what happened when you met me. I saw you, Cody! I saw what you were like when you went back to your car after visiting the psychologist. You were a wreck. Now, are you going to start telling the truth here, or should I just hang up?'

Cody feels the fight going out of him. He could continue lying, putting up a smokescreen, but what's the point? One slip, and Waldo will end the call, taking with him whatever precious nuggets of information he wants to trade. And besides, what harm can it possibly do to reveal the truth?

'Okay,' he says. 'I talked about you. Happy now?'

'What did you say?'

'I described the event. I talked about what you did to me and my partner.'

'Yes, but this was to a psychologist, Cody. Surely she was more interested in how it affected you mentally?'

'Yes. We talked about that.'

'How? What exactly did you say?'

'I don't remember *exactly*. I just made it clear that it had affected me.'

'Mentally?'

'What?'

'You made it clear that it affected you mentally as well as physically?'

'Yes, of course. Haven't I just said that?'

'But you haven't told me what you said to her about those mental effects. What did you say it did to you? How did you make it clear to her?'

'I don't know. She could just tell. She's trained for these things. She knows when—'

'Did you cry, Cody? In front of this woman, did you break down and cry?'

'No. Absolutely not. This was a calm and rational discussion. It was—'

'Did you cry? It's okay, you know. It's okay to cry.'

'I didn't cry. I just told her the facts. I—'

'You did, didn't you? You cried. Admit it. You—'

'Okay, okay! I got upset. I'd seen a good friend have his face cut off by a fucking lunatic clown, and I was a tad upset about it. Is that what you want to hear? Is it, you piece of fucking shit?'

There's a long pause. And then: 'You cried. Over me.'

He says this simply, almost as if he finds it unbelievable that he could have provoked such emotion.

'Well, there you go,' says Cody. 'That's my *Silence of the Lambs* moment. What do I win?'

The phone goes silent for an even longer period. Cody starts to wonder if Waldo is still on the line.

'It's in the post,' says Waldo.

'The post! You're sending me something in the fucking post?'

'Don't worry,' says the voice that would make anyone worry. 'I hand-deliver my post. Usually at night.'

There's a click, and now the phone line is definitely dead. Cody tosses the handset onto the sofa and races over to the window. He peers down at the street but sees only the dark hulks of stationary cars. He turns and runs out of the room, across the hall, down the stairs. He opens up his apartment door and runs across the landing, hurtles down the turned staircase to the ground floor. He sprints across the hallway, gets to the front door . . .

And sees it.

A small white padded envelope.

He opens the door anyway and checks outside. There is no sign of anyone here, just as he suspected. Waldo could have delivered his letter any time since Cody arrived home and is now long gone.

He retreats into his building, closing the door and picking up the envelope carefully by its edges. Printed on its front are the words 'To Nathan Cody'.

It occurs to Cody that he should safeguard any forensic evidence that might be on the letter, but he knows that Waldo is too careful to make such mistakes. Cody also knows that he's not going to turn this over to the police or forensics teams. This is his problem, and only his.

He feels the envelope all over. It contains something small and hard.

He heads back upstairs, his eyes on the gift from Waldo. He hopes that this isn't just a practical joke; that he really has been given something of value. Something life-changing.

His head is still swimming with thoughts of the telephone conversation. This is the first time Waldo has ever spoken to him. Even in the warehouse, he never said a word. That's significant. That has to mean something big.

And so what's in this envelope cannot be trivial. It must be important. It must provide a lead to Waldo, just as he was promised it would.

The envelope feels as though it is burning his fingers as he carries it up to his flat. He worries that it has been impregnated with something that will cause it and its contents to disintegrate if he doesn't open it soon.

He takes it into his kitchen, then grabs a knife from its block and climbs onto a stool at the breakfast bar. He continues to stare at the letter for a few more seconds, trying to prepare himself but not having a clue what he's preparing for. Taking a deep breath, he turns the envelope over, inserts the knife under the flap, and slices it open.

He pulls apart the sides of the envelope and peers inside. Surprised, he turns the envelope over and drops its contents onto his open palm.

It's a key.

A small steel key. The type of key that might be used for a padlock or a filing cabinet or a desk drawer. Attached to the key with a piece of thin twine is a label that says, 'The key to freedom'.

Cody is reminded of the *Alice in Wonderland* story in which Alice comes across various items with labels on them that say things like 'Drink me'.

He stares at the tiny key and wonders which rabbit hole it will take him down.

23

She worries that she may have missed them.

When she went home, she intended to stay there – to lick her wounds and live to fight another day. She intended to shower, slip on some clean, fresh pyjamas, and go to bed, filling her head with thoughts and memories of Matthew.

It didn't work out that way. She fumed all the way home. It mounted in intensity until she was incandescent, and no sooner did she walk through her front door than she realised she would be going out again. She stayed at the house only long enough to change out of her damp jogging bottoms, then she got back in her car.

Which is where she is now. In her car. Back at the same spot on the street she occupied earlier. But now her mood has darkened. Her husband is dead, and somebody in this pub knows something about it. No more pussyfooting around with these dickheads.

It's close to midnight. In the past half hour, nobody has gone in, but plenty have come out. There cannot be many customers remaining in there now. She can only hope that Freckles and Blinky didn't choose to leave the pub during the time she went home.

She continues to watch.

Two more people come out – a lad and his girlfriend. She's all over him, using him as a prop to keep her on her feet. Billy the bartender appears in the doorway, waves them off, and begins swinging the outer doors into place to lock up.

Shit.

But then Billy seems to hear a noise inside, and he turns. Two more figures appear. One of them claps Billy on the shoulder as he exits. The other still has a beer bottle in his hand.

It's the gruesome twosome. The dregs of this shithole of a pub.

She waits until Billy has disappeared inside and the two young men have made their way to the end of the block, then she gets out of her car and crosses the street. She remains a good distance behind her quarry; hardly anyone else is out at this time of night, and so she's in no danger of losing them.

When the pair turn up a side street, she picks up her pace. She jogs to the corner, then peers around it before continuing to follow. She is now only a few yards behind. Other than the three of them, the street seems deserted.

When Freckles and Blinky have to get into single file to squeeze past some cars that are parked across the pavement, Sara makes her move.

She increases her speed again, keeping her footfalls low and silent. As the men get past the cars and Freckles starts to move to the side of his friend again, Sara comes up close behind him.

The Belgian Takedown is one of its names. It involves reaching down and grabbing the ankles of your opponent, then yanking them towards you while simultaneously ramming your shoulder into the back of the opponent's legs. The enemy has no choice but to go down hard, and with his ankles still in your grasp, you are in a prime position to aim repeated kicks into his groin, or to climb onto his back and take him out of action.

When Sara applies the manoeuvre to Freckles, his face hits the pavement with a resounding smack, and the bottle in his hand smashes, spraying beer and splinters of glass towards his comrade.

Sara decides to dispense with the groin-kicking for Freckles.

Blinky is not so fortunate.

When he turns to see what all the commotion is, his eyelids are working more furiously than ever, and his mouth drops open in surprise and confusion.

Sara steps towards him, snaps a powerful kick directly into his crown jewels.

She hears the sharp intake of breath as Blinky clutches at his privates and staggers backwards. Then she finishes him off with a spinning roundhouse kick that almost takes his head off. He flies into a hedge and bounces off it again, landing spreadeagled on his back, unconscious.

Sara whirls to see Freckles clambering to his feet, blood gushing from his flattened nose. The top of the broken beer bottle is still clutched in his hand, and it's clear he intends to use it.

His drunken lunge is slow and awkward. Sara has no trouble sidestepping it, trapping his outstretched arm and then throwing him across her body and onto the ground. There's a crunching noise as he hits, and Freckles cries out. Sara jumps on his back and twists his arm up behind him. She wrests the broken bottle from his hand, then holds the jagged edge to his neck.

'Remember me?' she asks.

'I remember. The foreign bird.'

'That's me. Tell me about Metro.'

'He'll kill me.'

Sara presses the glass harder into his neck. 'I'll kill you if you don't. I'm not fucking about here. Who's Metro?'

'He . . . He works for Joey Pearce.'

'And who's Joey Pearce?'

'Everyone knows who Joey Pearce is.'

'Pretend I don't.'

'He runs things round here. You don't mess with him.'

'And what does Metro do for him?'

'He's an enforcer.'

'What does that mean?'

'He does all the dirty jobs. He . . . He collects payments. He steps in when there's trouble. That kind of thing.'

'Does he ever come into that stinking pub you were just in?'

'Sometimes, yeah. Not very often, though.'

'Where else might I find him?'

'I . . . I don't know.'

She jabs him with the bottle again. 'Think!'

'There's a few places Pearce owns. Try the Texicana pool hall. Or Jaeger's Gym. Or maybe Antarctica.'

'Are you being funny?'

'No! It's a club in town. He often goes there.'

Sara looks around. Blinky is still flat out. Across the street, a light goes on in a window.

'One more thing,' she says. 'The next time you're tempted to treat a woman like the shit on your shoe, think about this moment. Some of us bite back, arsehole.'

She gets to her feet. Freckles groans but makes no attempt to move. She turns and walks back towards her car, tossing the broken bottle over a hedge at the end of the street.

24

So that's another sleepless night.

Cody sometimes wonders how he manages to stay looking so young, given the countless hours of rejuvenating slumber that have been stolen from him. He knows he looks shattered this morning, though; his bathroom mirror was keen to point that out.

He spent most of the night staring at the key – not something he would ever have thought he would end up doing. A book, yes. A box-set of DVDs, possibly. But not a key.

It's not even an especially interesting-looking key. It doesn't sparkle or feel as though it possesses magical powers. It's just a plain, ordinary key of less than impressive dimensions.

He has looked around his apartment for things that it might possibly open, and come up with nothing. He's beginning to feel that the trade he made to obtain it was a very one-sided affair.

And yet . . .

This is the key to freedom. It says so, right there on the label. That's special, right? Has to be. Most keys don't even pretend to lay such bold claim to fundamental human rights.

So what does it set free? Cody wonders.

Me? Is this some kind of arty-farty symbol of my being released from the shackles of clowndom?

No. It has to be more grounded in reality than that. Waldo doesn't work in the abstract. He likes people to see and touch his art. To *feel* it, however excruciating and mind-destroying it might be.

So the key opens something. Pandora's box, perhaps – filled with the world's evils awaiting their release by the idiot detective gullible enough to unlock them.

Cody is still thinking about these weighty matters when he arrives at Stanley Road police station in Kirkdale. But as he walks through the door, he sees the desk sergeant and two uniformed officers gathered around a monitor, laughing at something.

'What's the joke, lads?' he asks.

The sergeant looks across at Cody, then nods for him to join them. 'Take a look at this,' he says.

Intrigued, Cody moves around to the front of the monitor. On the screen is a paused grainy video of a dark street scene.

'You know those two scallies,' says the sergeant, 'Kieran Willis and Lee Hassell?'

'Doesn't everyone? What about them?'

'Watch this.'

The sergeant mouse-clicks the video play button. For a few seconds nothing happens, but then a figure comes into view from the right, closely followed by another, swigging from a bottle.

'Is that them?' Cody asks.

'Certainly is. Are you watching?'

A second later, a third figure enters. Smaller than the other two, and wearing a hooded cardigan with the hood up, it closes in like a shark on the person Cody now knows to be Lee Hassell.

Cody watches as Hassell is suddenly pitched forward to face-plant the pavement.

'Oh, shit!' he says.

'The best is yet to come,' says the sergeant.

Cody's eyes widen as he observes the close combat. He finds himself gasping as Willis is dispatched with the kicks. He swears as Hassell closes in, brandishing what looks like the top half of his bottle, but then almost cheers as the hooded figure throws him to the ground and disarms him.

And then, as the assailant seems to interrogate or threaten Hassell, Cody realises something.

He says, 'Is that—?'

'A woman. Yup.' The sergeant is wearing a broad grin now. 'Can you believe it? Lee Hassell and Kieran Willis getting their arses kicked by a girl!'

But that is no longer the only question on Cody's mind. There is suddenly a clenching sensation in his stomach as he stares at this video. He leans forward to get a better look, but the figures are so small, the pictures so grainy. He can't quite make out the woman's face, but there's something about her build and those stray locks of blonde hair escaping from the confines of her hood.

'Where did you get this?' he asks.

'It's on YouTube. It was caught on the CCTV camera of a business premises last night, and it's already gone viral. Incredible, eh?'

'Yeah, but I mean where exactly did it happen?'

'In Bootle. Just around the corner from The Tar Barrel.'

The Tar Barrel. Just a few minutes' walk from Matthew Prior's office building. That can't be sheer coincidence.

'Has anyone looked into this?'

The sergeant stares at Cody as if he's taking all the fun out of the moment. 'We've asked some questions. We know it's Hassell and Willis, but there's no way they're going to admit to having the crap kicked out of them by a woman. And just between us, Cody, I wouldn't have thought catching their assailant would come high on our list of priorities. I know a lot of coppers who'd like to shake this woman's hand.'

Cody nods.

But he knows where he'll be going later.

25

Cody finds it difficult to concentrate. His wearied mind is being torn in two different directions. Waldo sits right up there, of course. Cody keeps seeing mental images of that grotesque clown mask, its grin filled with insanity and a thirst for blood. Cody keeps reaching into his jacket pocket to finger the key, as though that might help to divine its purpose. His eyes dart to his own desk drawer, and then across the room to the filing cabinets. Would it fit one of those, he wonders? How could I possibly go around checking all the locks in here without someone noticing?

And now there is the other issue. Sara Prior. That had to be her on the video. But why? What the hell has she got herself involved in?

He becomes aware that Blunt, at the front of the room, keeps glancing his way as she speaks.

She's on to me, he thinks. She knows I'm not quite with it. Her patented Cody radar is working at full tilt right now.

'Moving on to forensics,' says Blunt, 'we've had some progress there. The DNA in the hair follicles matches that in the saliva found on the bottle of water, so it was the same person. Unfortunately, it hasn't matched anything in our databases, so we still don't know who that person is. Moving swiftly back to positives, the wax used on the hair has been identified as a product called Head Art, manufactured by Head Action Limited. I've sent round a list of outlets for you to check. We've also got something on the red woollen fibres. It's almost certain they came from a man's sweater that was being sold in branches of Marston's up until about a year ago. Again, you've been sent a list of shops.'

She pauses and surveys her audience. 'That's pretty good going, folks. We know a hell of a lot about at least one of the killers. We know what they wore, what they did with their hair, where they shopped, what their fingerprints look like, and even the structure of their DNA. Hell, if we were a bit further into the future we could probably clone the killer right here. Unfortunately, we can't do that. What I'm trying to say, people, is that all of this wonderful evidence we've got is bloody useless to us unless you can haul in someone we can test for a match. Cody, what did you get from speaking to the people where Matthew Prior worked?'

Cody forces his mind back on track. Under the watchful glare of Blunt, he delivers a brief summary of the interviews with Lewis Fulton and Ann Staples.

'So,' says Blunt, 'there was friction between Prior and his boss? Enough to provide a motive for murder?'

'Well, friction of a kind, yes. If Ann Staples is to be believed, then Fulton seems to be a bit of a dick and a bully. There are probably several people who would like to kill Fulton, but I still haven't heard anything that would put Matthew Prior in anyone's sights. He seems to have been the most inoffensive man on the planet.'

'Maybe, but he certainly got in somebody's bad books.' Blunt looks pensive for a second. 'Judging from Prior's house, the killers were searching for something, and they were pretty desperate to find it. Maybe the only thing Prior got wrong in their eyes was not giving up what they were after. That could work in terms of what we've heard about Prior's personality. Maybe he died because of the strength of his integrity and not because of a flaw.'

Cody nods. 'Could be. It would be a great help to know what this Holy Grail was, though, and whether it was actually found by the killers.'

Blunt casts her gaze to the back of the room. 'Grace, any light you can shed on this, given that Prior's computer is the only item we're certain was taken?'

As always, Grace Meade gets to her feet before responding. 'As I mentioned, there isn't a lot we can do without the laptop itself. I'm still talking to HCU about accessing Prior's internet records from his service provider, but that could take a while. Even if we eventually get them, they might not tell us very much.'

Blunt sighs and drops her attention back on Cody. 'What about Sara Prior? You spoke to her again, yes?'

'Yes,' Cody replies. Images of the recently viewed video flash into his mind. 'I, er, I didn't find anything to suggest she's involved.'

Blunt stares at him. 'Did you ask her about why she didn't mention her army background?'

Those images. Sara sneaking up in the night like a ninja assassin. Disarming and disabling two young, fit men. That karate kick. That judo throw . . .

'Yes. She just didn't think it was relevant, and I have to agree with her. Most ex-army personnel don't go around murdering people when they return to normal life. In fact, you could argue that they're the very people who are more likely to stay away from violence because they're so aware of its effects.'

'Sara's husband dumped her. That could be a good motive.'

'He didn't dump her. They were temporarily separated because Matthew had anxiety issues. And even if he had dumped her and she was mad about it, how would she go about finding people willing to nail her husband to the floor and trash his house? I don't think people like that advertise in the *Yellow Pages*.'

'And what about the message?'

'The message?'

'Yes, Cody. The recorded message on the phone. You were supposed to ask her about that, too.'

'I did.'

'And?'

'Nothing. She said she doesn't know what it means.'

'And you believe her?'

'Well . . . yes.'

Blunt continues to pierce him with her stare. 'I'm afraid I don't share your faith. First of all, we don't know enough about this woman to say categorically that she isn't acquainted with people who would be willing to kill on her behalf. They don't have to come from Rent-a-Murderer. They could be friends of hers – army buddies. Secondly, Matthew Prior recorded that phone message because he knew it would mean something to his wife. I don't believe she's so thick that she can't figure it out. Do you?'

'I . . . She's not thick.'

'No. She may even be downright devious and manipulative. Possibly even homicidal. I don't want us to get complacent about this woman. She's not getting the all-clear just yet.'

Cody nods. A part of him wants to argue. Another part of him sees Sara Prior bent over a man she has pinned to the ground, the jagged edge of a bottle pressed into his jugular.

26

Metro Mackenzie pounds the bag with blows that could knock out a mule. He's been here for an hour, sparring, skipping, weight training. It's how he likes to start his day. Makes him feel ready for anything. And anyone.

Metro's real name is Samuel, but nobody calls him that. He hasn't been called it in so long he doesn't even respond when he hears it now.

He got the nickname 'Metro' as a teenager when he was into graffiti. He was quite the artist in his day. His canvases of choice were in the railway sidings and depots of the Merseyside underground system. The biggest prizes were the trains themselves. Get your work on one of those, and it would be carried right across the network for everyone to see and remember.

There were turf wars, of course, but Metro was never afraid of a little confrontation. On one occasion he caught a rival artist covering up Metro's tag with his own. Metro beat him up, stripped him naked, and left him tied to a lamppost on the platform, a huge letter 'M' sprayed across his face.

Those were the days.

His life is very different now. His art is less refined. Resculpting someone's face doesn't require the same finesse and attention to detail.

He continues to pound the bag, even as he hears the approach of footsteps behind him.

'All right, Ozone,' he says.

A figure shuffles round to the front, where he can be seen.

'How'd you know it was me?' says the arrival.

'Are you serious?' Metro asks.

Ozone is also not this man's real name. It derives from his penchant for dousing himself in vast quantities of anti-perspirant, body spray, foot deodorant, hair product, and aftershave. Ozone Fisher likes to smell nice and doesn't give a toss that he makes the air unbreathable for everyone else in his vicinity.

He likes to look good, too. He prefers leather jackets and highly polished shoes to sportswear, his thick hair slicked into precisely the right position, and his teeth gleaming. He brushes and flosses after every meal, just as his mother told him.

'Wanna see something funny?' Ozone asks.

Thump.

'You're not going to take your clothes off again, are you?'

Ozone looks hurt. He reaches into his pocket and takes out a top-of-the-range iPhone. 'It's a video.'

Thump.

'It's not another one of those cat videos, is it? You know I can't stand them.'

'Better than that. This one's got Kieran Willis and Lee Hassell in it.'

Thump.

'Oh, yeah? Doing what, exactly? Can't be anything more stupid than the stuff they usually get up to.'

'Oh, this one is. They'll never live this one down.'

Thump.

'Go 'ead, then. What is it?'

'This is a video of the pair of them getting the shit kicked out of them.'

Metro is suddenly interested. If this is a move by some opposition muscle . . .

'Who does the kicking?'

Ozone shows his pearly whites. 'You'll never believe it.'

Metro stops hitting the bag. He feels like landing one on Ozone instead.

'Are you gonna fucking tell me, or what?'

'It's a girl.'

'What is?'

'The one who does them in. It's only a fucking girl.'

And now Metro is *really* interested. 'Show me.'

Ozone plays the video for him on his iPhone. He laughs hysterically, but Metro doesn't join in. Metro is more concerned with studying this woman's moves and appreciating her skill and power.

'When was this?' he asks.

'Last night, just after they'd had a few bevvies in the Barrel. Awesome, isn't it?'

'Do we know what it's about?'

Ozone puts his phone back in his pocket. 'Ah, now that's where it gets even more interesting. Apparently, this woman – whoever she is – was in the Barrel some time before the fight, and she was asking about you.'

'Me? Why?'

'Didn't say. It was you she wanted, though. You dumped any blonde bunny-boilers lately?'

Metro ignores the question. 'I think you need to pay a visit to Lee Hassell. Find out what he said when he was acting like this woman's bitch.'

Ozone grins again, as though he'd been hoping for a mission like this.

When he's gone, Metro stares at the bag, but in his mind's eye he still sees the video.

He didn't tell Ozone, but he's been expecting something from this girl. Just not so soon, and not so dramatic. She's got some tasty moves on her. Could be more of a problem than he thought.

But all problems are solvable.

Thump.

27

Cody is shrugging on his coat, walking along the corridor, when he meets Webley coming the other way.

Shit.

'Hang on,' she says. 'I'll get my coat.'

'No, it's okay,' he tells her.

She halts. 'Well, we need to talk to Fulton, don't we?'

'Fulton?'

'Yes. After what Ann Staples told us, we should look into this possible animosity between him and Prior.'

'Oh, yeah. We can do that later.'

'So . . . where are you going now?'

'I need to talk to someone else.'

'Okay,' she says, but she doesn't budge.

'I'm off to have another word with Sara Prior.'

'Sara Prior? Well, okay. All right if I come with you?'

'I, er, I don't think that's necessary. No point in making this more difficult for her than it needs to be.'

'More difficult than . . . Cody, you did hear what the boss said earlier, didn't you? About turning up the heat on Sara?'

'I heard it. And don't you think I'm perfectly capable of doing that?'

'I . . . Well, what about bringing her in? Put her in a formal interview situation? Maybe we'd get more out of her that way.'

Cody shakes his head. 'This way's fine. See you later.'

He starts to move away, but she grabs hold of his arms. 'Cody, I really think—'

'Don't, Megan. I know what I'm doing. Can I go now?'

She releases him, and as he turns to leave, he knows he's just shattered a piece of her trust in him.

Sara seems surprised to see him, but not unhappy about it. More *hygge* than Scandinavian chill.

She makes him tea again. Resumes her cross-legged position on the sofa opposite him.

'Has there been some progress on the investigation?' she asks.

Cody is unprepared for this most natural of questions. 'Sorry? Oh. Yes. We've been analysing forensic evidence, and we're following up some leads from those. We've also been talking to the people Matthew worked with. They've been really helpful.'

'Good. Do you have any suspects?'

Other than you? Cody thinks.

'No strong suspects at the moment, but we're hopeful.'

She nods in a way that signals it's the answer she was expecting.

'How have you been managing?' he asks.

'As well as can be expected. It's not easy.'

'No.' He pauses. 'Do you mind if I show you something?'

'What is it?'

'It's a video. It was taken last night.'

She sips her tea. 'All right.'

He puts down his tea and moves across to her. Sits down and takes out his mobile phone.

As he plays the video, he searches her face. She gives nothing away, but then this woman has been trained to withstand the most severe forms of interrogation.

'I don't understand,' she says when the recording finishes. 'What is that?'

'I was hoping you could tell me.'

She looks directly at him. 'I'm not sure what you mean.'

'The attacker in that video is a woman.'

'Yes, I gathered that.'

'It looks a bit like you.'

'Do you think so?'

'Yes, I do. Do you have a dark hoody like that?'

'I do, but don't a lot of people? Don't you?'

'What this woman did to those two lads was ... *unusual*, to say the least. I don't think there are many women who are capable of it.'

She smiles. 'There you go again with your gender stereotyping, Sergeant Cody. Have you heard yourself? You find a video of a woman overcoming two young men, and automatically assume there is only one woman in the country capable of such a feat? What century is this, Sergeant?'

'Your background isn't the only reason I came to you.'

'It isn't?'

'No. This fight was caught on a CCTV camera in Bootle, just a few minutes from where your husband worked.'

'Ah, I see. So, two lads get beaten up in Bootle, my husband worked in Bootle, so it must be me – is that what you're saying?'

'You need to add into the mix that the woman in the video looks like you.'

'No, she doesn't.'

Cody sighs. 'It was late at night. The lads had been drinking. One of them still had a bottle in his hand. My guess is that they had just come out of a pub called The Tar Barrel. Have you ever been in that pub?'

She shakes her head emphatically. 'No.'

'You seem very definite.'

'I have never been drinking in any pub in Bootle, so that's an easy one. Next?'

'What about your husband? Did he ever drink in there?'

'I doubt it, unless it was with people from work. I certainly never went there with him.'

'So if I showed your photograph to the staff and customers at the pub, they wouldn't recognise you?'

'I don't see how they could.'

It was a bluff, and she's called it. Cody knows only too well that the regulars at The Tar Barrel wouldn't give the time of day to a copper.

'Mrs Prior—'

'Sara.'

'Sara. The two lads in that video are nasty pieces of work. They're involved in drugs and gangs. Making enemies out of them wouldn't be a wise move.'

'It's a good job I haven't, then, isn't it? I'm sorry, but did you want a biscuit with your tea?'

Cody looks across at his cup where he left it on the table. 'I don't suppose you've had any blinding flashes of insight into the meaning of the message that Matthew left on your phone?'

'I'm afraid not. It makes no sense at all.'

'You will let us know if you figure it out, won't you?'

'Of course. It might be important.'

'Hmm,' says Cody. And then: 'Sara, I want you to understand that we really are doing everything we can to catch Matthew's murderers. But if there's a vital piece of information being kept from us, then it could greatly hinder the investigation.'

'I fully understand.'

'I also want to stress that we're dealing with highly danger-ous people here. You saw what they did to Matthew. I think you're a very brave woman, but there's a fine line between bravery and foolhardiness. I don't want to see you ending up like your husband.'

Sara puts down her empty cup. 'You're a good man, Sergeant Cody. I have no doubt you will do everything to find Matthew's killers. But please don't worry about me. I can take care of myself.'

Cody smiles at her and hopes that she isn't overestimating her own abilities.

Sara sees Cody out of the house and goes back inside. When he gets to the street and starts walking to his car, he can't stop thinking about her. She is one impressive woman. Capable of killing, yes, but not a murderer.

And how do I know that? he asks himself.

She's definitely up to something, isn't she? That was her in the video – I know it was. Sneaking around at night, beating up scallies. I should report my suspicions to Blunt. Get her put under surveillance. Find out what the hell she's playing at.

So why don't I intend to do that?

Because she's not a murderer.

No, there's more to it than that.

It's because ... It's because she's like me. There, I said it. She knows something about whoever killed Matthew, just as I know something about the people who mutilated me and killed my partner. She's not revealing that information, just as I choose not to. She's undertaking some secret mission against her enemy, just as I am. She's dealing with past trauma, just as I'm trying to do.

She's me. Sara Prior is me.

That's how I know.

28

Ozone Fisher doesn't like the smell of this place. These old blocks of flats always stink. Too many people crammed into too small an area. You get the mingling of stale food, animals, rotting garbage, cheap air fresheners and bodily functions. It's disgusting. How can people live like this?

As the lift finally arrives and the doors squeal with the effort of opening, he expects to be hit by another wall of stomach-heaving odour. Needs must, though, because no way is he walking up fifteen flights of stairs.

A large middle-aged woman with a limp bundles herself and her shopping trolley out of the lift. She takes a look at Ozone and wrinkles her nose. He takes it as a signal that things aren't pleasant in there. He steps inside and takes a cautious sniff, and is surprised to find that it's not pungent enough to penetrate his barrier of freshness.

He presses the button and experiences a jolt as the lift drags itself wearily back up the shaft. While he waits, he keeps his back to the door and studies his warped reflection in the finger-smudged steel. He's happy with what he sees.

When the door opens on the fifteenth floor, the bottom of the lift doesn't quite line up with the corridor, and Ozone catches the toe of his shoe on the steel edging.

'Shit!' he says.

He crouches to study his shoe. There's a definite scrape there. 'Fuck!'

And now he's in a bad mood that will colour his actions for the rest of the day.

He finds the right door, raps on it sharply. While he waits, he breathes into the palm of his cupped hand, then takes a good sniff of the captured gases.

Could be better, he thinks, but this isn't exactly a date. It'll do.

When he hears the chain being put on the door, he slips his hands into the pockets of his leather jacket.

The door opens a fraction. An eye surrounded by a cluster of freckles appears in the crack.

'All right, O!' says Lee Hassell. 'What's up?'

'Open the door, Lee,' says Ozone.

'Why? What's going on?'

'Just open the door.'

'Er, yeah, okay. Hang on.'

The door closes again. The chain is taken off. The door opens.

And now Ozone can see that Hassell's nose is twice its usual size and bent to one side, and that a crusted scab has formed on his lip.

'You on your own?' he asks.

'Er, yeah. My nan's gone out to bingo.'

'Then I'll come in.'

'Oh. Er, yeah, sure.'

Hassell steps out of the way, allowing Ozone to pass.

Ozone looks around the flat. It's full of nan stuff. Ornaments and knitting and faded cushions and crossword magazines. He takes a seat on the sofa and hears the springs whine in complaint.

Hassell bounces around nervously in front of him. 'What's happening, O?'

'You tell me. That's a heck of a schnozz you've got on you there.'

Hassell touches his nose gingerly. 'Yeah. I, er, I fell over, like. I was a bit pissed.'

'Have you seen a doc? It looks broken to me.'

'Nah, it's fine. Look, do you want a cup of coffee or something? My nan's got custard tarts in the fridge. I'm sure she won't mind if you have one.'

'No, thanks. Sit down, will you, Lee? You're giving me eyestrain the way you keep bobbing about.'

'Yeah. Sorry. Yeah.'

He takes a seat on a winged chair by the window, but his legs are still restless.

'Have you seen anything of Kieran Willis lately?'

'Kieran? Yeah, I had a few bevvies with him last night. That's when this happened.' He points to his nose.

'I imagine he's got a bit of a sore head today.'

Hassell looks at Ozone as though he's trying to work out how much he already knows.

'Probably. We did have a bit of a session, like.'

'Whereabouts?'

'The Barrel.'

'Is that where you fell over?'

'No. That was outside. I tripped on a broken pavement or something. I should sue the council.'

He smiles as he says this. Ozone doesn't.

'Meet anyone else while you were in the pub?'

'Oh, just a few of the lads.'

'What about women?'

'Women?'

'Yeah. You know. The opposite sex. The curvy ones who smell nice.'

Hassell pauses for far too long. 'Actually, now you come to mention it, there was this one bird. I think she was foreign. That's right – it's coming back to me now. She was asking about Metro.'

'Metro?'

'Yeah. Don't worry, though. Me and Kieran had a quiet word with her. She won't be going there again.'

'Are you sure about that?'

'Dead sure. We got the message across all right.'

'I can believe it. I bet she got out of there sharpish.'

'Too right she did.'

'Never to be seen again.'

'Is right. Stupid bitch.'

Ozone doesn't move. He remains on the sofa, legs crossed, hands still deep in his pockets. His eyes bore into Hassell, who can't return his gaze.

Eventually he says, 'I take it you haven't seen the video.'

Hassell's eyes are suddenly blinking as furiously as those of his drinking buddy. 'Video? What video?'

'The one of you pair getting the shit kicked out of you last night. By a girl.'

'I, er . . . what?'

'I'd show it to you, but to be honest, I can't be arsed. You can take a look yourself later. You're a celebrity, Lee. For all the wrong reasons, like, but you're definitely a video star now.'

Hassell goes quiet, which Ozone thinks is probably the wisest move right now.

'Before we go any further,' says Ozone, 'you need to understand the rules.'

'Rules?'

'Yeah. The first one is no more lies, okay? The second is no leaving anything out. I've already spoken to Billy and others who were in the pub last night, and I've had a quiet word with Kieran.'

'You've spoken to Kieran?'

'I have. Despite what he may have told you, he was fully conscious when he was lying on that pavement. He was just pretending to be out so that he didn't get another kicking. He heard pretty much every word of what was said between you and the girl. And now I want to hear it from you.'

It's a bluff. Ozone hasn't been to the pub and hasn't spoken to Kieran Willis, but he's relying on Lee here being too dumb and too scared to question it.

'All right,' says Hassell.

'Good. So tell me what the fight was about.'

'Nothing. I mean, we hadn't hurt her or anything. We just spoke to her in the pub, that's all. And then, when we left, she jumped us.'

'Okay. And then what?'

Hassell squirms. 'See, this is when it gets a bit fuzzy, like. I smacked my head hard on the ground. I'm not quite sure—'

'Lee.'

'Swear to God, I'm not trying to pull a fast one. It's just a bit hazy . . . Wait, I remember she was asking about Metro again.'

'Asking what?'

'Who he was, and where he could be found.'

'And you said what?'

'I tried to frighten her off again. I told her Metro works for Joey, and that if she had any sense she'd leave well alone.'

'You brought Joey Pearce into the conversation.'

Hassell seems suddenly to wish he could retract his previous statement. 'Yeah, but like I say, it was only to scare her off. I mean, nobody in their right mind would want to mess with Joey, would they?'

'Then what?'

'How do you mean?'

'You said she asked where she could find Metro. Did you tell her?'

Hassell flashes him a look of incredulity that such a thing should even be considered. 'Don't be daft. I'm not that stupid.'

Ozone punctures him with his gaze again. Watches him wither in his chair. 'Lee, we can do this the easy way or the hard way. What's it gonna be?'

Hassell starts to chew his lip, but winces when he bites into the scab there. 'I might have mentioned one or two places.'

'Such as?'

'The pool hall. The gym.'

Ozone nods. 'The pool hall and the gym.'

'And maybe the club in town.'

'The club. Anything else? His home address, maybe?'

'I don't know his home address. Look . . .' He pulls down his collar to reveal some small scratches on his neck. 'She had a broken bottle. She was going to slit my throat. She's a fucking head-the-ball. What was I supposed to do?'

Ozone keeps a cold glare on him for another few seconds. Then, abruptly, he gets to his feet. His hands are still in his pockets.

'Are you going?' Hassell asks.

'I'm going,' says Ozone.

Hassell gets out of his chair. His relief is evident. 'All right, O. I'm really sorry about last night, okay? Tell Metro I wasn't trying to cause him any trouble.'

Ozone stands his ground, facing Hassell. 'There's one more thing before I go.'

'Yeah? What's that, then?'

And now Ozone brings his hands out of his pockets. He watches Hassell's gaze as it drops to those hands, as it takes in the sight of all the large, chunky, glinting rings on the fingers.

Ozone knows that he can be arrested for carrying a knuckleduster. Not for wearing rings, though. Lots of people wear rings.

Hassell's Adam's apple bobs, and then he looks up at Ozone. 'Do you have to? I mean, is there anything I can do to make up for it?'

'Sorry, Lee. Orders. You know how it is.'

Hassell's eyes shift left and right, and for a moment Ozone thinks he's contemplating making a break for it. Which would be idiotic.

Hassell says, 'Can we, er ... Do you mind if we do it in the bathroom?'

'The bathroom?'

'Yeah. If that's okay. Easier to clean up afterwards. My nan's just had a new carpet fitted in here.'

Ozone looks down at the carpet. It's beige. Spotless.

'Sure,' he answers. 'I wouldn't want to upset your nan.'

When he's done, Ozone uses the phone in the flat to call for an ambulance. He gives his name as Lee Hassell and says that he's just fallen down a flight of concrete stairs.

As he leaves the flat, he pulls his jacket to one side and sniffs his armpit. All the exertion has made him perspire, so now he'll have to go home, shower, and freshen up again.

Personal hygiene is so important.

29

As usual, Cody drives. It gives him something on which to focus. Being a passenger allows him too much time to think.

Webley is thinking right now.

He can tell. She goes quiet when something's on her mind, and being quiet isn't in her nature. Eventually, when she's built up a good head of steam, she'll let it out.

'So,' she says. 'How'd it go with your friend Sara?'

Thar she blows, thinks Cody.

'She's not my friend. And it went fine, thank you for asking.'

'What was it about?'

'What do you mean?'

'I mean the desperate rush to speak to her. What was the urgency?'

Cody shrugs. 'You heard Blunt. She thinks Sara Prior knows more than she's saying.'

'And does she?'

'I don't think so.'

'You don't think so. You made a mad dash over to Sara Prior's house because you don't think she's in this thing up to her neck. That makes a lot of sense.'

'It wasn't a mad dash. I was ticking another thing off the list.'

'It looked like a mad dash to me. Why couldn't it have waited until after we'd seen Fulton again?'

'We're going to see Fulton now, aren't we?'

Webley lapses into silence again. Then: 'Why didn't you want me to go with you?'

'There was no need. You've seen the action list. There's a million other things we need to follow up.'

Another pause. 'Cody, what's going on?'

'What do you mean? Nothing's going on.'

'Yes, there is. I know you. You act weird at the best of times, but at the moment you're at the top of the weird charts. You're Weirdy McWeird from Weirdsville. Talk to me.'

Ha, he thinks. The things I could tell you. About Waldo; about the key sitting in my pocket right now; about the shit Sara's getting involved in. Megan Webley, you don't want to be in that world.

'There's nothing to say. Everything's hunky-dory. I'm just doing my job.'

'Yeah, right,' says Webley.

Lewis Fulton seems a tad irritated that they've turned up at his door again.

'Is everything okay?' he asks them. 'Did you talk to Ann?'

'Yes, we spoke to her,' Cody says. 'As you know, some of my colleagues have spoken to your other staff too. That's why we need to clear up a couple of things with you.'

It's Ann who has pointed the finger, but Cody doesn't want it rebounding on her.

'Oh?' says Fulton. 'What kind of things?'

They're in the meeting room again, only Fulton doesn't seem as much at ease as he did last time. Not so much of the slouching.

'There seemed to be a general sense that things weren't entirely . . . *friendly* between you and Matthew Prior.'

'What? I'm not sure what you mean. What have they been telling you?'

'They seemed to think you had a habit of belittling Matthew.'

'Belittling him? What? Seriously? I told you yesterday: I had the utmost respect for Matthew. His work was exemplary.'

'I'm not talking about his work. There's a feeling that you objected to him on a more personal basis.'

Fulton's mouth drops as he switches his gaze to Webley, and then back to Cody. 'That's ridiculous. What exactly are they saying?'

'We'd like to hear it from you, Mr Fulton.'

'Hear what?'

'What you thought of Matthew. You said yesterday that you didn't like him.'

'No . . . wait. You're twisting my words. I didn't mean I hated him. I just meant I didn't see him as a friend. He wasn't someone I'd go out for a pint with.'

'Why not?'

'He just wasn't. I'm sure it's the same for you. I bet you pick and choose who you drink with, right?'

'So who do you go drinking with? Anyone from work?'

'Sometimes, but not on a regular basis. It tends to be birthdays and special occasions like that. I'm their boss, don't forget.'

'Where do you go? The pubs round here? The Tar Barrel?'

'Not that dive, no. If I go anywhere near here, it tends to be the Wetherspoons.'

'But not with Matthew?'

'Sometimes he'd be there, but he wasn't much of a socialiser. He wasn't into drinking.'

'What was he into?'

'I've no idea. Like I say, he wasn't a mate. Look, I'm not sure where—'

'Do you like sports, Mr Fulton?'

This from Webley. Fulton turns to look at her.

'I'm sorry?'

'Sports. Do you like sports?'

'Yes, I suppose so.'

'Do you do any yourself?'

'Yeah. Quite a bit of squash. A weekly game of football.'

'What do you think of men who aren't into sports?'

'I don't think anything. That's their choice.'

'You don't think they're a bit namby-pamby? A bit girly?'

'No. Not at all.'

'Would you ever criticise someone for not being into sports or drinking?'

'Of course not.'

'What if they don't talk about women much?'

'That's fine too. I don't—'

'Did you ever make fun of Matthew for being like that?'

'No. Don't be ridiculous.'

'You never suggested he was a bit effeminate?'

'No! I would never do that to anyone.'

'That's not what we heard.'

Pure shock on Fulton's face now. 'From who? Who told you that? Was it Ann?'

'We're not at liberty to say who—'

'I can't believe it. I'm gobsmacked.' He stabs his index finger into the table in a show of fury. 'You know what, we've got formal channels for this kind of thing. If someone wants to make a complaint, they should do it in the proper way, not go spreading rumours and gossip that can land people in trouble. This is unbelievable.'

'Did Matthew ever make a complaint?'

'No. Of course not. And if you don't believe me, you can go to Human Resources and ask them. We take things like that very seriously. It would have to be investigated and fully documented. Go ahead if you like – speak to HR.'

'What about an informal complaint? A private conversation between you and Matthew. All off the record.'

'No. Nothing like that. Not once in all the time he worked here. Matthew wasn't exactly the life and soul of the party, but he seemed happy enough in his work.'

'Again, there are some who would disagree with you. There has been a suggestion that he was quite upset at some of the things you might have said to him.'

Fulton shakes his head in apparent disbelief, but then he suddenly seems to decide on a change of tack.

'Look, I can be a bit ... laddish sometimes, okay? A bit blokeish. It's just the way I am. And maybe Matthew found that a bit intimidating. I have no idea. But I can assure you that

I never deliberately set out to – what was your word? – *belittle* Matthew. He was just a guy who worked here in the office. That was the full extent of our relationship.'

'What about his wife?' Cody asks. He catches Webley glancing at him as he tosses in this question.

'Sara? What about her?'

'You mentioned her a couple of times yesterday. I got the feeling you like her.'

'Yes. As a person. Yes. She's nice.'

'Nice? You mean attractive, right?'

'Well, that too. She's good-looking, yes.'

'Ever come on to her?'

'What? No. She's— no.'

'Ever meet up with her when Matthew wasn't there?'

'No. I only met her a few times, and that was back when Matthew first started working here.'

'What about since they split up?'

'I didn't know they'd split up until you told me yesterday. But to answer your question: no, I haven't ever seen her without Matthew being present.'

'Ever been to her house?'

'No.'

'What about Matthew's new place?'

'No. I didn't even know he'd moved out.'

'So we wouldn't find your fingerprints or DNA in that house?'

'No. How could you?'

'Mr Fulton, would you be willing to come into the station and give us your fingerprints and samples of your DNA?'

Fulton stares at Cody for a long time. 'W-why?'

'I thought that would be obvious. To eliminate you from our enquiries.'

'Do I . . . Do I have to?'

'No, you don't have to. All we're trying to do is to make it easier for you and for us. Assuming everything you've told us is true, and the forensic samples you provide support that, then we can put these rumours about you to bed and we'll never need to bother you again.'

Fulton mulls it over for a while longer. 'No. I don't want to do that. If I don't have to give you those samples, then I'm not going to.'

'Mr Fulton—'

'That's my final word. You said it's my right to refuse, yes? Well, then, I'm exercising my rights.'

'That's fine,' says Cody, but in a tone that makes it clear to Fulton that this isn't over.

Webley says, 'Mr Fulton, do you own a maroon woollen sweater?'

'A maroon sweater? No. It's not really my colour.'

'Ever shop at Marston's?'

'Sometimes. Not for a while.'

'How long is a while?'

'I don't know. Six months, maybe.'

'When did you last have a haircut?'

'At the end of last week. Friday, I think.'

'It's nicely shaped. Do you put wax on it?'

'Yes. What's that got—?'

'What brand do you use?'

'I don't know. I'd have to look in my bathroom cabinet. Look, how many more questions—?'

'No more questions, Mr Fulton. For the moment.'

'We'll see ourselves out,' says Cody.

'What do you think?' Webley asks on the stairs.

'I think he's a little shit who gets a kick out of bullying his employees. But as for nailing them to the floor . . .'

'Why'd you ask about The Tar Barrel? Of all the places you could have picked, that seems the least likely for a guy like Fulton.'

'Dunno. It was the first local that came to mind.'

'It'd be the last on my list.'

As they exit the building, Cody's mobile rings. He pulls it out and answers it without even checking who it's from. He hears, 'Hello, Cody.'

It's Waldo.

30

Cody tries to regain his composure, but he knows his shock has already splashed itself across his face. Webley has seen it and is giving him questioning looks.

'Hold on,' he says into the phone. Then to Webley: 'I've got to take this. Wait for me in the car.'

She eyes him with suspicion, but starts walking away, glancing back every few yards.

Cody brings the phone to his ear again. 'How did you get this number?'

He's had many weird calls on his landline, but this is the first time Waldo has ever contacted him on his mobile.

'You haven't said hello yet, Cody. It's only polite.'

'Fuck you. How's that for polite? Answer the damn question.'

'Your number is one of the most trivial things I know about you. I've been in your apartment, don't forget. I've looked through your possessions, your files, your life.'

'Which begs the question, how did you find out where I live?'

'Surely you don't want me to reveal the secrets of all my tricks? I'm a clown. This is a circus. Just believe the magic and enjoy the ride.'

'The ride to freedom, you mean? Do I need a key for that?'

'Ah, you got my little present. Excellent. You may be needing it soon.'

'How about telling me what it's for?'

'Don't worry, Cody. Even someone with the limited IQ and imagination of a police officer will be able to work it out. Give your brain time to work on it.'

'And to what do I owe the pleasure of today's call? Feeling bored?'

'On the contrary, you've kept me very busy.'

'Doing what?'

'Making my next move. Setting things up for you.'

'Meaning?'

'Patience, Cody. You know how this works. *Quid pro quo*, as Hannibal Lecter might say. Tell me something new about yourself.'

'Didn't you just say you already know everything about me?'

'Indulge me. I like to hear how you see things.'

'What kind of things?'

'Why don't we do what we did last time and begin with the day's events? Are you having trouble paying your taxes, Cody?'

He knows, Cody thinks. He knows I'm at the tax office.

He looks up and down the street for any sign that he's being watched. The only eyes he sees on him are those of Webley sitting in the unmarked car along the street.

'How do you know where I am?'

'I followed you from the police station. It wasn't difficult. I've done it many times. Got it down to a fine art now.'

'Are you still here, watching me?'

'Ah, that would be telling, wouldn't it? Besides, we're straying off-topic. What were you doing in the tax office?'

'Investigating a case. That's what I do, in case you don't know. I catch criminals. Murderers like you.'

'Is that what this is, then? A murder case?'

'Yes. And that's all you get to know about it.'

'I'm not interested in the details of the case, Cody. I'm interested in you, and how you deal with things. I want to know how your mind functions. So tell me: what did you think when you saw the victim in this case? How did you feel?'

Cody goes quiet.

'Cody? I need an answer if you want your next little present from me. And don't bother lying, because I'll know about it, and then the game will be over.'

Cody believes this. If Waldo keeps following him around, then he may have tailed him to Matthew Prior's house and will have seen Blunt preventing him from entering.

'I . . .'

'Yes?'

'I didn't view the body.'

'You didn't? Why was that?'

'Because my boss instructed me not to.'

'Really? How very interesting. Why, Cody? Why weren't you allowed to go near the body?'

'Work it out, Waldo. If you're such a criminal mastermind, you work it out.'

A deathly chuckle. 'I think I already have. It's connected with your visit to the psychologist, isn't it? Your superiors are concerned about your mental state, your sanity. Is that it? Is that what they're so worried about?'

'As I already told you, it's standard procedure. After what I went through on my last case, they're being cautious.'

'No, no. I don't think they are. I think they're seriously worried. I think you've been displaying signs of mental instability. You're falling apart. Your mind is disintegrating. You can't take much more, can you, Cody?'

Cody looks up the street again. Sees Webley gesturing to him through the windscreen.

He turns his back on her.

'Here's all you need to know about me,' he says into the phone. 'You did me some serious damage, okay? I'll admit it. But you know what's helping me to keep my shit together? You, Waldo. You. Because while you're out there, I will be looking for you. And I won't rest until I find you. Play all the games you want, because life won't be as much fun when I get hold of you.'

A full-blown laugh now. 'I love it! Even through the tears, you display strength. You have the true clown spirit. You make a worthy opponent.'

'That's very reassuring. Now, are we done here? Because, you know, I've got work to do.'

'Please, don't let me stop you. We'll speak again soon.'

'Wait. Is that it? What the hell happened to *quid pro quo*?'

'All good things come to he who waits, Cody. Be seeing you.'

'Wait—'

But he's talking to thin air.

He puts his phone away and looks back towards Webley. She raises her hands in a gesture of impatience.

He walks back to the car. Opens the door and gets behind the wheel.

Webley says, 'What was that, your stockbroker?'

'Sorry. Urgent call.'

'Problem?'

'Nothing I can't handle.'

She stares at him. 'You need help?'

'Nope. It's fine.'

'Are you sure?'

'I'm sure. Why all the questions?'

'I'm just wondering if there's something you need to get off your chest.'

'No. Really.'

'Okay,' she says. And then: 'I have something for you.'

And now it's his turn to stare. What is she saying?

Webley reaches to the pocket in the passenger door. Takes something out. Holds it up in front of him.

His mind races to find meaning. To impose some understanding on the impact of Megan's involvement in this.

She's holding a Jiffy envelope. Exactly like the previous one he received. The same typed message across its front: 'To Nathan Cody.'

Quid pro quo.

31

He sits frozen, dumbfounded. Why is Megan handing him an envelope? Surely she can't have a connection to Waldo.

'What's this?' he asks, doing his best to sound casually intrigued.

'You tell me,' Webley says. 'It was under the windscreen wiper.'

He takes it from her. Slips it into his pocket.

'You're not going to open it?' she asks.

'I'll do it later.'

He puts his key in the ignition and fires up the engine, hoping he won't get a follow-up question.

'Why later?' Webley follows up. 'Why not now?'

'It can wait. It's not important.'

'So you know what it is, then?'

'I think so.'

He depresses the clutch, puts the car in gear.

'Hold on, Cody. Turn the engine off, will you?'

'What? Why?'

'Just turn the frigging engine off and talk to me for a minute, okay?'

He does as he's told. Wonders how he's going to worm his way out of this.

'What?' he says.

'Seriously? You have to ask? Somebody leaves an envelope with your name on it under the wipers and you're surprised that I want to discuss it?'

'I told you. It's nothing.'

'If it's nothing, show me.'

'What?'

'Show me what's in the envelope.'

He shakes his head. 'I'm not opening the envelope, Megan.'

She goes silent for a few seconds. He's hurting her with his secrecy, but he can't do anything else. He could open the envelope, sure, but what if its content is not just another key? And even if it is a key, what if it has a tag again, and this time the tag holds a lot more information than the previous one?

He can't risk it.

'Why not?' she presses. 'Why won't you open it? Is it something incriminating?'

'Is that what you think?'

'I don't think anything, Cody. You're not giving me anything on which to base any sensible thoughts. But you can't blame me for asking the question.'

'Actually, I think I can. Why is that the first thing that jumps to your mind?'

Her eyes flare, hurt turning to anger. 'All right, put yourself in my shoes. Let's turn this thing around. Suppose we come back to the car. There's an envelope waiting for me, with my name on it. I put it straight in my pocket, refusing to tell you what's in it. Now, are you saying you wouldn't find that just a little on the suspicious side? Because if you are, you're a liar.'

'It's an envelope, Megan. That's all. Nothing earth-shattering. I've been expecting it, so I know what's in it.'

'You do, huh? Okay, so how did they find you?'

'Who?'

'Whoever delivered the frigging package! In case you'd forgotten, we're on an assignment, in an unmarked police car. How the hell did the courier know to leave the envelope here? Are they psychic?'

Cody turns away from her, shaking his head. He is fully aware he has no good answers, and every word he utters just adds to the depth of the murky hole he's in.

'I don't want to get in an argument about this, Megan.'

'I'm not trying to start an argument. I'm trying to get you to talk to me, because you know what? I think you're in trouble.'

'I'm not in trouble.'

'No? Who was the phone call from just now? The one you didn't want me to overhear.'

'Nobody. It was nobody.'

He risks another glance in Webley's direction, and sees how her eyes glisten.

She slumps back in her chair. Grabs her seatbelt and yanks it. It catches with the tension, and she has to pull it several times to latch it into position.

'I've had enough of this bullshit,' she says. 'You want to run away, then go ahead. Just fucking drive.'

The awkwardness hangs in the air between them as Cody drives back to the station. As he parks up, Webley is out of the car before he has even put on the handbrake. She storms off, not waiting for him to catch up.

Cody turns off the engine. Takes a deep breath. Then he reaches into his pocket and takes out the envelope.

He studies it for a full minute before tearing it open and emptying the contents out onto his palm.

Another key. It's bigger than the previous one. A Yale, for a front door or similar.

Like the other one, this also carries a label attached to it via white twine. The label says, 'The key to life.'

Cody reaches into his jacket pocket for the first key, and places it next to the newest addition to his collection.

The key to freedom and the key to life. Very profound.

But what do they open?

32

The pool hall stands on an industrial estate, next to a tyre fitters' on one side and a computer repair place on the other. Its gaudy orange sign reads, 'American Pool. Licenced Bar. Delicious food.'

Sara pushes open the door and walks in. She is greeted by the aroma of beefburgers and the click-clack of the games in progress. She stands there for a few seconds, eyeing up the interior. Most of the tables are empty, but a few are attended by sun-starved young men swigging from beer bottles and lining up their shots. At the bar, a man who is too old to be wearing his baseball cap backwards puts down his towering monstrosity of a burger and wipes his mouth with a napkin, spreading tomato relish across his cheek.

From out of the shadows, a short, pot-bellied man with flabby jowls and sad eyes waddles across to her. He wears a skin-tight polo rugby shirt over a physique that suggests he doesn't play rugby.

'All right, love. What can I do you for?'

Sara has heard the deliberate grammatical mistake many times. She no longer finds it amusing.

'You work here?'

'That's what they tell me. Not exactly rushed off my feet at the moment, though.' He eyes her up and down. 'You're not here for a game, are you?'

Sara wonders whether there is something about pool players that he can spot at a glance. Perhaps it's her physique – just not built for knocking balls into holes with a stick.

'I'm looking for someone,' she says.

'Someone in particular, or will I do?' He emits a high-pitched laugh as he says this, but again she doesn't see the funny side.

'Not unless your name is Metro.'

The smile is instantly crushed from his lips, and she knows she has uttered the magic word. She said it loud enough for everyone to hear, and she notices the wave it generates across the room. Postures stiffen, faces become grave, eyes bore into her.

'Never heard of him,' says the man.

'Yes,' she says. 'You have.'

The man swallows, then looks around him. It is very quiet here now. Not a shot is being played.

'Now look, love. I don't know what you've been told, or where you got your information, but there's nobody of that name here.'

'Uh-huh,' she says. 'My mistake. In that case, I think I'd like to play a game with your balls.'

'My . . .' He swallows again. 'My what?'

She points to the table closest to the bar. 'Your cute little ball game. Show me how it's played.'

'You, er, you have to hire the table.' He points to a sign by the door. 'There's an hourly rate. You need to—'

'Will this cover it?' she asks, pulling a ten-pound note from her pocket.

The man checks in with his observers again, who remain impassive, and then he gingerly plucks the money from Sara's outstretched fingers.

'It'll do for a start,' he says. He moves to the table and takes two cues from the rack. Hands one of them to Sara. She takes hold of it and studies it like it's an alien object. She decides not to tell the man that she spent a good deal of her leisure time in the army playing pool.

'Thank you,' she says.

'You're welcome. Now watch how I do this.' He takes one of the balls from the triangle, lines it up with the cue ball and the centre pocket, then bends into position. 'See how I'm bridging my hand like this?' he asks.

'Yes, I see.'

'Now what you want to do is gently tap the cue ball so that it hits the other one and knocks it into the pocket.'

He takes the shot and pots it nicely. Around the room, others relax back into their games.

'Fancy a go now?' the man asks.

'Why not? It looks easy enough.'

She waits while the man lines up the balls again, then she bends over the table and spends time trying to copy the man's stance.

'Does this look about right?'

She notices how the man's eyes instantly abandon their task of trying to see down her top.

'Er, yeah. Just relax now. Keep your eye on the ball. When you're ready, slowly pull back and gently—'

Sara lets fire with one of the most powerful shots she has ever attempted. The cue ball springs from the table, cannons across the bar and smashes into the bottles of spirits lined up on the shelves. The bartender leaps back with a yelp as he is showered in glass and alcohol, while Sara's instructor pulls at his hair in disbelief.

'*Gently!*' he yells. 'I said gently!'

'Sorry, sorry. Let me try again.'

Before she can be stopped, she stoops and attempts another shot. This time her cue rips a two-foot gash in the cloth.

Sara straightens up from the table in mock surprise, swinging her stick wildly. Its tip strikes the fluorescent light overhead, causing it to explode into a million fragments.

'For fuck's sake!' cries the man.

Sara runs to the next table. 'This one will be better,' she declares.

'No,' says the man. 'No.'

But Sara has already ripped through the cloth on this one too.

And then she knows her fun is over. The bartender has left his post and is storming towards her, as is a more muscular guy who has just come through a door marked 'Staff only'.

'That's it!' says the bartender. 'Out!'

Sara remains where she is, still holding on to the cue. She maintains a face of pure innocence.

The bartender's first mistake is in grabbing her arm. She twists it from his grasp and says, 'Don't touch me.'

The bartender's second mistake is in repeating his first mistake.

Sara whips the cue up between the man's legs. He releases her arm and grabs his crotch, while emitting a shrill cry.

Sara cuts off the noise by ramming the end of the cue into the man's mouth. Staggering back, he brings a hand up to his mouth to staunch the flow of blood and broken teeth.

'Fucking bitch!' says the jock who was in the back room. He attempts to rush her from behind, but Sara stops his charge by spearing his solar plexus with the other end of the cue. She spins, taking the stick in an accelerating arc that catches the man on the side of his head and sends him reeling backwards. He hits one of the pool tables and falls onto it, sending the balls into a clacking chaos of Brownian motion.

Sara becomes aware of the clientele closing in on her. They are cautious but loyal to the owners of this place. She brings the cue above her head, whirls it rapidly in a huge swishing circle to keep them at bay. When they have taken a few steps back, she holds her weapon across her body and squares up to them.

'Anybody else like to try their luck?' she asks.

There is no direct answer. Just groans and whimpers from the two men she has put out of action.

Sara turns slowly on her heel, eyeing up her audience for signals of intent. She has had enough experience to know when danger is imminent. Nobody here wants a repeat performance of what they have just witnessed.

She points the cue tip at the man in the rugby shirt. He looks terrified.

'You,' she says. 'Where's Metro?'

'I . . . I have no idea.'

She takes a step towards him, and he raises his hands in surrender.

'Honestly,' he says. 'I haven't seen him here in days.'

'You know how to get a message to him, though, right?'

The man opens and closes his mouth.

'*Right?*'

'Y-yes. I can do that.'

'Then do it. Tell him I want to see him. Tell him Antarctica, midnight. Okay?'

'Antarctica. Midnight. O-okay.'

Sara starts moving towards the door. The men in her way part to let her through. She pushes open the door, then slams it shut behind her.

Only when she has left the industrial estate does she toss the cue onto a rubbish skip.

33

Cody hardly touches his meal. He sits at the breakfast bar, pushing the food around his plate. He can't take his eyes off the two keys lined up in front of him.

The key to freedom and the key to life.

What the hell are they supposed to mean?

He picks up the most recent key and studies it. It's just an ordinary-looking Yale key. He has already compared it with his own keys, and it doesn't match any of them.

But what if . . . ?

He jumps off the stool, dashes out into the hall, down the staircase to his apartment's front door. He unlocks it and goes out onto the landing. Puts the lights on.

From here on down in the building, the rooms all belong to the dental practice run by Simon Teller, Cody's orthodontist landlord. To Cody's right, there is a passage to a small kitchen. On the left of the passageway, opposite an opening to the stairs leading downwards, are a couple of doors to surgeries. They are usually locked.

But they have Yale keyholes.

Cody tries his key in the first of them. His heart stops when it fits.

A weapon, he thinks. I should have brought a weapon with me.

But it's too late now. He's here, and he will have alerted whoever might be inside.

He tries turning the key.

It doesn't move.

Shit.

He tries again and again, but without luck. The key doesn't open this door.

He moves on to the next door. Same result. The key will go in, but won't turn.

Cody heads downstairs to the ground floor. More doors to surgeries and reception rooms. He tries the key on all of them, but he can't even insert it all the way in these locks. The only door he ignores is the one leading down to the basement, which has a completely different type of lock.

Cody sighs. Why give him keys to locks he can't even find?

He trudges back up the stairs. When he passes through his apartment doorway, he makes sure to lock the door and set the alarm.

Sometimes he loves the peace and solitude that being the only occupant of a massive Georgian building brings him. Other times he hates it. Hates being way up here, unaware of what foul deeds might be taking place below.

But he knows that he can't move into other accommodation. Waldo has found him here. Waldo will come seeking him again.

And so here he waits.

Sara Prior contemplates violence.

There was a time when she looked at it very differently. It was just a part of the job. What she was doing to restore peace and law and order often necessitated extreme force.

She thought she had put all that behind her.

Alone in her house now, she wonders whether she went too far in that pool hall. Did she overstep the mark?

But all she wants is answers. They could have tried to help her out. They could have said something like, 'Mr Metro isn't here right now, but let us arrange an appointment for you.' They didn't have to lie. They didn't need to put more obstacles in her way.

But what about my own actions? she thinks.

Did I need to inflict such damage, not only on possessions, but also on flesh and bone?

And yet what choice do I have? Accept their lies and walk away? Where will that get me?

My husband has had six-inch nails driven through his body. From beyond the grave he has told me that the man called Metro was somehow involved in that. If he didn't do it himself, he knows who did.

That's what I have to remember. That's why I can't feel sympathy for anyone trying to protect Metro.

And it's why I can't stop now.

Metro Mackenzie surveys the damage.

The glass has been cleared away, but the rips in the cloth covering the pool tables gape open like massive wounds. Mike, the bartender, has gone for emergency treatment on his teeth. Andy is wearing enough white cloth around his dented skull to fashion a turban. And Phil – well, he looks nervous enough to start throwing up.

'What happened?' Metro asks.

'She . . . she asked about you,' says Phil.

'Me? She used my name?'

'Yes. Of course, I told her I didn't know anyone with that name.'

'Then what?'

'She said she wanted to play a game of pool. She paid for a table, and then she started smashing the place up.'

Metro nods. He wanders over to Andy. Looks into his bewildered eyes.

'So what happened to you?'

Andy shrugs. 'I've never seen anything like it. She was so fast.'

'A woman. You and Mike were both beaten up by a woman.'

Andy shrugs again.

Metro shakes his head. This is getting beyond a joke.

He turns to Phil again. 'Did she give you any reasons for all this?'

'She asked me to give you a message. Said she wants to meet you at Antarctica tonight.'

'Why?'

'She didn't say.'

'Did you ask her?'

Phil doesn't respond, but Metro has already guessed the answer. The man was too shit-scared to question the woman.

'There's video.' This from Ozone, standing over by the bar.

'Show me.' Metro heads through the door for staff, closely followed by Ozone. Once in the back office, Ozone replays the security video of the earlier drama.

Metro studies it carefully. This woman is good. Really good. Strong, fearless and skilled. He'd have her in his crew before any of the spineless idiots out there in the pool room.

But, of course, that's not what she wants. She wants vengeance. She wants answers.

He can't let her have those things.

She's not the type to give up easily, though. She has made that very clear.

And so she's going to end up getting hurt.

A shame, but there you are. Go around biting people, and sooner or later you're going to have to be put down.

34

It has been a while since she went clubbing.

Matthew was never into it. She tried to convince him on numerous occasions, but he would always give her a list of why he hated it so much. The noise, the closeness of others, the way everyone was out to impress. Plus, he hated dancing. He was too self-conscious. On the infrequent occasions he permitted himself to indulge, he simply shuffled from side to side, his arms out in front of him like he was carrying an invisible tray.

But then the slow songs would come on, and she would come to him, and they would embrace. And then his movement was more natural, his fear less palpable.

There will be no dances like that tonight.

The sign couldn't be any less like the one that was above the pool hall. It is lit up in a dazzling white, zappy font. It reads, 'Antarctica – the coolest place in town'.

She can hear the music from here. Or, rather, she can hear the beat. Feel it, even. A dull throb that carries along the pavement and up through her legs.

She has dressed for the part. A short black leather skirt and tight white top. Matthew wouldn't have approved. Not in the company of so many drunken, lecherous young males.

But she needs to blend in. Needs not to fall at the first hurdle: getting through the door.

The bouncer doesn't appear to think twice. 'On your own, love?'

'I'm meeting some friends inside,' she says.

He nods her in. He's more concerned about gangs of rowdy lads. An attractive, sober female isn't going to cause any trouble.

Or so he thinks.

She goes in. The music batters her, drowns her senses. She takes in the scene for a short while. Observes the mobs of lads, the gaggles of girls. Watches how they come together, drift apart, rejoin. Sees how they drink, how they laugh. How they make the most of their freedom, their youth, their energy.

At any other time, she would smile. She would get down on that dance floor and become lost in the moment. She wouldn't be looking for long-term company. She would just live.

But this is a different time. This is business. This is where she is in the state of mind she might have adopted in Afghanistan. Wary, alert. Ready for trouble.

She makes a beeline for the bar. No pot-bellied rugby-shirted types among the staff here. They look like students, all dressed in identical ice-white T-shirts with a small logo of a dancing penguin. One of them is showing off his skills at juggling bottles of spirits while he mixes a cocktail.

Sara catches the eye of one of the female bartenders, who hurries over.

'What can I get you?' she asks in an Irish accent.

'Hi,' says Sara. 'Is your manager here, please?'

'The manager? Hold on a sec.'

She goes to a door behind the bar, opens it, sticks her head inside.

A few seconds later, she comes back.

'He'll be out in a couple of minutes, okay? Can I get you a drink?'

Sara thinks about her desire to blend in. 'Do you do any non-alcoholic cocktails?'

'Sure. We do a fantastic Peach Bellini Mocktail. Believe me, you'll love it.'

'Okay. Sounds great.'

She waits while the drink is mixed. The Irish girl doesn't toss the bottles in the air like some of the others, but she clearly knows what she's doing.

When the cocktail arrives, accompanied by a beautiful smile, Sara tells the girl to keep the change from the money she hands over. The poor thing probably has no idea of the scum who run this place.

Sara sips her drink through a straw. It's as delicious as it looks. She keeps her eyes on the door, with frequent glances in the mirror at anyone approaching from behind.

When she has half-drained the glass, she signals the Irish lass to come over again.

'I'm sorry, but could you just check if the manager is on his way? It's been at least ten minutes.'

'Right. Hold on.'

She goes to the same door. Pops her head in again. This time she jumps back as though she's just been yelled at. She scuttles back to her customers, her cheeks reddening.

Sara decides it's time for more drastic action. But before she can hop over the bar, the door opens again and a man comes out. He has red hair and a full beard, and his whole face shouts anger. He looks towards the Irish barmaid, and she nods towards Sara.

The man stands in front of Sara, rests his hands on the counter. 'Can I help you?'

Sara decides he needs to go on a customer relations refresher course. She looks at the name badge pinned to his white shirt. It says, 'Iain.'

'I hope so, Iain,' she says. 'I'm looking for someone.'

Iain gestures helplessly towards the crowd behind her. 'Good luck with that. There's a lot of people here tonight.'

'I think you'll know him. His name is Metro.'

Iain pretends he hasn't heard her over the music. 'It's what?'

'Metro. As in the underground railway.'

He shakes his head. 'Never heard of him. What's his real name?'

'I don't know. He's supposed to be meeting me here.'

Iain fills his cheeks with air and blows it out. 'Not sure I can help you there. Sorry.'

'I think you're wrong, Iain. I think you can help me.'

He stares at her. 'Look, as you can see, we're very busy. You're welcome to stay, have a few drinks, a dance. But I hope you'll understand if I get back to work now.'

'Are you on your own back there?'

'Yes, and I'm up to my eyeballs in it. Now if you don't mind—'

'Make some phone calls.'

'What?'

'Call your boss. Your boss's boss. Go as high as you can.'

'Why the hell would I do that?'

'Because hell is what will happen if you *don't* do that.'

He studies her intently. Tries to work out how serious this is.

'I can have you thrown out right now. You know that, don't you?'

'Yes, I do. I also know that you'll be in big trouble if you do.' She lets that sink in, then adds, 'Look, what's the harm? A phone call. If they tell you to get rid of me, I'll leave.'

Iain mulls it over. 'What do I say to them?'

'Tell them Metro has an appointment with me, and that I'm waiting.'

'And you are?'

'Tell them I'm the one who was at The Tar Barrel and the pool hall. Tell them I'm not going away until they talk to me.'

Iain strokes his beard, shaping it to a point. 'Wait there,' he says.

'Just what I was planning to do,' she answers.

He disappears into the back room. While she waits, Sara catches a couple of inquisitive glances from the Irish girl.

Five minutes later, Iain comes back.

'You get your wish,' he tells her.

'Which is?'

'You get your meeting.'

'Who's coming? Metro?'

'You get your wish, okay? That's all I've been told to say. It could be a while, though, so do you mind?' He points back at the door.

Sara raises her glass. 'Knock yourself out, Iain.'

She smiles at the Irish girl. Says, 'Same again.'

35

Cody drifts in and out of consciousness. His mind is too occupied with thoughts of the two keys and the messages attached to them. It starts to conjure up all kinds of fanciful theories as to their meaning, and what they might unlock. He pictures safes, doors, cupboards, cabinets, vehicles and padlocks. He gets into deep philosophical discussions with himself about life, freedom and other grandiose concepts.

None of it helps.

But then his phone rings.

It's the middle of the night. One o'clock, to be precise. He knows who this will be, and his pulse begins to race at the thought.

He picks up the receiver. Presses the call answer button.

'Hello?'

'Hello, Cody.' That deep synthesised voice again. 'I didn't wake you, did I?'

'Actually, I was dreaming. I had my hands around the neck of a clown. It was the best dream I've had in ages.'

'Then I apologise for interrupting.'

'No problem. Sometime soon, I'll pick up where I left off.'

'Did you get the present I left for you on your car?'

'I did, and it's not even my birthday. Have to say, I've had better gifts, though.'

'No, Cody. You really haven't. For you, this will be the best gift ever. You will appreciate this one more than anything you've ever had before.'

'Really? Because so far I'm not feeling very appreciative.'

'I take it you haven't figured out what the keys are for, then?'

'No. But then isn't that what you wanted? I'm sure you didn't set out to make this easy for me.'

'You're right. I didn't. But I think it will get a lot easier with the next key.'

'There's another one? How many of these damn things are there?'

'Just one more. But you know what you have to do to get it.'

Cody sighs. 'I'm seeing my shrink again in the morning. I've got all the psychobabble I need right now.'

'Sorry, Cody, but that's the deal. Are you ready?'

'What do you want to know?'

Waldo pauses. Then: 'Have you ever heard of the trolley problem?'

'The what? The *trolley* problem?'

'Yes.'

'Sure. It's when you get the one with the wonky wheel at Sainsbury's.'

'Very droll, Cody. The trolley problem is a thought experiment in morality. It makes you think about how you would behave in a particular set of life or death circumstances. Want to hear more?'

'Do I have a choice?'

'No.'

'Then I'm all ears.'

'Good. We're talking about a railway trolley here. What our American cousins might also refer to as a streetcar. Do you know what I mean?'

'I think so.'

'Then picture this. The trolley breaks free of its moorings. It's running down the hill, gathering speed. It's getting faster and faster, building up momentum. It's becoming a missile.'

'I can see it now,' Cody says sarcastically.

'At the bottom of the hill is a group of ramblers. Six people, and they're all walking on the tracks. They're heading away from the trolley, and they can't hear it hurtling towards them.'

'That's bad.'

'I'm glad you agree. Fortunately for them, you can save their bacon.'

'I can?'

'Yes. You can't warn them, because they're too far away to hear you. But you're standing next to a lever that can be used to switch the trolley onto another line.'

'Must be their lucky day. Mine too. I get to be the hero.'

'Yes. Perhaps.'

'Only perhaps?'

'Yes. You see, Cody, there is another rambler, standing on the other railway track. You can divert the trolley and save the six, but in doing so you will certainly kill the one. So what do you do?'

Cody thinks about it. Despite his antagonism, he finds himself curiously involved in the dilemma just outlined for him.

'Let me get this straight. If I do nothing, six people will die. If I pull the lever, only one person will die.'

'That's it in a nutshell.'

'Okay. Then I pull the lever.'

'Are you sure? You don't want to spend more time thinking about it?'

'No. It's a no-brainer. It's six versus one.'

Cody hears the deathly chuckle again. 'So you're going for the utilitarian argument. The greatest good for the greatest number of people.'

'That's how I roll.'

'But if you weren't there to pull the lever, or chose not to intervene, it would be the six who would be killed.'

'Yes, but I am there, right? I can do something about it.'

'The situation is not of your making. You didn't create it. Shouldn't you just let events take their course?'

'Not if it means the death of six human beings.'

'All right. Let's spare a thought for the other guy – the one whose death you've just determined.'

'If we must.'

'We must. There he is, minding his own business. He means nobody any harm. Maybe he's a vicar, or he gives huge amounts to charity. Maybe he's a brain surgeon. Maybe he's working on a cure for cancer. He has family. A loving wife. Children. Then you come along, and you take it all away. You wipe him off the map with a flick of a switch. Do you think that's fair?'

Cody hesitates. 'Life isn't fair. Sometimes tough decisions have to be made.'

'Would you be willing to explain that to his wife? Could you look her in the eye and tell her you decided to play God? Tell her that you sacrificed her wonderful, charitable, cancer-curing husband because you thought it was expedient?'

'If I had to. Six lives have been saved because of what I did. Decisions like that are made all the time in real life. In times of war, for example. We kill to protect others.'

'And so that's your final answer?'

'Yes.'

'Eliminate the one, or even the few, to save the many.'

'Yes.'

'Every single time?'

'Yes. How often do I need to say it?'

Another pause, longer this time. 'All right, Cody. Same scenario, with one minor change.'

'Go on. Enthral me.'

'The lonely rambler. It's not a brain surgeon or a cancer specialist. It's not even a stranger. It's Detective Constable Megan Webley.'

The twist hits Cody between the eyes. 'What?'

'I think you heard me. The lone person on the track is Megan. So now what, Cody? What's your answer now?'

'I . . .'

'Yes?'

'I don't know.'

'I think you do. You know exactly what your decision would be.'

'What I know is that this is a ridiculous game. I don't even know why I'm going along with it.'

'Yes, you do. You know the answer to that one too. It's because you need what I have to offer. So come on, Cody. What's it to be? Pull the lever and kill Megan Webley? Or allow six human beings to perish?'

'I can't answer that.'

'You have to. The trolley is on its way, Cody. Faster and faster it goes. Any second now it will be too late, the decision will be out of your hands. Is that what you prefer? To wash your hands of this? To let those poor people die? All six of them? Or ten? Or twenty? To allow them all to be crushed like insects? Or do you kill Megan? One of your few remaining friends in life. Your confidante. Your ex-girlfriend. A simple act, Cody. Just a quick pull of the lever. She'd never know. She'd have no time to hate you for it. Quickly now. Time's running out. Five, four, three, two—'

'She lives. Megan lives. All right? Happy now?'

'Say it again.'

'You heard. I choose to save Megan.'

'Are you sure? A minute ago you took the opposite decision. You made the utilitarian choice. Sacrifice the one to save the many, you said. Every single time, you said.'

'I know what I said.'

'So you admit you were wrong?'

'It's not a question of right or wrong. It's a question of ... context.'

'Context? Interesting. That's very interesting, Cody.'

'I'm glad you think so.'

'I do. And we'll talk more about this.'

'When?'

'When you've taken delivery of the third key.'

'And when will that be?'

'You have mail.'

The line goes dead. Cody tosses the phone aside, jumps out of bed. He pulls on a T-shirt, jeans and a pair of trainers, then grabs the extensible police baton he always keeps by his side at night. He runs out of the bedroom, down the stairs. Turns off the alarm and goes out onto the landing. Flies down the next set of stairs and across the hallway. He reaches the front door.

There is nothing here. No envelope. No delivery of any kind.

He unlocks and opens the door. A blast of cold air hits him, as though a ghost has just rushed past. But there is nothing on the steps, nothing on the street.

Waldo is toying with him. That's what he does.

Cody locks up. He trudges back upstairs, turning lights off as he goes. He reaches the first floor, turns onto the landing. Heads towards the door to his apartment.

And then he sees it.

The earlier ghostly chill is inside him now, rushing through his veins.

Waldo has been here. Inside the building. He stood just here, a single door's width away from Cody's own living space.

The envelope is taped to the outside of the door, the words 'To Nathan Cody' in deathly black on its bone-white surface.

36

She has waited over an hour. Still no sign of Metro, or anyone who might be able to tell her anything about Metro. There have been a couple of attempts to chat her up at the bar, but they gave her no trouble when she told them she was waiting for her Thai boxer boyfriend.

She signals the Irish girl over again. The girl points to Sara's empty glass and says, 'Fancy another?'

'No, thank you. Do me a favour, will you? I know he bit your head off last time, but would you mind getting your manager out here again, please?'

The girl looks with trepidation towards the rear door.

'Tell you what,' says Sara. 'When you've done that, you can get me a glass of tap water.' She passes across a twenty-pound note. 'And you can keep the change.'

'Tap water's free,' says the girl.

'I know,' says Sara.

The girl takes the money, nods, then goes over to the door. She knocks, puts her head through, says a few words, then runs back to her station.

A few seconds later, Iain reappears. 'You still here?' he says.

'I'm still waiting. You promised me a meeting.'

'Nobody turned up yet?'

'No, Iain. Nobody has turned up.'

'Well, I'm sorry, but I just passed on what was told to me.'

'No worries, Iain. But here's what we're going to do now. You're going to call whoever you called before, and this time you're going to tell them I want to speak with them directly. Then you can pass the phone to me.'

'Why would I do that?'

'Because if you don't, you'll have to explain to your boss why you are the one to blame for the consequences.'

'What consequences?'

'All you need to know, Iain, is that it won't be pretty. Look into my eyes. Can you tell I'm not fucking around with you?'

Iain locks eyes with her for several seconds. She can see his uncertainty.

'I'll make the call,' he says.

He skulks away to his office. Comes back a minute later, phone in hand. He passes it to Sara. She brings it to her ear, puts a finger in her other ear to dampen the pounding music.

'Hello?' she says. 'Who's this?'

'More to the point,' says a male voice, 'who the fuck are you? And what do you think you're doing, going around threatening and attacking people?'

'I take it you've heard what happened outside The Tar Barrel, and also at your shitty little pool hall.'

'I heard. I've even seen it. You're a one-woman army. I'm impressed. What I don't know is why you're doing all this.'

'Then give me a chance to explain. Come here and talk to me, like you promised you would. Prove to me you're not pissing your pants at the thought of sitting next to me.'

'Christ, you've got some balls, haven't you, girl?'

'Bigger than yours, it seems.'

The man laughs. 'I'm on my way. Keep a seat warm for me.'

The phone goes dead. Sara hands it back to Iain.

'Get what you wanted?' he asks.

'Not yet. But I will.'

Another key.

Of course it is.

This one is bigger and heavier than the others. Designed for a sturdy mortice lock.

But it's the tag it carries that preys on Cody's mind: 'The key to your deepest fear.'

Cody isn't sure he wants to unlock anything containing his deepest fear. Such a thing can stay in secure confinement, thank you very much.

But still it sets him thinking.

What *is* his deepest fear? And where might it be kept?

He can think of a lot of things that have frightened him. A good proportion of them have scared the bejesus out of him. Does he have a worst, though? Can he single one out for that honour?

But Waldo didn't mean it literally. He wasn't referring to all the horrors that have whirled and swooped in Cody's brain at night. He was referring to something more concrete. Something that, if Cody encountered it, would be certain to knock all his other terrors to the bottom of the rankings.

The earlier phone conversation worries him. All that stuff about the trolley problem. About when ending a life can be right, and when it can be wrong. It makes him especially anxious that Webley was brought into the discussion. Why her? Obviously, Waldo has done his research, and is aware that Webley is special to him, but was there more to it? Is it her life that could be a lever's pull away from being extinguished?

It occurs to him to give her a ring, just to check on her. But then he looks at his clock and sees that it's almost two in the morning. She wouldn't appreciate a call at that time. Moreover, she's already suspicious enough about Cody's actions. A phone call right now would be the cherry on top.

As if sensing it is being thought about, Cody's phone blares into life. He jumps, then answers the call.

'Hello, Cody. How are we doing?'

'How did you get into my building?'

'You found the third key, then?'

'Did you hear me? I asked how you got inside.'

'I've been there before. Don't you remember? I come and go as I please. I could come up to your apartment right now if I wanted. Would you like me to do that?'

It's a good question. When the person you fear and detest most offers to meet you face-to-face, what do you answer? How sure can a man be that he can defeat the devil?

But Waldo isn't a demon. He has no magic. He is a man. He is flesh and blood.

'Any time,' Cody answers. 'Any time you like. I'm ready for you.'

Waldo laughs. 'Be careful what you wish for, Cody. But perhaps you'll get that wish. After all, you've got all three keys now.'

'What am I supposed to do with them?'

'You use them to find me. Isn't it obvious?'

'Not exactly. I don't know what these keys are for.'

'Think about it, Cody. Think about it. I'll be waiting, but you haven't got forever. This is a time-limited offer. If you want to join me in the fiery depths of hell, you'll need to get a move on.'

37

Another hour passes, and Sara feels her fury mounting. She can't ask the Irish bartender to pester her boss again – the poor girl would probably lose her job. And her thoughts of jumping over the bar and crashing into that back room aren't going to get her very far either. The security staff would be on her in a heartbeat. In a fair fight she can take care of herself, but she wouldn't stand a chance against half a dozen burly bouncers.

But then the door opens. Iain comes towards her. He has the phone again. This time he looks almost pitying. He holds the phone out to Sara.

'It's for you.'

Sara takes the handset and puts it to her ear. 'Hello.'

'Go home,' says the voice. The tone is much more serious than it was earlier.

'We have an agreement. An appointment.'

'We have nothing. *You* have nothing. Go home, little girl, before you get hurt.'

'You don't want me to do that. That would be the wrong decision.'

'Don't tell me what the fuck I want. Go home now.'

'You've seen what I can do.'

'I've seen fuck all. You got the drop on a pair of drunks and used an offensive weapon on a couple of dickheads. You do a mean ballet spin in the air, but that's it. Don't start thinking you're ready for the big boys, because you're not.'

'If I go now, it won't be the end. I'll be back.'

'With that accent, you even sound like Arnold Schwarzenegger. It doesn't make you a terminator. Anyway, you're boring me now. *Hasta la vista*, baby.'

The call ends. Sara looks across at Iain. She offers the handset to him, and he accepts it almost apologetically – as if taking it from a woman he knows has just been dumped by her boyfriend.

'What now?' he asks. 'Are you going to kick off?'

She thinks about it. It hasn't gone the way she hoped. She thought she had done enough. Inflicted enough damage to make them sit up and listen. She assumed they would agree to the face-to-face because they would want to iron things out. It's why she chose here – a public place with lots of witnesses. Instead, they have dismissed her, belittled her, flicked her away like a bug, and she doesn't know what to do about it. She has no plan B.

She shakes her head. 'Don't worry. You don't need to whistle for your dogs. I'm going home.'

He nods. His earlier anger with her has dissipated, to be replaced by sympathy.

'If it's any consolation, I think you're doing the right thing. I don't know much about the people who run this place, but I've heard stories. You don't want to get on the wrong side of them.'

Sara slips off the barstool, slips the strap of her bag onto her shoulder.

'Problem is,' she says, 'they've already got on the wrong side of me.'

She's exhausted and dispirited when she arrives home. Metro has been toying with her. Treating her like a child.

She is starting to wonder that he might be right – that she isn't his equal. In the army, she was used to being in control of a situation, but she always had the backing of a tightly-knit, armed-to-the-teeth team. She's on her own now. Nobody to cover her back. Perhaps she needs to start realising she's not invincible.

She still needs to know why Matthew was killed, but she no longer feels assured of achieving that aim.

Sara unlocks her front door, steps inside.

She feels the wrongness even before she sees it.

When she snaps the light on, the carnage couldn't be any more obvious.

In the hallway, every picture has been pulled from the wall and smashed onto the floor. The telephone table is on its side. The lightshade has been smashed, leaving only a naked bulb on its cord. Right across the wall, the word 'SLAG' has been spray-painted in black.

She steps through the broken glass on the floor. Sees more spray-paint in the stairwell. It says, 'BITCH.'

She goes into her living room, puts the light on there.

More devastation.

The curtains ripped from the pole. Her chairs and cushions slashed to ribbons, leaving foam and feathers strewn across the floor. Vases broken, television overturned, books and candles thrown around the room. Streaks of paint on the walls, the furniture, the floor and even the ceiling. Wall-paper pulled away in long strips.

And there's a smell, too.

She realises it's that which alerted her when she first entered the house.

Not an unpleasant odour. Aftershave, perhaps. Or deodorant.

It's stronger here, though. Almost as if—

She turns too late. The fist smashes into the side of her face with immense force. She staggers backwards and trips over something and falls. Her head is filled with a pandemonium of light and colour and sound, but she has the presence of mind to keep rolling on the floor, away from her attacker. She jumps to her feet, blinks to clear her eyes . . .

And sees the gun.

38

She's not about to argue with a SIG Sauer P220. She has seen first-hand what 9 mm bullets can do to a human.

The man behind the gun is well-built and smartly dressed. Leather jacket, dark trousers, shiny shoes. He looks capable of handling himself even without a gun. The line of chunky rings on his fingers glimmers at her, and she brings her hand to her cheek to assess the damage they caused. She winces at the pain, and when she brings her hand away, it is slick with her blood. Her head is still buzzing, and she feels the need to vomit.

'Sit down, Sara,' he says.

She feels sick enough to acquiesce, but finding a seat left amid the devastation is another matter. She knocks some books off the sofa to reveal a ripped cushion, its interior stuffing bursting out of it. She plonks herself down on it nonetheless.

'Are you the one they call Metro?' she asks.

The man laughs. 'No, darling. He wouldn't waste his time on this shit. I'm just the messenger.'

'So what's your name?'

'You can call me Ozone. Everyone else does. I don't mind. It's because I like to smell nice, see. People say I'm doing my best to destroy the ozone layer. Me, I couldn't give a monkey's. We're all going to die anyway, right? Some quicker than others.'

'I recognise your voice. We spoke on the phone earlier.'

Ozone nods, smiles. Waves the gun playfully in her direction. 'Spot on, darling.'

'You kept me waiting deliberately, didn't you?' She indicates the room with a sweep of her arm. 'So that you'd have time to do all this.'

'Again, spot on. I think I've done a pretty good job here, don't you?'

'And then you told me to come home, so that you could attack me.'

'Guilty as charged. You should join the police, love. You're a right little Sherlock.'

'Your own detective skills aren't bad either. You know my name, where I live. Or did you get all that from Metro?'

Ozone shrugs. 'Metro didn't get to where he is by being in the dark. Anything he doesn't know, he makes it his business to find out. Especially when he knows someone is out to get him.'

'He's scared of me, then?'

'Not scared, no. Let's just say he likes to err on the side of caution. And who can blame him, eh? People aren't always what they seem. You, for instance. Who would think you could stand up to a roomful of men in a pool hall? Shitting hell, girl, that was some show you put on there. I was seriously impressed.'

'Thank you. Put down the gun and I'll give you another demonstration.'

'No, that's okay. Seriously, I don't think you could take me, but it's late and I'm tired after trashing your house. You have some nice stuff here by the way. Used to, anyway.'

'Did you need to break it all?'

'Did you need to break teeth and bones? You see what I'm saying, right? If you knock down a wasps' nest, you shouldn't be surprised when you get stung.'

Sara feels a tickle on her neck as a line of blood oozes down it. A wave of nausea washes over her again.

She says, 'I'm not doing this for fun. Do you know why I'm doing it?'

'I know you're the one whose husband was murdered, and so I'm guessing you think Metro had something to do with it.'

'Did he?'

'No. But I'd say that even if he had.'

'What about you? Were you involved in my husband's death?'

'Same answer, darling.'

'You seem to know how to use a gun. You could have been the one who shot him in the head.'

A broad grin from Ozone. 'Nice try, babe.'

'What do you mean?'

'You pretend he was shot to death, I go along with it, and then you know I had nothing to do with it. Only he wasn't shot in the head, was he? He had a lot of holes in him, but not one of them was caused by a bullet. To be honest, I'd have paid good money to see that. What was it like?'

Sara holds back her surge of anger. 'You could have rescued yourself there. You could have gone along with the gunshot story and pretended you knew nothing about the circumstances of my husband's murder.'

Ozone leans his free arm on the mantelpiece. 'That's because I don't need rescuing. I don't really care what you believe, and neither does Metro. All we care about is you staying out of our hair.'

Sara understands then. These men aren't stupid. The reason they aren't denying flat out that they killed Matthew is that they want her to believe they are capable of such atrocities. They want her to be scared of them.

But whether they did it or not, they have access to insider knowledge that Sara doesn't. Outside of the police, there are few who know precisely how Matthew died. That alone makes Metro a man still worth talking to.

'And this is your attempt to frighten me off?'

Ozone sighs. 'Look, girl. I'm trying to help you out. You're a foreigner, so maybe you don't know how things work over here. You're getting in the faces of people who won't think twice about hurting you. Keep it going and you'll end up the same way as your husband. He's dead, and there's nothing you can do about it, so just go back to Norway or wherever and get on with your life.'

'Denmark.'

'What?'

'I'm from Denmark. And I'm not going back. Not yet.'

Ozone shakes his head slowly, almost mournfully. 'Then there's no more to be said.'

For a split-second Sara expects him to bring this to a close by shooting her dead. But he doesn't. Instead, he starts walking towards the door, his shoes crunching on glass.

'He could put an end to this,' she says, stopping him in his tracks. 'Metro. He could stop this. All I'm asking is for him to meet with me and talk.'

'We all want things we can't have,' Ozone says. 'Maybe you should think about what your husband would have wanted.'

He leaves then. Sara hears the click of the front door – a surprisingly gentle sound given the mayhem that has been wrought in the rest of the house.

She jumps up from the sofa and runs to the front window, just in time to see a black Mercedes being driven away. She returns to the sofa and fishes her mobile phone from her bag, then opens a notebook app and types in the car licence plate number.

For a moment, the decisiveness feels good. She's taking action, preparing to fight back.

But then despondency takes over. She lowers the phone, looks around her. Takes in the demolition of all that she and Matthew built together.

What am I doing? she thinks. What is the point?

She walks across to a display cabinet. Its doors yawn wide open, the glass panels in them shattered. Its contents now lie at her feet. She reaches down and picks up a walnut-framed photograph. As though imprisoned behind the dagger-like shards of glass still clinging to it, Matthew smiles out at her. He looks so happy, so full of life. But then she notices how the glass has ripped a jagged hole in his head.

Maybe you should think about what your husband would have wanted.

Unexpectedly profound words from a man who goes around wrecking lives.

And perhaps not ridiculous advice.

Would you want this, Matthew? Would you want me risking my life to find your killers? Or would you plead with me to go back to Copenhagen and try to find happiness once more?

She knows the answer. She can hear the words from his mouth as if he were standing here next to her.

And it tears through her heart.

39

Cody has already accepted that sleep isn't on the agenda tonight.

When his mind isn't working on the puzzle of the three keys, it's worrying about the fact that Waldo has been in the building again. He was there, just one storey down, taping an envelope to the fucking apartment door, for Christ's sake!

Nobody could sleep knowing that.

He often wonders what he would do when finally faced with Waldo. He'd like to think that he'd beat the crap out of him. But sometimes he's not sure. He's not entirely certain of his own fortitude in facing up to the evil creature who has featured in so many of his nightmares. He worries that he would freeze, or run away, or scream, and all of those shameful outcomes frighten him as much as the prospect of the encounter itself.

But now he may get a chance to find out. Waldo has invited Cody to meet him on his own turf, to join him in the 'fiery depths of hell'.

Cody doesn't know where the fiery depths of hell are, but they don't sound pleasant. He pictures them as being in the bowels of the earth. Fire and brimstone and all that shit. Bubbling cauldrons. Tortured souls screaming for mercy. Monstrous demons ripping the flesh from their victims.

And clowns, of course. Clowns have their rightful place in hell.

A thought suddenly occurs to Cody. A possibility.

More than a possibility? Shit. If it's true . . .

He picks up the most recent key. *The key to your deepest fear.* What if . . . ?

He doesn't want to believe it, but he has tried everything. If nothing else, he needs to rule this one out.

He picks up the other two keys and pushes all of them into the pocket of his jeans. Grabbing his baton, he heads down the turned staircase that leads to his apartment door. He turns off the alarm and unlocks the door. He puts on the lights, walks slowly down the next staircase, constantly alert for noises.

When he reaches the hallway, he doesn't keep going towards the front door. Instead, he turns and walks to the left of the stairs, towards the rear door. There, he makes one last turn, so that he is facing the brown door that is beneath the main staircase.

The door that leads down to the basement.

Cody has stood at this door many times. It is always locked, but he has often been convinced that he has heard sounds coming from the other side. Tiny, scratching sounds. Mice or rats, perhaps. Whatever, the thought of passing through this doorway has always unnerved him.

Simon Teller once told Cody that he has never got round to doing anything with the basement. It was once a beer cellar, apparently, back when the building was used to house a British Legion social club. Now it holds the boiler and little else.

At least, that always used to be the case.

Cody reaches into his pocket. Brings out the largest key. This wasn't in his possession when he was trying all the doors with the Yale. But this door doesn't have a Yale lock. It has a mortice.

Cody inserts the key into the hole in the door.

A part of him desperately wants this to provide the answer to the puzzle set by Waldo. At the same time, he knows he will feel a huge sense of relief if the key doesn't work. Sometimes, defeat can be a mercy.

He twists the key.

It turns. The latch opens with a satisfying mechanical *kerchink.*

The fiery depths. Your deepest fear. The clues were there all along.

40

Cody's system steps on the gas, accelerating his heart rate. He whips his baton in the air, extending it to its full length.

With his other hand, he turns the handle and pulls on the heavy door. Its hinges squeal as it opens.

Ahead lies blackness. A slight breeze of stale air escapes from its prison and pushes at Cody, as though warning him to keep away. He blinks, straining to see into the gloom, then reaches out and feathers his hand up the wall. It feels coarse and slightly damp. His fingers locate a switch, and it is with a sense of relief that he flicks it on and banishes unseen terrors.

He is facing a rough-hewn wooden staircase leading down to a white concrete floor below.

Cody moves on to the first step. It seems solid enough. As he treads on the next step and releases his hold on the door, he realises that it is on a massive spring that causes it to close behind him.

He hopes it will open again when he returns. Especially if he is fleeing.

He keeps moving. Step after cautious step. Nothing jumps out at him, and he hears no noises other than his own breathing and footfalls.

When he gets to the bottom, he pauses and tries to calm his breathing. He is in a large open space. The concrete floor is dusty and gritty. The bare, unplastered walls have been whitewashed. There are two doors to the right and two to the left. Only one of the doors is closed.

Cody investigates the open rooms first. In each case he finds the light switch, then turns it on before jumping inside with his baton at the ready.

The two rooms to his left contain only some cardboard boxes, old furniture and discarded dental equipment. The room at the front and right of the house is where he finds the boiler, currently quiescent. Shutters cover the windows that can be seen below street level from the outside of the building.

Only one more room to check out. And Cody just knows that this isn't going to be easy on his nerves.

He walks over to the closed door. Puts his ear to it. He remains there for a full two minutes, just listening. He thinks he hears a tiny metallic noise, but he's not certain.

And now he wishes he were armed with more than a baton. A machine-gun, perhaps.

Cody thinks to himself, What's on the other side of this door? A person? If it's a person, could he have heard me?

The door looks substantial, and the walls are certainly thick. It's entirely possible that my arrival has gone undetected.

He looks at the keyhole. It's a Yale. Cody finds the next key in his pocket. Reminds himself that its tag reads, 'The key to life.'

There is something living on the other side of this door.

Shit, shit, shit.

He tries to decide what to do. He thinks, Should I bang on the door and order whoever's in there to come out? Yeah, but what if they don't? What do I do then? Or should I announce that I'm coming in, with several other cops and police dogs as back-up?

Or maybe the stealthy approach is better. Try to catch them by surprise.

I could die here, he thinks. If I handle this wrong, I could end up dead.

But then if Waldo had wanted me dead, he could easily have done that by now. Why bother with all this rigmarole if that was his aim? No, this isn't about killing me.

Famous last words.

He settles on the softly-softly approach.

Approaching the door again, he brings the key up to the hole. His hand is shaking, and he has to rest his forearm against the door as he lines up the key.

Slowly, with infinite care, he starts to insert the key.

It's not even warm down here, but he is starting to perspire. His hand feels clammy, and he worries that his fingers will slip on the key and give the game away.

But he presses on. A millimetre at a time. Despite the glacial movement, there is still a minute noise of metal on metal. Maybe it can't be heard through the thick door, he reasons.

Or maybe the sound is magnified by the large chamber beyond, and *everything* can be heard, including the fear in my breathing and my heartbeat.

And then it's in. The key can go no further.

Cody pauses. Focuses on taking long, deep breaths.

You can still walk away, he tells himself. You can make an emergency call to your police colleagues. Tell them you heard strange noises, and you believe that somebody has barricaded themselves in here. Let *them* do the dangerous stuff.

But you can't do that, can you? Because that wouldn't be playing the game, and Waldo will have prepared for that eventuality. He will never trust you again, and may never give you another opportunity to act as his opponent.

So you have no choice. You have to go in.

And before he can start talking himself out of it again, he is turning the key and he is pushing the door wide open and he is frantically searching for the light, and when it comes on he is ready and waiting to deal with whatever and whoever might be in here.

Except for this.

He is not ready for this.

He is not ready for the clown supreme, Waldo himself, in the centre of the room, staring right back at him.

41

Cody reacts.

Which is to say, he doesn't consider his next move. Doesn't put an iota of conscious thought into it.

It's a knee-jerk response. He sees the one thing he detests more than anything else he knows, the thing that is imprinted on his brain as a symbol of all that is wrong and hurtful in his universe, and his sole automatic impulse is to annihilate it.

His self-questioning about what he might do in this situation is answered. He rushes forward, baton raised, ready to strike – not once or twice or any number in single digits, but until this thing in front of him is mush at his feet.

He has no fear, no thought for his own safety. His passions have moved beyond that. He will slay this monster, and nothing will get in his way.

Except . . .

Waldo running.

This he does not expect.

Waldo running and shrieking in terror, being chased by Cody around the room until his body comes to a sudden jolting halt and he falls to the floor and raises his arms above his head and cries out not to be hurt, please God, no, don't.

And Cody can't do it. He stands over the clown, who is now something substantially diminished in stature and menace from the image in Cody's brain, and he cannot hit him. He cannot bring his baton down even once on this pathetic, snivelling creature before him. Even though he suspects a trap – because that's how Waldo rolls – Cody's baton-wielding arm waits in vain for its command.

Cody yells. Lets out all his breath and frustration and anger into the disgusting rubber face of his foe. And then he takes hold of the mask and tears it away and flings it to the far side of the room, wishing that it was Waldo's head, his actual, complete head that he was casting aside after the triumph of a glorious battle.

But there is no glory in this. All that is left is a man. A mere mortal. He is about thirty years old – a similar age to Cody – and his eyes are filled with both tears and utter terror.

'Please,' he cries. 'Don't hurt me.'

'Who are you?' Cody shouts. 'Are you Waldo?'

'Wh-who? I-I don't know what you—'

'Waldo! Don't fuck with me! Are you Waldo?'

'N-no.'

'Then who?'

'I-I can't say. I—'

Cody finally brings down his baton. But it's a shadow of his previously intended strikes. A crack against the man's thigh that will merely bruise.

'Do not fucking mess with me. Understand?'

'Yes, but I . . . I'm sorry, but I can't tell you. He said—'

Another smack with the baton. This time on the man's upper arm.

'Who said? What did he say?'

'That he'd call you. It's why they brought me here.'

'Who brought you here?'

'The other clowns, of course. He said you'd know that. He said you were expecting—'

'Wait! Wait! What did you say?'

'That you knew. You were expecting me.'

'No. Before that. The other clowns. Did you say the other clowns?'

'Yes. But you already know that. You . . .'

Enlightenment dawns, and the shock of betraying himself frees the tears from his eyes.

'You *didn't* know, did you?' he asks.

Cody straightens up, tries to make sense of all this.

'You're one of them. One of the four clowns.'

The man says nothing, but it is clear from his expression that he suspects he may have already signed his own death warrant.

'Which one?'

Nothing.

'Which fucking one?'

The man shakes his head, too terrified to answer.

Cody moves closer to the man, now huddled in a foetal position on the floor. He takes the baton in both hands, raises it above his head.

'Are you Waldo?'

'Please. I don't know who Waldo is.'

'The man who cut off my toes. The man who sliced the face off my partner. Are you that man?'

'No. I swear. I didn't do those things. I couldn't. I was there, but—'

'You were there. You admit that much. You helped. That makes you responsible. That makes you guilty. What you did to me . . . What you did to my partner . . .'

And suddenly Cody is crying too. He hates that it is happening to him, but he can do nothing to prevent it. The tears are streaming down his cheeks.

He takes a few steps backwards, as if hoping that the distance will give him some objectivity. That it will allow him once again to find the anger that is so rightly his. That it will empower him to administer the justice he has longed for.

But all he gets is tears.

He wipes them violently from his cheeks in an act of self-loathing.

'What the fuck is this?' he says. 'What the fuck are you doing here, in my house? In my own home? Why did you come here?'

'I don't know. Really, I don't. He said you'll get a call. It will be explained to you.'

'Who? You keep saying "he". Who do you mean by that?'

'The man you want. Waldo? Is that what you call him?'

'What do *you* call him?'

'I . . . I don't know his name.'

Cody advances again. 'Bullshit! You worked with him. You must have talked to him. You must have seen him.'

'No. Please. Wait for the call. It will all be explained.'

'I want it explained now, by you.'

'I-I can't.'

Cody glares down at him. Debates his next move. This is so absurd, so beyond the realm of what is ordinary. He is not equipped to deal with this macabre bizarreness.

He paces the room, and as he does so he becomes more aware of his environment.

The room is at the rear of the house. Like the other rooms, its window is shuttered. In addition, a metal grille is bolted over the window, presumably to prevent people breaking in to steal thousands of pounds' worth of booze when this was used as a cellar. Looped around the bars is a thick metal chain. The chain runs along the floor and terminates at a shackle around the clown's ankle. It was the chain becoming taut that caused the clown to fall when he was trying to evade Cody.

Cody walks back to look more closely at the shackle. He sees that it is kept closed with a padlock. He reaches into his pocket and pulls out the third key.

The key to freedom.

Cody realises now that this key will open the padlock and free his captive.

But he has no plans to do that.

Not until he has heard what Waldo has to say.

42

'Stand up,' Cody commands.

'W-why?'

'Just do what I fucking tell you to do, okay?'

The man scrambles to his feet.

'Over there,' Cody says. 'Hands up against the wall.'

The man does as he is told. Cody kicks at the man's legs, forcing them apart and taking his balance away should he decide to try anything. Cody then searches the man, turning out the pockets in the man's navy-blue overalls and patting him down. He finds some house keys, coins and a wallet that contains money but no means of identification. Cody stuffs them all into his own pockets.

'You ready to tell me your name yet?' he asks.

The man doesn't reply. Doesn't even turn his head to look at him. Cody punches him hard in the kidneys and the man collapses to his knees.

'That's just for starters. That phone call had better come soon. And you need to start praying that it helps you, because right now I am this close to beating the life out of you.' He holds his finger and thumb a millimetre apart and shoves them under the nose of the man.

Then Cody leaves. He closes the door, removes the key from the lock and ascends the wooden staircase. At the top, he relocks the door to the basement and removes that key too. He wants to be certain that his captive stays where he is.

Only when Cody reaches his apartment at the top of the building does he collapse his baton. Surprises seem to be the order of the day, and he's had his fill of them.

He goes into his kitchen because it's the door nearest the stairs. He needs to sit down, to think, even though his brain is mush.

He hauls himself onto a stool at the breakfast bar. He looks straight ahead of him.

And then his eyes mist over and he begins to sob.

He doesn't know quite why, but he cries like a baby. And when he's done, he wonders whether this is all a dream. Wonders if all he has done tonight is sleepwalk from his bed to the kitchen.

Because this seems so incredibly unreal, and he is so incredibly exhausted. He feels like he could go back to bed for a full day.

And yet that can't happen. He has unresolved business. Such as a homicidal clown in his basement.

He almost laughs out loud at that thought. A killer clown? In my basement? Really?

But it's not funny, of course. In fact, it could be a monumental turning point in Cody's life. That's as serious as it can get.

He wonders if he will let the clown live.

Before the solemnity of that thought can sink in, Cody's phone rings. It's the call he has been told to expect. The call that could explain everything.

He answers it. Says, 'This better be good.'

'Hello, Cody,' says Waldo as usual. 'I've called several times. Do I take it that you've been a little . . . busier than usual?'

'Who is he, Waldo?'

'Ah, you found him, then. It took you long enough.'

'I found him. Who is he?'

'Didn't he tell you?'

'He said he was one of the clowns.'

'Then why are you asking me? You know who he is.'

'What's his name?'

'You mean he didn't introduce himself? How terribly un-British.'

'His name, Waldo.'

'Let's just call him Clueless, shall we? I think that would be a good name in the circumstances.'

Clueless the Clown. Yeah, very apt. But Clueless Cody is even more apt.

'And he's here why?'

'Because your wish is my command. Because this is what you have always wanted. You want the clowns who hurt you. The clowns who killed your partner. The clowns who have ruined your life. I'm handing this one to you on a plate. Do with him what you will.'

'And you're handing him over to me because . . . ?'

'Because I'm feeling generous. I think you deserve a break.'

'Why?'

'You're such a cynic, Cody. All right, how does this sound? I'm giving you a break because eternal suffering gets boring really quickly. You're becoming inured to it, and I'm starting to lose interest. This way, you bounce back for a while, thinking your life has been turned around, and then I take the hugest of pleasures in knocking you off your perch again. How's that?'

'It sounds more like you. Which means I probably shouldn't believe a word of it.'

'Ha! Good response. But the fact of the matter remains the same. I'm a clown down, and you're a clown up. Make the most of it.'

'How do I know he's really one of you?'

'I'm sorry?'

'You're telling me he was one of the four. How do I know that's true?'

'What did Clueless say?'

'He said the same. Doesn't make it so. He could be as warped as you are.'

'Indeed he could. So perhaps now you've hit the nail on the head. Perhaps that's what this game is all about.'

'What are you saying?'

'The trolley problem, Cody. The trolley problem.'

'Shit. Not that again.'

'I'm afraid so. But we'll add another little twist this time.'

'Fab. I do love a good twist.'

'I knew you would. So, our trolley is on its way again, speeding towards our group of walkers on the railway line. This time, though, you're not able to divert it onto another track.'

'I'm not?'

'No. That's because you're observing all this from a bridge that runs over the line.'

'I bet I get a good view from there.'

'You do. And you're not alone. Next to you is another man.'

'Do I know him?'

'No. He's not a friend or a family member. You've never met him in your life. The only thing you know about him is that he's fat.'

'Fat?'

'Obese. Enormous. Gargantuan. Big enough, in fact, to stop that trolley in its tracks if he were to be dropped in front of it.'

'Oookay. And now I see where you're going with this.'

'Well done, Cody. So what do you do?'

'Is that a serious question?'

'Why not? All you have to do is push this guy off the bridge. He's a saddo, a loser. Nobody will miss him. You, however, will be a hero for saving all those lives.'

'No. I can't do that.'

'Why not? Earlier on, you were perfectly happy to kill one stranger to save several. What's the difference now?'

'I don't know. It's just . . . different.'

'Is it? A pull of a lever or a push of a body. The outcome is the same.'

'That's as may be, but my actions are different. I'm more involved. I'm physically acting on the guy instead of a switch. And I'm up close and personal with him. He's not just some remote figure in the distance.'

'Interesting. So you're not going to do it? You let the group below die?'

'Yes.'

'Final answer?'

'I'd like to say yes, but why do I get the feeling it isn't?'

'Because there's another twist.'

'You do surprise me.'

'Here it is: the man next to you is the guy who interfered with the trolley in the first place. He's the one who set it free. He's the one who will be responsible for the deaths of those people on the line. Unless, of course . . .'

'Unless I push him.'

'Yes.'

'Then . . .'

'Go on.'

'Yeah. I'd do it. I'd push him. He had it coming.'

Waldo's laugh is as long as it is disturbing.

'What's so funny?' Cody asks.

'You, Cody. You are. Don't you see? Don't you realise how full of contradictions you are? You don't know when to kill and when not to. Sometimes it's right and sometimes it's wrong. Life and death aren't always black and white. There is so much grey.'

'The moral of this story being?'

'That you have to do what feels right to you. There is no right or wrong. There are only differences of opinion.'

'I don't think that's always true. Hitler was wrong.'

'Not in his eyes. And not in the eyes of the millions of his followers. To him, the extermination of the Jews was doing his nation a service. He simply had a difference of opinion with those who eventually defeated him.'

'Look, Waldo. We could debate this all day, but I'm tired and I've got a clown in my basement. What's this important message you want to give me?'

'You've had it, Cody. You've had the message. It's simply that you now have to decide how far your morality will let you go.'

Cody suddenly has a sinking feeling in his stomach.

'What do you mean?'

'I mean that the man you have in your basement knows more than he's saying. Much, much more.'

'Such as?'

'Such as who I am, and where you can find me.'

Cody goes silent for a few seconds while he absorbs this. If it's true, then for the first time since the clowns captured him, Cody could be on the verge of getting his hands on Waldo.

'He says he doesn't know you.'

'Do you believe him?'

'No.'

'I thought not. But I'm not surprised he said that. He wants to save his skin. He will deny everything. He may even stop talking altogether.'

'Then what's the point of this? Why hand him over to me?'

'Because you're a resourceful man, Cody. And what we've just established through our entertaining little chat about the trolley problem is that you are as conflicted as everybody else on this planet. You will do what you need to do.'

'You mean torture him? Is that what you're suggesting?'

'I'm not suggesting anything. That's for you and your morals to decide. For all I care, you can set him free. You have the keys. But if you do that, you will never find me. I told you right at the beginning that I was giving myself up to you, but you're going to have to work for it. You're going to have to make your prisoner talk. So what's it to be, Cody? Pull the lever, or not?'

43

When the call ends, Cody puts the phone down and rubs his eyes. He is so tired, so mentally drained. What makes it worse is the enormity of the decisions with which he is now faced.

He has never been in a situation even remotely like this. He has been a captive before, and knows the suffering it entails, but he has never been the prison warden. Yes, he has handcuffed criminals, and yes, he has locked them up in custody cells, and yes, he has played his part in their being put behind bars for long sentences, but this is not like that at all. This is not a part of his duty as a police officer. This is, in fact, very much outside the law. This is false imprisonment. And if he does what Waldo has indicated he might do, it could just be the thin end of a wedge from which there would be no going back.

But Cody knows he cannot simply waste this opportunity. What he has got hidden several floors below is not merely a man; it is a treasure trove of secrets. Handled properly, it could fulfil Cody's deepest desires. It could take him directly to the mysterious figure he knows only as Waldo.

But then Cody's mind flips back again. You're a policeman, he tells himself. You promised faithfully always to uphold the law. It's the code you live by. It sits at the very core of what you are. No matter what he may have done, you cannot keep that man locked up downstairs. You certainly cannot act as his judge, jury and—

Executioner?

Really, Cody? That's in your thoughts? You would kill this man?

Cody slams his palms down on the breakfast bar and jumps off the stool so abruptly he knocks it over.

Shit!

He doesn't know what to do, what is right. Waldo's little mind games, his stupid trolley problem, have turned Cody's brain to porridge. He feels like he is swimming against a tide, getting nowhere, when all he wants to do is stop and drift.

He goes to the sink, turns on the cold tap, splashes water on his face. He needs to be awake to deal with this. The night is dwindling, the shadows retreating. He has work ahead of him shortly – the demands of a conventional day that seem so mundane in comparison with this night-time carnival.

But what then? What will he do when the cover of night has deserted him, when he can no longer act unseen and unheard?

I'll worry about that when it happens, he thinks.

Then he picks up his baton and his keys – his three special keys – and heads downstairs once again.

When he enters the makeshift cell once more, the man Waldo referred to as Clueless gets up from the floor. He stands with his back to the wall, his eyes wide with fear.

Cody lets him stew for a while. He paces up and down in front of the man, glaring at him unrelentingly.

'Did you . . . Did you get the phone call?'

Cody lets several more seconds elapse before replying. 'Yes, he called. Your friend called. He had a lot to say.'

'About me?'

'About you. About the role you played. About what you did to me.'

'I didn't do anything. I was there, but I didn't do anything. I didn't hurt you or your partner.'

'You were there. That's enough. That makes you responsible.'

'No. I—'

'You acted as one. You had weapons and you used force. If Waldo had come on his own, without the back-up of you and the others, we could have dealt with him. Your support enabled him to do what he did.'

'I didn't know it would get that bad.'

Cody's barked laugh is mirthless. 'Yeah, right. That's what they all say. You were just along for the ride. You didn't know what you were letting yourself in for. You'd be amazed at how many times I've heard that bullshit.'

'So . . . so what are you going to do?'

'Do? Well, that depends on you, doesn't it?'

'Me?'

'Yeah, you, Clueless. That's how Waldo referred to you, by the way: Clueless the Clown. He seems to hate your guts almost as much as I do. Why is that, I wonder?'

'I don't know.'

'Whatever. He hates you enough to hand you over to me, so life as you know it is over. You may as well start telling me the truth.'

'I've told you the truth.'

'You've told me fuck all. You haven't even told me your real name. But you know what? I'm not that interested in you. It's your boss that I want.'

'I told you before: I don't know anything about him.'

'And I told you that you're a lying little toe-rag.'

Cody walks over to the man. He rests the tip of his baton on the man's shoulder.

'You can probably tell from my mood that I don't give a shit about you. I don't care if you live or die. So here's how this is going to work. If you're helpful to me, I'll go easy on you. If you're not, well, look around you. Nobody will hear or see what I do to you. Nobody knows you're here. I could kill you now, dispose of your body, and nobody will be any the wiser.'

'You wouldn't do that. You're a police officer.'

Cody laughs in his face. 'It's because I'm a police officer that I know exactly how to get away with it. Do you want to test me out? Well, do you?'

'No. Please . . .'

Cody turns and walks away. The man's imploring tugs at Cody, finds some pity within him. He doesn't want that. He can't afford to show compassion towards this man, can't risk displaying any signs of weakness that might embolden him.

He summons up his fury again before he turns around once more.

'Let's start again, shall we? What's your name?'

'I can't tell you that.'

'Why not? What harm would it do?'

'Waldo told me not to.'

'Waldo isn't here. I am. And I'm ordering you to tell me.'

'You don't understand. Waldo is everywhere. He would find a way of getting to me. I can't risk that.'

'No, it's *you* who doesn't understand. What I will do to you is worse than anything Waldo could ever do. I'm in no hurry. I will keep you here for as long as it takes, and I will make it as painful for you as it needs to be.' He pauses. 'But I'll make you a deal.'

'Deal? What kind of deal?'

'A swap. You for Waldo. You tell me how to find Waldo, and I'll set you free.'

The man hesitates. It's for only a fraction of a second, but Cody notices.

'N-no. I can't.'

'I have the key to that padlock in my pocket. I can release you from that chain at any time. All I want is Waldo. Give him to me, and you'll never have to see me or him again.'

And now the hesitation is longer. 'You'd do that? You'd let me go?'

'Yes.'

'And all I have to do is tell you about Waldo?'

'Yes. That's all you have to do. You can go anywhere you like after that. You can leave the country, for all I care. All I want is Waldo.'

The man lowers his head. Brings his chin down to his chest so that Cody can no longer see his face.

Cody finds himself willing the man to take the deal. Come on, he thinks. Save yourself. Do something to make up for what you did to me.

The man's shoulders begin twitching, and at first Cody thinks he's sobbing, as though the agony of indecision is tearing him apart. But then he raises his head again, and Cody sees that he's laughing, silently at first, but then he takes an intake of breath and lets out an almighty roar of hysterical laughter, and it twists into Cody's gut, burns him inside.

'What are you laughing at?'

But the only response he gets is more of the same, tears now running down the man's cheeks.

The tears of a clown. Humour infused with darkness. Amusement tinged with horror.

Cody snaps. He runs at the man, grabs him by the throat, slams his head back against the wall.

'What the fuck are you laughing at?'

'You. You are so fucking naïve, so innocent. It's all bluff. You're not going to hurt me. You haven't got it in you.'

Cody bangs the man's head against the bricks again. He pulls back his right arm, the baton clutched in his fist.

'You can't, can you?' says the man. 'You can't do it. You don't work like that. You may as well let me go now.'

'I'm not letting you go. Not unless you talk. The best you can hope for after I've finished with you is a long spell in prison.'

'Really? On what evidence?'

The words take Cody by surprise. He realises he hasn't thought this through. He wants to believe that he can be forceful enough to extract either a confession or the goods on Waldo out of this man. Failing that, he would put him under arrest and call in his police colleagues.

But suddenly there is doubt in his mind.

'What?' he says.

'You don't think I'm going to admit anything in public, do you? What I've said in this room stays in this room. I'm not repeating it. If you think you can convince a judge to lock me up, then good luck with that. What are you going to do, tell him you've been given the word of the clown-in-chief?' He swivels his bulging eyes to indicate the room. 'And how are you going to explain all this? What will you tell the judge about the reasons for keeping me in your basement – especially if I come out of here with cuts and bruises? Hardly makes you look like the injured party, does it?'

Cody hates this newly found confidence in the man, who has quickly turned from a snivelling coward into an assured negotiator.

You're allowing him to gain the upper hand, Cody tells himself. He's losing his fear of you. You need to be more intimidating. Where's your killer instinct? Remember what he did to you. Remember that he's responsible. He took away your flesh and your bones. Remember what he did to Jeff? Remember how Jeff screamed for his mother? Remember that look on his face before it was separated from his skull?

Cody tightens his hold on the man's throat. The man brings up his hands and tries to loosen the grip, but Cody's strength is fuelled by his anger. He pulls back his baton again . . .

And then he lets the man go.

He's right, thinks Cody. I can't do this. No matter how much hatred I feel inside, it won't come out in violence against a man who can't fight back. That's not me.

He turns his back on the man. Starts heading towards the door.

The attack comes without warning.

The first Cody knows about it is the arm around his neck and being pulled down to the ground. His knees slam into the concrete, and then the man is on top of him, flattening him on the floor. The arm grip tightens, cutting off Cody's airways, the blood supply to his brain. He can't get either of his own arms free to fight back, and it is as though there is a python coiled around his neck, squeezing ever more tightly as Cody's field of vision begins to fill with sparkles and dots and patches of dark that will soon merge into complete blackness.

He tries to roll, to the right and then the left. Manages to draw up his right leg enough to push down on the ground and complete the turn. With his opponent under him now, Cody begins punching backwards with his elbow, spearing the man's abdomen. He hears grunts of pain, but the grip on his neck remains in place. Cody brings his foot up, slams it down into the man's leg and rakes his shoe down his shin. As the man shrieks, Cody rolls again and this time is able to get his legs beneath him and, with a yell of effort, heaves himself up from the floor, the man still clinging to his back.

Cody launches himself backwards, slams the man into the wall. Once, twice with his elbow into the man's gut again, then he throws his head back, hitting the man in the face.

The grip loosens. Cody tears himself away and whirls on the man.

And then Cody is gone. He abandons control. Hands himself over to a whirlwind of fists that pummel and batter until his opponent crumples to the ground. And still Cody doesn't stop. He drops to his knees, grabs the man's chain, wraps it around his neck. He pulls and pulls, because all he can see now is the hated mask of Waldo, and he so needs it to stop grinning at him, to stop taunting him.

It takes him too long to realise that Clueless the Clown is not fighting back. There is no longer any resistance. There are no more cries of pain, whimpers of protest. There is just silence.

Cody scrambles along the floor, away from the prone, inert figure. He looks back at the body, and then at his own blood-coated knuckles.

And he wonders what he has become.

44

Cody sits on the floor in silence, his senses completely focused on the figure just feet away. He watches for the slightest of movements – the rise and fall of the man's chest or the twitch of a finger. He listens intently for a groan, a murmur, a breath.

He waits in vain.

A realisation takes root and grows within him that he has become what he has always battled against. A criminal. A murderer.

He has taken a life – the thing he swore an oath to protect. He has no excuses. He can hardly claim self defence against someone he was keeping locked up in his cellar. And besides, his response was disproportionate. The man didn't need to die.

That should be the worst of it.

Committing murder should be what he regrets most about this total fuck-up. He feels ashamed that it isn't. What truly saddens him is that he has just severed his connection to Waldo. With Clueless now gone, he is back to square one.

What, he wonders, does that say about me? What does it say that my sense of loss is built on such a selfish foundation?

And what do I do now?

Give myself in? Should I make a call now to DCI Blunt? Throw myself at her mercy?

There would be no mercy, of course. Blunt would do her job. She's a professional. She will hate it, but she will do what must be done.

But then there's the alternative. I get rid of the body somehow. Hide it and pretend none of this happened. Is that possible? Am I capable of doing such a thing?

The options fly around in Cody's brain – unfamiliar birds he thought could never exist there. He can't believe he is seriously considering ways to evade justice.

And then something happens to take the urgency of decision away from him.

The man coughs.

It's a short, sharp exhalation at first, but then it builds. The man clutches at the chain, tugging it away from his neck as he struggles to find air. He coughs again and again, scrambling to his knees in an effort to make it easier to breathe.

Cody stands, but doesn't move towards the man. He wants to offer help, but at the same time he needs his opponent to believe that he is a hard-knock, a bad-ass, who really isn't going to think twice about killing him.

The fight for breath eventually becomes easier and the coughing fit subsides. Clueless sits with his back to the wall again, rubbing his neck. It's a while before he seems to notice that Cody is there in the room.

'You could have killed me,' he says.

'You jumped me,' Cody answers. 'You were asking for it. What were you trying to do? Get the key?'

Clueless doesn't reply, but it's the obvious motive.

'And then what?' Cody asks. 'Kill me? Finish off what you started in the warehouse? Torture me a little more, maybe? Tie me up and snip off some more toes, a few fingers?'

The man shakes his head, and winces with pain. 'I told you. I'm not like that. I just want to get out of here.'

'You really think I should let you go? After what you did to me?'

'I think . . . I think what you're doing is wrong.'

'Oh, so now I'm the one in the wrong?'

'Yes, and you know it. You're doing exactly what Waldo wants you to do.'

Cody knows that there are stinging barbs of truth in those words. He accepts that he's on a slippery slope towards committing unspeakable acts.

He needs time to think, to reflect. He needs some moments of calm and objectivity.

'What I do here is my choice, not your boss's,' he says. 'Don't underestimate me, and don't for a second believe that I won't go much further than I already have.'

And then he leaves the room, wondering how committed he is to the warning he has just issued.

The normality of his apartment seems so remote. As he sits in his living room, he tries to absorb his day-to-day life. He scans the vast array of books he has amassed over the years – all that knowledge, that expression, that poetry. He stares at the shapely guitar on its stand and tries to recall the feel of it in his hands, the gentle sound of its strings. But it's as if he has been tainted so much that he can no longer fully appreciate these wonderful, magical possessions. This environment contrasts so starkly with what he experienced down in Waldo's 'fiery hell'.

He has made a mug of tea, but it sits untouched on the table in front of him, a dark film forming on its surface. He is too lost in thought. He needs someone with whom he can discuss this. Not Waldo, who has his own poisonous agenda, but someone impartial.

But he already knows what they would say. They would tell him to take his captive into police custody. They would tell him that he if he does that now, he may just avoid getting himself into trouble. And what is more, it is simply the *right* thing to do. The man in the basement is still a man. He has rights. He has feelings. He has—

Fuck that.

He has no rights. He gave those up when he attacked me with his mates. I should have choked the life out of him when I had the chance. But I didn't. He lives, and that makes him useful to me. I still have a chance of getting to Waldo.

And so it goes. One ear and then the other whispered into by the tiny angel and devil on his shoulders. He listens carefully to each, and fails to make up his mind.

And time is running out, he thinks. Soon I will need to get washed and dressed and go to work. The dental practice downstairs will open. The building will fill up with orthodontists and nurses and hygienists and patients. How the hell will I get Clueless out of here before then?

As if to provide him with an answer, Cody's phone rings.

He answers it, in full knowledge of who will be on the other end.

'What now?' he asks.

'Top of the morning to you, Cody. You do know it's morning, don't you?'

'Yes, I know.'

'Good. And do you have the answers you want from our man Clueless?'

'I'm working on it.'

'Tick-tock, Cody. I already told you: this is a time-limited offer. You need to get a move on. What has he told you so far? My name? Where I live? How I put the gang together? How we broke the cover of you and your partner?'

He leaves a pause after each question, and Cody doesn't fill any of them.

'Oh, Cody. What a disaster. An opportunity like this, and you're wasting it? Surely you can do better than this?'

'You're beginning to sound like my old schoolteacher. Now, is this call for a reason, or are you just being a nuisance?'

'It's a courtesy call. A status check, if you like. And it sounds to me like you could do with a little help.'

'If it's from you, I'll pass, thanks.'

'Now don't be like that. I'm being genuine. I can help you.'

'Help me how?'

'Let me speak to him. Our mutual friend in your basement.'

'No.'

'Why not? What have you got to lose?' Waldo pauses. 'He is still alive, isn't he? I mean, you haven't diverted the trolley already, have you?'

'He's alive. But I don't think he'll want to speak to you.'

'See, that's where you're going wrong, Cody. Lesson number one: don't think about what *he* wants; this is about what *you* want. Your concerns have to be paramount. You have to regard Clueless as a worm, a bug, a nothing. If he's not bending to your wishes, you have to step on him, grind him under your heel. Do you understand?'

'Okay, then. I'll put it another way: *I* don't want him to speak to you.'

'Lesson number two: listen to those more experienced than yourself. If I say so myself, I'm an expert in these matters. I can get people to talk, whether they want to or not. I can make Clueless talk to you. All I need to do is have a quiet word in his ear. How can there possibly be a catch in an offer like that?'

'I always prefer to see the Terms and Conditions. Until then, the answer is still no.'

'Your loss, Cody. Or perhaps the loss of our clown friend. I'm trying to make it easier on both of you. At least do me the honour of mulling it over. I'll tell you what. Go downstairs again, but take your phone with you. Take another long look at your prisoner and think about my offer. I'll call back in precisely fifteen minutes from now. Whatever decision you make then will be final.'

And then the line goes dead once more.

45

Cody doesn't know why, but every time he comes into this basement room, he expects more. More than just a pathetic, miserable wretch sitting on the cold white floor.

Cody doesn't know what to do with him. Without a wink of sleep, he has no energy, no drive. He would love to retire to his bed for a full ten hours before facing a return to this room. But of course that's impossible.

He hates this man. Hates him with a vengeance. But does he have it within himself to use extreme measures to tease out his information? Is he willing to dole out excruciating physical and mental agony to get to the data locked up inside this creature?

He doesn't think he can do that.

Which is why, when the phone in his hand jumps into life, he already has his answer ready.

'Fifteen minutes precisely,' says Waldo. 'So what's it to be?'

'You can talk to him,' Cody says. 'I'm passing you over now.'

Cody approaches the man, who draws away in fear. He holds out his phone.

'W-what?' says the man.

'Your boss. He wants to speak to you.'

The man shakes his head.

'*Talk to him!*'

The man reaches out, takes the phone, puts it to his ear.

Cody takes several steps back but keeps his eyes on Clueless.

'Yes,' says the man. 'Yes. I understand.' He listens some more.

And then his face changes suddenly. It creases up. Tears spring from his eyes. He lets out a low moan. 'No. Please . . . No. I can't . . . *Noooo!*'

Cody springs across the room, snatches the phone.

'*What did you say?*' he cries. 'What the hell did you say to him?'

'Ah, hello again, Cody. I simply did what you don't seem to be able to do. I asked him to give you some information. Why don't you listen to what he has to tell you?'

Cody looks again at the man, whose eyes are now wide in terror. His lower lip is trembling, as though under tension from the words it has been ordered to shape.

Waldo is still buzzing in Cody's ear. 'Keep the line open, Cody. I want to confirm he tells you what he knows.'

Cody slowly lowers the phone, but doesn't end the call. 'What is it?' he asks. 'What have you got to say to me?'

The man's jaw opens and closes a couple of times. And then: 'They were my ideas.'

'What were?'

'To . . . to use the garden loppers. On your toes. And then to use the knife on your partner's face. They were . . . they were my ideas.' Hastily, he adds, 'But I didn't do it. I didn't think anyone would really—'

But Cody is no longer listening. He is already storming out of the room, his head filled with a pounding and roaring he has never experienced before. He slams the door closed behind him, races up the wooden stairs, into the hallway, up the next stairs to his apartment door, up the last flight of stairs into his apartment. He takes the steps two – sometimes three – at a time. The effort means nothing to him. He is unaware of his heavy breathing, his accelerating heart rate. He knows only the rush of blood and craziness in his head.

He goes first to his bedroom, where he picks up his police handcuffs. Then to the kitchen, where he opens up the cupboard beneath his sink. He drags out his toolbox and opens it up. He starts pulling out items, flinging them to one side, until he finds something suitable. He holds it aloft, studies it for several seconds.

It's a hacksaw.

He is not thinking now about consequences, about ramifications. He doesn't care for such niceties. This is a mission based on blood lust.

He heads back down all those stairs, still refusing to allow logic to poke its goody-two-shoes head through his baser instincts. He yanks open the door to the basement, thuds heavily down the wooden steps, flings open the last door between him and his intended victim.

The briefest of glances tells the man that this could be his end. He sees the madness in Cody's eyes, and he sees the glint of the handcuffs and the weapon held together in Cody's hand, and it is clear that he expects the worst.

He tries to run, but there is only so far he can go. He is chained to the bars over the window, restricting his movement within the room.

Cody closes in, forcing him into a corner. And when the man makes a last-ditch attempt to slip past, Cody grabs the chain and pulls with all his might. The man almost somersaults onto the concrete, and then Cody is on him, and all that Cody can think of is what was done to him, how his toes were snipped from his feet, and how his partner Jeff suffered so horrendously, and now he has one of the people responsible, has him here in this room, with nobody else able to see what happens next. And Cody is intent on exacting his revenge, there is no doubt in his mind that he will do that. And so he sits on the back of the squirming figure and starts to force the man's hands behind his back, and even though the man has the strength of self-preservation, Cody has the greater strength of a need to dispense justice denied to him for too long. He gets the arms into position, snaps on the handcuffs. And now the man is powerless except for the breath he has left, and he uses that breath in cries and pleas that go unheard, not only because the rest of the building is empty, but because Cody himself is deaf to them. They cannot, will not, be allowed to stop him.

Cody does not pause. He spins around on the body beneath him. He moves his weight down to the man's legs, lifts one of his feet. He grabs the shoe, yanks it off without even undoing the laces, peels away the sock in one quick motion.

Then he picks up the hacksaw.

This is it, he thinks. An eye for an eye, a tooth for a tooth.

A toe for a toe.

A face for a face.

46

He brings the hacksaw blade to the man's smallest toe. This is how it started for Cody. Cold steel edges wrapped around his toe, just waiting for the merest flicker of effort to bring them together, severing flesh, snapping bone.

'Who's Waldo?' he cries.

'Please. I don't know. I don't know anything. Please don't . . .'

'Who's Waldo?' Cody repeats.

'I told you. I don't know. I swear to God.'

Cody presses the blade into the button of flesh, begins to cut. A trickle of blood flows. Screams intensify.

And Cody realises that some of those screams are his own.

He flings the hacksaw across the room. Clambers off the man, who is now sobbing for mercy.

Cody sits on the floor, next to the window. He wraps his arms around his legs and draws them in, then rests his chin on his knees. He stares ahead at his captive, waits for the thunder and lightning in his head to move away and for precious calm to return.

So that's it, he thinks. It's over. I can't do it. I can't become what it takes to win this. And maybe that's a good thing. Waldo is trying to make me be like him, and he hasn't succeeded. So maybe I do win after all.

Who am I kidding?

That is so much philosophical bullshit. Waldo gets away with it again. Even this guy – whoever he is – gets away with it. I can't keep him here. And even if I did, I won't get anything out of him. I've already proved to myself that I'm not a torturer.

So either I put him under arrest, in the tissue-thin hope that we can pin something on him in a formal police investigation, or else I let him go. Those are the choices, right? What else is there?

As he contemplates his options, Cody's gaze drifts to the man's shoe. It seems curiously symbolic – the forlorn remnant of a lost battle. Like a museum relic of war or persecution. Except that this particular shoe is brand new. Still has the sticker on the sole.

Cody reaches out and pulls the shoe towards him, dragging it across the dusty floor. He picks it up and studies the sticker.

'Walgrave and Palmer. Sale price £49.99. Last pair!'

And Cody has an idea.

He slips his hand in his pocket and takes out his phone. Uses its camera to take some photos of the shoe. Then he puts the shoe down and goes across to Clueless, who is still face down and handcuffed, his head turned away. Cody grabs him by the shoulder and flips him over. The man turns his face away, as if fearful of being struck. Cody grabs a fistful of shirt and hauls the man into a sitting position.

'Smile,' says Cody.

'What?'

Cody holds up his phone. Clueless doesn't smile, but Cody snaps a shot anyway.

'What . . . what's that for?'

Cody puts his phone away. 'You're going to have to stay here a while.'

'What do you mean? How long?'

'Until I say so.'

'What about you?'

'I'm going to work.'

'Work? You're leaving me here all day?'

'At least. Make yourself comfortable.'

'I can't . . . I mean, you can't . . .'

'I can do what I like, Clueless. If you want this to end sooner, you'll need to give me some answers. Willing to do that?' He waits for a few seconds. 'Thought not.'

Cody retrieves his hacksaw and his baton from the floor. Heads towards the door.

'Wait,' says the man. 'I need . . . I need to pee.'

'I'll get you a bucket.'

'My hands . . .'

Cody nods. 'Okay. I'll be right back.'

'And . . . and I'll get hungry and thirsty.'

'Jesus Christ! Where do you think you are? The Crowne Plaza? You do realise I very nearly started chopping off your toes, don't you?'

Cody gets no reply. He leaves the room, locking it behind him. He goes up to his apartment, then returns with the key to the handcuffs, a bucket, a bottle of water, and two bags of crisps.

As Cody unlocks the cuffs, the man says, 'Crisps? That's it?'

'It's all I—' Cody realises what he's doing. 'What the fuck! You want them or not?'

'I was just saying—'

'Yeah, well don't. Jesus!'

Cody leaves him again. Makes a further trek up the stairs to his apartment. When he gets there, he is hit by a tidal wave of exhaustion. He never sleeps well, but he could really do with an hour or two in bed. The exertion, the stress, the emotion, the adrenaline have all taken their toll.

But now it is morning. A dark, drab March morning to be sure, but morning nonetheless. He needs to get ready for work. He needs to shower, shave, dress, eat, and then turn his focus to the job ahead without letting it drift to what he's left behind in his basement.

So that'll be interesting.

He checks the calendar on his mobile phone for the day's appointments and gets his next shock of the day.

His first meeting is with the police psychologist.

He thinks it's not likely to go well.

47

Sara Prior wakes in the hope that it has all gone away.

Wouldn't it be wonderful, she thinks, to put the light on and see a perfect bedroom? My pictures, my flowers, my clothes, my ornaments – all in one piece, all in their rightful places.

But her hopes are quickly dispelled when her fingers eventually find the lamp switch.

The words 'FUCK YOU' stare back at her in neon orange from the far wall. Her broken pictures are in a pile in the corner of the room, following a half-hearted attempt last night to restore some order. One door of the wardrobe yawns open, hanging precariously from its broken hinges. Stuffing from the mattress and feathers from her pillows are strewn far and wide across the room. She had to cover the wrecked mattress with several thick blankets to make it comfortable enough to lie on last night.

She sits up and swings her legs off the bed. Pushes her feet into her thick slippers before risking the walk across a carpet glistening with countless fragments of broken glass.

She goes out onto the landing and into the bathroom. Putting the light on, she moves straight to what is left of the smashed mirror in the cabinet above the sink.

It's worse than she thought.

The band-aid is still in place and seems to have stemmed the bleeding. She cleaned the wound last night and didn't think it was deep enough to require medical attention.

But her face!

Her cheek is massively swollen, making it difficult to open her left eye, and the whole area is badly bruised. A real shiner, as the English call it.

She turns away from the devastating sight in the mirror to survey the devastation in her bathroom instead. The contents of her cabinet are here, as are the contents of the airing cupboard; it's as if they have exploded out from their confinement to fill a vacuum. The towel rail has been yanked from the stud partition wall and then thrust end-first through the plaster. Ozone has had a whale of a time, as the English might say.

Where to begin? How to even start to fix this? Especially being alone, without Matthew to help her. It's such a mammoth task.

Images of Matthew's house come back to her. The chaos there was of a similar level to that created here. It makes her suspect that Ozone was involved in both. The difference this time is that Ozone wasn't searching for anything; he was simply sending a message.

And the message has struck home.

Ozone was right. The game has been stepped up. Now she is facing thugs with guns. She can't beat those odds.

She wonders about going to the police. She still has Sergeant Cody's card. She could call him. Give him Ozone's name.

But what good will that do? Ozone will have been careful not to leave forensic evidence behind, and he will deny everything.

Even if it could be proven that he was in this house, it wouldn't prove a connection to Matthew's murder.

Besides, she would then have to explain how she found her way to Ozone in the first place. If anything, her own actions would probably land her a heavier jail sentence than Ozone might get for vandalism.

So where does that leave her?

She tries to put the deep thinking to one side for a while. She strips off, takes a shower, then returns to the bedroom and throws on some old, comfortable clothes.

The conversation she had with Cody seems laughable now. *Hygge?* Look at it. Look at this shithole.

She goes down to the kitchen. Steps across a puddle of broken eggs. Picks up one of the few undamaged bowls from the pile of crockery on the floor. Finds a cereal box that still has enough content for a minimal breakfast, and a milk carton that hasn't quite been drained.

She eats standing up, because the barstools are covered with ketchup and mayonnaise and flour. She would like some tea, but is no longer certain where to find it.

When she has finished breakfast, she decides she may as well begin work on the room she's in. It will take a long time just to make it liveable in here. Longer term, she will need to replace all the broken items and have the whole place redecorated.

Especially if she's going to sell up.

That thought came to her last night, and it's not going away. There is nothing left for her here now. She can't have Matthew, and she can't have justice for Matthew. She hates herself for being so defeatist, but there it is. A soldier has to know when to advance and when to retreat.

She places her cereal bowl on the counter next to the sink. She can't even wash it until she has removed all the crap from the basin.

But first thing's first.

She goes out to the hall and picks up the phone. She's almost surprised to discover it's still operational. She flicks through the contacts, dials a number.

'Hello,' she says after a wait. 'Yes, I'd like to book a flight, please . . . Copenhagen . . . This evening.'

48

He walks into Falstaff's office acting as though he's as bouncy as Tigger. Just bursting with *joie de vivre*.

Falstaff is having none of it. She sees through his façade, he can tell.

'How are you this morning, Nathan?' she asks.

'Cody,' he says. 'I prefer Cody.'

'Yes, I'm sorry. So how are you?'

He shrugs. 'Fine.'

'Good. Although . . . you look a little *fraught*.'

Understatement of the year, he thinks. I look like shit. My eyes are red raw, my skin looks like old paper, and I'm having trouble stringing sentences together.

'I'm really busy at work. Early days of a murder investigation, we don't get a lot of sleep.'

'How much sleep, exactly?'

'I'm sorry?'

'Last night. How many hours of sleep did you manage to get?'

'A few. Enough. I'll catch up when we've solved the case.'

'That's a tough way to live. Doesn't it take its toll?'

'I'm young enough to cope.'

Falstaff nods knowingly. She looks down at her notes. 'Just to recap, we were talking about your encounter in the warehouse.'

'Yes.'

'The clowns.'

'Uh-huh.'

Yes, doc, I remember the clowns. I've recently been on a refresher course.

'You got quite upset talking about it.'

'It was a traumatic event. I expect you'd be worried if I hadn't got upset about it.'

Just throwing that out there, he thinks. Not trying to bring you round to my way of thinking or anything . . .

Falstaff doesn't pick up the ball by revealing her thoughts. She says, 'I want to move on now to the child abduction case you worked on recently. The one that put you in hospital. Can you give me a brief run-down on what happened to you?'

He takes a deep breath, then rattles through the tale. The words just seem to tumble out of their own accord, and he's not sure if they are making any sense, but Falstaff keeps on nodding like one of those dogs you used to see on car dashboards. He decides that Falstaff would be a good name for a dog.

When he's done, she says to him, 'That's quite a story. You like to lead an eventful life, don't you?'

You don't know the half of it, he thinks.

'Trouble seems to go out of its way to find me,' he says.

'So it seems. That must have been traumatic too.'

'It was. Not as bad as the other incident, but yeah, it wasn't a barrel of laughs.'

'Did you find it brought back memories of the previous events?'

'How do you mean?'

'Well, did it lead to nightmares? Anxiety? Depression? Perhaps even hallucinations?'

All of the above, Cody thinks. 'I had some bad dreams, but other than that, no. I was assessed during my stay in the hospital.'

Falstaff seems unimpressed by that. Cody gets the feeling she doesn't like to have her opinions influenced by those of her peers.

'And you've been all right since your release?'

'Right as rain.'

He wants to laugh as he says that. Anyone can see what a wreck he is right now.

'No anxiety?'

'No, none.'

He catches her glance towards his leg as he answers, and he realises his leg is bouncing up and down. Practically vibrating. He makes it stop.

'All right,' she says. 'Do you mind if we talk about your family?'

'No, go ahead.'

He relaxes a little. It's a welcome diversion from the topic of clowns.

Speaking of which . . .

He wonders what Clueless is doing now. Contemplating his future? Munching on crisps? Trying to escape?

He can't escape. There's no way he can break through that chain.

There are the bars over the window, though. Are they strong enough? The bars themselves, yes, but what about the screws holding them to the wall? They've been there for many years. Is it possible he could pull them away?

No, don't be ridiculous. He's not breaking out of there.

But does he need to? Isn't it possible he could alert somebody else? The dental practice is just one floor above, and there will be a lot of people up there now. He could shout to them. Would they hear, though? The floor above the basement must be pretty solid. It must be—

He realises that Falstaff is staring at him, and that she is waiting for the answer to a question.

'I'm sorry,' he says. 'What was that?'

'I was asking you about your relationship with your family. Do you get on well with them?'

No point lying about this, he thinks. 'Not really, no.'

'Could you elaborate on that?'

'Well, it's mainly my dad. He has a thing about the police, and so when I decided to join them, he basically disowned me.'

'Do you see the other members of your family?'

'Not much. I love my mum and sister, but they live with my dad, and I'm not welcome there, and my mum is under strict instructions not to see me anywhere else.'

'Do you just have the one sibling?'

'No, I've got a brother too.'

'And what about him? Do you see much of him?'

'No.'

'Same reason? Only you didn't mention him.'

'Different reason. Let's just say that his day-to-day activities are incompatible with mine as a police officer. The less I know about what he's up to, the better.'

'Okay. So to sum up, you have virtually no family support?'

It sounds a harsh judgment, but it's essentially true.

'Yeah, you could say that.'

'Did they rally round when you and your colleague were attacked, or when you were recently hospitalised?'

'Rally round would be putting it too strongly. I saw my mum and sister a little. That's about it.'

'How did that affect you? Emotionally, I mean?'

It kills me, he wants to say. It tears me apart that it's so difficult to go back to the place of my birth, my upbringing. It makes me crumble inside to know that my own father detests what I do, and by extension, me for doing it. It makes me want to cry every time I see my mother hide her feelings for fear of estranging her husband.

'I'm used to it,' he says. 'They're never going to change.'

Falstaff lets it go for the moment. 'What about other people in your life? I see that you're not married, but do you have a partner?'

'Not at the moment.'

'No? Why is that?'

Cody can't get used to the directness of the questions. Nobody else would ask him these things, but slap a doctorate on someone and they think they can quiz you freely.

'Life is too busy.'

'Really? I mean, I don't doubt that your job is a demanding one, but there's a life to be lived outside it, right? So there's no one special?'

'Nope.'

'Okay. Tell me what you do for fun.'

'I read. I play guitar. I jog and work out.'

'They're all very solitary pursuits. What about your social life?'

'I go out occasionally.'

'Yes? What sort of thing? Restaurants, pubs, clubs?'

'That kind of thing.'

'When was the last occasion?'

'I, er . . .'

'A week ago? A month?'

'I, er, I'm not sure.'

She stares at him for a long time. Cody realises his leg is jumping again and puts his hand on it to keep it under control.

'What did you do at Christmas? I take it you didn't go to your parents' house.'

'No. I was working.'

'On Christmas Day?'

'I drew the short straw.'

'Yes, but not the whole day, surely? You must have had some downtime, some time to celebrate?'

'I was . . . I was too tired. I didn't do much.'

'And New Year's?'

'Same story, I'm afraid. Hazard of the job.'

'All right, but I hope it's not always like this. Has there ever been a love interest in your life?'

'Sure,' he says. I'm not a total loser. Just ninety per cent of one.

'Care to tell me about it?'

'I was engaged. Her name's Devon.'

'That's a pretty name. When did it end?'

'About nine months ago.'

'I'm sorry to hear about that. Do you mind telling me why you split up?'

I could, he thinks. I could tell you about the infinite patience she displayed in trying to deal with my sleeplessness and mood swings, and my loss of romantic interest in her. And I could tell you about how I woke up one night thinking she was Waldo, and how I then proceeded to strangle her. I could tell you all that, but of course I'm not going to.

'It . . . it just wasn't working.'

'In what way?'

Oh, can't you just leave it alone now?

'The pressures of the job, I suppose.'

'Yours or hers?'

'Mine.'

'I see. From what you've told me, there are a lot of negatives to this job of yours.'

'It can be stressful, sure. But it can also be the best job in the world. I wouldn't change it for anything.'

Just letting you know, doc, in case there's any doubt.

'Not even for the sake of your fiancée?'

Touché. You asked for that one, Cody.

'That wouldn't be me. Devon got engaged knowing what she was getting into.'

Falstaff nods. 'When did things start to go wrong between the two of you? Before or after your encounter with the clowns?'

Here we go.

'After.' Then he adds, 'Months after.'

The time span doesn't sway Falstaff. 'Do you think there was a connection?'

Something strange happens to Cody as he tries to come up with an appropriate response. It's as if the word 'connection' causes his brain to start concentrating on those associations. Suddenly he is back in the bedroom with Devon. He has his hands around her throat – no, Waldo's throat, because this is Waldo's rubbery visage he can see. The razor-sharp, brown-tinged teeth, the rotting flesh. And he continues to squeeze, even when his mind suddenly transports him to his basement and he's with the man called Clueless now, but still with Cody's fingers around his neck, and he is tightening his grip, cutting off the man's lifeblood and air, whispering to him to die, die, die, you bastard, you fucking—

'Cody! Are you okay?'

He snaps out of his trance. Sees that his fingers are digging hard into his thighs. He blinks several times.

'What?'

'It looked like you zoned out for a few seconds there.'

'Sorry. Just thinking about your question. A connection? No, I don't think so.'

It's a crap answer, an untruthful answer, and Falstaff knows it. But Cody is too thrown to embellish it.

I'm too tired for this shit, he thinks. My head is so screwed up it's starting to play tricks. The last thing I want to happen when I'm sat in front of a shrink.

Falstaff continues to press. 'Are you certain about that? You see, it's the timing that concerns me. You went through an awful ordeal at the hands of those men, and then a few months later your relationship with your fiancée started to fall apart. Quite often, post-traumatic stress can give rise to problems months or even years after the event itself. Do you understand why I'm asking?'

Yes, I'm not a fucking child. Get off my back.

'Yes, I understand. And no, I still don't think it's connected. Break-ups happen. I imagine divorces and separations are probably more common among police officers than in many other professions.'

Falstaff neither denies nor confirms the statistic. She just stares at him for a while, as though trying to look behind his face.

I've seen behind a face, he thinks. Literally. I mean *literally!* I have seen what actually exists behind someone's face.

Cody's fingers are digging into his legs again. He takes a deep breath. Lets it out slowly and silently in the hope that Falstaff won't notice.

But you notice everything, don't you, doc? You see all my thoughts and fears. I don't stand a chance here.

She says, 'There's something else I'd like to ask you about before we end the session.'

'Okay.'

She glances at her notes again. 'You worked on a case last October. A serial killer who was leaving dead birds on his victims.'

'Yes, I did.'

'I've been given some information about an operation that took place during that investigation, when you volunteered to search an abandoned building down at the docks.'

Bitch!

How could she? Not Falstaff. *Blunt.* How could she do this to me?

'Okay,' he says.

'The report mentions that you suddenly abandoned the search and raced out of the building.'

Cody remembers it well. He had a panic attack. The clowns were there. Or at least he imagined they were. He lost control and fled the scene.

'I thought I saw someone. I thought they were trying to evade capture.'

'You were wearing body cameras and a microphone, is that right?'

'Yes.'

'And they didn't pick up any signs of another person?'

'No, they didn't.'

'And when you left, and a task force went into the building, they didn't find anyone either, is that correct?'

And then it happens again. Waldo is here, in this room. It's not Falstaff interrogating him, but Waldo. He is staring out maniacally from behind the desk.

'I, er, yes. That's right. But I believed I saw . . .'

'Yes?'

'I believed I saw . . .'

'What did you see?'

I saw *you*, Waldo. *You* were there, hiding in the shadows, waiting to cut my face off, just as you're doing now. You are waiting for me to slip up, to drop my guard, and then you'll jump across the desk, leap across it like a warty toad, and you'll land on me and you will open your slimy mouth and—

Cody jumps to his feet. The chair overturns and crashes to the floor.

'Cody! Cody!'

'I . . . I . . . I have to go.'

And then he rushes out of the room. Gets out of there fast before he compounds the irreparable damage he has already done to himself. He races down the stairs and past the reception and out onto Rodney Street, and then he leans forward and dry-retches and listens to the roar of his world crashing down around him.

He staggers to the iron railings and grabs hold of them, focusing on the shock of their coldness in the hope that it will restore his senses. A kindly voice behind him asks if he is all right, and he turns to see an elderly woman staring at him with concerned eyes.

'Yes. Thank you,' he says.

He manages a weak smile, then points himself towards home and wills his shaky legs to take him there.

A few minutes, he thinks. Just a few minutes in familiar surroundings to calm myself down, to get my shit together again.

What is the matter with me?

But he knows the answer to this. He has had a panic attack. He is suffering from overload. Too much stimulation of his tortured, exhausted brain, like it is being shotgun-blasted with horrific sensory input.

The walk home takes only a couple of minutes, but it seems like an eternity. It feels as though everyone he passes stares at him in wonder, as though every vehicle on the road slows down for its passengers to rubberneck at the spectacle of him.

He eventually reaches the haven of his building and is alarmed for a second as to why the front door is open. But of course the dental practice is open now. Cody's own working pattern usually keeps him away from the building in these hours.

He turns the handle of the internal lobby door and steps into the hallway.

And realises something is wrong. Very wrong.

Simon Teller sees Cody and moves towards him. He is tall, handsome and wealthy, and Cody always struggles not to hold those things against him. But he has given Cody a roof over his head, and for that Cody is grateful.

'Hey, Cody,' says Teller. 'Everything okay?'

Is it that obvious? Cody wonders. One glance is all it takes to see how much I'm suffering?

'Yeah. Why?'

'Well, I don't normally see you here this time of day.'

'Oh. No. I had a local appointment. Thought I'd pick up a couple of things while I was here.'

'Not another orthodontist, I hope?'

'What? No.' He forces out a laugh, but it sounds absurdly false. His focus is too much on other things.

Like the man standing behind Teller, for example.

He does not know this man. Has never seen him before in his life. He is short and bald, and has a large mole in the cleft of his chin. But that's not what interests Cody.

What concerns Cody is that the man is wearing blue overalls. A bit like those being worn by Clueless the clown.

He isn't a clown, though. It is clear in his earnest expression and the way he is checking his watch that he takes his job extremely seriously.

Teller seems to detect the man's impatience. 'Gotta go,' he says to Cody. 'Drop in again for a coffee or something. It'd be good to catch up.'

Cody nods. He watches Teller go, escorting the tradesman.

Leading him towards the door to the basement.

49

Cody finds himself trailing after the two men. He has no alternative.

'Is there a problem?' he asks. He tries to sound jovial and not particularly worried, but he is so tired. Pretending seems to involve so much energy.

'Just the annual boiler service,' Teller answers. 'Why? You haven't had a problem with the heating, have you?'

'No. All good. To be honest, I've never even given a thought as to where the boiler is in this building.'

'It's down in the basement. Probably the best place for it. It's a bit of a noisy old beast.'

'You know what? In all the time I've lived here, I've never once been down to the basement.'

'It's not very exciting. Bit spooky, actually. Do you want to take a look?'

'Sure. I can spare a few minutes.'

Teller digs a large bunch of keys out of his pocket and quickly finds the one to unlock the cellar door.

I've got one just like that, Cody thinks. The key to my deepest fear.

Teller pulls open the door, finds the light switch, starts to lead the way down. Cody follows behind the two men. When he gets to the whitewashed, windowless chamber below, he finds it difficult to keep his eyes from being drawn towards the only locked door.

'As you can see,' Teller says, 'not much down here.' He beckons the engineer. 'Boiler's through here.'

Cody continues to dog the steps of the others, his head swivelling as he continues to check the closed door.

Clueless must be able to hear us out here, he thinks. His chain prevents him from reaching the door, but he could shout, he could call out. And how will I explain that one?

The heat from the boiler room hits Cody as soon as he reaches the doorway. The boiler itself sits high on one wall, clinging to it and looking down on them. It roars angrily as it sucks gas into its furnace and strains to push scalding liquid through the arteries of the building. Teller seems reluctant to go anywhere near it.

'Bloomin' 'eck,' says the engineer. 'That certainly is a beast.'

'Still going strong, though,' says Teller. 'We'll leave you to it.'

He heads out of the room, nodding at Cody to follow him. 'Never have trusted that thing,' he whispers. 'It's going to blow up one day and take the whole street with it.'

'Thanks,' Cody says. 'I'll sleep easier at night knowing that.'

Teller shows his bleached teeth, and it's as if the whole space lights up.

'Did I tell you this used to be a cellar, back when there was a social club here?'

'You did.' He starts to head towards the stairway, hoping that Teller will do likewise.

Teller doesn't budge. 'Pity they didn't leave any booze behind.' He starts gesturing towards the various rooms. 'I think that one was where they kept the barrels for the stuff that was on tap. The delivery men used to roll them down from the street above. And that one was where they kept the crates of beer bottles and the wines and spirits. As for this one . . .'

He starts moving towards the closed door. It seems to Cody that every organ in his body starts clenching.

'I should get to work,' he says. He takes another couple of steps towards the staircase, but Teller doesn't take the hint, and Cody knows he cannot leave the orthodontist down here to discover his prisoner.

Teller continues with his guided tour. 'This room was a small office. For a caretaker, I think. When I moved in, it still had calendars on the wall with pictures of naked women.'

He laughs as he digs out the keys from his pocket again. He selects one, inserts it into the keyhole.

'It's okay,' says Cody. 'I really have to go now.'

Teller tries to turn the key. It doesn't move.

'I've got too many bloody keys on this keyring. Hang on.'

He starts flipping through the keys, searching for the one he needs. Cody's hand slips automatically into his pocket and touches his own key. He wonders if it's the only one, but he can't take that chance.

'Simon. I can't hang around. My boss will have a fit. And haven't you got patients to see?'

Teller checks his watch. 'Shit, yes. Another time, okay? You can have this room if you need more space.'

Cody finds his fake laugh again. 'If you think I'd be able to relax in an empty basement with only that boiler for company, you've got another think coming.'

'You've got a point. Let's get out of here before the beast gets annoyed at you for saying that.'

As Teller puts his keys back in his pocket, Cody wants to breathe a loud sigh of relief. He allows Teller to go ahead of him up the wooden staircase, mainly so that he can act as an obstruction should Teller be tempted to change his mind and turn around.

Then, before he leaves, Cody takes one final lingering look at that locked door.

50

Cody isn't even aware of his drive to work. One minute he's leaving the apartment; the next he's at Stanley Road police station. His mind is a maelstrom: questions mixed with emotions stirred in with the surreal.

Regrets, he has a few. And yes, they are worth mentioning, because basically he has just fucked up his career prospects. Falstaff will have written him off as a basket case. Okay, she won't use those words exactly, but that will undoubtedly be the gist of her report. How could it be otherwise? Given the way he disintegrated before her very eyes, how can she possibly recommend that he be allowed to continue in his current role?

So there's that.

And then there's what to do about Clueless. He can't keep him imprisoned for ever. For one thing, it's against the law.

What's happening now? I mean, right now, in the building?

Has he started shouting and screaming for attention? Has the boiler man heard him and reported it to Simon? What if Simon has decided to unlock the door anyway?

That's going to fuck up not just my career but my liberty. They'll throw away the key. My own 'key to freedom' isn't going to be much help there.

And yet . . .

Why didn't Clueless make a racket when he had the chance?

He knew we were just outside the door. He could easily have made his presence felt. Why would he want to remain undetected in that room?

It can only be because of Waldo. Waldo has something on him. He's able to apply pressure even from a distance. Look at how Clueless went to pieces when his boss spoke to him on the phone. A few words were all it took. That's how powerful, how formidable Waldo is.

When Cody enters the police station, he senses he is being watched and assessed. He tries to act normal, but coppers have a practised eye for these things, honed from years of observing people struggling to compensate for the effects of alcohol or drugs. He knows his own eyes are weary and bloodshot, his posture a little less upright, his reactions a little slower than usual.

What worries him most is that he may have another episode like the one he experienced with the psychologist. The strain he is under now could easily trigger one.

If Waldo appears any time soon, he thinks, here in this station, then I'm done for.

It's yet another way in which my career might end.

Face it, man: shit creek is a beauty spot compared to this.

When he gets upstairs to the home of the Major Incident Team, again he feels all eyes are on him. This is the second time he has shown up for work so late, and on this occasion he looks like he's been through a meat grinder.

His good friend Neil 'Footlong' Ferguson is the first to voice his concern. 'You all right, mate?'

'Yeah,' Cody says. 'You?'

'Yeah. Only, you're looking a bit rough. Did you go on a bender without me last night?'

Cody finds a smile. 'Wouldn't cheat on you like that, would I? Nah, I just couldn't sleep.'

'Right,' says Footlong, patently unconvinced. 'Well, you'd best get some matchsticks under those eyelids of yours. The boss said to send you her way when you got in.'

Cody looks towards Blunt's office. It's already on his to-do list to have a head-to-head with her, but he was planning to wait until he was a bit more composed. Now it looks as though his hand has been forced.

He nods at Footlong, then heads towards Blunt's office. He raps on her door and then pushes it open. He's surprised to see that Webley is in there too.

'Sorry, ma'am,' he says. 'Shall I . . . ?' He jerks his thumb into the space behind him.

'No, Cody. Come in.'

He takes the long walk across her carpet. It feels like the 'green mile': the condemned man's journey to the electric chair. The brows of both Blunt and Webley are furrowed as they study his approach.

'Are you okay, Cody?' Blunt asks.

He pretends to be surprised by the question. 'Fine.'

She stares at him for a while longer, then says, 'Right. Take a seat.'

He wants to be petulant about it and say, *No thanks, I'll stand.* But he doesn't. Instead he lowers himself onto the proffered chair and wonders what this is all about.

Blunt turns to Webley. 'Tell him what you've just told me.'

Webley clears her throat. 'This morning I made a phone call to Ann Staples. You remember, the woman who—'

'Yes, I know who Ann Staples is,' he interrupts, but then realises how sharp he has just sounded.

'Good. That's . . . good. So then you might be interested to hear that I asked her a few things about her boss.'

'Lewis Fulham,' says Cody.

'Fulton. Lewis Fulton.'

'Yes. Him.'

Webley glances at Blunt, then looks at Cody again. 'One of the things I asked her about was Fulton's clothing.'

'His clothing?'

'Specifically, whether she ever remembers seeing him in a maroon woollen sweater. Her answer was a very definite yes. She saw him wearing one just before Christmas.'

'She remembers that?'

'Women notice things like that, Cody. She remembers it in particular because it was exactly the same colour as a collar she'd bought as a Christmas present for her cat.'

Cody mulls this over – no mean feat given the chaos in his head right now.

'Fulton told us he never owned a sweater like that. Said it wasn't his colour.'

'Uh-huh. And that's not all that Ann Staples told me.'

'Go on.'

'I asked her whether Matthew Prior had ever said anything about Fulton coming to his home. According to her, Matthew said it had happened a couple of times. Once when he was still living with his wife, and then to his new place when he moved out.'

'Did she know what the visits were about?'

'Apparently, the first visit was when Matthew wasn't at home. Only Sara was there. Matthew was away on work business, and Fulton would have known that.'

'Interesting.'

'On the second occasion, Fulton dropped off some work documents at Matthew's place. According to Ann, Matthew complained to her that it could easily have waited until after the weekend.'

Cody nods. He knows this is an important development, but he's finding it difficult to summon up the appropriate level of enthusiasm.

Blunt says, 'Good work on Megan's part, don't you think, Cody?'

Cody realises she is supplying the words he should have uttered. His nodding becomes more vigorous.

'Yes, definitely. Nice one, Megan. We should ... we need to talk to Fulton again.'

He sees how Megan frowns when he stumbles over his words. Then her gaze drops to his hands, and he realises she has noticed the grazes on his knuckles. He quickly covers them up with his other hand.

'Bring him in this time,' says Blunt. 'Put him in unfamiliar territory. I want him to know we mean business now. No more pissing about.'

Webley stands, ready to leave. She looks down at Cody, expecting him to do the same.

Cody turns to Blunt. 'I'd like to discuss something else, if that's okay.'

'Does it involve Megan?'

'No.'

He glances at Webley as he says this and sees her irritation at being left out. When she exits the room, she closes the door a little more firmly than is necessary.

'You sure you're all right, Nathan?' says Blunt.

He hates it when she calls him Nathan. He believes she does it when she wants to disarm him.

'Actually, no. I'm not.'

'Thought as much. What's up?'

'I had another session with the psychologist this morning.'

'Oh, yes. How did it go?'

'It could have been easier. I could have done without your contribution.'

'Explain, please.'

Cody sits up straight in his chair. He's just getting started.

'I don't like having to see a shrink, especially when I don't think it's necessary. They ask all sorts of personal, ridiculous questions that have no bearing on anything whatsoever, and all because they have this compulsion to slot us into one of their neat little pigeonholes. But you know what? I'm willing to go along with the whole charade. If it helps to convince you and the force that I can do my job, even though I've never presented you with any evidence to the contrary, then I can put up with the stupid mind games.'

'So what's the problem?'

'The *problem* . . . the problem is when my superior officer goes out of her way to make things difficult for me. The problem is you doing your best to sabotage my career. That's what the problem is.'

Cody can hear his own voice rising in both tone and volume. He knows he should contain his anger. He should reach out, gather it in and push it back inside. But it's too big a force to embrace, and it seems to be growing in strength.

'Nathan, you know as well as I do that the sessions with the psychologist were unavoidable. After all you'd been through—'

'I'm not talking about the sessions. I'm talking about your personal input. Your little anecdote about the time I carried out the search of that building at the docks.'

A light seems to switch on in Blunt's eyes. 'Ah, that.'

'Yes, that. What was that all about? I mean, why did you think it necessary to even mention it?'

Blunt sits back, as if to provide a distance that will allow some calm to intervene.

She says, 'As your commanding officer, I made the referral to Falstaff. As part of that referral, I was asked to comment on any aspects of your behaviour that have given me cause for concern in the past. To be perfectly honest, Nathan, I was spoilt for choice. There were others I could have mentioned, but that's the one I settled on.'

'But I explained my actions to you at the time. I told you what I thought I saw and heard.'

'Yes, you did. But the cameras and microphones told a different story. Either you made a simple mistake, or else it was symptomatic of something more serious going on – something I couldn't ignore.'

'And you chose the latter? Why? Why not just go with my explanation? Why bother to mention it to Falstaff at all?'

'Lie, you mean? Pretend I have no concerns about you? I'm sorry, but that's not how this works. The whole point of your sessions with Falstaff is to get you properly checked out. We're not going to do that by working with falsehoods.'

'But what you told her is a falsehood. I'm perfectly fine, but all you've done is put doubt in her mind about me. You've put my job on the line, and for what? What the fuck does that achieve?'

Blunt leans forward again. Closes the gap to achieve an intimacy.

'Listen to me, Nathan. If you were anyone else in front of me right now, I'd chuck you out of my office and have you on a disciplinary charge. You are skating on very thin ice. You want me to be honest? Then here it is. Here's what I think. You have problems. It has been clear to me for a long time that you have issues. What I don't know – what I'm not qualified to assess – is how serious those issues are. That's where Falstaff comes in. I have used her before and I trust her professionalism and ability. She will tell me – she will tell both of us – if you need help. And if that's the case, I will go to the ends of the earth to make sure you get that help. This isn't about trying to end your career. You are without doubt one of the best coppers I have ever worked with. It's about looking after you. It's about caring.'

She stops then, not least because it seems to Cody that her voice is choking. That was a heartfelt speech, and it has robbed Cody's fury of much of its venom. He wonders not only *how* she manages to accomplish such bomb disposal, but *why*. What is it about their relationship that causes her to make such allowances for him?

But, in the end, what does it matter? Falstaff's report is going to be so damning that he'll be out of here seconds after Blunt reads it. There'll be no 'helping' from Blunt then, none of her 'caring', because in that instant he'll be seen as too much of a liability to be allowed within a hundred yards of any criminal investigation.

He gets up from his chair. 'I've got to go. I've got crimes to solve.'

'Yes, you do,' says Blunt. 'And long may it continue.'

51

Lewis Fulton isn't happy about being subjected to more questions. He's even less happy about being brought in to the police station to answer them.

'This isn't ideal, you know,' he tells Cody and Webley. 'We're getting towards the end of the tax year. It's a busy time for us.'

'We understand,' Cody says. 'And we'll keep it brief. Just to be clear: you're not in custody. We're not charging you with anything. That means you're free to leave at any time. Right now, you're just helping us with our enquiries.'

'I've already told you, I don't want to give any DNA samples or whatever. I can still say that, right?'

'Yes, you can still refuse. All we want to do for now is clear a few things up.'

'Couldn't we have done this back at my office?'

'It's better that we do it here. The investigation into the death of Matthew Prior has reached a critical phase, and we need to make sure we do everything by the book.'

Pure bullshit, of course, but it seems to have the desired effect of putting a red-hot poker up Fulton's arse.

'Oh,' he says. 'Oh. I didn't realise.'

'Yeah, so if you'll bear with us . . .'

'Sure. Okay.'

Webley fires the first salvo. 'The last time we spoke, I asked you about a maroon woollen sweater, and you told us that you'd never owned one.'

'Yes, that's right. I said it wasn't my colour.'

'You have a good memory. That's exactly what you said. Do you still stand by that answer?'

'Of course. Why wouldn't I?'

'Well, it's just that we are in receipt of a report that suggests otherwise.'

'Suggests . . . I'm sorry, what do you mean?'

'I mean there's a claim you have been seen wearing a sweater matching precisely that description.'

'What? What are you talking about?'

'Do you deny it?'

'Damn right I deny it.'

'This would have been not long before Christmas. Maybe you thought you'd wear something more colourful to get in the Christmas spirit?'

'No. Not at all. I don't own a red sweater. Never have and never will. Who the hell told you this?'

Webley ignores the question, and puts another of her own. 'You told us you sometimes shop at Marston's. Is that right?'

'Yes, but only sometimes.'

'Could you have bought such a sweater there?'

'No, I couldn't. And the reason I know that is because I haven't bought such a sweater anywhere.'

'So if we were to go with you to your house right now, we wouldn't find a sweater like that hanging up in your wardrobe?'

'Not unless you've planted it there, no.'

The intentional slur does nothing to help Cody's mood. He says, 'Or any fibres?'

'What?'

'A woollen garment like that will shed fibres, especially onto the clothes next to it in a closet or a drawer. Are you saying we wouldn't find any fibres like that?'

Fulton hesitates for a fraction of a second. 'Yes, that's exactly what I'm saying.'

'Because forensic technology is so advanced now, if there's a fibre to find – on the carpet, in the washing machine, between the floorboards – then our guys will find it.'

'I ... I don't recall ever wearing anything of that colour. I mean, maybe I've got something with a *bit* of that colour in it. Do you know what I'm saying? Not the whole jumper, but maybe there's a *bit* of red in there somewhere.'

'Sure. I get you. But we don't just consider colour. Our technicians will compare fibre length, thickness, cross-section, the chemical composition of the dye – all that. We can match fibres precisely.'

'I see.'

'Yes. But you've never had a sweater like that?'

'No.'

Cody stares at him. Leaves him in no doubt he's under the microscope.

Webley breaks into the awkward silence. 'Something else I asked you about was whether you ever went into Matthew Prior's home. You told us you never did. Again, do you want to stick with that answer?'

The hesitation is longer this time. 'I . . . yes. I don't recall ever going into Matthew's house.'

'Which house?'

'I'm sorry?'

'The one in Halewood, where he used to live with his wife Sara? Or the one he moved to in Aintree?'

'I don't think I've ever been in either of them.'

'You think that, or you know that?'

'I . . . I'm pretty sure of it.'

'Okay. Because again the information we've been given recently conflicts with your answer.'

'Then my advice would be that you need to start getting your information from a more reliable source.'

Cody decides to take a gamble. 'I think Sara Prior is a pretty reliable source.'

Fulton blinks as he switches his gaze from Webley to Cody. 'What?'

'I think I would trust her to remember whether you ever set foot in her house.'

'Is . . . is that what she told you?'

'Is it the truth?'

'It . . . it might be.'

Bingo.

'So you have been to the Priors' house?'

'Yes. Just once.'

'What was the reason for your visit?'

'I . . .'

'Yes?'

'I wanted . . . Look, has Sara already told you about this?'

'We want to hear your version.'

There's a long pause. And then: 'I wanted to see Sara. Alone. I mean, without Matthew.'

'Why?'

'Because . . . because I liked her. I thought I could get to know her better.'

'Why?'

'Isn't it obvious?'

'You were hoping to have an affair with her?'

'Well, maybe not an affair. I suppose I wanted to check out their relationship, see if it was on the rocks.'

'And was it?'

'No.' He shakes his head. 'No. If anything, they seemed like the perfect couple. I never went back after that.'

'How blatant were you with Sara? Did you come out and tell her you were interested in her?'

'God, no. I'm not stupid. I just acted like a friend.'

'Did she see it that way?'

'I hope so. I mean, she didn't throw me out or anything.'

'Didn't she wonder why you'd turned up when Matthew was away on business?'

'I made something up. I told her I was just passing, and thought I'd drop in. I said I'd forgotten about Matthew's work trip.'

'So she wasn't upset by your visit?'

'No. Did she say she was?'

'Any idea what she said to Matthew about it?'

'Not in detail. He mentioned it to me the next time I saw him, but he didn't seem bothered by it.'

'Are you sure? No animosity?'

'No. None.'

'So why did you lie to us? Why did you tell us you'd never been to Matthew's house?'

'Isn't it obvious? Matthew was murdered. Telling you that I was doing my best to chat up his wife some time before that doesn't exactly look good for me, does it?'

Webley takes the reins again. 'And what about Matthew's new place? When did you go there?'

Fulton looks puzzled. 'I never did. I already told you that.'

'Once again, we've heard otherwise.'

'And once again, your information is completely inaccurate. As I said to you when we first met, I didn't even know Matthew and Sara had separated.'

'Do you know where he was living when he was murdered?'

'I do now, but only because it's been in all the news reports. I had no idea before that. Matthew certainly didn't file a change of address with me.'

'So you didn't drop in on him to hand over urgent work documents?'

'No. I've never done that with anyone who works for me.'

'Why would Matthew say you did?'

'Did he? When? Who did he tell— Oh, hang on! Have you been talking to Ann Staples again? You have, haven't you? The sneaky bitch. The sneaky little—'

'We're not at liberty to divulge our sources, Mr Fulton. We just need to know if it's true that you visited Matthew at his Aintree address.'

'Categorically no. I never went to that house. I was never aware that Matthew was living there. Anyone who says different is a liar.'

'It was you who told us you'd never been to Matthew's previous address.'

'Well, yes. But I've owned up to that now. I've come clean. I'm not lying about Matthew's new address, and I wasn't lying about the sweater.'

'So we won't discover any forensic evidence to suggest you visited the house where Matthew was found dead?'

'No. Definitely not.'

'You say you're coming clean. Now's the time to get everything out in the open.'

'I swear. I haven't been there. Ever.'

Webley looks across at Cody. He says, 'There's one way we can clear this up, of course.'

'What's that?' says Fulton.

'You could volunteer to give us your fingerprints and a DNA sample. We could compare it with the evidence we have from the crime scene.'

'You asked me for that before.'

'And you said no. You can still say no, or you can do something to help both us and yourself. Why not take yourself off our radar while you have the opportunity?'

Fulton looks at each of the detectives in turn. Cody fully expects a negative answer again. This man doesn't like the police, he resents being accused of involvement in a crime, and he seems to feel the whole world is against him. Even if he is innocent, he will probably say no just to make things awkward for everyone else.

'All right,' says Fulton. 'I'll do it.'

They leave Fulton alone in the interview room for a few minutes. Outside, Webley says to Cody, 'What do you think?'

'Not sure. He may be clean. On the other hand, he may have had help killing Prior, and is gambling on the hope that the forensic evidence we have belongs to one of his associates.'

Webley nods. 'We'll know soon enough.'

'Yeah. You mind taking care of the prints and samples?'

'Sure. You off somewhere?'

'There's a couple of things I need to take care of.'

'Connected with the case?'

'Kind of.'

'Well, do you fancy letting me in on it?'

'If it pays off, you'll be the first to know.'

She gives him a look he remembers well from the time when they were going out together. A look that says, *You're hiding something*.

'Cody, are you sure everything is all right?'

'Yes!' he snaps. 'I'm fine. Why does everyone keep asking me if I'm okay? Jesus!'

And then he turns and marches away, his mind raging at this latest step on his path to self-destruction.

52

Walgrave and Palmer is almost an anachronism on Castle Street in the city's business district. It sits discreetly between its brasher neighbours, relying on reputation and word of mouth for its clientele rather than gaudy neon announcements as to its presence. No loud music blares from its doorway: one has to step across the threshold to be bathed by its soothing violin concertos. Inside, there are no training shoes or, heaven forbid, flip-flops. The air is suffused with the aromas of supple Italian leather and high-grade polish. Where many other shoe shops employ gum-chewing, floppy-haired, tattooed youths who barely know a left foot from a right, this particular emporium is staffed only by its owners: the esteemed Mr Walgrave and the erudite Mr Palmer.

As Cody approaches the counter, he is acutely aware that the pair are studying him intently. They look to be in their late fifties, and both are smartly attired in three-piece suits – one a slightly darker shade of grey than the other. Cody is willing to bet that the shoes they are now wearing bear not a single scuff mark, in direct contrast to his own shabby, misshapen footwear. He is also willing to bet that Walgrave is the one on the left, and that they always stand in that configuration – the Ant and Dec of the shoe world.

'Hello,' says Cody, in a somewhat hushed tone. He feels like he's in a library.

The first man nods his head, as though he is meeting royalty. 'Good morning, sir.' He turns to his colleague. 'A ten, wouldn't you say, Mr Palmer?'

'Most definitely, Mr Walgrave.'

'I'm sorry?' says Cody, wondering what his score is for, and whether the scale goes higher than ten.

'Your shoes, sir. Size ten, if I'm not mistaken.'

'Oh,' says Cody. 'Yes. I'm a ten.'

'And forgive me for saying so, but you exhibit a noticeable ambulatory perturbation. An over-compensation for some anomaly, perhaps?'

'I'm sorry?' Cody says again.

Walgrave lines up his hands in front of him, then shifts them so they are askew, as if that might explain things. 'There is a distinct imbalance when you place your feet, as if you are experiencing some slight difficulty in walking.'

'Oh, that. Yes. I have some toes missing. Two on each foot.'

'That would certainly account for it. How unfortunate.'

'An impediment indeed,' says Palmer.

Walgrave turns to his left again. 'Very amusing, Mr Palmer. Greek?'

'Latin.'

'Yes, of course.'

'I'm—' Cody begins, then realises he was about to say sorry for the third time. 'Excuse me?'

'Mr Palmer was making a little joke. The word impediment, you see, derives from the Latin word for foot. It means literally to have a shackled foot.'

An image of someone else with a shackled foot jumps to Cody's mind.

'From that root we also get the words biped and pedal,' Walgrave continues.

'And also pedestrian, pedicure, pedestal and centipede,' says Palmer.

'But not paediatrician or paedophile.'

'No. They *are* from the Greek. The word there means "child".'

'I see,' says Cody. 'Anyway, I was wondering if you could help me.'

'We most certainly could, and it would be our pleasure so to do. Although, it's a pity you didn't come to us some time ago.'

'It is?'

'Yes. Those items currently encasing your fortune-stricken feet are not doing anything to correct the situation.'

'In fact,' Palmer adds, 'they are making it much worse.'

'In time, your gait will deteriorate, and you will begin to suffer pain in your legs and then your back.'

'If we intervene now, however, there is much we can to do to improve matters without sacrificing aesthetic quality.'

'You misunderstand me,' says Cody. 'I didn't come here to buy shoes.'

The two men go quiet, and stare at Cody as though he has just spoken in an alien tongue. Cody reaches into his jacket and produces his warrant card.

'I'm a police officer.'

'Ah,' says Walgrave. 'A member of the constabulary.'

'One of our boys in blue,' says Palmer.

'We see many of your colleagues here. As I understand it, your occupation entails a considerable amount of walking. The health of one's feet is of paramount importance in a job such as yours.'

'Yes,' Cody says, 'but that's not what I've come here about. Just a sec . . .' He reaches into his pocket again, takes out his phone and finds a photograph of the shoe belonging to Clueless.

'Do you recognise this?'

Both men bend forward in unison, as though they are about to embark on a synchronised Olympic dive.

'Ah, yes. The Oxbridge Endeavour. A very fine shoe. The manufacturers make use of a unique—'

'This was a sale item. Last pair in the shop, at £49.99.'

'Absolute bargain! Rest assured that you won't find a shoe of that quality at a better—'

'Do you know who bought it?'

'I can do better than that,' says Walgrave, holding back his excitement. 'I know who bought the pair!'

The two men laugh uproariously at the joke, but Cody has attached himself solely to the fact that he is getting close to knowing who Clueless is.

'And?'

'Sir?' says Walgrave when he regains his composure.

'The man who bought these shoes. Who was it?'

'Well, sir, as I'm sure you will appreciate, discretion is our watchword here at Walgrave and Palmer. Our loyal customers shop with us on the express understanding that any information they impart will be treated with the utmost confidentiality.'

Jesus, thinks Cody. This is like something out of a John le Carré novel.

But he knows he won't get very far by trying to get tough with these two. They would demand he take the formal route, and there's no way he can obtain a warrant for an unauthorised jaunt like this.

'Look,' he says. 'I work for the Major Incident Team. That should tell you that this is a serious matter, and time is of the essence. I really wouldn't be bothering you if it wasn't urgent.'

Walgrave and Palmer exchange glances.

'Perhaps there is a way,' says Walgrave.

'I'm listening.'

'Perhaps if sir were to become a member of our exclusive clientele, thereby entering into the cadre of gentlemen who appreciate the ethos we embody here at W and P . . .'

'I'm sorry?' says Cody, not realising he has just made the third such utterance.

Palmer leans across the counter and peers down at Cody's feet.

'You want me to buy some shoes?' Cody says.

'We would like you to immerse yourself in the Walgrave and Palmer experience. We would like you to take measures to improve the health and wellbeing of your feet, your posture, your whole body. We would like you to—'

'Right! I get it. Okay. But first the name.'

Walgrave closes his eyes for a second, as if reading a name on the back of his eyelids.

'Those shoes were bought by Mr Keenan. Mr James Keenan.'

Cody flips to the next photograph on his phone.

'Is this him? Is this Keenan?'

'Not the most flattering image of him, but yes, that is indeed Mr Keenan.'

'I don't suppose you have an address for him?'

'We have his telephone number.'

'But not his address?'

Palmer raises a finger. 'If I may interject. It was once my most earnest ambition to become a detective.'

Walgrave looks astonished. 'I didn't know that about you.'

'Yes indeed. In my youth I lived vicariously through the likes of Hercule Poirot and Sherlock Holmes. Perhaps I may be permitted to put some of the skills I acquired to the test now?'

'Be my guest, Mr Palmer.'

Palmer opens a ledger on the counter. He flips through the pages, runs his finger down a column, jots a number down on his notepad. Next, he smiles, reaches beneath the counter and, with a flourish, brings a book into view.

It's a telephone directory.

A few seconds later, Palmer is reading out Keenan's address. He slams the book shut in triumph.

Walgrave offers a smattering of applause. 'Bravo, Mr Palmer.'

'Much appreciated,' says Cody. 'You've been a great help. Thank you so much.'

He puts his phone away, begins to step away from the counter. He is stopped by the sight of the two men bending forwards and peering at his feet again.

'I believe we concluded that sir takes a size ten.'

53

Webley suspects that Cody will blow his top when he finds out.

Well, fuck him.

If he insists on acting so weird, then he should expect others to react appropriately. And this is appropriate.

She gets her first shock when the front door is opened. Sara Prior's face is a mess. The large plaster on her cheek strains to contain a bulge the colours of a stormy sky. Her eye is half-closed.

Webley's mind jumps to the image of Cody's grazed knuckles.

No. Surely not.

Webley holds out her warrant card. 'Mrs Prior? We haven't met. I'm Detective Constable Megan Webley from the Major Incident Team.'

'Hello,' says Sara. 'So you work with Sergeant Cody?'

'Yes, that's right. We're both investigating the murder of your husband.'

Although it doesn't always seem that way, she thinks.

'I see. Have you come to give me some news about the case?'

Good question, Webley thinks. What have I come here for?

To check up on Cody – that's why. I've got much better things to do, but that arsehole has driven me to this.

'Do you mind if we talk inside?'

'It's . . . it's not very convenient at the moment.'

Sara keeps the door only slightly ajar as she says this, her body obscuring Webley's view of the interior of the house.

What is going on? Is Cody in there with her? Is that where he's disappeared to?

Webley makes a show of wrapping her arms around herself. 'It's a bit nippy out here. I wouldn't mind a cup of tea while we chat.'

Sara thinks about this for a while. Reluctantly it seems, she opens the door wider and steps aside.

'Thank you,' says Webley. She steps across the threshold and immediately her mouth drops open. 'Holy shit.' She turns to Sara behind her. 'What the hell happened here?'

Sara folds her arms. 'Somebody broke in.'

'And your face?'

Sara brings a hand to her cheek. 'This? No. I fell. I tripped over the mess.'

Webley looks again at the devastation. Uninvited, she walks through to the kitchen and then the living room.

'Is the whole house like this?'

'Pretty much.'

'Have you reported it? To the police, I mean?'

'I don't want to report it.'

'What do you mean? Why wouldn't you report this?'

'What would be the point? I think there are people who blame me for Matthew's death. That's why they did this. If you catch the real killer, they will know they got it wrong. That's enough for me.'

Webley shakes her head. 'I'm sorry, but this is still a crime. Whatever their reasons, somebody has broken in and trashed your house. I would strongly advise you to report this.'

Sara merely shrugs, and with that gesture whatever sympathy Webley might have held for this woman is washed clean away.

'Sara, what's really going on here?'

'I don't understand.'

Webley waves a hand to indicate the chaos. 'This isn't someone who thinks you killed your husband. You might get a brick through your window, but this is several levels above that. And that eye of yours? Somebody hit you, didn't they?'

'I told you. I fell.'

Webley takes a few steps towards Sara. She says, 'You know who killed Matthew, don't you?'

'No. I—'

'This was a warning from the killer, telling you to back off.'

'No.'

'Well, it's either that, or else you're involved. You had a hand in Matthew's death. And before you say it, yes, I know you were thousands of feet in the air when it happened. You've got the perfect alibi. Very convenient, really.'

'I don't need an alibi. I had nothing to do with it.'

'Whatever. You know more than you're saying. Some of us are working our butts off trying to help you. Day and night we are doing everything we can to catch the person who hammered nails into the body of your husband. You could help us, but you choose not to. I hope you can live with that. I don't often say this to the family of victims, but it's very possible that, in this instance, we are not going to catch whoever did this, simply because we don't have enough information. Think about that, Sara. When you're ready to talk, give me a call.'

Furious, she starts to walk away, but then Sara stops her.

'Is that the only reason you came here? To make accusations? Did Sergeant Cody send you here to do this?'

The mention of Cody's name pours petrol on Webley's flames. 'No, DS Cody did not send me here. For some strange reason, DS Cody seems to think that you can do no wrong. He seems unable to see what should be obvious to a blind person. I don't know what spell you managed to cast over him, but it's not working with me. I came here for one reason only, and that's to get to the truth. At some point you need to decide if that's what you want too.'

The new shoes are a revelation. Expensive, but wonderful. He can't fault them for either comfort or looks. He's not certain, but he does feel as though they gently coax him to walk more properly. They even make him feel taller.

It's almost a shame to cover them up.

He is standing in the lobby of Keenan's house, the front door now firmly shut behind him. Getting this far wasn't difficult. He simply marched straight up to the door as though he were a visiting salesman, then rang the bell with his elbow. When it wasn't answered, he checked that nobody could see him in the porch, then donned a pair of blue latex gloves and used Keenan's own key to open the door.

From the small bag he brought with him, Cody takes out a full crime scene outfit and puts it on: suit, overshoes, hairnet, and mask. He's not sure what the fate of Clueless – or Keenan, as he now knows him – will be, but if the police ever inspect this house, he doesn't want them to find any evidence that might point them in his direction.

He begins his search.

The problem is that he's not sure what he's looking for. He came here hoping for some kind of lead to either the identity or whereabouts of Waldo, but he has no idea what form it might take.

He spends nearly half an hour looking for it.

What he discovers from looking through the various documents in drawers and boxes is that Keenan lives alone, he has an MA in Business Management, he makes his living as a financial advisor, he plays tennis and squash, and he's a fan of Elton John.

At the same time, it nags Cody that he's not getting a complete picture here. It's almost as if this record of Keenan's life has been subtly edited, like a redacted transcript. For example, there are no photographs of family or partners. There is no address book. There are no highly personal letters to loved ones.

It occurs to Cody that Waldo et al may have already been here and sanitised the place, in the same way that they took away Keenan's phone and all forms of identification.

But then Cody finds the laptop.

It's in a drawer of the farmhouse-style kitchen table. Not the most obvious place for high-tech equipment, but Cody can picture Keenan pulling up a chair to work at this space.

Cody picks up the laptop and stares at it for a few seconds. He's not *au fait* enough with computers to delve into the secrets it may hide.

But he knows someone who is.

54

It doesn't come as a major surprise to find that Webley is waiting for him when he gets back to the station. His departure was sudden and unexplained to say the least. The problem he has now is that he hasn't put any thought into a reason for his absence.

'Have you got a minute?' she asks him.

'Sure.'

'In private.'

He nods and follows her out to one of the interview rooms. Webley closes the door and turns towards him.

'Do you mind if I ask where you disappeared to earlier?'

'I was just following up on a couple of things.'

'Oh. Okay. Is it all right if I ask what they were?'

'It was nothing. A shot in the dark. It didn't lead anywhere.'

'Well, was it connected with the Matthew Prior case?'

'Megan, what is this? Do we need to switch on the interview recorders? Do you want to caution me?'

'Don't be a twat, Cody. I'm trying to help you.'

'Really? Is that what this is? Because it's starting to sound like you've been promoted to inspector while I've been out.'

'Don't bring rank into this. You might be my sergeant, but you're also my friend. What the hell is going on with you?'

'I told you. I was checking out some stuff.'

'That's nice and specific. I'm glad it was work-related and not, say, just popping out to buy new shoes.'

Cody looks down at his shiny new footwear. Idiot, he thinks. Why didn't it occur to you that somebody would notice?

'I threw in an early lunch break while I was in town. Bought some shoes while I was at it.'

Webley throws her arms up. 'Well, that's just great. So nice to see how preoccupied you are with this case.'

'Don't patronise me, Megan. I'm working as hard as anybody else on this investigation, if not harder.'

'Really? Then I suppose you'll know all about Sara Prior.'

'What about her?'

'That she's been in a fight.'

Cody blows air out of the side of his mouth.

'You've heard, then. How did you find out?'

'Wait, what? You *know*?'

'Yeah. I was going to tell you, but . . .'

'But what? You didn't think it was important enough? The woman looks to me like she might need stitches. Her house is a war zone. She—'

'Hold on, hold on. What are we talking about here?'

Webley stares at him. 'Sara Prior. She's been punched in the face. Her house has been vandalised. What is it *you're* talking about?'

'Not that. I thought you were talking about something else.'

'What exactly?'

'Nothing. Has Sara reported it?'

Webley loses it then. 'Forget it, Cody. I'm not playing by your rules anymore. I'm not giving you everything while you give me nothing in return. You want to know about Sara, go talk to her yourself.'

She opens the door and storms off in the direction of the ladies' toilets.

Cody decides it's best not to follow.

55

She sees everything.

There are advantages to having a desk in a dimly lit recess at the back of the room. From here she can see all the comings and goings. This is her theatre.

Grace Meade is an intelligence analyst. A civilian, but still a key member of the Major Incident Team. At least, that's what they tell her. She's not always convinced. Self-doubt has always been her crippling nemesis.

She's had her moments, though. No denying that. Made a couple of vital contributions that have helped to crack cases that were beyond the capabilities of the experienced detectives.

Even those of Sergeant Cody.

She watches him most of all. Not in a creepy, stalker way, but because she admires him greatly. She likes to watch how he works, how he manages his more junior colleagues.

He has an interesting past, does Cody. She often suspects it impacts on him more than he lets on. He seems unusually tired today. Stressed. Grace knows about stress. Anxiety follows her everywhere she goes. She noticed that Cody came into work late again this morning, and she wonders if that might have something to do with his demeanour.

It's the interplay between the various characters in this room that most interests Grace. DCI Blunt, for example, presents a masterclass in how to run a tight ship when she addresses her team. Yes, she can be scary at times, but Grace has learned so much from her about how a woman can maintain control of a room that is predominantly filled with highly assertive men.

She wishes she could bring herself to be a bit more like Blunt.

And then there are the frequent exchanges between Cody and Webley. A microcosm of human behaviour right there. To the casual onlooker, much of it consists simply of interactions arising from the job – a constable reporting to, or seeking advice from, her sergeant. But Grace sees below that surface. She sees how close they get when they stand next to each other. She sees the contact – nothing overtly sexual; just a feather-light touch of an arm, the fleeting press of a hand into the small of the back.

She wonders what will become of their relationship. Will it blossom or wither?

Probably the latter, if recent events are anything to go by.

Even before Webley approached Cody at his desk, Grace could tell that something was awry. Webley kept staring at the door, clicking her biro while waiting for him to arrive. And, as soon as he appeared, she was on him like a sparrowhawk, digging in her talons and dragging him out of the room.

Okay, Grace thinks, maybe I'm being a bit unfair on Webley there. But something has happened. She's not looking his way any longer. If anything, the pair are doing their utmost to avoid all eye contact with each other.

But not with me, though.

There he goes again! Cody, glancing round to look at me. Why does he keep doing that?

And now he's decided to stand. Perhaps he's going to make it up with Webley, or he needs to talk to Blunt, or he just fancies a coffee, or—

No. He's heading in my direction. What could he possibly want with me? But here he is. Right next to me. Leaning forwards. Whispering.

'Can I have a quiet word, Grace?'

Grace nods, and then Cody beckons her with a head tilt to follow him out of the room, and now she's flustered, she doesn't know what this is, doesn't know why it's all so secretive.

For a few seconds she doesn't move. She would like to think that this is something good, something that might require her to pop a Tic-Tac into her mouth, but her lack of self-worth is already opening holes in that thought. What have you done wrong? it asks her. Why are you in trouble?

She gets up. Sees that Webley notices, which both pleases and frightens her. Then she goes in search of Cody.

He's in the corridor, just outside the door. He's looking left and right to ensure nobody is watching.

Calm yourself, she thinks. You know what happens when you build your hopes up. They always come crashing down. Expect the worst, because that's what you always get.

But then Cody says, 'I need to talk to you.'

'All right. Have I done something wrong?'

'No. Nothing like that.'

'Is it about a case?'

'No. I just need to talk, but not here.'

Grace gestures towards an interview room. 'We could go in there.'

Cody shakes his head. 'We can't do it here. You don't have any plans this evening, do you?'

Grace has to fight to keep her jaw in place. Plans? Me? What kind of plans would I have?

'No. I'm available.' She regrets using the word 'available' as soon as it leaves her mouth.

'Would you mind if I called in at your house after work?'

'Er . . . okay. I mean, if you really want to.'

Cody brings out his phone. 'Great. What's your address?'

She tells him, and he types it in.

'Brilliant! Thank you, Grace. I'll see you later.'

He moves away, heads back to his desk.

Grace is already making a mental note to pick up a bottle of wine on the way home.

56

Sara Prior pushes her car down the outside lane of the motorway. She just wants to get to the airport now. Hop on that plane, drink some gin and forget about all that she's leaving behind her.

A part of her wonders if she'll ever come back. Her father knows lots of people in the UK. He could arrange to pack up her things and ship them out, and then sell the house.

She knows it doesn't look good. Fleeing the country like this will only cast extra suspicion on her.

Well, tough shit. Let them extradite me if they can. Might be better if they concentrate on finding the real culprits, though. That'd be a refreshing change.

They're not going to catch them. They're not competent enough. And no, Detective Constable Webley, I'm not to blame for that. Even if I told you what I know, you still wouldn't get anywhere.

What do I know, anyway? A name. Metro. That's about it. I've never met him, I've never seen him, I don't know his real name. I don't even have proof he was involved in Matthew's murder.

So what would you do with that information, Detective Webley? Find him? Talk to him? Release him when he tells you a pack of lies?

I could do better myself. I'm already doing better than the police. I can go outside the law, and that's what's needed here.

So why am I running away? Why have I let the murdering bastards win? Am I too scared of the odds stacked against me? A man with a gun – what's that? I've been up against whole armies with guns, grenade launchers and complete fanaticism.

What was it that Detective Webley said?

I came here for one reason only, and that's to get to the truth. At some point you need to decide if that's what you want too.

All right, Webley. You're right about that one. I need to decide if I want the truth.

It's at that point that 'Heroes' by David Bowie starts playing over the car radio. Memories flood in of her and Matthew belting out the words together in this very car. She listens carefully to the lyrics.

And makes her decision.

She moves over to the inside lane. Comes off at the next junction. Drives all the way around the roundabout and rejoins the motorway to head back home again.

Grace Meade is nervous as hell.

When's the last time I had a man inside this house? she thinks. Well, how about never. Plumbers and joiners and the weirdo who reads the meter don't count.

The wine is in the fridge. She has also bought some nibbles from Marks and Sparks, just in case. I mean, he may not have had time to eat. He's a busy guy, with big cases to solve. Making time for (gulp) little old me is quite an honour. The least I can do is offer him nibbles.

She has changed out of her work clothes and into a dress, and now she worries that she's gone too far. Would something more casual be better? But then again, why not make the effort? If it all goes wrong, at least she won't be able to blame it on looking like a slob.

No, she thinks, I would have to blame it on my personality instead. Because of course I'm going to say something stupid, or else I won't know what to say, or else I'll spill wine down my dress or drop food in his lap or—

Stop it! Stop panicking. Deep breaths, now. Deep breaths. Think about something soothing. Something like—

Oh, shit. Oh, shit. Did you hear that? That was the doorbell. He's here. Cody is here.

She starts running to the door. Slows down only at the last moment when she remembers she's supposed to be relaxed about this.

She opens the door. He is still in his work suit, and there is a bag slung over his shoulder. Why would he bring a bag?

'Hi, Grace,' he says. 'You look great.'

'Thank you,' she says. She would add, 'So do you', except that he doesn't. He looks like he's been knocking back cheap vodka on a park bench. Feeling the need to find a compliment, she says, 'I like your new shoes.'

Cody looks down at his feet. 'Oh. Yeah, thanks.'

'Comfy?'

'Yes. Best pair I've ever had.'

'Good. Good.'

There's a silence, and then Cody points into the hallway behind her. 'Shall we?'

It suddenly strikes Grace that she is supposed to be breaking the long-established tradition of not having a man inside her house.

'Oh. Yes. Please come in.'

Fluttering around him like a butterfly, she escorts him through to the living room – now the cleanest and tidiest it has ever been.

'I've got some wine in the fridge,' she says. 'Would you like a glass?'

'No, thanks, Grace. I'm driving.'

'Then perhaps something to eat? You must be starving.'

'No. I'm fine, thank you.'

Great, thinks Grace. So that was a wasted trip to the supermarket.

Cody sits at one end of the sofa. Not wanting to seem presumptuous, Grace sits at the other end, a gulf of cushion between them.

'So . . .' she begins. 'I'm intrigued. Do you often visit the homes of people you work with?'

Cody smiles. 'Not often, no.'

She glances at Cody's bag. Thinks, Please don't let this be about work.

'Is it about a police investigation?'

A shake of the head. 'No. No, it's not.'

Good answer. So what's in the bag, Cody? A present?

'Then what?'

Cody watches her for a few seconds, as if building himself up for whatever's coming next.

'This isn't easy,' he says. 'I don't even know if I should be here.'

You should definitely be here, she thinks. For as long as you like. We could watch a movie. I've got popcorn in the kitchen cupboard.

'Sounds serious,' she says.

'It is, and it needs to stay confidential. Just between the two of us. Nobody at work can ever hear about it. I know that's asking a lot of you, and if you say you can't do it, I'll walk away right now.'

Oh, God, she thinks. Oh, God. *The two of us*. What a great phrase.

'I can keep a secret.'

'I was hoping you'd say that. I couldn't think of anyone else.'

She can't prevent a frown from creasing her features. She thinks, Am I the last resort here? The bottom name on a long list of possibles and maybes? Like the one who's always left at the end when teams are being picked?

'Anyone else for what?'

Cody finally reaches for his bag. He unzips it. Brings out something sleek and shiny.

It's a laptop, and Grace wants to scream.

How could I have imagined it might be anything but a computer? Why did I permit myself to entertain a glimmer of hope that my life won't always revolve around computers?

But deep down, she knows. She knows this is how everyone sees her. She's the computer geek at the back of the room. Got a problem involving technology? Speak to Grace. Need a date tonight? Don't ask Grace. Not unless you think she might know someone who is attractive, has a personality, and isn't so desperate.

But she keeps her cool. Suppresses her anger and humiliation as she always does in front of others. They will put in an appearance later, when she's away from sympathetic smiles and pitying eyes.

Plus, this is Cody. It's impossible to get annoyed at Cody.

'I was hoping you could take a look at this for me,' Cody says.

'In what way? Is it broken?'

'Not that I know of. I want to know what information it holds.'

'So it's not yours?'

'No.'

'A friend of yours?'

'No.'

'But you said it wasn't connected to a case.'

'That's right. It isn't.'

'Then . . . I'm sorry, Cody, but I'm not sure what's going on here.'

'To be honest, it's probably better that you don't know all the details.'

'Why? Will I be breaking the law?'

'You? No. As far as you're concerned, you're simply helping a friend who's having problems with his laptop.'

'And what about you? Are *you* breaking the law?'

'It might be better if you don't ask me that question.'

'Then let me put it another way. Are you in trouble?'

'I . . . I need help. And I need it quickly.'

'How quickly?'

'Like now. Tonight. Tomorrow could be too late.'

'Tonight? That's not a lot of time. I mean, if there's any kind of protection on this machine—'

'I understand. I'm not asking you to do the impossible, just to have a go.'

'Can I ask who it belongs to?'

'A guy. You wouldn't know him.'

Grace studies her hands as she crosses them on her lap. It's a while before she speaks again.

'I'll do it,' she says. 'But only because I trust you. I don't think you would get involved in anything illegal, and I don't think you would deliberately involve me in anything that might get me in trouble.'

'I wouldn't do that, Grace. I have no idea what's on this computer. For all I know, it could be games, photos, music. I just need to know more about the owner: the names of his contacts, suspicious emails – anything.'

She nods. 'I'll take a look. No promises, mind.'

Cody smiles as he puts the laptop on the sofa between them. 'You're beautiful, Grace. I owe you one.'

She thinks to herself, He said I'm beautiful. I don't think a man has ever said that to me before.

Cody takes a card from his pocket and lays it on top of the laptop. 'I've written my mobile number on the back. Call me as soon as you know anything, no matter how trivial it may seem.' Then he stands up.

'You're going already?'

'I have to. I've got a lot to do.'

She stands and faces him. She hopes for a hug before he leaves. Maybe a peck on the cheek.

Cody brushes past her.

'I'll speak to you later, Grace. Thank you. You don't know how much this means to me.'

And then he's gone, and Grace is left staring down at her mute, unfeeling companion for the night.

'Twas ever thus.

57

Cody half expects there to be a huge police presence outside his building, just waiting for him to show up and explain why he's been keeping a clown in his basement.

But there's nothing. The building looks as empty and ghostly as it always does on a dark evening.

Something within Cody urges him to turn his back on this and walk away. Just get as far away as possible. Let the man in there die and rot.

But he knows he can't do that. Waldo wouldn't let it play out in that way. There are scenes in Waldo's movie still to be directed.

Cody puts his key in the lock of the glossy black front door. He turns the key, pushes the door open. Inside, the usual gloom, the aromas of dental hygiene, the rush of water through the central heating pipes. The boiler man obviously did his stuff.

Cody puts on a light and walks straight through to the rear of the building. He stops at the basement door beneath the stairs. He tries the handle and finds that it is locked. He takes out his key.

A few minutes more won't make any difference, he thinks.

He returns the key to his pocket, then trudges up the stairs to his apartment. There, he undresses, showers, and puts on some jogging bottoms and a sweater. He knows he should eat, but he can't face it; knows he should sleep, but that his brain won't allow it.

Grabbing his keys, baton and phone, he heads downstairs again. This time he traipses all the way down to the basement. At the locked door of the room holding Keenan he pauses and listens. He's not sure what he's expecting, but he gets no surprises. Not a hint of life or death.

When he unlocks the door and enters, he finds Keenan sitting on the floor again, his back to the wall. The water bottle and crisp packets lie empty next to him.

'You've been gone a long time,' says Keenan.

'I've got better things to do with my time than spend it all on you.'

Keenan forces out a laugh. 'That's not the impression you gave last night. Seems to me I'm the most important person in your life right now.'

'Keep thinking that if you want, James.'

At the sound of his name, Keenan tenses. 'What?'

'I said you can keep believing you're useful to me. I'm not so sure anymore.'

'You called me a name.'

'Oh, that. Yes. James. James Keenan.'

'H-how . . . Where did you hear that?'

Cody holds up his phone and waggles it. 'Your friend Waldo called. He told me a lot about you. Where you live, who your friends are, what you do for a job. I must say, I didn't have you down as a financial advisor. Not the most exciting job in the world. Is that why you chose the clown act as a sideline? Spice things up a bit?'

'You're lying. Waldo wouldn't have told you all that.'

'No? To be honest, I think he's become bored with you and this whole game. He wants to bring it to a conclusion. You see, he got it wrong. I haven't acted the way he expected, and so now he's thinking up new rules.'

'What new rules?'

'I don't know yet. He's going to call me again tonight. He wants me to come looking for him, so he's going to give me some more clues.'

'And what about me? What part do I play?'

'You don't. You've become redundant, James. The plan is to hand you back to Waldo.'

Keenan tries to hide it, but terror jumps into his eyes. 'You can't do that. He'll kill me.'

'Not my concern, James. I gave you a chance to cooperate, but you turned it down. You snooze, you lose.'

Keenan gets to his feet, his chain jangling as he moves. 'That's not right. You can't do that.'

Cody starts moving back towards the door. 'Too late. It's happening. The next time this phone rings, you're out of the equation. See you later, James.'

He leaves the room, locking it behind him, then leans back against the door and closes his eyes for a minute. He has hope now, where before he had nothing: Keenan might break, and Grace might find some vital information on his computer.

What he tries not to think about is where he will be if neither of those pays off.

58

It has taken Sara hours to find him, but it could have been worse. She was prepared to do this for days – weeks even. The army taught her the virtue of patience when it comes to warfare.

That scumbag in Bootle gave her a list of three locations: the nightclub, the pool hall and the gym. She has been driving between all three, watching and waiting. She knew he would turn up at one of them eventually.

And now here he is, outside the gym. Climbing out of his big black Mercedes. Sniffing his armpits before opening up the boot and pulling out a grey sports bag.

She observes from her own car across the street as Ozone walks to the front door of the gym. It's almost ten o'clock now, and the gym is closed, but Ozone takes out a key, opens up, and steps inside.

Sara pulls up the hood of her cardigan and gets out of her car. She puts her hands in her pockets as she looks up and down the deserted street, then marches swiftly across to the gym. She tries the front door, but finds it locked. To the right of the building is an alleyway. She follows it for a few yards, nearly craps herself when she is suddenly bathed in yellow light.

The light is from within the building. Through the frosted glass and security mesh she can make out the movement of a blurred figure. A few seconds later she hears a metallic slam, like that of a locker door.

She hopes that Ozone isn't about to undertake a late-night gym session, but then the light goes out again, and she doubts he would bother to do that if he were staying.

She races back to the front of the building and waits by the door. Less than a minute later, she hears noises coming her way. She flattens herself against the adjoining wall, flexes her fingers.

As Ozone appears in the doorway, Sara spins into view. She shoots out her right hand, the fingers and thumb forming a V-shape that strikes hard into Ozone's throat. He staggers backwards into the building, clutching at his neck. Before he has time to think about a response, Sara runs straight at him and launches a kick into his chest. Ozone flies further backwards and hits a rickety wooden chair behind him. The chair collapses and he crashes to the floor amid the wreckage. He tries to roll away from her, reaching towards his waistband. Sara picks up an arm of the broken chair, then swings it hard onto Ozone's wrist as he tries to point his gun at her. She hears a sharp crack of bone, and then the clatter of the gun hitting the floor.

Ozone screams in pain. 'My arm!' he splutters. 'You broke my fucking arm!'

Sara retrieves the pistol, points it at Ozone. 'You broke my fucking house. That makes us even.'

Ozone rubs his wrist and then his bruised Adam's apple. 'Not even close, girl. You've just earned yourself a death sentence. What the fucking hell do you think you're doing?'

'I want to know where Metro is.'

'I don't know where he is.'

Sara cocks the hammer of the SIG. 'I may have earned a death sentence, but I'll take you out first. Where's Metro?'

Ozone puts his good arm up in surrender. 'Seriously, I don't know.'

'Don't move,' says Sara. She backs up to the front door and closes it, then approaches Ozone again.

'Get up.'

'What?'

'You heard me. Stand up.'

Ozone struggles to his feet, wincing with the pain.

'In there,' says Sara, gesturing to the locker room.

'Why?'

'Just do what I say.'

Ozone staggers through to the locker room that he must have been in a few minutes earlier. Sara keeps a respectable distance behind him.

'Put the light on. Good. Now, which locker?'

'I don't know what you're talking about.'

'The locker you put the bag into. Which one was it?'

'Bag? What bag?'

Sara takes a step towards him, aiming the gun at his forehead.

'You were a big man when you had this gun pointed at me in my house. But do you want to know what I think? I think you've never actually shot anyone. The difference between us is that I have. I know what it's like to splatter someone's brains all over a wall, and I won't hesitate to do it again.'

'Yeah, well this isn't a fucking war zone. You can't get away with that shit here.'

'No?'

Sara suddenly lowers her aim and fires a single round into Ozone's foot. The blast reverberates around the room, but Sara doubts there will be anyone outside to hear it.

Ozone screams again and drops to the floor. 'You shot me! You fucking shot me, you stupid bitch!'

Sara aims at his head again. 'And I'm going to keep on shooting until you answer my questions. So, which locker?'

Clutching his foot, Ozone chin-points to a large, waist-high locker in the corner of the room. Unlike most of the others, which are coin-operated, this one is secured with a combination padlock.

'What's the code?' she asks.

'I'm injured,' he whines. 'I need a doctor.'

Sara points the gun at his other foot. 'What's the fucking code?'

'Two, seven, seven, nine.'

Sara moves across to the locker. She faces Ozone while she enters the combination. The padlock snaps open. She unhooks it, pulls the door wide, then drags out the sports bag it contains.

'So what do we have here?' she says.

Ozone says nothing. He is too busy grimacing and swearing.

Sara kneels down, unzips the bag, pulls it open.

Money. Lots of it. Bundle upon bundle of used tens and twenties.

Sara steps across to Ozone again. 'I'm guessing that this money is intended for Metro, right?'

Ozone nods.

'So how will it get to him?'

'He'll pick it up.'

'In person? When?'

'I don't know. Could be any time. Tomorrow, the next day, next week.'

Sara sighs. 'Pick a leg.'

'What?'

'I'm going to shoot out one of your kneecaps, so pick a leg.' She lines up the gun with Ozone's left kneecap. 'This one?'

'Tonight! Okay? Tonight. He'll pick up the money tonight. I swear I don't know exactly what time, but it should be in the next couple of hours.'

'Will he be alone?'

'Yes. He always comes alone for the money.'

'Then I suppose we'll have to wait.'

'I can't wait. I need a doctor.'

'Don't worry,' Sara says. 'I'll take care of you.'

59

Cody is getting sick of waiting. Literally. His tiredness, his lack of appetite, his adrenaline are all conspiring to turn him into a quivering mass of jelly, incapable of rational thought and the ability to act.

He wants to go downstairs and confront Keenan again, but he knows he has to leave him to stew a little longer. If he appears too desperate for information, Keenan will detect it and clam up.

Cody picks up his phone, jabs in a number and waits for an answer.

'Hello?'

'Hi, Grace. It's Cody. I was just wondering if you'd managed to get anywhere with that computer?'

There's a short silence, which Cody immediately interprets as disappointing news.

'The problem is that the hard drive is encrypted. If I can crack the encryption, I should be able to see everything it contains, but that's easier said than done.'

'I see,' Cody says, although he doesn't really. 'But it's possible, right?'

'Theoretically, yes. In practice, it's not looking good.'

'Grace, I really need this.'

'I understand. I don't know why you need it, but I appreciate the urgency. I'll do everything I can.'

'I know you will. Call me. As soon as you have any news – I don't care what time it is – call me, okay?'

'Of course. You have my word.'

'Thank you, Grace. You don't know how much I appreciate this.'

'Any time, Cody.'

He says goodbye and ends the call.

And then he goes back to the sickness of waiting.

Metro Mackenzie is thinking about the girl when he pulls up at the gym. Sara Prior. He will remember her for a long time to come.

She was a definite nuisance, but he admires her for it. If he's honest, he'd hoped for a bit more from her. She seemed made of sterner stuff.

Ozone did the trick, as he always does. He can always be relied upon. Metro recalls how Ozone phoned him up earlier today and gave him the news. He was characteristically succinct:

'It's done. She won't bother you anymore. Not sure it was wise to tell her that we know how her husband died, though.'

'But you did, right?'

'Yeah. I did what you said.'

And that was that. Job done. Metro could get back to doing what he does best, which is collecting money, for others and himself, and Ozone could carry on doing what he excels at, which is following orders. Ozone doesn't need to understand complexities; he just needs to obey.

DAVID JACKSON | 337

Like now, for example.

As soon as he walks through the door to the gym, Metro knows that his deputy has been here. Even up against the odour of stale sweat, Ozone's scent cloud prevails. He has been here and carried out his instructions, no questions asked.

Metro makes his way to the locker room. He could do it with his eyes shut, simply by following the whiff of Ozone, which seems even stronger than usual tonight.

Metro goes over to the locker. Like an expert safecracker, he rubs his hands together before starting to enter the combination into the padlock, but he does so with the anticipation of further riches. The Abba song 'Money, Money, Money' runs through his head.

He removes the padlock, swings the door wide . . .

And is greeted with the sight of Ozone Fisher, crouched inside the locker, his hands covered in blood, his eyes staring widely, madly.

'What the—'

Metro takes a step backwards, trying to take this in, trying to make sense of this craziness through the mist of fear that is starting to billow into his mind.

He takes another step back. Halts when he feels the cold barrel of a gun pressing into the nape of his neck and hears the echoing click of a hammer being cocked.

Sara so wants to pull the trigger. If she were certain that this man Metro was responsible for Matthew's death, she would have no hesitation.

But, as yet, she's not certain. All she has to go on is that this man's name was mentioned in a letter. It's not enough.

'You know who I am?' she asks.

'Yes,' says Metro. 'You're Sara Prior.'

'You know why I'm here?'

'You want to know about your husband.'

'Did you kill him?'

'No.'

'Do you know who did?'

'No.'

Sara pulls back her arm, then rams the butt of the pistol into the back of Metro's skull. He goes down to the floor. Turns and sits there glaring at her while he tries to staunch the blood flowing from his wound. She gets a better look at him now. He's lean and muscular, with eyes that beam contempt – for her and for everything that gets in his way. She doesn't find it hard to believe that he would have killed Matthew simply for bumping into him.

He says, 'You don't learn, do you, girl?'

'Oh, I learn very quickly. You, on the other hand, keep making the same mistake of underestimating me. Take a look at your faithful hound there. See how quiet and subservient he is in his kennel? I tamed him. I can do the same to you.'

'You know what? I actually believe you could. What do you want from me?'

'How did you know my husband?'

'I didn't.'

Sara fires the gun. It chews up concrete an inch in front of Metro's groin. Still in the locker, Ozone jumps in fear.

Sara says, 'The next bullet will be slightly higher. I'll ask you again. How did you know Matthew?'

'Swear to God, I didn't. Honestly, I'm not lying.'

'Then why would Matthew give me your name?'

'When did he do that?'

'He sent me a letter before he died. He knew he was in danger, so he wrote to me. He mentioned you, and said you could be found in The Tar Barrel.'

'I don't know why he said that. I'd never heard of Matthew Prior until—'

'Until what?'

'Until I read about him in the papers.'

Sara advances swiftly on Metro. Puts the gun to the top of his head. 'No, that's not what you were about to say. Until what?'

'Until—'

Metro doesn't finish his sentence. He moves quickly, unexpectedly. He grabs Sara's gun hand and pushes it away from his head. The gun goes off, the bullet punching a hole in one of the lockers. He tries to drive his other fist up into her solar plexus, but Sara twists and takes it in the side of her abdomen. The pain is excruciating, but as Metro tries to get to his feet, she brings her knee into his face. He starts to fall back, and as he does so Sara yanks her gun arm free, then whips the weapon across Metro's face. He lands heavily on his back, blood gushing from his cheek.

Over at the locker, Ozone is halfway out. Sara points the gun at him. 'Get the fuck back in there.'

Panting heavily, she stands over Metro and takes a two-handed combat stance, the gun pointing squarely between Metro's eyes.

'You have five seconds to tell me what you know, and then I pull the trigger. Five . . .'

Metro spreads his arms. 'Hey, girl, you don't even need to get to four. I'm done. This isn't worth losing my life over.'

'Then talk.'

'I'm talking. I never met your husband, okay? And I don't know who killed him. But I heard things, all right? In my line of work, I hear things.'

'What kind of things?'

'I heard that your husband was killed because he had something I would find valuable.'

'What are you talking about? Matthew was just a civil servant. He worked for the tax office. What possible item could he have that would interest you?'

'I really don't know, but I was about to find out.'

'What do you mean?'

'A message was left for me at the club. I'm supposed to turn up alone at an address tonight to find out what's on offer.'

'What time?'

'Two in the morning.'

'And you were planning to go?'

'Fuck, no. Not without back-up. My plan was to sit it out, wait for the guy to contact me again, and then suggest a meeting on my terms.'

'What's the address?'

'Are you serious?'

She moves the gun a few inches closer.

'Okay,' he says. 'You're serious.'

He reels off the address, and she pins it at the front of her brain.

'Do you want to change any details of your story?' she asks.

'No. It's the God's-honest truth. Swear on my mother's life.'

'Well, we'll find out, won't we? Take off your jacket and empty your pockets.'

'Why?'

'Just do it. Nice and slow.'

Metro does as he's told, piling up his possessions on the floor next to him.

'Move over there,' she tells him.

When he has shifted away a safe distance, Sara moves to the pile and picks a twenty-pence piece out from the loose change.

Watching her closely, Metro says, 'What's that for?'

'To open the locker next to your friend there. He's about to get a new neighbour. I'm taking your keys to this place, too. If any part of your story turns out to be bullshit, I will come straight back here and empty this gun into both lockers. If you've told the truth, someone will find you in the morning.'

Metro looks incredulous. 'You really expect us to spend the whole night in these lockers?'

'Think of it as an opportunity to reconsider your lifestyle choices.'

'My lifestyle? What about yours? You know you're dead, right? Whatever way the thing with your husband works out, your days are numbered.'

60

Grace Meade stares at her computer screen and eats the nibbles that were intended for Cody. Waste not, want not, she thinks.

The wine is still in the fridge. She hates to drink alone; it just makes her more depressed. And anyway, she needs to stay awake and focused on the task at hand. The alcohol can wait until the next time a man comes into her house. Ten-year-old wines are supposed to be more prized, aren't they?

Cody won't come back here, except maybe to stand at the doorstop while she hands the laptop back to him. After this disaster, he'll have no reason to think she can help him in future.

Okay, maybe disaster is too strong a word. Nothing has actually gone wrong. This was always going to be a difficult nut to crack. No, that's not true: it was always going to be an almost impossible nut. Cody was just expecting too much.

Sometimes, though, you get a stroke of luck. That's what she was pinning her hopes on. A weak encryption algorithm, or a way to get to the decryption key.

Imagine that, she thinks. Imagine what Cody would say – how he would react – if I were to show him all the secrets contained on this machine. He would worship me.

But my life isn't like that. I don't get lightning strikes of good fortune. All of my achievements, such as they are, have been attained through sheer hard work. And hard work won't cut it in this instance. Even the unbelievable computing power at my disposal isn't cutting it.

She is not working directly on the laptop Cody supplied. That's not what one does. Instead, she has cloned its disk drive and launched an assault on the copy. To assist her, she has employed the services of the university supercomputer.

Well, employed isn't quite accurate. Hijacking or press-ganging might be more fitting terms. She has to be careful, though: there are some clever bods at the university who would take exception to her misappropriation of their precious computing resource.

But their high-tech equipment is no better than a corner-shop calculator right now if it can't solve this problem. It might not solve it even if she had weeks of computing time, and she has only hours. Hours that are already ticking away rapidly.

'I'm going for a shower,' she tells her computer. 'When I come back, I want answers, okay? No excuses. Cody is relying on me.'

She rises from her chair. Yawns and stretches. Heads upstairs.

In her bathroom, she fills the washbasin and begins removing her make-up. She spent a long time on her stupid make-up this evening, for all the good it did. Did Cody notice? No. Or if he did, it made no difference.

Getting into this computer would make a difference, though. Has to. Cody is a man who appreciates results. He likes people who get things done.

She opens her mirrored cabinet, takes out a fresh bar of soap. Stoops over to wash her face. It stings her eyes. She grabs a towel and dries herself off. She straightens up, closes the cabinet.

And sees the reflection of the clown standing behind her.

61

Cody wakes up.

Which is a hell of a surprise, because he doesn't remember going to sleep. One minute he's sitting there staring at his phone and willing it to ring; the next he's wondering why it's disappeared from his hand.

The reason it's no longer in his hand is that it's now on the floor, and when he picks it up and checks the time it displays, he sees that he's been out not for a minute but a whole hour.

He groans, then gets up from the sofa. He doesn't feel refreshed; if anything, he feels groggy and out of touch with reality. His mouth is dry and his eyes are struggling to focus.

But he knows what he must do.

Grace hasn't called. It seems unlikely that she will pull any rabbits out of the hat for him tonight. That leaves Cody with only one possible way to get to Waldo.

He goes to the bathroom first. Takes a pee. Washes his hands and splashes cold water on his face.

Next, the kitchen, where he collects his usual equipment – the keys and his baton.

He whips his arm forward, extending the baton.

I could use this, he thinks. I could break every bone in that stupid clown's body, and he would talk. He would have to talk.

And then I'd know where Waldo is. I could find him and I could break every bone in his body too. And then—

And then what?

Would you be happy with that, Cody? Is that what you want?

I don't know what I want. Happiness is not the goal here. I want . . . I want . . .

Justice?

Maybe. But more than that I want . . .

Answers.

Yeah, that's it. I want answers. I want to know why Waldo has chosen me to play his stupid game. I want to know why he hasn't just killed me outright. I want to know what plans he has for me in the future. I want to know what he gets out of this. I want to know which other people he has targeted, and what the outcomes were.

I want to know a million things, and I can only get them from the mouth of Waldo.

And then maybe I can rest.

Cody doesn't like the fact that Keenan is smiling. He's just squatting there on the floor like a Buddhist monk, a smug grin on his face.

Cody feels his grip tighten on the baton. He could wipe away that grin with a single swipe. It wouldn't be hard. Go on, Cody, do it. Hit him. Show him he can't laugh at you.

'What's so fucking funny?'

Keenan shrugs. 'Nothing.'

Cody flicks the baton open again. Takes several steps towards Keenan.

'I said what's so funny?'

Keenan seems to sense the seriousness of his predicament. His smile fades.

'Not funny. I've seen the light, that's all.'

'Divine intervention? Good. You might need some help along those lines where you're going.'

Keenan shakes his head. 'No, it's nothing religious. I just realised you were bluffing. Waldo didn't call you. There's no arrangement to hand me over to him. You were trying to scare me. Nice try.'

'What makes you think it was a bluff?'

'Because if Waldo wanted me, he'd have me by now. There'd be nothing you could do to stop it. He wouldn't need your agreement. And that stuff you found out about me? The photograph, right? The one you took on your phone. I don't know how you did it, but somehow you traced me using that photo.'

Cody begins to walk slowly around the room, tapping his baton on the whitewashed walls.

'So what if you're right,' he says. 'You think that helps you somehow?'

'I think it means you're running out of options. You want Waldo so badly it hurts, but you're starting to accept that you can't get to him through me. You also know that you can't take me into police custody. For one thing, there's no evidence against me; I'd walk within minutes. For another, you'd have to explain why you kept me locked up in your cellar, and I don't think you want to do that. And finally, you can't keep me here much longer. I was nearly discovered today. Tomorrow, someone might come along and open that door.'

Cody continues to tap his baton. 'You've certainly put a lot of thought into this. Let's suppose all the above is true. What's your conclusion?'

'That you'll have to let me go.'

'You really want that? You want to be out in the open, with Waldo on the loose?'

'I'll have to take my chances.'

'Uh-huh. And what about me?'

Keenan furrows his brow. 'What do you mean?'

'I mean, what do I get out of it? If I let you go, where's my closure? See, what you don't seem to appreciate is that the only thing that's been keeping me going since you and your clown friends took away my toes and my colleague is the thought that one day I might end up in a position exactly like this. Just you, me, and nobody watching.'

Keenan's mouth twitches. 'It's not me you want. You want Waldo.'

'You're right. I do want Waldo. But I've been doing a lot of thinking too. And what I've come to accept is that I have to settle for second best, because that's all that's on offer. If I let you go, I throw that all away.'

'So . . . what's the solution?'

'That we end this now.'

It's all he has to say, because Keenan understands what it means. And what Cody realises about himself is that he's not bluffing. It's true that he has run out of options. Grace isn't going to ring, and he can wait no longer. Waldo was right when he told him that he needs to think of Keenan as an irrelevance, a bug fit only for squashing.

I'm tired, Cody thinks. I need an end to this.

'Look,' says Keenan, 'I already told you. I didn't actually hurt you. I didn't kill your partner. That wasn't what I thought—'

Cody raises his baton and brings it down fast. It skims the top of Keenan's hair and smacks against the wall behind him.

'YOU WERE THERE! YOU ARE RESPONSIBLE!'

'No! I was there, yes. But I didn't think it would go that far. I didn't know that—'

'You suggested the loppers! You suggested using the knife!'

'It was . . . I was making stuff up. Waldo asked us to dream up horrible tortures. I didn't really think he was capable of—'

'You didn't try to stop him, though, did you? None of you did.'

'You don't understand. Waldo isn't someone you say no to. He does whatever he wants.'

'Well, now I do whatever I want, okay? Now it's my turn.'

'You can't . . . kill me. You're a police officer. You can't—'

'WAS! I *was* a police officer. I'm about to lose that too. That's what you and your clown friends have done to me. I have nothing left. No life, no peace, no career. Nothing except an opportunity to fix this one small thing.'

He raises the baton again. Tears sting his eyes and there is a burning in his heart. The fire spreads to his arm. He can feel the rage there, a power that could split this man's skull in two. There is no rationality now, no empathy. What lies before him in this dank basement is vermin, an insect that needs eradicating. One simple quick action will do it. He will open his mouth and he will roar and he will bring all his might down on this infestation.

And then Cody's phone rings.

At first he is not sure what the noise is, where it is coming from. It intrudes into his consciousness, makes him aware of his surroundings. He sees the cowering figure beneath him, feels the coiled energy in his arm, the hatred in his soul.

He takes a step back, then another. It seems to him that the blood slowly drains from the bulging veins in his arms, neck and temples.

He lowers the baton. Takes the phone from his pocket and answers it almost absent-mindedly.

He listens to what he is being told, and it changes everything.

62

Cody knocks and rings for several minutes before he gets an answer. When the door is finally opened, it is obvious that Grace is distraught. She is shaking, and her cheeks are glistening with tears.

'Oh, Grace,' says Cody.

He steps into the house, gives her a hug.

'Come on,' he says. 'Let's go and sit down. Tell me all about it.'

He leads her through to the living room and sits her on the sofa. He sits right next to her, no expanse of cushion between them this time.

'What happened?'

'Cody, I'm so sorry. He took the computer. I had no choice. He was . . .'

'Tell me from the beginning. How did he get into the house?'

'I don't know. I was trying to get into your laptop, and then I went upstairs to get washed. He came up behind me, Cody. He just—'

She starts sobbing, her words swallowed up. Cody grabs a box of tissues from the coffee table and hands it to her.

'It's all right. He's gone now. He got what he wants, and he won't come back.'

'He . . . he was wearing a clown mask. A disgusting creepy mask, with sharp teeth and blood. I started screaming, but then he put his finger to the lips of his mask, and in his other hand he was showing me a huge knife. I thought he . . . I thought he was going to . . .'

'Shush now. You're safe, okay? He didn't hurt you, did he?'

'No. He didn't actually touch me. I just . . . Cody, he frightened the life out of me. I didn't know what to do. I still don't.'

'Did he talk to you?'

'Yes. And that was weird, too. He must have rigged a microphone or something in his mask, so that his words came out in this freaky monster voice.'

Cody thinks about the voice he has listened to over the phone. He wonders how many others have had it inflicted upon them.

'What did he say to you?'

'He said something like, *Here are your instructions. Obey them and you won't be hurt. Lock yourself in the bathroom and stay there for ten minutes. After that, you can come out. Do it now.*'

'Is that what you did?'

'Yes. I was glad to get away from him. To be honest, I think I was in there for longer than ten minutes. When I came out, I went downstairs and saw that the computer had been taken, along with the cloned disk drive.'

'Did he take anything else?'

'No. I don't think so. I haven't checked properly. I called you straighaway.'

'Have you called anyone else?'

'No. I-I was going to phone 999, and then I thought about the computer and about how secretive you were about it, and I thought that if I called you, then at least you could come over and . . . and . . .'

Cody feels the relief. He doesn't know how he would have explained this to other coppers.

'Thank you, Grace. You did the right thing.'

'Did I? I'm not so sure.'

'What do you mean?'

'I mean I don't know what I've got myself involved in here. I trusted you. I didn't think this would be dangerous. But now I—'

'Grace, listen to me. I didn't think it would be dangerous, either. Please believe me when I tell you that I had no idea this would happen.'

'How did he find me? How did he get my address?'

'My guess is that he followed me.'

'Why? What's going on, Cody?'

He thinks carefully about his response. He feels he owes her an explanation, but at the same time he doesn't want to endanger her further.

'It's complicated. I can't explain.'

Grace's look is withering. 'I'm not stupid, Cody.'

'I didn't say you were. I would never—'

'I've read the news reports. I know what happened to you before you joined MIT.'

'Grace, I—'

'Four men, wearing clown masks. And now the guy tonight, also in a clown mask. That's not a coincidence, is it?'

Cody knows he can't avoid the truth. 'No. It's not a coincidence.'

'The men who attacked you were never caught. They're back again, aren't they?'

Regret washes over Cody. He wishes now he had never come to Grace for help. Wishes he could keep the reappearance of the clowns to himself. But it's out now. Finally, it's out.

'Grace, you can't tell anyone about this.'

'We have to. Cody, these men murdered a police officer. It's your duty to report them. Mine too. You can't expect me to keep quiet about this.'

'Grace, please. I'm getting close to these men. I can catch them. I just need a little more time. If we report this, they will disappear into the woodwork. Please. I'm begging you. Can you not just pretend tonight never happened?'

Grace stares down at the bundle of tissues clutched in her fist. 'Who else knows about this? About the clowns coming back?'

'Nobody.'

'Nobody? Not even Megan?'

'Not even Megan. You're the only one, Grace.'

'This means a lot to you, doesn't it?'

'No. It means everything to me. To be honest, I'm already on the verge of losing my job over it.'

Grace shakes her head. 'Please don't say that. You're the best detective on the force.'

Cody smiles, and he sees how Grace blushes at her own remark.

He says, 'That's kind of you, but I'm not sure it's anywhere near the truth. I seem to be making a lot of fundamental errors lately.'

'You need help. You can't do this alone. Maybe . . . maybe I could help you?'

Cody takes hold of Grace's hand. 'I've asked too much of you already. I can't put you at risk again. I couldn't live with myself if anything bad happened to you.'

And now Grace is burning up furiously. But Cody means every word of it, and he needs her to know that.

'Compared with what you go through in your job, I suppose tonight was nothing, really. A man in a mask – so what?'

'Don't put yourself down. He came into your house. He had a knife. That's enough to scare the bejesus out of anyone. Actually, I think you're coping surprisingly well.'

For the first time, Grace finds a smile. 'Okay,' she says.

'Okay what?'

'Okay, I won't tell anyone about tonight.'

'Grace, I—'

'Don't say any more. Just put the kettle on.'

63

Sara isn't convinced.

Something about this place doesn't feel right. Why would Metro be told to come here?

Of course, one option is that he wasn't. He could have been lying through his teeth. In which case Sara will be paying him a return visit at the gym, and she won't be happy. In fact, she will be downright livid. Perhaps livid enough to start blasting holes in those lockers.

On the other hand, how could this be a trap? Metro didn't know he was about to be hijacked at the gym, so how could he have set something up at this address? And now that he has been stuffed into a locker without his phone, how could he warn anyone of her imminent arrival?

The remaining alternative is that he was telling the truth when he said he was instructed to come here tonight to discover what precious item Matthew had in his possession. If that's so, any trap that might be in place here would be for Metro, not Sara. That could give her an advantage.

To be on the safe side, she still has Ozone's gun, with a lot of rounds left in the magazine, and she's fully prepared to use it if she has to.

But still this choice of venue seems curious.

She gets out of the car. Pats the gun that is in the waistband beneath her hoody.

She goes for a short walk first. Up and down the street, checking out the geography, working out escape routes. She doesn't expect a firefight, but who knows?

Finally, she makes her move.

She ascends the few short steps leading up to the front door. Studies the intercom system. The address Metro gave her was for the top floor, but there is no name against the bell-push for that floor.

What seems really odd to her is that the other floors are occupied by an orthodontal and dental practice.

And Rodney Street seems a very strange part of town to arrange a meeting with a murderer.

She thumbs the button. Waits.

She expects a voice, a brief interrogation at least. Instead, the intercom buzzes back at her and the door clicks open.

She pushes the door. It swings smoothly aside. Beyond, the lobby is black.

Sara steps inside. She finds a light switch and puts it on before closing the door behind her. Then she takes out her gun and heads towards the staircase.

She moves silently and cautiously up the stairs, constantly checking ahead for surprises. At the top of the stairs she steps through a doorway onto a landing. She finds another light switch and puts it on. There are doors here that lead to dental surgeries, but also one that looks as though it will take her up to the top storey. She creeps towards it, the gun stretched out ahead of her. She gets to the door. Reaches for the handle.

'Hello, Sara.'

She whirls. Sees the figure that has mystically materialised behind her. A man, yes, but also something more than a man. He is a *presence*, and all that he represents is depicted in his mask of pure evil.

'Congratulations, Sara,' he says, his voice eerily metallic. 'You win.'

She wants to shoot, but she also wants answers. His words have thrown her.

I win? What do I win?

But she has no time to voice her question, because something hits her hard in the side of the head, and she goes down and the gun flies from her grasp, and she feels hands on her, strong hands that hold her down while something sharp pierces her neck.

And it seems to her, before her world turns black, that she has not won. In fact she has lost everything.

64

It seems to Cody that he has lost everything.

He is about to be declared unfit for duty and kicked out of his job, and his chances of laying his hands on Waldo have diminished to near zero.

What's left? Where do I go from here?

He expects the worst for his mental state. If his career really is coming to an end, and all hope of catching Waldo is gone, then he foresees a spiral of depression and instability. He will have nothing left to live for.

He locks up his car. This time of night, Rodney Street is quiet, peaceful. The various practices are empty, their windows black with lifelessness.

He wonders what people would say – how the media would react – if the news ever broke that a serving police officer was keeping another man shackled in his basement. What a story that would be.

And that's another problem, of course. What to do about Keenan. Torture him? Kill him? Release him? None of these choices is palatable to Cody, but isn't that what Waldo intended all along? This is what the discussion of the trolley problem was all about: a choice between impossible alternatives.

Cody opens his front door, as he has done thousands of times. He would normally head straight upstairs, to his cosy apartment with its books and his guitar and his solitude. The rest of the building he usually sees as merely a pair of shoulders supporting his fortress of thought and reflection.

On this occasion he continues straight to the rear of the house, his fingers caressing the keys he has kept with him ever since this saga began.

He unlocks the cellar door, snaps on the light, descends the wooden staircase. He moves to the door on his right – the make-shift prison with its solitary chained and hungry inhabitant, like something out of the dark ages.

Did I really do this? Cody thinks. Did I really go along with this whole charade?

He takes out the next key. Unlocks the door. Turns on the light switch.

The differences scream out at Cody.

Keenan is not sitting on the floor, hunched and miserable. Not this time.

Keenan is standing in the middle of the room. He stands tall and unmoving, facing Cody.

That's if it *is* Keenan.

Because the biggest difference of all right now is that Keenan is wearing his clown mask again.

What stares back at Cody is a face of pus and blood and rotting flesh containing a needle-toothed smile that chills Cody's blood.

And what it takes Cody too long to realise is that when he first encountered this apparition, he removed the mask and threw it to the far side of the room.

Out of Keenan's reach!

And what it also takes Cody's exhausted mind far too long to comprehend is the implication of this. Which is that Keenan – or Clueless, or whoever else this is now – is no longer wearing the chain around his ankle.

All of this crowds into Cody's brain at once, defying him to make sense of it, challenging him to react accordingly.

But it is too late.

The clowns are upon him.

They come up from behind, sneaking out from the other rooms of the basement. They attack him in force, wrestling him to the ground, putting a sack of rough cloth over his head, tying his hands behind his back. He cries out, and they respond with clownish giggles. They strike him – fierce punches and kicks to his abdomen, his ribs, his kidneys. It feels as though his internal organs might burst with the pummelling.

Someone sits on his back. The sack covering his face is lifted, just enough to let him see, and his head is yanked back by the hair. An iPad is pushed in front of his face. It shows him a video feed of Sara Prior, and he cannot for the life of him understand what she has to do with any of this. And yet there she is: she appears unconscious, and a gun is being held to her temple. And when the iPad is taken away, Cody gets a view into the room again. He sees Keenan on his knees. He is holding a large white envelope bearing the words, 'HERE'S WALDO!' Standing behind Keenan is another of the clowns. He has a knife to Keenan's throat.

Cody knows then that he is being presented with a choice. It's the trolley problem again, but now for real human stakes.

The hood is pushed back in place and Cody is dragged to his feet. They begin tossing him from clown to clown, each one punching or kicking him again before sending him on his way to the next. He spins blindly, taking his punishment, his ears bombarded by the eerie high-pitched squeals of glee.

'What's your decision, Cody?'

It's Waldo's synthesised voice. Cody has no way of knowing whether he's here in the basement or elsewhere.

Another punch into his side. Cody groans.

'Everything about me is in that envelope, Cody. You can have it. But the trolley is on its way. It's heading towards Sara Prior. You're at the lever. Pull it and you save her, but lose me. What do you do?'

A kick to his knee. A sharp jab into his stomach. He drops to the floor and is pulled back up.

'She's going to die if you don't do something. You can save her life. The lever, Cody. Pull it or not?'

More blows. He wants to throw up inside the sacking.

'It's almost too late, Cody. She will die in the next few seconds. Decision time! Save her or catch me. What's it to be?'

Another fist lands on his left side.

'Last chance, Cody. Pull the lever or—?'

'YES!'

Everything stops. The noise stops. The hurting stops.

'Yes!' Cody repeats. 'I'm pulling the lever.'

More silence for several seconds. And then a sudden flurry of movement. Heavy footsteps going up the wooden staircase. The slam of a door.

Cody waits. Listens to his own panic-filled breathing and the pounding in his ears. Wonders if the game is still on, if the *coup de grace* is about to be administered. Waits for Waldo's final pronouncements.

But nothing happens.

'Hello?' he says. 'Are you there?' He raises his voice. 'Keenan? Are you still here?'

He gets no answers.

He bends forwards and shakes his head from side to side in an attempt to remove the suffocating hood. When it doesn't come off, he sinks to the floor and tries to push his head far enough forward to grip the cloth between his knees, but finds he can't quite manage that either.

Realising he will have to free his hands first, Cody spends several minutes navigating his way to the staircase. He gets there after twice bouncing off walls. His plan is to make his way to the dental practice kitchen on the first floor, find a knife, and cut through the ropes binding his hands.

Climbing rickety stairs blind and without the ability to put out one's hands is both tricky and worrying. Cody blows out air in relief when he gets to the top. Putting his back to the door, he takes hold of the handle and turns it.

The door has been locked. And, to make matters worse, Cody can't get to the key in his pocket.

He traipses downstairs again, which is even scarier than coming up. When he is certain his feet are on solid concrete again, he slides down the nearest wall and begins working on the cord around his wrists.

It takes him almost an hour of straining and pulling and chafing to get free. When he finally yanks off the hood, he sees that his wrists are red raw.

What he also sees is that the door to the room that contained Keenan is wide open, and that there is no longer any sign of its inhabitant.

Cody gets up, goes into the room. No clowns, no masks, no chains. Even the crisp packets, water bottle and bucket have disappeared. There isn't a single minuscule clue that anyone has been in this room recently.

Except . . .

It's small, but red stands out clearly against white. His arms clutched across his burning ribcage, Cody hauls himself to the spot on the wall.

It's a single fingerprint. In blood. Cody doesn't know who it belongs to – Keenan himself? Waldo? – but he knows it will match the one found at Matthew Prior's place.

Everything is connected. Waldo's game is bigger than anything Cody ever imagined, though there is much he still does not understand.

He digs out his mobile phone, then finds a number. He dials it, making sure first of all to withhold his caller ID.

'Hello? Who is this? *Who is this?*'

He ends the call. Sara Prior is safe. Upset, by the sounds of it, but safe.

Waldo stuck to the rules. A real-life trolley problem. He put Cody in front of a lever that allowed him to save Sara Prior. But Cody knows full well that in pulling that lever, he diverted death into the path of James Keenan.

He's not sure how he feels about that.

65

When the insistent ringing of his phone eventually grabs the attention of his consciousness, it seems to Cody that he has been in a zombie-like existence for a period of time that could have been minutes or hours. All that went before that no longer feels real.

His caller puts paid to that.

'Hello, Cody. You managed to accomplish a Harry Houdini act, then?'

'Fuck you,' Cody says.

'That's no way to treat a friend. Because I think we can regard each other as friends now, don't you? We've been through so much together lately.'

'Fuck you.'

'If your needle is stuck in that groove, Cody, I'll hang up now, but I thought you might like a word or two of explanation.'

'Explain what? Explain why you killed James Keenan? I assume he is dead by now.'

'Oh, yes. Very much so. You chose to pull the lever.'

'Don't try to put his death on me. Are you at least going to own up to the murder of Matthew Prior?'

'Ah, so you figured that out, then?'

'I figured it out. Prior was a clown too, wasn't he?'

Cody hears a slight intake of breath. 'Very good, Cody. I'm impressed.'

'It's the only thing that makes sense. You didn't pick Sara Prior at random to show me on that iPad. She was somehow a key player in this all along. And then there was the bloody fingerprint at Prior's house and my basement. You want to explain that?'

'All in good time. But yes, you're right. Both men were there at our little get-together when you lost your toes and your friend lost a bit more than that.'

The confirmation of Cody's suspicion still comes as a shock. They were there, he thinks. Both of them. Prior and Keenan. They formed half the team that practically destroyed me.

'Why?' he asks. 'Why would they do that? One worked for the tax office and the other was a financial advisor. How did you get them involved in killing people?'

'You see, there *are* things you want explained. But that's the fun of it. Where would be the challenge in recruiting psychopathic killers to do my bidding? Far more interesting to push Mr or Mrs Average into doing things they would never normally consider.'

'And how did you find your two Joe Averages?'

'The way tech-savvy people like me find most things these days: I went internet shopping. I went looking for people who were letting it be known that their lives were dull, and who craved a little more excitement. They wanted someone who could take them by the hand and lead them into situations they never dreamed they could cope with. I offered them the opportunity to go into dangerous and unknown territory, and yet remain perfectly safe.'

'There's a big leap from that to torturing and killing cops. Why not just take them bungee jumping?'

'That wasn't quite the experience they craved. Matthew and James were social misfits. Good at their jobs, but not brave with other people. They took their aggression out on computer games and social media, but wouldn't say boo to a goose in real life. What they needed was to be shown how to find their courage in the midst of other people.'

Cody considers what he was told about Matthew Prior. He certainly fitted that mould: a man afraid of others, ashamed of his inability to be more like his own wife.

'Okay, but cop killing?'

'It took a while to get to that stage. I was a patient teacher. We started with smaller things, like beating up a drug addict who had robbed a pensioner of her savings. You should have seen the pleasure on their faces after they had landed their first blows. They were truly liberated. By the time it came to you and your colleague, they were completely gung-ho. Admittedly, I had to bend the truth a little.'

'How so?'

'I didn't tell them you were working undercover. I told them you were bent cops, making money through drugs and gun-running. They loved the thought of putting a stop to that.'

'If it was all going so well, why kill them?'

'We hit a snag. A crisis of conscience. When Prior and Keenan discovered the truth about you, they decided they were going to hand themselves in to the police. Naturally, I couldn't allow that to happen.'

Cody finds himself nodding as he listens. It explains Prior's sudden change in behaviour, and why he couldn't focus on his marriage. He couldn't live with what he'd done.

'So you murdered Prior. Why not just bump off Keenan at the same time? Why the run-around?'

Waldo laughs. 'Do you really need to ask, Cody? I'm a clown! I'm all about fun, fun, fun! I need games to play, people to manipulate.'

'And so you thought of me. Should I be flattered?'

'You were intimately connected to Prior and Keenan, so of course you were a natural choice. But I also thought that Sara Prior would make an admirable contestant.'

'Contestant? Is that what we were?'

'Certainly. It was a race, which Sara won. Your own goal was to find me – *Where's Waldo?*, remember? – but you failed miserably at that. Sara's goal was to find the person responsible for her husband's death.'

'Meaning you again.'

'Meaning *you*, Cody. Prior died because of his pangs of conscience about *you*.'

Cody ignores this latest attempt to shift the blame on to him. 'So then how did Sara win?'

'She was given a puzzle to solve. That initial phone call from her husband wasn't made of his own free will. He was already in my hands at that stage. He was told exactly what to say. That in turn led her to a letter, written by me but signed by Prior. I won't bore you with all the other details, but to win the game, Sara had to turn up at an address given to her by a man called Metro Mackenzie. I assume you've heard of him?'

Cody's head is swimming. It all makes sense now. It explains why Sara was getting into fights with Mackenzie's lackies, why her house was trashed.

'How did you persuade Metro to go along with this?'

'Persuading anyone to do anything isn't hard when you have the right information. In Metro's case, I found out that he has been skimming money from his employer, one Joey Pearce. My deal with Metro was that I wouldn't tell Pearce about him if he played along. All he had to do was hand over the address if and when Sara got to him and forced him to do it. He thought Sara didn't stand a cat in hell's chance, but she proved him wrong. When she got to your address, the game ended, and so did your opportunity to find me.'

'Wait. *My* address? She came here?'

'Yes. While you were out looking after your computer nerd friend. Which, by the way, was also set up by me. There never was anything on that computer for her to find. And that label on Keenan's shoe?'

Cody's heart sinks. 'You deliberately chose not to remove it.'

'Quite. Well done for using it to find his address, though. I had faith in you.'

Cody feels numb. It's almost as if his every action has been predestined, or at least anticipated. As though he has had no control whatsoever.

'How did you make sure that Keenan didn't just confess everything to me?'

'Simple threats. He knew what I'm capable of. Remember when you handed him your phone so that I could speak to him? At that point I gave him a little reminder of what he would face if he didn't obey me. I played him a recording of Matthew Prior's screams as the nails were being driven into him.'

'You really are a charmer, aren't you?'

'I have my moments.'

'All right. So we played a game, and I lost. Now what?'

'There will be other games, other chances. But don't feel so badly about this one. Two of the men who attacked you are now dead. You must take some satisfaction in that.'

'There are still two more to go. When I've got you, then I'll be satisfied.'

'The glass is half empty, eh, Cody? Look at it that way if you must. But, as I said, there will be other opportunities for you to redeem yourself. Not for quite a while, though. I've got other fish to fry. In the meantime, I'm sending you two consolation prizes. Keep an eye out for them.'

'What kind of con—?'

'Until the next time, Cody.'

The line goes dead. Cody stares at the phone. Waldo was right: two clowns dead could be considered a victory of sorts.

But somehow Cody isn't feeling triumphant.

66

He gets into work much later than usual, but everyone seems too busy to notice. Something has happened, and Cody suspects it owes much to the actions of Waldo.

His eyes are drawn to Grace first. She looks up from her computer, nods, then gets back to work.

When Webley realises he has arrived, she rushes over to him. He tries to straighten his posture, to hide the fact that his body is covered in bruises and that it feels like his intestines are about to prolapse.

'Hey,' she says.

'All right,' he answers. It's not much of a reconciliation, but it's a start.

'You've missed it all.'

'Missed what?'

'Suicide. Guy by the name of James Keenan. He put a chain around his neck, padlocked it to a railway bridge and then jumped minutes before a train came through. He obviously wanted to make doubly sure.'

Clever, thinks Cody. Hang him with the same chain to explain away any marks I might have left on his neck, then smash him to bits to help mask the injuries he sustained in our fight.

Cody pulls a face. 'Nice. But isn't that one for BTP?'

Webley smiles. The British Transport Police would normally handle an incident at a railway track, but she clearly has a surprise up her sleeve.

She hands Cody a sheet of paper. 'Copy of the suicide note he left.'

Cody takes it from her. It's a scan of a document that has been handwritten, presumably by Keenan while under the watchful and threatening eye of Waldo.

I have killed a man, and now I need to pay the price.

He was a beautiful man, and his name was Matthew Prior. The mistake I made was falling in love with him, but for a short time I really thought we might be happy together. In the end, Matthew decided he wanted to go back to his wife, and I couldn't accept it.

I killed him in the most horrible way possible, and then I tried to make it look like a burglary.

What I did was wrong, and I'm deeply, deeply sorry.

I can't make up for what I did, but I hope I can be forgiven.

'Short but sweet,' Cody says. 'Does it all add up?'

Webley's look tells him it's an odd question. 'So far. We've found a maroon woollen sweater at his home address, plus hair wax that matches the type found at the scene. His hair's the right colour, but we'll have to wait for the lab to get back to us on a precise match, along with a DNA comparison.'

Cody nods. He knows the hair and DNA will match. Waldo will have made certain of that. There will also undoubtedly be a pair of shoes in Keenan's closet that match footprints left at the murder scene.

'What about the fingerprint?'

'Yeah, that's the one fly in the ointment. It doesn't belong to Keenan.'

'Really?'

Cody is genuinely puzzled. It's not like Waldo to make such a basic mistake.

'We think maybe Keenan had help. God knows if we'll ever work out who it was.'

You won't, thinks Cody. You won't.

'So Lewis Fulton is in the clear, then?'

'Yup. Ann Staples came clean. She had it in for him. She told lies about the sweater and about Fulton going round to Matthew's place in Aintree, purely to drop him in the shit. He was a workplace bully all right, but not to the extent she made out.'

Cody looks round the room. He wonders if it's his last day here. He'll miss it so badly, but perhaps he doesn't belong here anymore. The team hasn't changed, but he has.

'Sara needs to know about this,' says Webley.

'Yes. Yes, she does.'

'I thought ... well, I thought you might prefer to tell her yourself.'

Cody looks her straight in the eye, and the rest of the room blurs and fades.

'Yes, it's probably better coming from me.'

'Cody, are you okay?'

'I'm fine.'

'And us? Are *we* okay? You and me, I mean.'

'We're more than okay. We're great.'

Webley blinks, and a tear escapes.

'That's what I hoped you'd say.'

67

This is hard, Cody thinks when Sara Prior opens her door. Hard pretending I know nothing when in fact I know everything.

He feigns surprise at seeing the wound on her cheek, feigns shock when he sees the state the house is in. When he asks her about it and she says it was nothing, he doesn't press it. What would be the point?

In the living room, he gets straight to business.

'There's been a development in the investigation into your husband's murder,' he says.

'I see,' Sara answers.

'In the early hours of this morning, a man called James Keenan committed suicide. He left this note.'

Cody opens up his folder, slides out the copy of the note, and passes it across to Sara.

She reads it quickly. Hands it back. She seems dead to its content.

'You, er, you don't seem surprised.'

Sara stands up. 'I've had a note of my own.' She crosses to the sideboard, picks up a folded piece of paper, brings it back. 'This was put through my letter box last night.'

Cody opens up the note and reads it.

Dear Sara,

My name is James Keenan. You don't know me, and we have never met. This is difficult for me to write, but you need to know the truth.

I am responsible for the death of Matthew.

There, I've said it. If I could undo it all, believe me I would.

I also need to tell you that Matthew and I had a brief relationship. In hindsight, I realise that it was just a fling. Matthew was experimenting, I think. Testing his own boundaries. But I thought it was much more than that. I fell in love with your husband.

The problem was that Matthew wasn't prepared to return that love. After much soul-searching, he decided that what he really wanted to do was come back to you.

I couldn't have that. In a fit of rage, I killed him in the most brutal way possible.

I know that was bad enough, but I was also jealous of you. I wanted you to suffer for taking him away from me. And so I played a terrible game with you.

I forced Matthew to make that phone call to you. I left the letter for you in the library, after forcing Matthew to sign it. I paid Metro a lot of money to give you that address when you found him. And I paid men to attack you when you got there.

I don't know why I did all those things. I thought it would bring me some kind of satisfaction to play with you in that way, like a cat with a mouse. But the only thing it taught me was how much you loved him, and I know now how much he truly loved you.

I am deeply sorry for what I have done to you and Matthew. I know that's not enough, but by the time you read this note I will be dead.

Perhaps that will help to ease the pain.

Yours in repentance,

James Keenan

When he has finished reading, Cody says, 'I'm not going to ask you about the letter in the library, the man called Metro Mackenzie, all of that.'

There is a flash of surprise on Sara's face. 'Thank you.'

'But I take it that it explains the fight on video, the cut on your cheek, the mess your house is in.'

Sara says nothing in response.

'Strictly speaking, I should turn this note in as evidence, but then you'd have a lot of questions to answer. So I'm not going to do that either.'

She nods her gratitude.

'How do you feel about this?' he asks. 'The note, I mean.'

'You really want to know?'

'Yes.'

'I think it's bullshit.'

'I, er, I'm not sure what you mean.'

'I mean what I say. Matthew didn't have a sexual encounter with a man. That's ridiculous.'

'Sara, we found a heap of forensic evidence at Matthew's place to suggest that this man Keenan was there.'

'I don't care. Maybe he *was* there. Maybe he killed Matthew. But not because of any relationship gone wrong. I knew Matthew too well. That letter is pure bullshit.'

Cody finds himself on the verge of confession. He wants to tear the letter into shreds and share the real story with her.

But an important element of that truth would be that her husband was involved in the murder of one police officer and the torture and mutilation of another. It would entail informing her that Nathan Cody, the man now sitting in front of her, was a victim of her husband's desire for adventure and experience.

And so he keeps that truth contained within himself, like a radioactive element held behind a lead shield. Lets her live with the tissue of lies while he decays on the inside.

'So what now?' he asks.

'What now? You tell me. You're a detective on this case. You have your so-called evidence, you have your murderer, you have an explanation that ties everything up with a pretty bow. It makes a great story. I imagine that this is case closed as far as you are concerned. Or are you going to listen to the objections of an unconvinced, grieving widow and keep investigating?'

Cody issues no reply.

'I thought not,' she says.

He locks eyes with her for several seconds. 'What about you? What will you do now?'

'I think . . . I will go home. Back to Copenhagen. There is nothing here for me now.'

He simply nods, while trying not to show his sadness. He feels that he has let her down, that he has taken the coward's way out by adopting the official police line.

'I want you to know,' he says, 'that I did everything I could.'

He could say more, a million things more, but he leaves it there.

'I believe that,' she answers. 'And I'll never think otherwise.'

He smiles. Stands to leave. Says goodbye. When he gets to the front door, she gives him a hug and whispers to him that everything will be all right.

And for ever afterwards he will wonder what she meant by that.

68

The next few hours back at the station are spent tidying up, now that the case has been cracked. There are countless reports to file and phone calls to make, but there is an air of ebullience in the incident room. Detectives love to see a conclusion to an investigation, even when one or two loose ends remain. Cody notices that even Grace appears to have managed to budge her traumatic experience over to one side.

The phone call comes in the late afternoon.

'DS Cody.'

'Hello, Detective. It's Gem Falstaff here. I'm in the process of writing up my report on you, but I think it only right that I have a quick chat with you first.'

Shit, Cody thinks. This sounds ominous. And she's gone all formal on me: *Detective* instead of *Cody*.

'When were you thinking?'

'I need to submit my report tomorrow, so I was hoping we could do this as soon as possible. I can stay late in my office if you could pop in on your way home?'

'Uh, yeah, sure. Can you give me some indication—?'

'See you later then.'

She hangs up. Cody thinks that, for a psychologist, her ability to salve the mind of her client leaves much to be desired.

Cody doesn't put a spurt on to get there: he knows it's not going to be worth the effort. When he eventually arrives, Falstaff appears to be the only one left in the building.

She shows him brusquely into her consulting room. Not so much of the smiling now. Not so much of the attempts to make him feel at ease.

Just get it over with, he thinks.

Falstaff seems to receive the mental hint. She holds up a sheaf of A4 paper.

'This is my report on you. As you can see, I had a lot to say.'

'Should I take that as a compliment?'

She ignores the question. 'I won't bore you with all the technical jargon. In layman's terms, you're a mess.'

Her bluntness takes him by surprise.

'That doesn't sound good.'

'It's not. You have exhibited distinct signs of emotional instability, mental fatigue, delusion and anxiety. And that's in just two sessions. My considered judgment is that I have barely scratched the surface, and that there is a high probability you are suffering from post-traumatic stress disorder.'

Cody swallows hard, forcing back his objections. There really is no point in arguing the toss. Falstaff is the expert here, and moaning about her appraisal will only serve to antagonise a professional who already seems to have had a shitty day.

'I see.'

'I'm glad you do. That in itself makes you unfit to be doing the job you're doing, but you know what's worse?'

'What?'

'What's worse is the fact that you have the sheer temerity to sit there and pretend you don't know what's going on.'

'Excuse me?'

'Frankly, I think you ought to be ashamed to carry a warrant card. It's the bad apples like you who bring the police force into disrepute. You're an embarrassment, and if I had my way, you'd be in prison.'

Cody finds it almost too difficult to speak. 'Now hold on—'

'No, *you* hold on! You don't think you fooled me for a second, do you? Disguising your voice like that. I knew it was you all along. How did you find out, anyway?' She holds up a hand, stopping him from a reply he doesn't have. 'Don't bother. You're a detective. You have your seedy little ways of digging up the dirt on people. So well done, Sergeant Cody. Nice fucking job.'

It becomes clear to Cody then. At least partially.

Waldo.

This has all the hallmarks of the master clown's devious little fingers. He has unearthed something about Falstaff, something she doesn't want made public – an affair? Embezzlement? Professional misconduct? – and is using it against her.

Falstaff reaches down for something next to her, and for a second Cody fears she's going to bring up a shotgun. What she actually produces is a paper shredder. She slams it down on her desk, then holds up the sheaf of papers again.

'I wrote this report purely to get it out of my system. It contains what I'd really like to say, namely the truth. But as you aren't interested in being a seeker of truth, Sergeant Cody, here's what we'll do . . .'

She inserts the end of the report into the shredder. With an angry whine it snatches the papers from her grasp and chews them up.

'There,' she says. 'Happy now? And now if you don't mind, I'd like you to get the fuck out of my office, because I have another report on you to write. One that will paint a glowing picture of your mental health, as demanded. Just remember that I tried to help you. When you have a meltdown on the job, and a murderer walks free because of it, or one of your colleagues is injured or killed, remember that I was offering you a chance to prevent it. Now get out and leave me alone.'

Cody stands up. This is not how he expected things to go.

'Look, I—'

'*Get out!*'

He leaves. When he exits onto the street, he debates going back in. He hates the fact that his reputation has been so undeservedly sullied in Falstaff's eyes. He wants to clear his name, to convince Falstaff that he hasn't blackmailed her, that it was none of his doing.

The knowledge that it would be counter-productive leaves a bitter taste.

Waldo has saved Cody's career.

Three cheers for Waldo.

69

The conversation with Falstaff stays with him during the short trek back to his building.

A part of him is ecstatic. After all, he gets to keep his job. He gets to continue doing the thing he loves most. He should be grateful to Waldo.

But he is also fully aware that Waldo has done this for his own nefarious ends too. He wants – no, *needs* – Cody to remain a cop, and at some point he will return to cash in his chips.

But that's for the future. Weeks from now? Months? Years? Cody has no way of knowing, but the threat of it will always hang over his head.

He unlocks his front door and enters the building. So much has occurred here in recent days. So much unpleasantness. And yet now the place seems curiously serene.

He looks straight ahead towards the rear of the hallway. The basement door is there, skulking in the darkness beneath the stairs, waiting to reveal its secrets again.

Cody decides not to venture down there again for a long time to come.

On the way to the staircase, he collects the day's mail from the table against the wall. The dental staff always leave it there for him at the end of their working day. It's mostly junk, as usual.

He doesn't know what makes him do it, but he turns to look back towards the front door. There on the floor, pushed to one side when he entered, is a white padded envelope.

He walks back and picks it up. It's the same size as the envelopes containing the keys. As before, it bears the words, 'To Nathan Cody.'

He knows who it's from.

Waldo promised him two consolation prizes. The first will have been the intervention with Falstaff. This must be the second.

Cody doesn't open it immediately. He carries it with reverence all the way up to his flat, then places it down on the breakfast bar in the kitchen and stares at it for a full two minutes.

He's not sure he wants to open it.

Waldo's gifts tend to lead to other things, and right now he doesn't have the energy for a follow-up.

But the first consolation prize was good, right? Warped, but good. It restored his career. Perhaps this is also something desirable. Perhaps Waldo is trying to make amends for what he put him through.

Yeah, right.

He starts to open the envelope. Thinks to himself, If this is another damn key . . .

But it's not a key. It's a small white box. The kind of box that might contain an item of jewellery. On the top face of the box it reads, 'Thought you might want this back – W.'

Cody takes a deep breath. Opens the box.

At first, he's not sure what he's looking at.

When he's sure – when the horror before him crystallises – he leaps back off his chair and screams.

Later, when he is able to think coherently about this, he will realise that it makes perfect sense. He will realise that the clue tying together the two men, Prior and Keenan, was there from the very beginning.

The bloody fingerprints found at each scene did not belong to Keenan, Prior, Waldo, or anyone else.

In fact, they were not fingerprints at all.

Because what has been returned to Cody – what was presumably kept on ice for an occasion such as this – is one of his toes.

Acknowledgements

Thank you to all the various editors – Sophie, Margaret, Jennie and Jon – who have helped to hone and polish this book. You turn rocks into gems. To everyone else at Zaffre: you do an incredible job, often behind the scenes, and I want you to know how much I appreciate it.

Thanks also to Oli and the rest of the team at A M Heath. Your sterling (other currencies are available) efforts are incomparable, and I always know I can trust your advice.

To Lisa and the girls: I couldn't do this without your love and support – not to mention your understanding when my mind seems to be on a different planet ("Dad, I've already told you this"). Keep believing.

To other family, friends and faithful readers: Thank you for accompanying me on this journey. It would be a lonely trek without you. Next time, bring chocolate.

A message from David . . .

Dear Reader,

In several respects, *Your Deepest Fear* was a difficult book to write. My original idea for a story in which a woman is forced to conduct her own investigation into the death of her husband in the face of overwhelming opposition was, I felt, a strong premise. However, I was also conscious of the army of fans who desperately wanted to hear more about Cody's struggle against the nightmarish clowns from his past. Reconciling the two was quite a problem, but I hope I've managed to pull it off in this fourth book in the series.

Striking such a balance is always difficult when one is writing a series. Readers who have been there from the beginning feel invested in the characters and want to know more about their lives and experiences. On the other hand, there will be readers new to the series who simply want a page-turning tale that doesn't rely on lots of backstory. Satisfying these newcomers often involves a certain amount of summary of previous events that hopefully doesn't feel too repetitive to those who have already read about them. Whichever camp you're in, do let me know whether you think I've succeeded!

If you'd like to receive advance notice of new books before they appear, you might be interested in joining my Readers' Club. Don't worry – it doesn't commit you to anything, there's no catch, and I won't pass your details on to any third parties. It simply means you'll receive occasional updates from me about my books, including offers, publication news, and even the occasional treat! For example, sign up now and you'll be able to download an exclusive short story, completely free of charge. I won't bombard you with emails, but if you ever get fed up of me, you can unsubscribe at any time. To register, all you have to do is visit **www.bit.ly/DavidJacksonClub**.

Other ways of reaching out to me are via the contact page on my website, www.davidjacksonbooks.com, or on Twitter, where I exist as @Author_Dave. One way or another, I hope to hear from you soon, and that you continue to read and enjoy my books.

Thank you for your support.

Very best wishes,

David

If you enjoyed *Your Deepest Fear*, read on for an extract from David Jackson's bestselling novel

DON'T MAKE A SOUND

You can't choose your family. Or can you?

'A fast-paced and darkly disturbing thriller'
Clare Mackintosh

AVAILABLE NOW

1

'What are you up to?'

The words startle him. But then Malcolm Benson finds the mental echo of the chuckle he failed to contain. He turns from his place at the sink, the amusement still written on his face.

Harriet is at the table, mug of tea cradled in her small hands. It's her favourite mug – the one with Snoopy on it. He made certain to give her that one on this special morning. She has her eyebrows arched in that endearing way of hers. One of the features that first attracted him to her thirty years ago.

He flicks soap foam from his Marigolds, then touches a finger to the side of his nose.

'Wouldn't you like to know?' he says.

Her suspicions confirmed, Harriet lowers her mug to the raffia coaster.

'You're planning something.'

'I'm always planning,' he says. 'You know that. Planning and plotting.'

Her eyes shine at him. 'What is it?'

'You'll have to wait.' He faces the sink again. Dips his gloved hands into the suds. He knows she will be staring at the back of his head, trying to read his mind.

'It's not my birthday for another month,' she says casually.

He remains silent.

'Is that it? Something to do with my birthday?'

He looks at her over his shoulder. In her fifties, and yet still full of such child-like innocence and wonderment.

'It *is* a present. But not for your birthday. It couldn't wait that long.'

'Malcolm, you're teasing me now. Tell me. Please!'

He had been hoping to draw things out a little longer, but it wouldn't be fair on her. Besides, he's as excited as she is to bring it into the open. He has kept it to himself for far too long.

'All right,' he says. 'Wait there.'

He peels off his gloves and removes his apron. As he heads towards the kitchen door, he sees how Harriet claps her hands in anticipation.

He smiles as he walks all the way up to the tiny box room that is his study, and all the way back down again. This is a huge moment for both of them. The culmination of an immense amount of effort and patience.

He pauses before re-entering the kitchen. 'Close your eyes. No sneaky-peekies.'

'Okay,' she answers. 'I'm not looking. Promise.'

He walks through the door, his gift held out before him. Harriet has her hands tightly clasped over her eyes. There is a discernible tremor in her fingers.

'Right,' he says. 'You can look now.'

She parts her fingers. Slides them slowly down her cheeks. Her face registers puzzlement and then disbelief at the sight of the large, leather-bound book.

'It's . . . it's the album.'

He nods. He knows she's about to blub, and already a tear is forming in his own eye.

She lifts her gaze to lock with his. 'You haven't?'

'I have.'

'You've found one?'

He smiles.

'Oh my Lord,' she says. 'Oh my Lord. Show me, show me, show me!'

She leans across to drag one of the chairs around so that it's right next to hers. Malcolm sits down and places the album on the table between them.

'Are you ready for this?' he asks.

'Malcolm, you know how much I've wanted it. Open the book.'

He locates the silk tab inserted into the centre of the album. Opens the book at that position.

The reflected glow from the page lights up Harriet's face. Her hand jumps to her mouth. Tears spring from her eyes and run down the back of her hand.

'I hope those are tears of joy,' Malcolm says.

It's all she can do to nod her head as she continues to marvel at the contents of this treasure chest. This is better than any birthday.

She reaches out and turns the page. Emits a gasp. Malcolm studies her as she gets caught up in the dream. Watches her cry and smile and laugh as she turns page after page. He wishes he could do this for her every day.

The questions start to come then. Harriet wants as much information as she can get, down to the last detail. Malcolm is sometimes stretched to answer, but he does his best.

When Harriet reaches the last page, she goes back to the first. Gently touches a finger to the photograph affixed there. Malcolm knew she would love that one best of all.

And then a cloud of doubt seems to cross her features.

'This isn't just more teasing, is it, Malcolm? I mean, this is definite?'

'Oh, yes. You can see how busy I've been. Look at the photographs. It's all set.'

'All set? When? Soon?'

Malcolm strokes his chin. 'Well, that's the difficult part. These things take time. It's a question of logistics, you see.'

Her face drops. 'Oh.'

'So I thought . . . I thought *tonight*. Would that be soon enough for you?'

Huge eyes now. Eyes brimming with ecstatic incredulity.

'Malcolm!' She throws her arms around him, pulls him into her warmth. 'Malcolm, you are an amazing man. I love you.'

She releases him finally. 'It won't be dangerous, will it? I mean, you're sure you can do it?'

He takes her hands in his. 'It won't be easy. I'm not as young as I used to be. But yes, I can do it.'

She hugs him again. Returns her gaze to the album. And then something occurs to her, and she glances up at the ceiling.

'Can we tell her? Can we tell Daisy?'

'I don't see why not, do you?'

* * *

Daisy hears them coming upstairs, so she puts down her pencil and sits up straight. She knows how much they like it when she sits to attention.

She has been writing a story about a mouse. She has never been good at writing stories, and doesn't know much about mice, so it has been quite a challenge. She hopes they like what she has done. Later, she will do some more fractions, and then some reading. She has a very busy day ahead.

The door eventually opens, and as the adults enter she stiffens her posture even more.

She notices how much they are smiling this morning. In fact, this is probably the happiest she has ever seen them. She wonders what that might mean.

'Hello, Daisy,' says Malcolm.

'Hello, Daddy,' she replies.

Malcolm and Harriet sit opposite her at the small worktable. They are still smiling.

'We've got some news for you,' says Malcolm. 'Something we're very excited about.'

Daisy doesn't reply. She's not sure how she is meant to answer. She sits and waits patiently.

'Don't you want to know what it is?' asks Harriet.

Daisy nods, although she's not sure she does want to know.

Harriet looks at Malcolm and nods for him to break the news. Malcolm leans forward across the table. Gets so close that Daisy can see the blackheads on his nose.

'You're going to get . . .' he breaks off, leaving a huge gap of expectation, then – 'a little sister!'

Harriet flutters in her chair. Gives a little clap of delight.

Daisy, though, is still not sure how to react. She expects they want her to be as euphoric as they are, but somehow she cannot find it within her. Seeing their eyes on her, she opens her mouth, but no words emerge.

'What do you think about that?' says Malcolm. 'Isn't it wonderful? Just think of all the things you can share together.'

'You can show her your toys,' Harriet says. 'And you can read to her, and explain how everything works. Best of all, you won't be on your own anymore. You'll never be lonely again. How fantastic is that?'

Not wanting to cause an upset, Daisy frantically searches her mind for something meaningful to utter.

'What's her name?' she blurts out.

Malcolm looks at Harriet. Harriet looks at Malcolm. 'Good question,' they say to each other.

'Her name's Poppy,' says Harriet. 'A flower name, like yours. And she's blonde like you, too. And only six years old. She's adorable, and I'm sure you're going to love her.' She turns to Malcolm again. 'Isn't she, Daddy?'

They get lost in each other's eyes again, giving Daisy a chance to formulate her next query.

'When? When is she coming?'

'Another excellent question,' says Malcolm. 'Hang on to your hat, Daisy – it's pretty fast! How does tonight sound to you?'

Something lurches inside Daisy, and she has to fight not to show it. 'Tonight?'

She realises too late that there is a tone of negativity in her voice. She sees how Malcolm's lips quiver slightly as they struggle to hold on to their smile.

'Yes, Daisy. Tonight. That's all right with you, isn't it?'

'Yes, Daddy,' she answers quickly. 'I mean . . . I was just wondering where she's going to sleep.'

Malcolm looks across at the bed. He frowns, as though the problem had not occurred to him until now.

'Well, I'm afraid you'll have to share that bed for a short while. We'll sort something out.'

'Details, details,' says Harriet. 'We don't worry about things like that in this house. It'll all be fine. It'll be more than fine. It will be the best thing ever!'

It seems to Daisy that Harriet could explode with joy. She could suddenly burst apart at the seams and splash onto the walls and ceiling.

She closes off the thought. Stares down at her story in an effort to distract herself.

'So,' says Malcolm. 'That's our amazing news. I knew you'd be pleased, Daisy.'

Daisy doesn't know the word 'sarcasm', but the tenor of Malcolm's voice tells her she is not reacting the way he wants her to.

'Don't worry,' she tells them. 'I'm a big girl. I'll look after Poppy.'

It's the most positive she can be, and the most truthful. It seems to do the trick.

'Well, we'll leave you to do your schoolwork now,' says Harriet. 'I'll pop up later to see how you're getting on.' She wags a finger. 'Don't expect me to be much help today, though. I don't know whether I'm coming or going, I really don't.'

They leave her then, almost floating out of the room on the cloud they have created. She watches them go. Waits for the door to close. For the familiar noise that always comes next. The grating sound that seems to reverberate in the centre of her chest.

The sound of the bolts being drawn.

She is alone again. She spends so much of her time alone. Because of that, a part of her really does think that it will be wonderful to have another child here.

But she wouldn't wish that fate on anyone.

She looks around her bedroom. Sometimes she wonders how long it would take a visitor to work out the true purpose of this room were it not for the external locks. They would see the bed in the alcove across from the doorway. To the left of the door they would see the shelving unit containing books, toys and a flat-screen television. Next to that, the chest of drawers, on top of which sits a doll's house and more toys. In the middle of the room, the foldaway table and stackable plastic chairs.

Nothing particularly unusual.

But then they might question the absence of bulky wardrobes. They might wonder why, instead of storage, there is a small washbasin in one corner and what looks like a shower curtain in another. And when they peered behind that curtain they would probably be surprised to find that it hides not a shower but a manky old commode.

And, in an effort to shed some natural light on the puzzling features of this gloomy room, they might wish to draw back the window curtains, only to discover the wooden boards screwed in place behind them.

At that point they might finally realise that this is not merely a bedroom, a room in which to sleep. It is a room for *everything*.

It is a prison cell.

Daisy has learnt not to complain to the adults about her situation. To the people she calls Mummy and Daddy, but who are not her real parents.

This is not the place to bring another child, she thinks.

It wasn't the place to bring *this* child.

She is not sure precisely how long she has been here, but she has a rough idea. She was forced to celebrate her tenth birthday recently. And she knows she was seven when she was snatched.

That makes it about three years that she has been trapped inside this room.

2

'Is this him?'

Detective Sergeant Nathan Cody follows Detective Constable Megan Webley's pointing finger to its target. Through the grimy windscreen he sees a figure coming towards them along the pavement, hands deep in his pockets, collar up against the cold.

'Nope. Nothing like him.'

Ed Sheeran is playing on the radio. Cody taps his fingers on the steering wheel to the beat. He looks into the shop window next to the car. It's full of skimpy lingerie. He wishes he'd parked a bit further back.

'What about this guy?' says Webley.

Cody sighs. 'No. Look, are you going to ask about every bloke who walks past?'

'If I do, it'll be your fault.'

'Why is it my fault?'

'Your idea, wasn't it? Plus, you said he'd show up at five o'clock on the dot, and it's already three minutes past.'

'He'll be here. Have patience.'

Webley indicates how much patience she has remaining with an emphatic folding of her arms.

'I'm cold and I'm tired and I'm hungry. I had no lunch today.'

'You're not the only one. Bit of a mad dash to court, wasn't it?'

'You were very good, by the way. In court.'

'You think?'

'Yeah. That barrister met his match there. I could see the sweat running down from his wig, the arrogant git.' She gestures towards him, raising her eyebrows. 'I noticed you wore a new tie for the occasion.'

Smiling, Cody sits up and straightens it. 'Yeah. Like it?'

'No.'

'Oh.'

After a short pause she says, 'Do you ever miss the old days?'

Cody feels a hot flush coming on. He suspects she's about to bring up the time when they were a couple. Back when she had a say in what ties he wore.

'Which old days?'

'When you were undercover. Do you miss that side of it?'

Phew, thinks Cody. 'Yeah, sometimes. This is good too, though.'

'Ever think of transferring back?'

'Why? Fed up of me?'

'No. Just wondering. It used to be such a big part of your life.'

He shakes his head. 'Doubt it. I still like doing the occasional small job, but I don't think I could do it full-time again.'

'Because of what happened?'

Cody thinks carefully before answering. It's a natural enough question. For most people, the experience of four men in clown masks forcibly removing parts of your body and then gruesomely murdering your partner would be enough to persuade you to seek other avenues of work.

'Yeah, but not just for the obvious reasons. To be honest, I thought the move to Major Incidents would only be temporary, but it opened my eyes. I thought I'd miss the buzz of UC work, but I don't. I like our team, and I like the work we do.'

'Wouldn't be the same if I wasn't on it, though, would it?' She smiles, and he sees her dimples appear.

Before he can reply, Webley's phone rings. She glances at the screen. 'Footlong,' she announces, then answers the call.

Cody looks in his rear-view mirror at the unmarked car parked yards behind them. He can make out the face of DC Neil 'Footlong' Ferguson, lit by the glow from his own phone. Alongside him is another DC from the squad, Jason Oxburgh.

Webley listens, then turns to Cody. 'He wants to know how long we're expected to sit here. He wants to know if your CHIS for this op is reliable.'

CHIS is cop-speak for Covert Human Intelligence Source. An informant.

'Tell him my intel is impeccable,' says Cody, 'and that he needs to have a bit more faith.'

Webley passes on the message, then listens for a few more seconds before ending the call.

'What did he say?' Cody asks.

'Nothing.'

'Go on, what did he say?'

'He asked if you're doing your best to keep me warm in here.'

Cody turns away, shaking his head in despair, but he thinks that the heat returning to his cheeks should be more than enough to keep both of them warm.

He's glad of the distraction when he notices a movement through the car window.

'Aye, aye,' he says.

'What?' says Webley. 'Is it him?'

Cody continues to observe. He sees a woman at the cash machine. She has her purse in her hand, but has left her bag wide open. A young man in a dark tracksuit has begun moving up behind her.

Cody lowers his window. 'Fitzy, get over here!'

The young man jerks to attention. Hands in pockets, he saunters over to the car.

'All right, Mr Cody. How's it going?' He bends to look across at the passenger. 'All right, love.'

Cody has to stop himself from smiling. He knows that Webley will be bristling at being called 'love'.

'What are you up to, Fitzy?'

Fitzy shrugs. 'Nothin.'

'Didn't look like nothing. Looked to me like you took a very sudden interest in that woman at the ATM.'

'Oh, her! No, I was just keeping an eye on her, like, you know what I mean? Doing my bit as a good citizen. I don't think she realises there are certain types around here who might take advantage of a situation like that. Know what I mean?'

'Yeah, right, Fitzy. Glad to hear it. I'll put you in for the Pride of Britain Awards. Off you go, then. Chasing you through the streets is the last thing I want right now.'

Fitzy doesn't budge. 'What's happening here, anyway?'

'Nothing to concern you,' says Cody.

Fitzy grins, revealing a gap where one of his front teeth should be. 'Are you waiting for the coast to clear so you can take your missus in there?' He points behind him at the lingerie shop. 'It's okay, you know. These are modern times. No need to feel embarrassed, know what I mean?'

Webley leans towards Cody's open window. 'I'm not his missus. Now do one, before we nick you.'

Fitzy puts his hands up in surrender. 'All right, love. Just being friendly.'

It's then that the wheels seem to start turning in Fitzy's mind. He peers along the street towards the other unmarked car.

'They're with you, aren't they? What's going on? You gonna raid the frilly knickers place?'

'Something like that,' says Cody. 'Now go and bother some-one else, Fitzy. And stay out of trouble.'

Fitzy shrugs, then saunters away. As he goes past Footlong's car, he gives the occupants a little wave.

Cody closes his window.

'God,' says Webley, 'I could do with a drink after this. Fancy one?'

'No.'

'Why not?'

'It's February. I don't drink in February.'

'You don't drink any frigging month. I bet you didn't even have a drink at Christmas.'

'I'm sure you quaffed enough for the two of us,' he answers. But she's right: he didn't drink at Christmas. He spent Christmas alone, in his flat. While everyone else was carving turkeys and pulling crackers and getting pissed, he was tucking into a micro-waved curry and nursing an ankle sprained in the line of duty. He didn't tell Webley that, of course. He told her that he spent time with his parents and with his ex-fiancée, when in reality neither seemed overly keen to spread the festive cheer in his direction.

'Come on,' Webley urges. 'It'll be fun.'

'Nah, I'm knackered. I just want to put my feet up.'

'Christ, Cody. You sound like my nan, and even she manages to get out to t'ai chi and bingo every week. Are you sure you're not ninety-six beneath that boyish exterior?'

'Another time, Megs. Okay?'

She smiles at him.

'What?' he asks.

'Megs. You used to call me that all the time when we were going out.'

'Sorry.'

'No. It's nice.'

Hot flush time again. Cody is grateful when Webley's phone blares into life once more.

Webley answers the call. Listens. Says, 'Footlong again. Thinks we should knock this on the head. His suggestion is—'

'He's here,' says Cody.

'What?'

Cody points. 'He's going in now.'

He watches as a dark-haired man puts a key into the door of a shop front to open up, then disappears inside. Cody starts to get out of the car.

'We're on!' says Webley into her phone.

The four detectives assemble on the pavement, then head briskly in the direction of the shop.

Cody pushes open the door. Inside, the man he has been waiting for turns to stare at the new arrivals.

'What can I do for you?' the man asks.

Cody listens to the action taking place in the back room. He breathes in the odours.

His mouth waters in anticipation.

'Fish and chips four times, please. And can you make my batter extra crispy?'

* * *

Cody pulls rank and insists they eat in Footlong's car. The food is excellent, the company even better, but when the topic of a few beers is raised again, Cody declines. He drives back to his flat alone.

Home is the top floor of a Georgian building on Rodney Street, above a dental practice. The practice is closed now, so Cody has the building to himself. He could have invited his colleagues back here. He could have suggested they buy some alcohol on the way. Could have put on some music.

He did none of those things.

In his kitchen, he puts the kettle on, empties his pockets, and removes his jacket and tie. When he has brewed his tea, he takes a seat at the small breakfast bar.

He thinks about Webley. There have been a couple of occasions in recent weeks when she has suggested going for a drink.

Sometimes he wonders if she has an agenda, but then he worries that he is being arrogant. She's probably just being friendly.

Besides, there are barriers. Too many things in the way. The job, for one. Cody and Webley have to work together, to rely on each other.

Then there are the partners. Okay, ex-partners. Cody doesn't think there is much chance of his own ex-fiancée taking him back, but he expects that Webley will hook up with her bloke again. They have been apart only since Christmas. Time yet for a reconciliation.

And then, of course, there is the other matter. The thing he can't talk about.

Webley touched upon it earlier. The event that caused him to abandon undercover work. She knows how traumatic it was for him. How it led to horrific nightmares, hallucinations and a loss of control.

What she doesn't know is that they are back in his life.

The clowns.

They have made contact. They have been sending him weird messages. They have even been here, in his flat.

They have been quiet since Christmas, but he knows they'll come again. And when they do, it won't be pretty.

That's the real reason he can't allow Webley, or anyone else for that matter, to get too close.